The Urbana Free Library

To renew: call 217-367-4057
or go to **urbanafreelibrary.org**
and select **My Account**

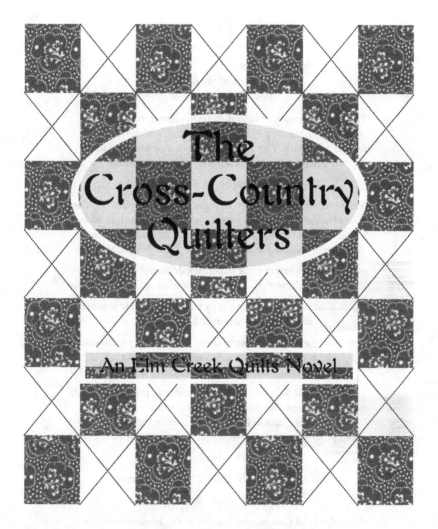

The Cross-Country Quilters

An Elm Creek Quilts Novel

Jennifer Chiaverini

Simon & Schuster Paperbacks
NEW YORK LONDON TORONTO SYDNEY

SIMON & SCHUSTER PAPERBACKS
A Division of Simon & Schuster, Inc.
1230 Avenue of the Americas
New York, NY 10020

First Simon & Schuster trade paperback edition September 2009
First Simon & Schuster All You Wal-Mart edition September 2009

SIMON & SCHUSTER PAPERBACKS and colophon are registered
trademarks of Simon & Schuster, Inc.

For information about special discounts for bulk purchases,
please contact Simon & Schuster Special Sales at
1-866-506-1949 or business@simonandschuster.com.

The Simon & Schuster Speakers Bureau can bring authors
to your live event. For more information or to book an event,
contact the Simon & Schuster Speakers Bureau at
1-866-248-3049 or visit our website at www.simonspeakers.com.

Designed by Brooke Koven

Manufactured in the United States of America

1   3   5   7   9   10   8   6   4   2

The Library of Congress has cataloged the hardcover edition
as follows:

Chiaverini, Jennifer.
The cross-country quilters : an Elm Creek Quilts
novel / Jennifer Chiaverini.
p. cm.
1. Female friendships—Fiction. 2. Quiltmakers—Fiction.
3. Quilting—Fiction. I. Title.
PS3553.H473 C7 2001
813'.54—dc21   00-046325

ISBN 978-0-7432-0257-2
ISBN 978-1-4391-4891-4 (pbk)
ISBN 978-1-4391-6733-5 (All You Wal-Mart)
ISBN 978-0-7432-1489-6 (ebook)

For
Marty and Nicholas,
with all my love

Acknowledgments

This book would not have been possible without the help of many friends and colleagues, including:

My agent, Maria Massie; my editor, the incomparable Denise Roy; her assistant, Tara Parsons; and publicist Rebecca Davis. I am privileged to work with such talented people.

My fellow quilters, who never fail to inspire me, especially the members of the Mad City Quilters, R.C.T.Q., QuiltNet, and QuiltersBee.

The members of the Internet Writing Workshop, especially Christine Johnson, Candace Byers, Dave Swinford, Jody Ewing, Lani Kraus, Rhéal Nadeau, and everyone in the Lounge.

The whole Orbitec crew and associated friends, especially Rachel and Chip Sauer, my first and best Madison friends.

My wonderfully supportive family, especially Geraldine, Nic, and Heather Neidenbach; Virginia and Edward Riechman; Leonard and Marlene Chiaverini; and the entire Riechman clan.

My beloved husband, Marty, without whom I would not be able to live the writing life; and Nicholas, my heart's treasure and constant companion during the writing of this book.

My heartfelt gratitude goes out to you all.

The
Cross-Country
Quilters

One

JULIA LOATHED retirement parties. Watching the guest of honor make the obligatory final curtain call evoked a predictable yet uncomfortable melancholy, but worse yet was the sense of the other guests' eyes upon her. She imagined their whispers: Isn't it about time we threw one of these parties for *her*, the dowager queen of the television drama? Doesn't she realize her time has passed?

As she raised her champagne flute to join the others in a toast to Maury, the man who had been her agent throughout her career, Julia forced herself to smile. Despite the critics' lukewarm appreciation of her talent, she knew she was a fine actress. No one would detect her dismay at realizing that she was one of the oldest people present, that she could no longer count on being the most beautiful woman in the room, that maybe it was best that she retire with some dignity instead of lingering on long past her prime.

No doubt the stars and would-be stars assembled there expected her own announcement soon, especially since *Family Tree* had just ended its lengthy run. She had hoped for at least another two years, but as the three endearing cherubs who played her grandchildren grew into sulky adolescents with various addictions and attitude problems, the program's once-spectacular ratings had begun a gradual but unmistakably downward slide. The final blow had come the previous winter, when the actor who played her son-in-law developed a particularly nasty infection in one of his pectoral implants. When his hospitalization forced them to shut down production for a month and show reruns during sweeps week, the studio heads decided not to renew any of their contracts. Most of the cast moved on to other projects, but for the first time in over two decades, Julia found herself facing a summer hiatus that threatened to extend indefinitely.

If she were planning to leave the business, this would seem to be the time to do it. Money wouldn't be a problem; she had invested her earnings so wisely that she wouldn't need to earn a paycheck to maintain her lifestyle—even with the ungodly amount of alimony she had to pay her third husband. But to retire now, before she had starred in a hit movie, something meaningful and important and true—that would be unbearable.

A handsome young waiter smiled as he offered her another glass of champagne. Drowning her sorrows didn't seem like such a bad idea, given that her series was over and Maury was abandoning her, so she placed her empty glass on the waiter's tray and took another. As she raised it to her lips, Maury caught her eye and inclined his head in the direction of his study. She took a hasty sip and nodded to indicate she would join him there. If he intended to scold her for drinking too much, she'd scold him right back. What was he thinking, retiring when she needed him so desperately?

"You look lovely," he greeted her, kissing her on the cheek as she entered the study. He closed the heavy door behind them, shutting out the noise of the party.

"Thank you, Maury. You look rather lovely yourself."

He grinned and tugged at the sleeves of his elegant tuxedo. "Evelyn insisted," he said. "I didn't want such an ostentatious send-off. I would have preferred eighteen holes and a quiet lunch at the club with a few friends."

"And disappoint everyone who wanted to bid you a proper good-bye?" Julia tried to keep her voice light, but she couldn't prevent some bitterness from slipping in. "It's not like you to put your golf game ahead of your friends."

"Now, Julia, don't be like that." He placed a hand at the small of her back and guided her to a soft tapestry-covered sofa in front of the fireplace. "You're going to be well looked after. Your new agent will be able to do more for you than I have these past few years."

The apology in his voice touched her. "I've had no complaints," Julia said, resting her hand on his arm. "There's no one in this world I trust more than you."

"Thank you, Julia." Maury cleared his throat and drew out his handkerchief. "That means a lot to me." Abruptly he strode over to his desk, and when his back was turned, Julia watched him fondly as he composed himself. Maury was a good man, one of Hollywood's last true gentlemen. He had been her first husband's oldest and dearest friend. He and his wife, Evelyn, had seen her through Charles's death, and the two foolish marriages and bitter divorces that followed. He had insisted that the producers of *Family Tree* audition her for the role of Grandma Wilson despite their complaints that she wasn't the right type. He had unraveled hundreds of management snarls and eased countless disappointments throughout the years. Maury was a true friend in a city that knew little of friendship and everything about opportunism and greed.

He tucked his handkerchief away and picked up a thin stack of papers bound by three gold brads. "What's this?" she asked as he placed the papers in her hands.

"A little farewell present. You didn't think I'd leave you without one last great project, did you?"

That was precisely what she had thought, but she wouldn't tell him that. She glanced at the top sheet of the script for the writer's name. "Who's Ellen Henderson? What else has she done?"

"You won't have heard of her. This is her first major motion picture."

"Oh, Maury." Julia frowned and tossed the script onto the coffee table.

He took up the papers and sat down beside her. "Don't 'Oh, Maury' me before you read it. This is the project we've been searching for. It has heart, it has warmth, and it has a fantastic part for you." He placed the script in her lap and closed her hands around it. "Trust me."

"Who's directing?"

"Ellen is."

The alcohol helped flame her temper. "This is your big plan for getting me my breakthrough role? I've won four Emmys and a Golden Globe, and you give me a script written by a nobody. How dare you, after all I've sacrificed?" The last words came out almost as a sob, which she tried to disguise with another sip of champagne.

Gently Maury took the glass. "Don't hold her inexperience against her. Two years ago her student film won an honorable mention at Sundance. Plus, William Bernier is producing."

Julia raised her eyebrows at him, her anger forgotten. "I thought he had a three-picture deal with—"

"He does. This will be one of those projects. We'll have all the perks and publicity a major studio can provide."

"That's not bad," Julia admitted, picking up the script. Even if the production fell through, Bernier would remember that she had been willing to take a chance on a neophyte director for his sake. Not every actress of her caliber would take such a risk, and it certainly wouldn't hurt to have a man like Bernier in her debt.

"I'll leave you alone to read it." Maury patted her knee and rose. "If you don't love it, I promise I'll go out there in front of all those people and tell them I'm canceling my retirement until I can find you the project of your dreams."

"Don't tempt me," Julia teased as he left the room, though she knew such an announcement would embarrass her more than it would him.

Alone in the restful silence of the study, she settled back on the sofa and decided to skim through the first few scenes. If nothing else, Maury's script would provide an escape from an evening of phony smiles and niceties and too much rich food. She read the cover page aloud to test the sound of the title. *"A Patchwork Life,"* she said, and winced. She wanted *Masterpiece Theatre,* and Maury had given her something so hokey it could have been plucked minutes before from a Midwestern cornfield. If Bernier was half the savvy producer his reputation claimed, he would change that title before releasing a single dollar. Shaking her head and expecting the worst, she turned to the first page and began to read.

Within a few minutes she forgot the party, the humiliating dearth of offers, the patronizing responses of the few movie producers who owed Maury too much to avoid returning his phone calls. A woman named Sadie Henderson and her life in pioneer-era Kansas drew her in until they became more real than the tapestry sofa beneath her, more vivid than the music of the orchestra and the celebration just beyond the study door. She could almost taste the dust in her mouth as the script transported her to the small prairie homestead Sadie struggled to build with her husband, Augustus. Her heart broke when Augustus died, leaving Sadie with two young sons. Alone, Sadie persisted despite grasshopper plagues and drought when other neighbors gave up and returned to homes back east. She shared Sadie's grief when she sold off cherished family quilts to raise money to improve the farm. Sadie then took in sewing from her more successful neighbors, running the farm by day and stitching her neighbors' quilts late into the night. Her quilting kept the family alive until at last, years later, the farm flourished.

Long after she finished the last page, Julia held the script to her chest, lost in the details of Sadie's hardship and triumph. In Sadie's place, Julia would have crumbled in a week. She longed to meet Sadie, understand the source of her strength, and somehow harness that power for herself.

The door opened, startling her out of her reverie. "Well?" Maury asked, sitting beside her.

"It was quite good," she said cautiously, testing him. "But who would pay to see a movie like this, old ladies and nuns? It's a little—well, I don't know. A little too squeaky-clean." She thumbed through the script, shaking her head. "Maybe you should see if Sally Field is available."

"How can you say that?" Maury protested. "You said you wanted something meaningful, something worthy of your talent. This story has all the pathos and character development you wanted—or at least I thought you wanted."

"Relax, Maury. I didn't say I wouldn't consider it; I'm just not sure what this will do for me."

"It'll get you an Oscar nomination, that's what it'll do," he said, but his voice had lost some of its distress.

"It does have some great monologues," she admitted, but suddenly a horrible thought struck her. "Which part did you have in mind for me?"

"Sadie Henderson, of course. Not when she's in her twenties, but after that. Bernier will get his best makeup people. I'll insist on it."

She was too relieved to notice Maury's implicit admission that, without makeup miracles, she was far too old to play anyone younger than a matriarch. For a moment she had feared that Maury intended her to play the cruel elderly neighbor who tried to buy up the Henderson farm.

"So are you interested or not? Just say the word, and I'll send this along to Anne Bancroft, Judi Dench—"

"I'm interested," she interrupted. She refused to entertain even for a moment the thought of Dame Judi collecting a golden statuette for a role Julia had declined.

"Then I have someone I'd like you to meet." Maury crossed the room, opened the study door, and ushered a young woman inside. She was slender and dressed in what was likely her best suit, but her unfashionable haircut and lack of makeup marked her as a breed apart from all the other young women at the party. "This is Ellen Henderson."

"Miss Merchaud, it is such an honor to meet you." The young woman approached and shook her hand. "I've admired your work since I was a little girl."

Julia twisted a wince into a smile. "That long, hmm?" The young woman's grip was strong and confident, and suddenly Julia realized something. "Your name is Henderson. Are you a descendant of Sadie Henderson?"

"She was my great-grandmother. My script is based on her diaries."

"I'm so delighted to hear that," Julia exclaimed, forgetting her reserve. She so wanted to believe that Sadie had been a real woman who had lived and breathed and walked the same world she walked.

"Your writing makes Sadie live again," Maury said.

Ellen blushed at the compliment. "It's the actor who brings the script to life. Miss Merchaud, there's no one in the world I'd rather have portray my great-grandmother than you."

Years in the business had taught Julia to suspect flattery. "And why is that?"

"You have this core of strength, this resilience. I've seen it in every part you've played, ever since Mrs. Dormouse in *The Meadows of Middlebury.*"

"You saw *Meadows*?" That couldn't be. Mrs. Dormouse was her first major role, but *Meadows* was a children's film that had quickly slipped into obscurity despite strong critical acclaim. Besides, Ellen hadn't even been born when it came out. For that matter, her parents had probably been too young to see it.

"My public library ran it during its summer film festival when I was in the fourth grade." Ellen gave her a shy smile. "I loved the book, but when I saw how actors brought all those characters to life, I was transfixed—and transformed. Especially when I saw how you made Mrs. Dormouse more real than she had been even in my imagination. That was the moment I knew I wanted to make movies when I grew up."

Ellen's genuine admiration hit home. "I'll take the part," Julia said, without thinking of contracts or box office or who might share top billing.

Ellen's face lit up. "Oh, Miss Merchaud, thank you." She seized Julia's hand and shook it again. "You won't regret this. I promise."

Julia laughed and eased her hand free. "I'm sure it will be a delightful experience." She raised her eyebrows at Maury, who recognized his cue.

"Miss Merchaud and I have some details to discuss," he said, showing Ellen to the door. "Why don't you go on out and enjoy the rest of the party?"

Ellen looked uncomfortable. "If you don't mind—if you won't be needing me, I think I'd rather go home. It's getting late."

As Maury promised her they'd be in touch, Julia wondered how long the awkward little wren had been forced to mingle among that crowd of peacocks as she waited for Julia to read her script.

When they were alone, Maury said, "You've just won her loyalty for life. Bernier took on the project on the condition that she would obtain a major star for the lead role."

"Really?" Julia felt a rush of pleasure at being considered a major star by a man like Bernier, but the sensation was quickly followed by anger that she had not taken the compliment in stride. Dame Judi no doubt heard such praise twenty times a day. "I wonder why she didn't mention it."

"She wanted to be sure you took the part because you truly loved her story, not because you felt sorry for her."

"If she keeps that up, this town will eat her alive." Still, the young woman's sincerity was oddly refreshing. Julia wished she had not been in such a hurry to dismiss her.

"She'll learn."

"The sooner the better, for her sake," Julia said. "So, when do we get started? Will we be shooting on location?"

"We'll have to for some of the exterior shots," Maury said apologetically.

"That's fine." Then she added, almost to herself, "Some time away would be good for me."

"I'm glad you think so, because I was planning to send you on a little trip."

"A week at Aurora Borealis?" Wouldn't that be just like Maury, to pamper her at her favorite retreat in Ojai.

"Not exactly. This will be more of a working vacation." He was smiling, but he still looked tentative. "You need to learn some new skills for this part."

"I already know how to ride a horse."

"But you don't know how to quilt, unless you've been keeping secrets from me."

"You know I don't keep secrets from you." Then she paused. "Do I really need to know how to quilt?"

He nodded.

"Can't we use a stand-in?"

"You need to know how to quilt for this role. It's important, Julia."

He said it so gravely that at once she understood what he would not admit aloud: He had won the role for her by telling William Bernier she already knew how to quilt. "I see," she said briskly. "I'll just have to learn, then. I might even enjoy it. Are you planning to bring a quilt tutor to the set? Is there such a thing?"

"I had a better idea," Maury said. "I'm sending you to quilt camp."

Megan hadn't felt so frustrated and helpless since the afternoon Robby had come home from Cub Scouts with a black eye and a missing tooth. At first he wouldn't tell her what had happened, and when she phoned the scoutmaster, his only explanation was, "Some boys aren't cut out for the Cub Scouts. Why don't you try again next year, when he's thicker skinned?"

"This is the Cub Scouts, not the Marines," Megan had snapped.

"Tell that to your son. He threw the first punch."

Megan had been so flabbergasted by this obvious untruth that she could think of nothing to say, so she hung up. Her gentle, owlish son was among the smaller boys in his grade, and she simply could not picture him as an aggressor. He had few friends at school, but never before had he been beaten up by his classmates. More than anything she wanted Robby to be safe, healthy, and happy, but at that moment, she realized she couldn't protect him from everything. A bullying gang of seven-year-olds had bluntly defined the limits of her motherly powers.

As she tended Robby's wounds, the story came out, but only in defense against the scoutmaster's charges. Robby argued that maybe he had thrown the first punch, but the other boy had started it by teasing him. Robby had told some of the other scouts that his father never came to any scouting events because he was an astronaut working on top-secret research on the space station. When another boy loftily pointed out that Robby's explanation couldn't possibly be true since the space station was still being built, Robby told him that was just a cover story so other countries wouldn't know how far ahead of them the Americans were. "It's an international space station, you stupid liar," the other boy said, and in response, Robby slugged him.

Like all of Robby's stories, this one had a grain of truth in it, but only a grain. Although Keith was a corporate sales manager, Megan was an aerospace engineer, and one day the new technology she developed would be used aboard the space station. But although sometimes Megan wished her ex-husband had been shot into orbit, he and his new wife had made it only as far as Portland, Oregon.

That day Megan told Robby that hitting was wrong, and that if he became frustrated or angry, he should just walk away. Several times since, she had also explained—after making certain her son did understand the difference between reality and fiction—

how lies sometimes made people angry, because they didn't like to be deceived. "You don't need to exaggerate to get people's attention," she told him. "Just be yourself." Robby told her he had to tell stories because no one liked him just as himself. Megan patiently pointed to his bruises as evidence that they didn't seem to like him very much when he lied, either, and that in the future it might be better to err on the side of truth and caution. "If you like to make people laugh by telling a story, that's okay," she said, "as long as you tell them it *is* a story." Robby agreed, but it pained her to know that he thought no one would like him if he didn't put on an act. Maybe she was blinded by a mother's love, but couldn't everyone see what a sweet, sensitive, bright little boy he was? Couldn't the world appreciate him for that?

The Cub Scout incident had occurred two years ago, five years after Keith confessed to his affair and moved out. When she placed today's events in that context of misery, they seemed almost trivial. Why, then, was she so upset? This wasn't the first time she hadn't been invited to a party, although she never would have expected Zoe to exclude her. So few women engineers worked at their company that they all knew each other, and Megan had considered Zoe one of her closest friends at work. When she overheard Tina and Michelle discussing the Fourth-of-July barbecue at Zoe's house the previous Saturday, she first thought they were talking about a future event that she, too, would soon hear about from the hostess herself. But when Tina spotted her and both women abruptly stopped talking, Megan realized the truth.

Later, Zoe came to her office and tried, in her awkward way, to apologize. "There were only couples there," she explained. "I didn't think you'd have any fun, you know, being the only single person at a party full of couples."

Megan hid her disappointment behind a smile and assurances that she'd be delighted to join them next time, and if she needed an escort, she'd find one. Zoe looked relieved that she was taking it so well, never suspecting that after she left, Megan locked the door to her office and sat at her desk contemplating whether to burst into tears right there or climb out the window, flee for the sanctuary of home, and cry in private. She was a grown woman with a child, but she felt like she was back in high school. She regained her composure by reminding herself that she couldn't force people to include her, nor could she make them enjoy her company enough to excuse her involuntary single status. Nor could she resent Zoe when most of her other couple friends had also drifted away after Keith left. Maybe they feared divorce was contagious, or maybe they had always preferred Keith and tolerated her presence only because she was his wife. She would never know, because she wasn't the sort of person to confront others, even when they slighted her.

As she left work that afternoon, still unhappy, she decided that after Robby went to bed, she'd go online and vent her frustrations to her best friend, Donna. They had been E-mail pals for years, ever since they had met in an Internet quilting newsgroup. Whenever Megan needed to pour her heart out, Donna was there with patience and understanding, the same way Megan tried to be there for her. Often Megan wished that Donna lived nearby rather than in Minnesota, so that they could meet for lunch or go quilt-shop hopping like normal best friends. She wondered what that meant about her, that she was best friends with someone she had never actually met in person. Maybe Robby had inherited his social ineptitude from his mother.

As she pulled onto the long dirt driveway leading up to her parents' house, Megan checked the dashboard clock. She had arrived later than usual, but probably too early to say hello to her father, who at this hour would be closing up his hardware store in town. Her parents owned nearly ten acres sandwiched between two larger family farms, and although they still cultivated most of the property, the small farm had always been more of a hobby than a career. Megan treasured childhood memories of playing hide-and-seek with her father in the cornfield, the green stalks topped with golden silk towering above her head. Soon Robby would play there with his grandfather again.

She circled in front of the house and parked beside one of the outbuildings. Her father's two dogs bounded over to greet her as she climbed the stairs to the front porch. "Hey, Pete. Hey, Polly," she said, petting the golden retriever first and then the German shepherd. She heard laughter inside, and found Robby with his grandmother in the kitchen.

"Mom," Robby cried out. "Did you know when Grandma was little she had her own cow? It would come when she called it and everything, just like a dog." His grandmother caught Megan's eye and shook her head. Robby saw the exchange and quickly added, "It's just a story."

Megan's mother laughed affectionately and ruffled Robby's hair. "You're my little storyteller, all right." She hugged Megan in welcome, but then her smile faded. "What's wrong, honey?"

"Nothing. Just some stuff at work." It wasn't anything she wanted to discuss in front of Robby, and she wasn't even sure if she ought to confide in her mother. Her parents had raised her to be strong and independent, and she was ashamed to show them how meek and accepting she had become since Keith had left her. As hard as it had been for her staunchly Catholic parents to accept the breakup, it would be even more difficult for them to understand how deeply his betrayal still affected her.

But when they heard her father's truck pull up outside and Robby ran out to meet him, Megan found herself telling her mother what had happened. Her mother continued shelling peas, nodding thoughtfully as Megan perched on a stool and rested her elbows on the counter as she spoke. It was a scene that had played out many times in that kitchen since Megan was a child, first learning the painful truth that the whole world wouldn't cherish her the way her parents did.

"What did you do last Saturday?" her mother asked when she had finished.

"We took Robby to the county fair," Megan said. "You were there, Mom. Don't you remember?"

"Of course I remember, but I wasn't sure if you did. We had a great time, didn't we? Wasn't the weather perfect? Didn't Robby love the rides and the animals?"

Megan nodded, not sure where her mother's reminiscence was taking them.

"Well, then, seems to me this Zoe character did you a favor." Her mother finished the last of the peas and dusted off her hands as if brushing off both the chore and Megan's co-worker. "If you had gone to the party, you would have missed the fair. And for what? A party with too many rules to be much fun, or at least that's how it sounds to me."

"It's not missing the party that bothers me," Megan said. "It's being excluded."

Her mother's face softened. "I know, dear." She cupped Megan's chin in her hand for a moment, then patted her cheek. "My quilt guild is meeting at Dorothy Pearson's house tonight. Why don't you join me? Your father can watch Robby."

Megan squirmed. Her mother's invitation sounded too much like her father's offer to escort her to the homecoming dance sophomore year of high school, when none of the boys had been willing to ask her and she had been too shy to ask any of them. Her mother's friends were sweet women, but they had known Megan since she was in diapers and had never stopped thinking of her as a little girl. "Thanks, Mom, but I have some papers to read before bed tonight. I have a grant proposal due next week."

"At least stay for dinner."

Megan tried to picture the contents of her pantry, wondering if she had enough energy for something as simple as pasta from a box and sauce from a jar. Then she thought of her mother's home-made bread and baked chicken, and vegetables fresh from her parents' garden. "We'd love to."

When Megan and Robby returned home early in the evening, Megan knew before she leafed through the mail that Keith's child support check would not be there. The day had gone too badly to end on such a high note.

That's why she assumed the envelope from *Contemporary*

Quilting magazine was a subscription renewal notice and didn't bother opening it until two days later, when she paid her other bills. She would have opened it immediately if she had known that the renewal notice was in fact a letter informing her that her watercolor charm quilt had taken first prize in the magazine's annual contest, and that she had won a week's vacation at the famous quilting retreat, Elm Creek Manor.

"Way to go, Megan," Donna shouted as she finished reading the E-mail note. It was about time her best quilting buddy had some good luck come her way. They'd been friends for years, ever since they met on an Internet quilting newsgroup when Megan posted a frantic request for a certain piece of fabric. Everyone at her son's school had gone crazy over a Saturday morning cartoon called *Baby Dinosaurs,* and Megan's son was infatuated with a character named Little Trice, a pastel triceratops who somehow managed to look adorable clad in a bib and diaper. Megan had secretly begun working on a Little Trice quilt for Robby's birthday, but she had found only one yard of *Baby Dinosaurs* print fabric at her local quilt shop. She thought it would be enough, but she ran out when the quilt top was only half finished, and when she checked at the store, they told her the print had been discontinued. "All I need is a half yard more," Megan wrote to the other quilters in the newsgroup. "I'll swap anything for it, just name your price. Can anyone help me?"

Donna sympathized, for despite her compulsive fabric-shopping habit, she had often found herself in similar situations. She phoned all the quilt shops in her area code and finally found one that had two yards left on a remnant bolt. She drove an hour to St. Paul to buy it, then E-mailed Megan with the good news. A week after Donna mailed her the material, Megan sent her a box of beautiful Civil War–era reproduction fabric and a heartfelt thank-you note. Donna immediately sent her an E-mail message to tell her how pleased she was with the surprise, and Megan wrote back to let her know how the Little Trice quilt was progressing. Their correspondence continued over the Internet and through the mail, and before long, they had become confidantes. Donna knew everything about Megan's divorce and troubles at work, and Megan knew everything about Donna's eternal struggle with her weight and her two daughters' nerve-wracking journey through the teen years. Although they had never actually met in person, they were so close that Donna was as happy for Megan as if she had won the *Contemporary Quilting* contest herself.

After replying with a note of congratulations, Donna shut down the computer and returned to her sewing machine. The fourth bedroom had been the girls' playroom, but when they reached the age when they preferred to shut themselves away in their separate bedrooms, Donna had adopted it as her quilt studio. Even with the door open so she could monitor all the comings and goings in the house, she still had a sense of peaceful solitude, the perfect antidote to a hectic day.

"Mom?" Lindsay appeared in the doorway, slender and lovely in her denim shorts and pink top, her long blond hair pulled back into a ponytail. "Can I talk to you for a minute?"

Donna put down her quilt block and swiveled her chair around to face her eldest daughter. "Sure, honey. What is it?"

Lindsay crossed the room and took her hands. "Not here. Downstairs." Lindsay led her out of the room. "Dad's already waiting, and Becca's about to go to work. I want to tell you all at the same time."

Laughing, Donna allowed herself to be guided downstairs to the family room. Paul was sitting on the sofa; Becca sat on the floor beside him, glancing at her watch and looking bored. Exchanging a quick glance of puzzlement with her husband, Donna seated herself on the opposite end of the sofa so that Becca was between them.

Only then did she notice that Lindsay was wringing her hands and compulsively shifting her weight from foot to foot. "Lindsay?" Donna said, suddenly anxious. "What is it, honey?"

"I have an announcement to make." Lindsay took a deep breath. "Brandon and I are getting married."

Donna couldn't breathe. She groped for Paul's hand and squeezed it.

Lindsay looked around at her silent family. "Well? Say something."

"You're out of your mind," Becca said flatly.

Lindsay frowned at her, then looked at her parents, hopeful. "Mom? Dad?"

Breathe, Donna ordered herself, then gasped, "I don't know what to say."

Lindsay smiled nervously. "'Congratulations' would be nice."

"Congratulations," Donna and Paul said in unison, in a monotone. Becca merely groaned and let her head fall back against the sofa.

"But you like Brandon," Lindsay protested.

Donna said, "Of course we like him—"

"I don't," Becca said.

"—But this is a little sudden," Paul finished. "Your mother and I weren't expecting to hear an announcement like this so soon."

"Brandon and I have been dating for two years."

"I've had library books longer than that," Becca said.

Donna patted Becca on the shoulder to quiet her. "Have you set a date?"

"Well, I've always wanted a June wedding, and Brandon will have some vacation time then—"

"June of next year?" Donna shrilled.

"I know that only gives us eleven months to plan, but we don't want anything elaborate."

"What about school?" Paul asked.

"Brandon says I don't really need to finish. After medical school, he'll earn enough to support both of us."

"I don't believe I'm hearing this," Becca said.

Donna couldn't believe it either. "You're going to quit school a year before graduation?"

Lindsay hesitated. "Well, Brandon thinks maybe I shouldn't go back this year, either. He thinks maybe—as long as it's okay with you—we could take my tuition money and use that for the wedding instead."

"'Brandon thinks,'" Becca mimicked, then her jaw dropped. "You're pregnant, aren't you?"

"No, I am definitely not pregnant," Lindsay snapped. She looked close to tears. "Isn't anyone happy for me?"

Paul released Donna's hand and leaned forward to rest his elbows on his knees. "Sweetheart, don't you think you ought to finish college before you get married? You're only twenty."

"That's legal in this state, Dad."

"Finish college first," Donna pleaded. "There's nothing wrong with a long engagement. If it's meant to be, two years won't make a difference."

Donna saw something in Lindsay's eyes change then, as if she were closing some part of herself away from them, and a pang of uneasiness went through her.

"It makes a difference to Brandon," Lindsay said. "He wants us to get married now, I mean, right now. Elope. I talked him into waiting until June. That's the best I can do."

Donna didn't like the sound of that, but before she could say anything, Paul spoke. "I still don't understand why you have to give up school. If you have your heart set on getting married, we won't stand in your way, but can't you continue school, too? Think of everything you'll miss. Your classes, all your friends, all the fun you girls have—"

"Yes, and the drama society," Donna broke in. "What about the plays you were going to direct this year? You were looking forward to them. And that internship next summer. Professor Collins said you had a good chance of winning it."

As Donna spoke, Lindsay's cheeks flushed. "I know," she said.

"I know it's a sacrifice, but when you love someone the way Brandon and I love each other, you make sacrifices for him."

"What exactly is Brandon sacrificing for you?" Becca inquired.

Lindsay shot her a sharp look. "I'm leaving school because Brandon can't afford to pay for my last two years, and he doesn't feel right having my parents pay his wife's tuition." She took a deep, shaky breath and looked from Donna to Paul and back. "Please, I don't want to fight. Please tell me you're okay with this."

"Are you sure this is what you want?" Donna asked in a small voice.

"This is what I want."

"Then we'll make the best of it," Paul said.

"I don't want you to make the best of it," Lindsay said. "I want you to be happy for us."

She looked so miserable that Donna rose and embraced her. "We're happy if you're happy." As Lindsay clung to her, Donna caught Paul's eye and shook her head slightly. They could discuss this privately later and, she hoped, find some way to convince their daughter to reconsider.

"I still say you're nuts," Becca muttered.

Lindsay pulled away from her mother and turned to her sister. "I hope you'll be my maid of honor anyway."

"Maid of honor?" Becca considered. "Can I help pick out the dress?"

"Why? Are you afraid I'd stick you in something hideous?"

"That thought did cross my mind."

Lindsay laughed. "Yes, you can help pick out the style—but I get to pick the color."

"That's fair."

Lindsay turned back to her mother, tentative. "Will you help me choose a wedding gown?"

"You don't need to worry about that just yet," Donna said. "You have plenty of time."

"I know. It's just—well, now that it's official, I want to get it over with. The work, I mean. It'll be a lot of work, and I want to get started." Her smile trembled, and Donna knew what an effort it took for her to keep it in place.

Paul sighed and rubbed at his jaw distractedly.

"I know this is a shock, but you'll feel better once you get used to the idea," Lindsay said. "Brandon says his parents were surprised, too, but once they had some time to adjust, they were happy for us."

Donna wondered how long ago Brandon had told his parents. How long Lindsay had been engaged without telling her and Paul?

"You'll meet Brandon's parents soon," Lindsay promised. "They're coming to Minneapolis next month to visit him. I thought we could drive down and meet them for supper. That's on a Sunday, the fifteenth. The families should meet each other before the wedding."

"I can't," Donna heard herself say.

Lindsay's face fell. "What?"

"I can't." She could support her daughter here, at home, but she could not—she *would* not rush out and meet the other family and plunge into a frenzy of wedding plans as if she wanted this marriage to happen, when she didn't, at least not now.

"Why not?"

"I can't." August fifteenth. Why did that date sound familiar? "I'm busy that day."

"Too busy to meet Brandon's parents?"

"That's the week I'm going out of town," Donna said. "I know you've heard me talk about it. My friend Megan and I are meeting at quilt camp. Don't you remember?"

Lindsay looked dubious. "I guess I forgot."

"Well, that's the week. I'm sorry, honey, but I'll have to meet Brandon's family another time." Brandon was a nice enough young man—what she knew of him—but they were both so young, and she couldn't bear to see Lindsay throw away all her dreams for the future. Lindsay had begged them to be happy for her, but how could Donna be happy when her every instinct screamed that Lindsay was not?

She climbed the stairs and retreated to the sanctuary of her quilt studio, where she switched on the computer and sank heavily into the chair. As she waited for the system to boot up, she realized she'd have to confirm that date with Megan and ask her where exactly this quilt camp was, anyway.

Adam fumbled for the phone. "Hello?"

"Adam?"

"Yeah?" he mumbled, trying to clear his throbbing head. Last night his two best friends had shown up with a case of beer and a stack of videos—war movies, the kind where the hard-edged, tough hero died at the end by throwing himself on a hand grenade or by carrying a bomb into an enemy bunker to save his equally hard-edged, tough buddies. Natalie despised the genre, and if she had been present, they would have watched something else entirely. And that, his friends' message seemed to be, was precisely the point; watching movies with an abundance of pyrotechnics and high body counts was celebration of the male independence he had narrowly escaped losing. As if that was what he wanted, as if it were his choice.

"Good morning, honey. It's Nana."

Of course. Who else would phone so early on a Sunday morning? "Hi, Nana."

"Did I wake you, dear?"

"Yeah, but that's okay."

"You should be getting ready for church by now anyway."

He squinted at the clock. "Church isn't for another four hours." He sat up on the edge of the bed and yawned. "What's going on?"

"I need you to drive me somewhere next month."

He smothered a laugh. "It's a good thing you called me so

early," he said with mock solemnity. "If you'd waited until dawn, I might have been all booked up."

"Listen to how you talk to your grandmother," she scolded him. "I have no idea why you're still my favorite grandson."

"Each of us is the favorite, according to you."

"I can have more than one favorite. Now, about this ride. Are you free on August fifteenth or am I going to have to walk? That's a Sunday."

He felt a pang, picturing how that Sunday in August should have been spent—a leisurely breakfast on the patio with Natalie, an afternoon trip out to Amish country to look at the furniture she so adored, maybe a romantic candlelit dinner. But now . . . "I won't be busy."

"Are you sure?"

"Very sure. Where do you need to go?"

"It's time for my quilt camp again, remember? I always go during my birthday week. I need you to drive me there on August fifteenth and pick me up the twenty-first. That's a Saturday."

"Is this the camp in Pennsylvania?"

"Yes. Your sister took me last year, and she said to tell you it's your turn."

Now he remembered his sister complaining about the long drive to the middle of nowhere. "Why don't you fly this time?"

"You know I don't like airplanes," she said primly. "I would take the train, but the nearest station is a long drive from Elm Creek Manor. What do you suggest I do, take a taxi? I suppose I'll have to, if it's so much trouble—"

"It's no trouble," he assured her before she could get too excited. "I have a teachers' in-service at school the next day, but Sunday's no problem. I'll take you."

"And pick me up?"

"And pick you up." Why not? Anything was better than moping around the empty house. Maybe he should get a dog.

"Thank you. You're a good boy." She paused. "Do you want to come to supper tonight? I could make a nice pork roast."

"Thanks, Nana, but—"

"Dayton's only an hour north of you. Less than that, the way you drive."

"Maybe next week." He didn't feel up to seeing anyone that day. Or maybe for the rest of the summer.

Nana's voice softened. "Adam, I didn't forget what day yesterday was."

The reminder pained him. "You mean, what yesterday was supposed to have been."

"You're much better off without her."

"So I'm told."

"If she's that fickle, it's better you find out now rather than three or four years into it."

"Please don't criticize her."

"Why not, after what she did to you? I never liked her, you know."

"Yeah, I know." So did Natalie. So did the entire family and, if he knew his grandmother, all the ladies in her quilting circle and every other senior in her apartment complex. Nana had never been one to keep her opinions to herself, even when her words were sharp enough to cut. Yes, Natalie had her faults; he could admit that. She had a temper, and he never knew whether he would please her or set off a tantrum. But even now, when any sensible person would be too angry to remember any of her good qualities, just thinking about her made him ache with loss. He couldn't honestly say he still loved her the way he had before she broke off their engagement—his trust had been too badly damaged for that—but he still cared about her, and he missed her.

"My friends have granddaughters—"

"No, you're not setting me up," he interrupted. "I'm not ready. I mean it, Nana."

"I heard you," she said innocently. "But if I meet a lovely young woman and happen to mention my favorite grandson, and if she happens to be available . . ."

He was too tired to argue. After promising to come to dinner the next Sunday, Adam hung up the phone and slumped back into bed with a groan. This was supposed to have been his first full day as a married man. He should be sleeping peacefully in the bridal suite of the Radisson Hotel Cincinnati right now, his beautiful, dark-haired wife in his arms. He should be dreaming of their future, which had always seemed so full of promise. He should have risen just in time for a shower and breakfast before they left on their honeymoon. Instead Natalie and her sister were going to use their nonrefundable tickets to the Bahamas, and a call from his grandmother instead of a kiss from his bride had awakened him.

Adam closed his eyes and tried to go back to sleep. It wasn't even six o'clock in the morning, but already he knew he was in for a rough day. Maybe he *should* get a dog. Natalie hated dogs. Now that he was allowed to have one, he ought to get one, if only to convince his well-meaning but overanxious family and friends that he was getting on with his life.

Grace nodded as Sondra chatted about the two men she was dating, though she was only partially listening. For the most part her thoughts were on the television interview scheduled for later that morning, but in the back of her mind she fretted about the sewing machine and fabric stash left idle too long in her studio. She also worried about how tired she was, and how if the smell of relaxants and perming solution weren't so sharp in her nostrils, she might fall asleep. She tired so easily lately.

"Justine driving you to the station?" Sondra suddenly asked, speaking in a voice far too casual to be casual.

"Yes." Grace tried to catch her eye in the mirror. "Why do you ask?" Was it that obvious she rarely drove these days? She had walked to the salon, but her loft was only a few blocks away; surely that had not roused Sondra's suspicions.

"No reason." Sondra kept her attention on Grace's hair. "I was just wondering how she's doing."

"She's fine. Busy with school and Joshua, and volunteering at the women's shelter." Grace admired her daughter's commitment to social justice, but she hoped when Justine completed her degree and passed the bar, not all of her work would be pro bono.

Sondra trimmed a stray curl with the electric razor. "She seeing anyone?"

"Not that I know of."

"You sure?"

"Well . . ." Grace thought about it, and shrugged. "Of course. She would have told me."

"Is that so."

Something in her expression made Grace suspicious. "What do you mean?"

"I wasn't going to say anything—"

Though Sondra had raised the seat until Grace could barely reach the ground with an outstretched foot, she managed to spin the chair around so she could face her friend. "Tell me."

"If you're going to force it out of me, two nights ago I saw her and Joshua out at a restaurant." Sondra raised her eyebrows. "They weren't alone."

"You mean, a man was with them?"

"What else would I mean?" Sondra shook her head. "For someone who's not seeing anyone, Justine sure looked interested."

Grace's hopes rose. Since Joshua had accompanied them, maybe this mysterious man was his father—and maybe that meant Justine had decided to patch things up with him. Grace had always liked Marc and had been heartbroken when Justine told her in no uncertain terms that they wouldn't be getting married. Two-year-old Joshua was an angel, but the older he grew, the more he would need a father figure in his life. Maybe Justine had finally realized that. "Did you get a good look at him?"

"Mmm-hmm." Sondra spun Grace's chair around to face the mirror and tended her close-cropped hair with a comb. "Tall, nice eyes, good-looking. If Justine gets tired of him, she can send him to me. He's more my type, anyway."

Grace hid a smile. Sondra thought every handsome man was her type. "How so, exactly?"

Sondra gave her a pointed look in the mirror. "He's old enough to be her father, that's how."

"Are you sure?" Grace's heart sank. So the man wasn't Joshua's father but someone else—someone *her* age. "Justine's never had a thing for older men."

"You didn't see this particular older man."

Grace didn't need to see him. She mistrusted him already. What was Justine thinking? She was supposed to find a father figure for Joshua, not for herself. "Maybe he was a professor. Maybe they were discussing a school project."

"At a restaurant on a Saturday night? And why would she bring Joshua along instead of leaving him with his grandma?"

"I don't know." Distressed, Grace searched her memory for any hint Justine might have let fall about this strange new man. "I can't remember what she told me she was doing that night. I know she didn't say she had a date." Grace definitely would have remembered that. "How was he with Joshua?"

Sondra's eyes widened in injured innocence. "Do you think I spent my evening spying on your daughter?"

"Yes, I do. And I would have done the same for you."

"Joshua seemed to love him." Sondra brushed a few bits of hair from the back of Grace's neck. "Think of it this way: He's old, but at least he likes kids."

"And that makes it fine that he has one foot in the grave."

Sondra laughed. "I said old enough to be her father, not great-grandpa."

"That's old enough."

"A good man is a good man," Sondra protested. "What does age matter?"

"You know it matters, or you wouldn't have mentioned it."

"Well, maybe it does matter, but it shouldn't." Sondra removed the plastic drape and gave Grace a hand mirror so she could examine the back of her head. "All that counts is that Justine is happy, right?"

Grace frowned, knowing Sondra was right but not feeling any better about it. Her daughter was an intelligent young woman, but even intelligent people didn't always make sensible decisions where matters of the heart were concerned. Grace knew that as well as anyone.

What was worse was that Justine hadn't told her about her new friend. If their relationship had advanced so far that Justine would bring Joshua along on their dates, why hadn't she mentioned him to her own mother?

"Good luck," Sondra told her as Grace left the salon, but Grace wasn't sure if she was referring to the interview or to Justine's mysterious dinner companion.

She met her daughter and grandson in the park across the street from the salon. Justine was pushing Joshua in a swing, her dozens of long, glossy braids gathered in a silk scarf at the nape of her neck. She had the strong cheekbones and rich brown skin her mother and grandmother had also been blessed with, but her stubborn, independent streak had come from her mother alone, and her passion from the father she barely remembered. Joshua resembled Justine physically, but his studious, thoughtful temperament reminded Grace of his own father. Marc and Justine had been good together. She wished with all her heart that he had been the man Sondra had seen with Justine.

When Justine spotted her, she smiled and lifted Joshua out of the swing. Grace laughed with delight as he ran to meet her, and, forgetting herself, she bent over to swoop him up in her arms. "Oooph," she grunted, shifting him so his weight rested on her hip. "You're getting bigger every day, aren't you, honey?"

"Bigger and smarter and more mischievous," Justine said with a smile as she joined them, but Grace saw the concern in her eyes.

"I'm fine," Grace told her.

"I know." Still, Justine took Joshua from her arms, and Grace was more than willing to let her.

As Justine drove them downtown to the television station, Grace decided not to mention the little she knew of Justine's secret. Her daughter would have a fit if she knew her mother's friends were keeping an eye on her. Grace contented herself with asking, "If you were seeing someone new, you would tell me, wouldn't you?"

"Sure." Justine paused, keeping her eyes on the road. "Probably. It depends."

"On what?"

"On whether I thought you'd hate him on sight, on how serious I was about him. I wouldn't want to get your hopes up by introducing you to someone who wouldn't be around long." She glanced in the rearview mirror and lowered her voice. "That's why I don't introduce anyone to Joshua right away, either. I wouldn't want to hurt him by letting him get too attached to just anyone."

"That seems wise."

"It also gives me time to make sure the boyfriend understands that Joshua will always come first in my life—before myself, before my work, and definitely before him." She sighed. "That's probably why I don't date much. Not that I mind. My life is full already, and I'm not one of these sisters who thinks she has to have a man to be complete. I learned that from you."

"I think I taught you too well," Grace said glumly, thinking of Marc, but Justine merely laughed.

When they reached the studio, Justine left Grace in front of the building and went to park the car. Grace went inside, up the elevator to the second floor. She waited there for the producer, a thin, dark-haired white woman with a harried expression, who bustled in ten minutes late, full of apologies.

"I wasn't waiting very long," Grace said, but the woman continued on as if she hadn't heard, leading her through a maze of corridors so rapidly that Grace stumbled and nearly fell.

"You'll be on in five, right after local news and right before the weather. Your assistant sent over the photos, so we're all set." The producer paused for breath as she stopped outside a large, solid door. "You'll need to keep quiet until your segment. Try not to knock anything over."

"I'll do my best," Grace said dryly as the producer opened the door and led her inside.

The studio was cool and dark except for the end of the room where the set was located. The two news anchors sat behind the desk taking turns reading from the TelePrompTer. Grace had hoped to see the same woman who had interviewed her last time, but her usual chair was occupied by the blond woman from the morning show. Soon after, when the news went to commercial and the producer led Grace to a chair on the set, she realized with some dismay that the blond woman was her interviewer.

"Good afternoon. I'm Andrea Jarthur," the blond woman said, smiling and extending a perfectly manicured hand.

Grace shook it. "Grace Daniels." From behind, someone clipped a microphone to her jacket. "Thanks for having me on."

"It's my pleasure. I love your work."

"Thank you," Grace said, nervousness stirring. "You do know I'm not here to talk about my work, right?"

"Of course," Andrea said, smiling. "But if we have time, I might get to that, okay?"

"I'd prefer it if you didn't."

Andrea's eyebrows rose. "I've never met an artist who didn't like to promote her work. Surely you don't mean it?"

Before Grace had a chance to reply, the stage manager called out, "In five, four . . ." He held up three fingers, then two, and then one.

Andrea turned to one of the cameras. "Welcome back. With us now is Grace Daniels, the celebrated quilt artist from right here in the Bay area. Welcome, Grace."

"Thank you."

"I understand that you're the curator of a new exhibit of antique quilts at the deYoung Museum in Golden Gate Park."

"That's right. The exhibit is titled 'Stitched into the Soul: A Celebration of African-American Quiltmakers in—'"

"Is any of your own work included?"

"No," Grace said, somewhat sharply. "These are *antique* quilts."

"Of course. Tell us, what makes these quilts so special?"

"They're important not only as works of art, but as historical artifacts. These quilts were pieced by slaves for their own use, and therefore they help document what life was like for them." Mindful of the limited time, Grace briefly explained what could be learned from the materials used, the patterns chosen, and the condition of the quilts.

"That's fascinating," Andrea interrupted just as Grace was warming to her subject. "Especially since the domestic arts are undergoing a renaissance of sorts these days, aren't they? Hobbies like quilting are becoming so popular lately, but you were really out there on the cutting edge—pardon the pun—years ago, weren't you?"

"Actually . . ." *Hobbies?* Grace thought. *Domestic arts?* "What this exhibit shows us is that—"

"I think what your fans really want to know is, when will you next treat us to an exhibit of your own work?" Andrea smiled innocently. "I understand it's been over three years since you've had a show."

"Two years."

"Can you give us a little hint as to your current projects? And maybe tell us how soon we can expect to see your latest work?"

Grace forced herself to smile through clenched teeth. "I don't like to discuss my projects before they're finished."

Andrea's bright smile never faltered. "The San Francisco art community will just have to wait in suspense, is that what you're saying?"

"I . . . I suppose so. But in the meantime, the deYoung Museum exhibit is a fascinating look at an important part of American art and cultural history." Quickly Grace ran through the particulars. Her voice sounded clear and serene in her ears, but inside she was fuming—at Andrea, of course, for her questions, but also at herself, for allowing herself to be so easily shaken.

After the interview ended, Grace abruptly rose and left the set without returning Andrea's farewell. Justine met her in the lobby,

Joshua by her side. "How did it go?" she asked as Grace approached.

"I don't want to talk about it." Grace continued past her daughter and out the front door so quickly that Justine had to scoop up her son and hurry after her. Grace's heart was racing. Current projects—what current projects? How could she talk about her latest quilt when her latest quilt had been completed more than a year before? How could she admit that her well of creative inspiration—which she had once thought too deep to ever run dry—was as barren as her own future?

"I have to get away from here," she said, thinking aloud.

"The car's only a block away," Justine replied, baffled. But Grace hardly heard her. She had to get away from her loft, from her studio, from the museum where she faced questions like Andrea Jarthur's nearly every day, from everything familiar.

Suddenly a memory tickled the back of her mind, and she thought of her friend Sylvia Compson. Sylvia was running a quilt retreat somewhere in Pennsylvania. Perhaps Sylvia could provide the sanctuary Grace needed so her art might return to her while she could still hold a needle.

Two

JULIA MARVELED that the agency's chartered jet managed to locate the tiny airport at all, much less come to a halt before speeding off the end of the runway. She studied the view from the window with misgivings. Except for the control tower and a small one-story building she assumed was the terminal, all she could see were trees. Had Maury taken leave of his senses, sending her out into the wilderness like this?

"The limo should be waiting," the man across the aisle said. "I've kept your arrival a secret, but don't be surprised if there's a crowd gathered around. They probably get a limo in this backwater only once every twenty years."

Julia felt a flash of annoyance, not the first since meeting her new agent a week after Maury's retirement party. "I'm Ares," he had introduced himself when she joined him at the restaurant. After she seated herself, he had reached across the table and offered her his hand and a flash of white teeth. Maury would have stood as she approached, and he would have pulled out her chair for her and not returned to his own until he was sure she was comfortable.

"Aries, the ram?" she had said, shaking the younger man's hand.

"No." His grin had suddenly become fierce. "Ares, the Greek god of war."

"How interesting," Julia had replied, gingerly releasing his hand and thinking, *Oh, dear.* She had allowed her contract to revert to him because of his reputation for being ruthless, for doing anything it took to get his clients the roles they sought. She couldn't have picked an agent less like Maury if she had tried, but Maury's approach, as a gentleman bargaining honorably with other gentlemen on the strength of his word, had become as ineffectual as it was archaic and naive. It also didn't hurt that Ares was the nephew of one of Hollywood's most powerful directors. She didn't have to like him, she reminded herself, to work with him.

Still, she worried that his focus on getting the deal might blind him to the importance of good PR. She gave him a disapproving look and said, "People in towns like these watch movies. They also kept *Family Tree* at the top of the Nielsens for many years."

"Near the top, anyway," Ares acquiesced. "The top of the middle, at least."

Stung, Julia pursed her lips and unfastened her seat belt.

No crowd had gathered by the limo parked on the tarmac, but the sight did attract a few curious glances from other travelers. A group of four women—some in cheerful patchwork clothing, all younger than she—talked and laughed as they greeted each other on the sidewalk. As the limo drove through the parking lot, Julia lowered her sunglasses to get a better look, but suddenly the tinted window began to rise.

She turned to Ares, who had his finger on the button in his armrest. "We can't have the locals gawking at you."

Julia thought the women seemed too preoccupied to spare the

limo a second glance, but she removed her sunglasses and settled back into her seat, resigned.

For more than an hour they drove in silence past picturesque farms and rolling, forested hills. Julia lowered her window to take in the scenery, figuring they were surely isolated enough to satisfy Ares. Just when she thought she'd be stuck in that car with him until nightfall, the driver turned onto a gravel road that wound its way through a leafy wood.

"The least they could have done was pave the road," Ares grumbled. Julia hid a smile.

They crossed a narrow bridge over a creek so clear she could see stones at the bottom, and suddenly the trees gave way to a vast expanse of lawn. The road smoothed, and at the end of it Julia spotted a gray stone building with tall white columns and two semicircular staircases climbing gracefully to a broad veranda. She could see at least a dozen people—mostly women—unloading luggage or helping others carry their bags up the stairs, through the tall double doors, and into the house. With a pang, Julia suddenly remembered how much she had always hated the first day of school. Where would she sit in the classroom? Would she eat lunch alone every day? As lovely as this Elm Creek Manor appeared to be, Julia's stomach twisted at the thought of spending an entire week there, alone in a crowd. By instinct she slipped on her sunglasses again.

Sure enough, the clusters of women broke off their conversations and watched as the limousine came to a stop in front of the manor. When the driver opened the passenger door, Ares stepped out first and offered his hand to assist her. Julia took it ungratefully, suspecting it was a show for the crowd, who gaped as he escorted her up one of the semicircular staircases.

A woman older than she met them at the door. "Miss Merchaud?" she said pleasantly, without a trace of the awe or admiration Julia usually evoked from people outside the industry. "I'm Sylvia Compson. Welcome to Elm Creek Manor."

"Thank you." Julia followed her inside to a large foyer with gleaming marble floors and a ceiling three stories high. The furnishings spoke of wealth, but of good taste and comfort rather than excess. Perhaps Maury hadn't been so misguided after all.

"You must be tired after such a long trip." Sylvia led her to the center of the room, where three women wearing name tags sat behind a long table. "Let's take care of your registration and show you to your room." She eyed Ares with some skepticism and nodded to the driver. "Matthew will help you with your bags."

She signaled to a young man with curly blond hair, who smiled as he approached and reached to take the bags from the driver.

Ares put out an arm to stop him. "It's under control, thanks." In an undertone, he added to Sylvia, "We don't need the entire staff knowing where Miss Merchaud will be staying. Security. You understand." He shrugged at Matthew. "No hard feelings, buddy."

"Sure," the other man replied, and Julia had the distinct impression he was trying hard not to laugh.

"Matthew is our caretaker. I assure you, he's quite harmless," Sylvia said.

Julia removed her sunglasses and pretended not to notice the hush that had fallen over the other guests, who were no doubt stunned to see "Grandma Wilson" playing the prima donna. "Give him the bags," she murmured to the driver. He looked from her to Ares, uncertain. "I said, give him the bags." At last the driver complied, and she smiled an apology to Matthew. To her relief, the registration process went quickly, and soon she, Ares, and Matthew with her bags were following Sylvia upstairs.

"Your suite is in the west wing," Sylvia told them as they reached the second floor landing. "You'll have your own bath. I trust you'll be quite comfortable."

"Thank you," Julia said, watching as other women went from room to room introducing themselves and welcoming each other, as excited and happy as children at summer camp. A few greeted Julia as she passed; she smiled guardedly in response, wondering if they recognized her without her limousine and stage makeup.

Sylvia ushered them into the room and pointed out the closet, the bath, and her private phone. It was a large suite with a four-poster bed covered with a blue-and-red quilt pieced of homespun plaids. "It's lovely," Julia said. "Thank you, Sylvia."

"You're quite welcome. Now, if there's nothing else you need, I'll return to our other guests."

Ares held up a hand. "Before you go, let's establish some ground rules."

The older woman's eyebrows rose.

"Miss Merchaud's status may cause some excitement," Ares went on. "Ordinarily Miss Merchaud goes out of her way to please her fans, but this week is different. We can't allow her to be disturbed. For that reason, she'll take her meals in her room rather than the common dining area, and she will not participate in any of the camp activities other than classroom instruction."

Sylvia folded her hands. "All of our activities are voluntary, Mr. Ares."

"Just Ares. Also, is there any way Miss Merchaud could have private instruction rather than attending classes?"

"I'm afraid that's not possible."

"Then at the very least, she'll need a table to herself at the front of the classroom."

"I'm sure that can be arranged."

"Ares," Julia interrupted, "I don't think—"

"You'll also inform your staff and other guests that they are not to address Miss Merchaud or trouble her in any way."

Sylvia's mouth twitched. "Do I understand you correctly? You wish me to announce that no one may speak with her?"

"Unless she speaks to them first, yes."

"That's absurd, and I won't do it," Sylvia declared. Behind her, the young blond man coughed as if he were strangling back a laugh. "Miss Merchaud is a camper like everyone else here." She turned her piercing gaze on Julia. "And I'm tired of talking about you as if you weren't in the room. If you wish to ignore people who speak to you, that's your decision, but I won't offend my other guests by clamping muzzles on them."

"I never wanted that," Julia said, distressed. "This wasn't my idea."

"I'm pleased to hear that, because otherwise you'll have a dreadful time this week. What an idea—to come to quilt camp and refuse to make any new friends." She shook her head in disapproval and frowned at Ares. "You see, I have a few ground rules of my own. If they don't suit you, I'd be happy to return your agency's check."

"That won't be necessary," Ares said stiffly. "I'm sure Miss Merchaud will be able to adapt to the circumstances."

"Good." Sylvia returned her attention to Julia, her voice noticeably warmer. "If there's anything we can do to make your stay more enjoyable"—her eyes flicked to Ares as if getting rid of him would be a step in the right direction—"please inform someone on the staff." With that, she and Matthew left the room, closing the door behind them.

"What a crazy old bat," Ares muttered.

"I found her quite pleasant," Julia said. "And I do wish you had consulted me before deciding I should isolate myself in my room all week. Maybe I would have enjoyed—"

"You're not here to enjoy yourself. You're here to work."

"Observing quilters would help me prepare for my role."

"You can observe them during your classes. The less you interact with these quilters, the less likely you'll reveal the truth. The press releases for the film will promote you as an expert quilter. Do you want these old biddies running to the media with the real story?"

Julia laughed. "I doubt even the tabloids would be interested. As secrets go, it's not very sexy."

"You can't afford the risk. Maury didn't want to tell you, but Bernier agreed to give you this part only because he thinks you already know how to quilt. If he discovers you lied, you're out of a job, and I don't think I need to tell you how difficult it will be to find you another role this good."

"I appreciate your honesty," she said crisply. How could he be so hurtful, so undiplomatic? "I suppose you're right. When I'm not practicing my quilting, I ought to be learning my lines."

"Don't bother. Bernier wants a major rewrite. Wait until you have a final script."

"Ellen will be involved in the revisions, of course?"

"Who?"

"Ellen Henderson, the writer and director."

Ares looked confused. "Stephen Deneford is directing. I heard it from Bernier himself two days ago."

"I see." Julia wondered how Ellen had been informed of the decision. "But she's still the writer."

"I guess she might be consulted. You know how Deneford and Bernier are."

Julia shrugged as if she did, although she had met Bernier only once and knew Deneford merely by reputation—and surely no more than half of those stories could be true.

None too soon, Ares left her to settle into her room. The room felt oddly still when she was alone, the silence broken only by the little noises she made unfastening her suitcases and opening and closing bureau drawers. From the hallway came the sounds of the other women talking and laughing, and the sound of quick footsteps going from room to room. Julia wondered why all the other guests seemed to know each other already, when quilt camp had only just begun.

She sat on the bed and listened.

Donna had been at quilt camp for less than an hour, but had already unpacked her suitcase and had met one of her next-door neighbors and the woman across the hall from her suite on the second floor of the south wing. She had just returned to her room for a patchwork jacket she had promised to show a quilter from West Virginia when she heard a voice through her open doorway. "I'm here," an elderly woman called. "The fun can begin!"

"Vinnie!" several other women cried out, and a clamor of voices echoed down the hallway.

Donna peered outside to see what all the commotion was about. A thin woman in her early eighties was trying to make her way down the hallway, but was stopped every few feet by one welcoming camper after another. She wore a bright red skirt, white tennis shoes and top, and had a red baseball cap perched on a fluffy cloud of white hair. Donna liked her on sight, and was pleased when the young man carrying her suitcase eventually led her into the unoccupied room next door. Several other campers followed them inside.

Donna's other next-door neighbor joined her in the hall. "Vinnie's here," she said, delighted. "That means we'll have a party."

"Do you two know each other?"

"I met her here last summer. She was one of the first twelve guests of Elm Creek Quilt Camp, and she's come back each year since, always during the week of her birthday. The staff throws a big surprise party for her—only it's not such a surprise anymore, though Vinnie always pretends it is. She's a riot. Come on, I'll introduce you."

She took Donna's arm and pulled her down the hallway. Donna was enjoying herself so much that she could almost forget that at that very moment her husband was in Minneapolis with Lindsay, Brandon, and Brandon's parents. And where on earth was Megan? It was almost time for supper, and she hadn't checked in yet.

Megan pulled off the highway and followed the signs for food and lodging. She had been driving for hours, the past two with a growing suspicion that she had missed the correct exit. *Contemporary Quilting* magazine had awarded her a generous travel allowance, but instead of using it for an airline ticket and cab fare, she had put the money aside for Robby's back-to-school clothes.

Now she regretted her frugality. She had anticipated having several more hours of daylight to drive by, but she hadn't considered the rolling Appalachian terrain. The sun had descended nearly to the tops of the mountains behind her; if she had missed the proper turnoff with the sun shining, how could she expect to find it in twilight? Twice she had stopped to ask directions—but while one person had heard of Waterford but didn't know how to get there, the other had insisted there was no such town in Pennsylvania.

Frustrated, her stomach growling, she pulled into the parking lot of a diner, ruefully remembering the camp brochure's photos of the elegant banquet hall at Elm Creek Manor. She would grab a bite to eat, study the map and get her bearings, and be back on the road in a half hour—and with any luck, she would choose the right direction.

She seated herself in a booth so she would have plenty of room to spread out her map. After the waitress took her order, she traced her route with a pencil, referring to the printed directions Elm Creek Quilts had provided. When the waitress delivered her turkey melt with fries, Megan moved the papers out of the way and thanked her. On impulse, she asked, "Do you know how to get to Waterford?"

The waitress shook her head. "Never heard of it."

Megan's heart sank. "Thanks anyway." Her gaze fell on a plate in the waitress's other hand. She inhaled the fragrance of baked apples and cinnamon and decided she'd order a slice of apple pie when she finished her supper. She deserved some dessert, as consolation for the loss of her first day of quilt camp. Besides, with her luck, she might be wandering Pennsylvania's back roads until dawn. She would need the energy.

As she watched the waitress walk away, her gaze fell on the man sitting in the booth across the aisle—or rather, on his shirt. It was the exact shade of blue she needed for her latest project, a charm quilt composed of hundreds of equilateral triangles. Instead of using pieced or appliquéd blocks, Megan preferred to make one-patch quilts, in which all the pieces were the same shape. Varying the color, pattern, and value of the pieces could create dramatic visual effects, but indifference to fabric placement could easily result in a drab, uninspired quilt. And since a charm quilt by definition required that no two fabrics could be used more than once, she often spent weeks searching for the right material to finish a project. The gray-blue she now looked upon had eluded her for a month, even though her Internet friends had sent her swatches of the various hues in their collections.

"Did I spill something on myself?"

Megan looked up, startled, into the puzzled but smiling face of the man wearing the shirt. "Oh. I'm sorry," she stammered. "I was just admiring your shirt."

"Thanks."

Megan wished she had stared more discreetly, but he had spoken to her first, and she just had to have that blue. "Where did you get it?"

"It was a gift from . . . a friend."

Something in his voice told Megan his friend was a woman. "It's very nice," she said lamely. She hoped he didn't think she was trying to pick him up. "I . . . see, I'm a quilter, and I'm always looking for the right fabric."

"Say no more," he said, with a knowing grin. "My grandmother is a quilter."

Great, Megan thought. As if she hadn't met enough people who considered quilting the exclusive domain of little old ladies and people with too much time on their hands. She was tired of explaining her passion to those who didn't know any better, and decided not to bother trying to explain it to some stranger in a diner whom she'd never see again.

Megan returned her attention to the map as she ate, trying to figure out where she had gone wrong. According to her father's estimate, she should have reached the turnoff two hours ago. Should she backtrack or keep going east? She had seen a gas station across the street from the diner; maybe someone there would be able to direct her, although the responses she had received so far made that seem unlikely.

By the time she finished her sandwich, she had decided to give the gas station a chance—after dessert. She signaled the waitress, who approached with a slice of apple pie on a plate. "You read my mind," Megan said.

"What's that?" the waitress said, delivering the plate to the man in the booth across the aisle.

"Oh, I thought that was for me. I was just about to order a slice. Could I have it à la mode, please?"

"I'm afraid you're too late, honey. That was the last piece."

"Are you sure?"

The waitress looked tired. "You can check for yourself if you don't believe me." She jerked her head in the direction of the front counter, where an empty pie tin sat in the bakery case. "Would you like something else? Chocolate cake? Peach cobbler?"

"No, thanks. I was really looking forward to that apple pie."

"Here," the man said. "You can have it. I haven't touched it yet."

"Oh, no," Megan said. "Thanks anyway."

"No, really." The man got up and brought the plate to her table. "Take it."

"I'm not going to take your dessert."

"You're not taking it; I'm giving it to you." He set the plate on her table, smiling. "Go ahead. Enjoy."

"I don't want it." Annoyed, Megan pushed the plate toward him. "What planet are you from, that you offer perfect strangers in restaurants your dessert?"

"Cincinnati."

"No kidding," she said, without thinking. "Me, too."

"Really." He sat down across from her. "I live near Winton Woods. How about you?"

"Actually . . ." Involuntarily, she shrank back against the seat as his knees bumped hers. "I moved away when I was very young."

"To Pennsylvania?"

"Well . . ." She wasn't about to tell some strange man where she lived. She looked to the waitress for help, but the woman merely folded her arms and listened. "Look," she said to the man, in a voice she hoped was firm but not unkind, in case he was a nutcase or something. "I appreciate your generosity, but you ordered the pie first, so it's yours. I can't accept it."

He shrugged. "So we'll split it." He turned to the waitress. "Could you bring us another plate and fork, please, and a dish of ice cream on the side?" He looked questioningly at Megan. "Vanilla?" When Megan managed a nod, he turned back to the waitress. "Vanilla."

The waitress returned quickly with his order, and he deftly sliced the piece of pie and placed half on the new plate. "Here you go," he said with a friendly grin.

"Thanks," she said, resigned. "Do you want some of my ice cream?"

"No, thanks," he said. "When it comes to apple pie, I'm a purist. No ice cream, no cheese, no caramel—nothing to mar the pure simplicity of the apple and the pastry." With that, he took a large bite of pie, savoring the mouthful.

Megan watched him, her misgivings changing to amusement. "I had no idea it was possible to have such strong opinions about apple pie."

"You should hear my discourse on tiramisu."

Megan smiled and took a bite of the dessert—and found it just as delicious as its fragrance had promised. "It's wonderful. Thanks for sharing it. I'll pay half, of course—"

"Don't be silly. It's my treat."

"At least let me pay for the ice cream, since you're not having any." She gave him a practiced no-nonsense look that had proven most effective with Robby. "I insist."

"Fair enough." He glanced down at her map. "Are you planning a trip, or did you lose your way?"

"Lost my way. I don't suppose you know how to get to Waterford?"

"Sure. I just came from there."

She was so astonished she almost dropped her fork. "You have no idea how glad I am to hear that. I thought I missed the turnoff, and I'd have to turn around and go home."

"You didn't miss it. Head east for another hour and you'll see the sign. Here." He turned her map around and picked up her pencil. "The sign doesn't say Waterford, but it's the same exit as Two Rivers." He circled a spot on her map. "Go south for a few miles and you'll start to see signs for Waterford College. You should be there by seven."

"Thanks," she said, greatly relieved.

"Anytime." He signaled to the waitress, then shrugged apologetically. "Sorry to eat and run, but it's a long drive back to Cincinnati, and tomorrow's a school day."

"Oh. Of course." She felt oddly disappointed as he rose and took the check from the waitress. "Well, thanks again for the dessert and the directions."

"My pleasure." He left his check and a few bills on his table across the aisle. "Drive safely."

"You too."

Megan watched him leave the diner, then peered out the front window and watched him climb into a well-kept but older model compact car. Only as he drove off did she realize that she didn't even know his name. Not that it mattered. "Tomorrow's a school day," he had said, which meant he was probably a dad with children—a married dad with children. Then a thought struck her. It was the middle of August. Unless his children's school had a very strange schedule, they should still be on summer vacation, as Robby was—which meant that this nice-seeming guy was either lying to her or had a very bizarre sense of humor.

The evidence pointed to a friendly but rather odd man. *Too bad*, she thought, and put him out of her mind.

After the welcome banquet, Sylvia invited Grace to a cozy sitting room off the kitchen for a cup of tea and a chat. "I'm so delighted you accepted my invitation at last," Sylvia said after giving her a warm hug. "How many years has it been?"

"Five, I think," Grace said, easing herself down onto a sofa and taking the cup Sylvia offered her.

"That's right. Lancaster, wasn't it? The Quilter's Heritage Celebration?" Sylvia took a seat beside her, and her eyes had a faraway look. "And to think Elm Creek Quilts didn't even exist then."

"It's amazing what you've accomplished in such a short time."

Sylvia sipped her tea and nodded as if she agreed, as if, like Grace, she was amazed at the long journey that had taken her away from her beloved home and back again. When she and Grace first met, Sylvia had been estranged from her family for decades and had never expected to return to Elm Creek Manor.

Fifteen years before, Grace had been giving a lecture at the University of Pittsburgh on Civil War–era textiles and how they had inspired her own work. She created what she called story quilts, appliqué quilts that illustrated historical and sometimes autobiographical tales. Unlike the intricate, painstaking appliqué of the Baltimore Album style, her work more closely followed the folk-art appliqué tradition, with abstract figures representing people, places, moods, or ideas. That evening she displayed several antique quilts from her collection, including one pieced by a runaway slave who had settled in Canada. After describing the symbolism of the motifs the unknown quilter had used, Grace showed a quilt of her own, one she had sewn in tribute to the long-ago quiltmaker as Grace imagined her hazardous journey north to freedom.

At a reception following the lecture, Sylvia introduced herself and told her about the Civil War–era quilts she remembered from her childhood home, which had been a station on the Underground Railroad. Intrigued, Grace asked her if it would be possible for her to inspect the collection, and possibly include photos of them in the book she was writing.

"That's unlikely," Sylvia said crisply. "For all I know, the quilts might not be there anymore."

Taken aback by her sudden change in temper, Grace apologized, wondering what she said to offend. Sylvia shook her head and said, "No, I should apologize to you. You had no way of knowing what a sensitive subject this is for me." She went on to explain that she and her sister had had a falling out years ago, and that Sylvia had not returned to her family estate since shortly after the war.

"Vietnam or the Gulf?" Grace asked, wondering how long this estrangement had gone on, and if the sisters might reconcile soon.

"The Second World War."

With that, Grace's hopes that she might be able to view those tantalizing quilts in the near future evaporated. In the years that followed, whenever she ran into Sylvia at a quilting function, she inquired about her relationship with her sister as delicately as she could, and eventually her concern for the quilts transformed into sympathy for her aging friend, who seemed to be growing more brittle-tempered with each year the old resentments simmered. Grace and her sisters were so close that hardly a week passed when they didn't communicate at least by phone, and she found it hard to imagine anything they could do that would compel Grace to sever all ties with them. No wonder Sylvia seemed so alone, despite her friends and accomplishments; she had cast off all her ties to her own history, and in doing so, she had lost herself. When Grace learned that Sylvia's sister had passed away, she feared that Sylvia would never recover from the loss and from the knowledge that now reconciliation would never come, but Sylvia had surprised her. From the debris of her grief, Sylvia had built a new future for herself and had come home at last to reclaim her family's history.

"I didn't build Elm Creek Quilts alone, of course," Sylvia was saying. "I have some very dedicated helpers. The truth is, I'm all but retired from the business now. Two young women, Sarah McClure and Summer Sullivan, direct our operations these days."

"You haven't retired from quilting, I hope."

"No, no, I could never do that. Even with the business, I still

offer my opinion when asked—and often when I'm not asked—
and I sign off on all our major financial and development decisions. Lately I've been seeing a bit of the country, traveling with a
friend. I've spent more weeks away from Elm Creek Manor than
here this summer."

"I'm glad you happened to be in town the week I came."

"Now, Grace," Sylvia admonished. "Do you really think I'd
make myself scarce when you've come all this way? I couldn't leave
without finding out what's troubling you."

Grace almost spilled her tea. "What do you mean?" Carefully
she placed her cup and saucer on the coffee table. "I'm fine. I just
thought I would enjoy a week of quilt camp."

"Grace, dear." Sylvia fixed her with that knowing gaze Grace
remembered well. "We both know there's nothing our teachers
could show you that you haven't seen already. You should be a
teacher here, not a camper."

"I just needed a change of scene."

"Perhaps you do. I must say I've never seen you so tense. You
haven't smiled once since you walked through those doors." Sylvia
placed a hand on her friend's, and in a gentle voice, added, "But I
know there's more. What's wrong, Grace?"

Grace took a deep breath and tried to smile. "My muse has
fled."

Sylvia's eyebrows rose. "I see. And you thought you might find
her here?"

"I thought in new surroundings, with other quilters around to
motivate me, I might be able to reawaken my creativity." Grace
shook her head, hopeless, and cradled her teacup in her hands. "I
don't know. I'm probably grasping at straws, but I haven't started a
new project in eighteen months. Eighteen months! You know how
prolific I used to be."

A frown of worry creased Sylvia's forehead. "Can you think of
any reason you might be blocked? Did something happen eighteen months ago? Have you been under an unusual amount of
stress?"

Grace's heart pounded. Was she that transparent? "No, of course not. Just the usual stress." Sylvia looked dubious, so Grace blurted out the first plausible worry that came to mind. "Except for my daughter. She's seeing a much older man fairly seriously, and she didn't even tell me about him."

"But you've worried about Justine before, and your art hasn't suffered."

"I suppose that can't be it, then," Grace said, as if she didn't know precisely what the source of her anxiety was. But she couldn't tell Sylvia, not yet, not until she had no choice. "Maybe there isn't a cause. Maybe I've just run out of ideas and inspiration. But there must be some way to replenish myself even if I don't understand why I ran dry."

"If it's replenishment you need, I'll see that you get it," Sylvia said. "Perhaps I was wrong about our staff not having anything to teach you. Why don't you sit in on some of our advanced classes? We have some delightful workshops in color theory, photo transfer, computer pattern design—all sorts of exciting techniques to explore."

"Photo transfer?"

"Yes, techniques for transferring images from a photograph onto fabric. You've always been fascinated with quilts as historical artifacts and documenting quiltmakers' lives. Perhaps photo transfer could help you discover a new way to explore that area of your craft. And it's not just the information that might stir your creativity," Sylvia added. "The interaction with other quilters is what I find most invigorating about a class, whether I'm the student or the teacher. You never know what new ideas might come to mind when you brainstorm with other quilters."

"Yes, you're right." Grace felt a flicker of hope, and suddenly she realized that for the first time in months, she wasn't dreading the thought of approaching a stack of uncut fabric. "Sign me up."

Sylvia laughed. "Consider it done. But Grace, don't forget that the most important thing you can do this week is to relax and enjoy yourself. Think of your quilting as play, not work. Take the pressure off yourself and remember the joy quilting brings you. You have all the time in the world. Be patient and have fun."

Sylvia spoke encouragingly, but the words felt dull and empty to Grace. She didn't have all the time in the world. Despite the difference in their ages, she might have less time than Sylvia. Any project she began now might remain incomplete, like so many of the anonymous, abandoned relics from generations past she documented at the museum.

"Grace!"

Grace started and realized that she couldn't feel the teacup in her hand. Too late, she tried to hold the cup upright, but the warm liquid sloshed onto her lap. She gasped and instinctively tried to leap to her feet, but her ankle twisted under her clumsily, and she fell back onto the sofa.

"Goodness, dear," Sylvia exclaimed, handing her another napkin. She hurried into the kitchen and returned with a damp towel. "Did you burn yourself?"

"No . . . no, I'm fine." She wasn't fine. She was shaken badly, and her hand was still numb. She grasped the towel and tried to blot the tea stains from her slacks.

"Are you sure?" Sylvia's gaze was piercing.

"Quite sure." Grace laughed shakily. "Annoyed at myself for staining my favorite slacks, but otherwise unharmed."

"Hmph." Sylvia studied her a moment as if waiting for more, but when Grace said nothing, she sighed. "Well, you run upstairs and change, and I'll have one of my helpers wash those for you." She glanced at her watch and then out the window, where twilight was descending. "If you hurry, you won't miss our welcome ceremony."

"Welcome ceremony?"

"You'll see. You'll enjoy this. In fact, it might be just what you need to call that wayward muse back where she belongs." Sylvia rose, but she paused, looking down at Grace with a fond but troubled smile. "And if later you decide you want to talk, I'm always willing to listen."

Wordlessly Grace nodded and rose, wondering if anyone could keep a secret from Sylvia for long.

The sun was just beginning to set when a staff member named Sarah McClure knocked on Donna's door and invited her to the welcome ceremony. Donna joined several other campers in the hallway and followed Sarah downstairs. "What's the welcome ceremony like?" Donna asked Vinnie. "There wasn't anything about it in the brochure."

But Vinnie refused to tell her. "I won't spoil the surprise," she said. "You first-timers will have to find out the hard way, like the rest of us."

A young woman beside Donna asked, "Is it an initiation? It won't hurt, will it?"

She looked so alarmed that the others laughed, but secretly Donna had been wondering the same thing.

Just as they were crossing the foyer, one of the front doors swung open and a slender woman entered, carrying a suitcase. She had light brown, shoulder-length hair and looked to be in her early to mid-thirties. Her gaze traveled from the empty registration table in the center of the room to the group of quilters obviously interrupted in the middle of an activity. With dismay, she asked, "Is it too late to register for camp?"

Although Donna had never seen her photo or heard her voice, she knew at once who the latecomer was. "Megan?"

"Donna?"

Megan barely had time to set down her suitcase before Donna had raced across the room and embraced her. "Megan! It's so wonderful to meet you in person! I was afraid you had changed your mind."

"No, I just misplaced it temporarily." She laughed, but she sounded exhausted.

Sarah joined them and welcomed Megan to Elm Creek Manor. She led Megan to the registration table, and within a few moments, Megan had signed in and received her room assignment. "I'm sorry you missed the welcome banquet," Sarah said, "but I could fix you something to eat in the kitchen."

"That's all right. I stopped at a diner on the way." Megan looked at Donna and added in an undertone, "Wait until I tell you about *that*."

To Donna's delight, Megan's dry tone sounded exactly the way Donna had always imagined it, and suddenly she was certain that joining Megan at camp had been a good idea.

Donna waited with the others as Sarah took Megan to her room to drop off her suitcase. When the pair rejoined them, Sarah led the group through the west wing and outside, onto a gray stone patio surrounded by evergreens and lilac bushes. The other guests had gathered inside a circle of forty chairs, where they sipped glasses of lemonade or iced tea and munched cookies. Donna spotted Sylvia Compson standing somewhat apart from the group, chatting with another woman who looked familiar, although Donna didn't remember meeting her earlier that day.

Megan clutched her arm. "Is that who I think it is?"

"Who?"

"The woman over there with Sylvia Compson. Is she Grace Daniels?"

Megan's prompting stirred Donna's memory. "She could be."

"I'm sure it's her." Megan glowed with excitement. "I didn't know there would be famous quilters here."

"That's not the least of it. Rumor has it Julia Merchaud is here, too."

"Julia Merchaud, from television?"

"The one and only. I didn't see her myself, but other people on our floor swear they saw her go into the room at the end of the west wing."

"That's right across from my room," Megan gasped, then hesitated and scanned the faces of the other guests. "But why isn't she here for the welcome ceremony?"

"I don't know. I hope it's not because she's so high and mighty she can't associate with us commoners."

Megan laughed. "Maybe she thinks we'll pester her for autographs instead of letting her enjoy camp." Then she frowned. "Okay, I'll admit it; that's exactly what I was going to do. Maybe she's right to stay away."

"If we see her, we'll treat her like any other quilter," Donna resolved. "Unless she wants us to treat her like a big star. Then we'll just leave her alone."

Megan agreed, and, eyeing the table near the door, suggested they get themselves some refreshments before it was too late. Just as they picked up their cups and plates of cookies, Sylvia clapped her hands to get everyone's attention.

"Let's have everyone take a seat so we can begin," Sylvia said. "It's getting late and I don't want any of you nodding off during the ceremony."

The campers laughed, some nervously because they didn't know what was coming next, others because they were far too excited to sleep. Their voices fell silent as Sylvia lit a candle and placed it in a spherical crystal holder. She moved to the center of the circle and looked around at the faces of her guests. "One of our traditions is to conclude the first evening of quilt camp with a ceremony we call Candlelight. Originally we intended this as a way for you to introduce yourselves to us and to each other; we're going to be living and working together closely this week, so the sooner we get to know each other, the better. But our ceremony helps you to know yourselves better, too. It helps you focus on your goals and wishes, and helps prepare you for the challenges of the future."

Donna felt a thrill of expectation. Sylvia made it sound as if they were embarking on a journey together, when all Donna had planned for was a simple week of quilting with a friend.

Sylvia continued by explaining the ceremony. The campers

would pass the candle around the circle, and as each woman took her turn to hold the candle, she would explain why she had come to Elm Creek Quilt Camp and what she hoped to gain that week. There was a pause after Sylvia asked for the first volunteer. Donna froze, heart thumping, and relaxed only when a woman two seats to her left raised her hand. Since the candle would be passed clockwise, Donna would have some time to prepare her remarks. She certainly couldn't tell the truth, that she was at camp because she was too cowardly to face her daughter's engagement.

The first woman held the candle for a long moment in silence. Around them, unseen, crickets chirped in the gradually deepening darkness. "I'm Angela Clark, from Erie. I'm a new quilter. I've only made little things, pot holders and baby quilts. I came to camp to improve my skills because . . ." She took a deep breath. "My oldest son died in a car accident two years ago." A murmur of sorrow and dismay went up from the circle. "His best friend was driving. He was drinking—they were both drinking. He smashed the car into a tree. My son was killed instantly. His friend had a few broken bones, but otherwise he was fine." Someone murmured a scathing rebuke of the young driver. "No, you don't understand. I don't hate him. He made a terrible, terrible mistake, and my son paid for it. They both paid for it. My son died that night, but his best friend has been dying ever since, a little each day." She looked around the circle. "He's grieving, but he won't allow himself to heal. He can't forgive himself, and he can't believe that my husband and I and my other children have already forgiven him. He was Jeremy's best friend. Jeremy loved him as much as he loved his own brothers. I can't bear for him to be in such pain." She hesitated and lowered her eyes. "A lot of people want me to hate him, but I can't do it. I can never excuse what he did, but I want him to get on with his life. I've read about memorial quilts—the kind made from pieces of someone's clothing. I saved a lot of my son's T-shirts from school and other activities, and thought I would piece them into a quilt for my son's friend, to help him remember the good times he and Jeremy shared, and to help him find some closure. I don't know if it will work, but I'm going to try." With that, she passed the candle on to the next woman in the circle.

"I don't know how I'm supposed to follow *that*," the woman said in mock displeasure as she took the candle. "I just came because I saw an ad in a magazine." A smattering of soft laughter went up from the circle, and Donna felt the tension and nervousness leaving her as she joined in.

She listened as one by one the others told their stories. One woman had come to learn how to quilt the pieced tops her late grandmother had left her; another, noticeably pregnant, had come to enjoy one last trip on her own before assuming the responsibilities of motherhood. "Also because my husband's nesting instinct kicked in," she said with a naughty grin. "He decided to paint every room of the house, and the fumes make me ill. At least, that's what I told him." Everyone laughed as she passed the candle to Vinnie.

"My name's Lavinia Burkholder, but everyone calls me Vinnie—except for my grandchildren, who call me Nana. I came to celebrate my birthday. I have the distinction of being one of Elm Creek Quilts's first campers." She rose and bowed as to a round of applause, then handed the candle to the woman on her left.

Before long the candle came to Grace Daniels. Like most of the others, she held the candle for a long while before speaking. "I'm Grace Daniels, from San Francisco," she eventually said, confirming what everyone else there had already guessed. "I'm an old friend of Sylvia's. She's been after me to visit her camp for years now, and I finally decided to indulge her." She smiled at Sylvia as the others chuckled. But then her smile faded. "What do I hope to gain this week? Some inspiration, I hope. I feel like I've run out of ideas, and . . . and I hope to discover some here." With that, she handed the candle to Megan.

"My name is Megan Donohue, and I'm from Monroe, Ohio. I came because my watercolor charm quilt won *Contemporary Quilting* magazine's quilt contest, and the first prize was this trip."

She smiled at Donna. "I also came to meet my friend Donna, whom I met on the Internet." And with that, she passed the candle to Donna.

Donna smothered a moan of dismay. Megan's story had been the shortest one yet, and Donna had planned on at least another minute or two to come up with something to say. "I'm Donna Jorgenson, and as Megan told you, I came to camp to meet my Internet friend." Then she could think of nothing more.

She looked around the circle of faces. Some of them would become her friends that week, she realized, confidantes as dear to her as Megan. She thought of how they had opened their hearts, trusting in the sincerity and support of their listeners. How could she do any less?

"I also came because I'm a coward," she heard herself say. "My eldest daughter just got engaged to a young man my husband and I don't know very well. My daughter, though, I do know her, and something tells me her heart isn't in this marriage. It's just an instinct, but I don't think she's happy—and all I ever wanted was for my daughters to be happy, happy and safe." She confessed the rest. "I came to camp because it got me out of meeting her fiancé's parents. I know I'm just delaying the inevitable, but I want to buy my daughter time. It might be only a few weeks, but it might be enough for her to be certain that this is what she really wants."

"Don't underestimate your intuition," someone said. In the semidarkness, Donna was not sure who had spoken. "Our maternal instincts are there for a reason."

Others nodded and chimed in their agreement. Donna looked around the circle of concerned faces, and although nothing had changed, somehow she felt comforted. As she passed the candle to the next woman, Megan put an arm around her shoulders and whispered mournfully, "And here I thought you came just for me." She said it so comically that Donna had to laugh, although she was blinking back tears.

Before the next woman could begin her story, Grace leaned

over behind Megan and murmured, "You and I should talk." She gave Donna a knowing look. "I have a daughter, too."

Donna nodded, speechless. A world-famous quilter wanted to talk with her, Donna Jorgenson from Silver Pines, Minnesota. She had finally met her best friend and closest confidante in person. She had aired her fears to a circle of women who only an hour ago had been strangers, and they had taken her seriously, without judgment or ridicule.

She felt as safe as if she were at home surrounded by friends who had known her all her life.

The candle cast shadow and light around the circle as the next woman told her story.

After supper, with no one to talk to, Julia had gone through her yoga routine with extra care, then lay on the bed idly paging through the issue of *Variety* she had brought to read on the plane. Bored, she had tossed it aside and rummaged through her bag for the script and a notepad. Ares didn't want her to waste time memorizing lines that would probably change in the rewrite, but that didn't mean Julia would accomplish nothing that evening. She took a seat at the small desk in the corner and began reading through the script, noting each quilting technique that Sadie had used and Julia would need to learn. By the time darkness fell, she had finished the first act and had listed several unfamiliar terms on her notepad: basting, piecing, binding. Just then the voices had broken into her concentration and compelled her to go to the window to investigate.

For more than an hour, Julia had sat at her window, spellbound, listening as one by one the women shared the deepest secrets of their hearts with perfect strangers. How liberating that must feel, to unburden oneself without fear of rejection.

What would she have said when it was her turn to hold the candle, if she were spending the warm summer evening among them? She had come to Elm Creek Manor to learn how to quilt so that she could keep a movie role. She had to keep the movie role to breathe life into a stalled career. She had to revitalize her career or fade away into obscurity and become a has-been before she had ever truly made a difference, before she had ever participated in something worthwhile, something worth remembering. Something worth all she had sacrificed for her career—two marriages, her privacy, her pride when critics mocked her attempts to perfect her chosen art.

If only she could be as open and trusting as the women gathered in a circle beneath her window. Of course, none of them feared that one of the others would race to the tabloids with her deepest secrets. None of them worried that her failures would become fodder for late-night talk-show comedians. They could afford to trust each other.

Overcome by the sensation that she was intruding on an intimacy she did not deserve, she let the curtain fall back and withdrew from the window.

Three

DONNA AWOKE bleary-eyed and disoriented in the unfamiliar room. For a moment, as she tried to sort out the furniture and shadows, she thought she was in the bedroom she had shared with her elder sister as a child. The blue-and-white Dresden Plate quilt on the bed focused her memory. It was the first full day of quilt camp, and the clock on the night stand told her it was not quite five. Usually she needed an alarm to yank her out of sleep by seven. *I must still be on Minnesota time,* she thought, until the sleepy confusion left her and she realized that she had her time zones mixed up. At home it was not yet four.

Strangely enough, despite the travel and the excitement of the previous day, she felt as wide awake as if she had slept a full eight hours. Anticipation for the day ahead kept her from drifting off to sleep again, so she got up and dressed in her workout clothes. Silently she left her room and tiptoed down the grand staircase and across the foyer to the front door.

Outside the air was cool and misty, with the promise of

warmth as soon as the sun rose above the trees. Donna stretched her calf muscles, enjoying the solitude and the chirping of birds in the distance. Then, with a sigh, she descended the circular stone staircase and began walking briskly across the lawn and along the edge of a thick grove of trees, inhaling deeply and pumping her arms.

Sometimes she wondered why she bothered. Years of watching her diet and exercising regularly had not burned any of the excess baggage from her hips and thighs, and yet she stuck with it, stubborn and hopeful to a fault, as she was in everything. Lindsay encouraged her mother by urging her to think of the internal benefits to her heart and lungs, and not to evaluate her fitness by the number on a scale alone. Donna tried, but it wasn't easy to be proud of her low cholesterol and excellent blood pressure when her size fourteens no longer fit as well as they once had. "Maybe they shrank in the laundry," Paul would say when she fretted, and she had to bite her tongue to keep from retorting that his clothes had been in the same load, and they still fit him fine.

She hadn't planned to stick to her morning workout routine at camp, but seeing Megan motivated her. Megan, nearly as slender as Lindsay, wouldn't blame pregnancy for her weight gain, unlike herself, who clung to that excuse although her babies were now sixteen and twenty. For some reason Donna had assumed that Megan would be closer to her own size. Maybe Megan had thought the same thing about Donna, and was dismayed to learn that her Internet friend was so pudgy and out of shape.

Knock it off, she ordered herself. She was at camp; she was supposed to be relaxing. If she kept up with those miserable thoughts, at breakfast she'd be tempted to wolf down a foot-high stack of pancakes for comfort. If she wanted to make herself miserable, instead of contemplating her ever-widening thighs, she ought to think about Lindsay.

Lindsay. Donna's heart plummeted with such force that she quickly shifted her thoughts to her schedule for the day. After breakfast, she and Megan would meet for the first of a week-long series of color theory classes. Lunch followed, and then she would attend an appliqué class while Megan took one on miniature quilts. Donna was disappointed that they hadn't chosen all the same classes, but consoled herself with the thought that they had most of their seminars in common. She was especially looking forward to the watercolor workshop. Megan had already mastered the art of using small pieces cut from large-scale prints and arranging them so they blended together in the style of an Impressionist painting, and Donna hoped to pick up some tips from her. It wasn't by accident that Megan had won the *Contemporary Quilting* contest.

Her muscles now warmed from the exercise, Donna paused to stretch by a wood rail fence that, she assumed, indicated the northern border of the property. Last night, Sylvia's verbal tour of the estate had located the gardens to the north, but somehow Donna had missed them. Maybe the gardens were within the grove of trees she had just circled. She walked along the fence until she came upon a break in the trees. There she found a path of the same smooth, gray stones she had seen by the manor. At this end, the path was untended—probably unused, judging by the weeds and grass growing between the stones. Hoping she wasn't breaking any camp rules by straying off the more well traveled parts of the property, Donna pushed a branch aside and followed the path into the trees.

Fortunately for her arms and legs, which were acquiring a few scratches from the undergrowth, the path grew wider and more clear as she continued. Before long, she glimpsed a white wooden structure, that, as she drew nearer, she realized was a gazebo. Then the trees opened into a clearing, and Donna stopped short—a pace away from tumbling into tiered flower beds carved into the hillside. From the top terrace she was eye-level with the gazebo's gingerbread molding, and she heard the splash of water somewhere beyond it. As the fragrance of flowers wafted to her, she looked around for the source of the sound—and found instead a series of stones artfully arranged along the edge of the hill as if nature had built a staircase there.

As she followed the stone path, more of the garden came into view: a black marble fountain in the shape of a mare prancing with two foals, and beyond that, four large, round planters filled with roses and ivy. The planters were larger at the base than the top, the lower halves forming smoothed, polished seats. Donna spotted someone sitting on one of those seats.

Grace Daniels.

She sat staring straight ahead at a bed of decorative grasses, not quite facing the gazebo. Donna almost called out to her, but the other woman's stillness held her back.

The trail to the manor resumed just past the spot where Grace was sitting, but Donna deliberately kept her distance. When she reached the edge of the garden she glanced back, tempted to remind Grace of her invitation to talk about their daughters. She bit her lip and considered, then decided to continue in silence. If Grace had wanted company, she would have called Donna over. Even if somehow Grace hadn't seen her as she passed in front of the gazebo, the sound of her sneakers clomping on the stone would have been hard to miss.

Grace's heart sank at the sound of footfalls, and in her peripheral vision she spotted someone on the other side of the gazebo. *Please turn around and go away,* she thought, but the figure emerged and began descending steps Grace hadn't seen in the hillside. She stared fixedly ahead, pretending she hadn't noticed the newcomer. It was one of the other campers, the plump woman with the Upper Midwest accent. *Leave me alone, leave me alone,* she thought, clutching her hands together in her lap.

She stiffened as the sound of footsteps grew louder, then relaxed as they continued past and fell silent. Grace took a deep breath and leaned back against the cool stone seat. Finally, someone who respected her privacy, who didn't insist that she talk all the time. That Candlelight business had been bad enough. If she had wanted a support group, she would have signed up for the one at the hospital.

Her fingertips were numb again. The pins-and-needles sensation had intensified since that disastrous meeting in Sylvia's sitting room. She felt her heart begin to pound, and rising panic stole over her. Quickly she closed her eyes and pictured herself in her favorite place: a restful spot in Santa Cruz, hiking through a redwood forest, emerging from the shade of the trees on the edge of a bluff overlooking the sparkling waters of the Pacific Ocean. She inhaled deeply and imagined the wind, the feel of the sunlight on her skin, the faintly sweet odor of moldering leaves, the smell of decay and new life.

She exhaled, trying to blow out all her anxiety with the breath, just as she had been taught. This time, the exercise worked, and she felt her pulse returning to normal.

She was not having a relapse. She was fine.

It was the fatigue and stress of travel, that was all. She had gone to bed too late and risen too early. She was not getting worse. She had plenty of time.

Julia overslept.

She had forgotten to set the alarm clock and, still jet-lagged, did not wake until someone knocked on her door. "Miss Merchaud?" a woman called. "Breakfast."

Julia scrambled out of bed and snatched up her robe. "Just a minute." Hastily she finger-combed her hair as she went to the door. She hoped the woman in the hallway didn't have a camera. The *National Inquirer* would pay big for a shot of her with mussed hair and no makeup. Holding her robe closed at the neck, she opened the door a crack, only wide enough to see a brown-haired young woman holding a covered tray, looking back at her inquisitively.

Julia had the younger woman place the tray on the desk and ushered her out again as quickly as possible. She wasn't hungry, but she nibbled on an English muffin and ate most of the fruit, leaving the omelet untouched. The coffee was suitably strong, though she missed her cinnamon cappuccino. Oh, well. As Ares had said, she was there to work. She could endure a week of roughing it.

She showered quickly, but dressed and applied her makeup with care. In the hallway, the muffled sounds of other campers making their way downstairs had faded, and a glance at the clock told her she would have to hurry. She grabbed a pen and the notes she had compiled the previous night but, with an effort, forced herself to leave her sunglasses on the dresser.

Her registration papers included a map of the manor, and she followed the directions downstairs to the ballroom, which had been partitioned into classrooms with folding screens decorated in patchwork. The last of eleven women to arrive, she found Quick Piecing with barely a moment to spare. The instructor—the same young woman who had brought Julia her breakfast—had already begun her introduction as Julia slipped into a seat at the back of the room, grateful that she had a table to herself. She would have been mortified if the teacher had made another camper change places to accommodate Ares's demands.

The teacher, Sarah, passed out the first lesson, instructions on quick-piecing quarter-square triangles. "First, you'll need to pick a light fabric and a medium or dark," Sarah said. "Cut a six inch by twelve inch rectangle from each fabric using your rotary cutter, and then lay the two fabrics with right sides facing, the light piece on top."

As Sarah spoke, Julia watched with alarm as the other ten students reached into their bags and brought out folded bundles of fabric, plastic rulers, and odd-shaped tools that resembled pizza cutters. Was she supposed to have brought her own fabric? She glanced around her tabletop—a sewing machine, a gridded plastic mat, no fabric—and her face grew hot. Obviously she should have brought fabric from home; everyone else was prepared. She looked to the front of the classroom in dismay, but Sarah was already walking around the room observing her students as they layered fabric on their mats and happily sliced away at it with the pizza cutters.

"Is everyone ready to go on?" Sarah called out. Julia's meek "No" was lost in the chorus of affirmatives. "Okay, then, next I want you to take your pencil and, using your ruler, draw a grid of two-inch squares on the back of your light fabric."

A ruler. Julia snatched up her notebook and quickly tore out a sheet of paper. The pages were eight and one half inches by eleven; she could fold it into sections and estimate an inch. Then she remembered the gridded plastic mat and scooted her chair closer to it. To her relief, she saw that the grid was marked in one-eighth-inch increments along two edges. Folding her paper to strengthen it, she lined it up against the edge of the mat and began marking off inches. By the time her makeshift ruler was completed, the rest of the class had already proceeded to the next step. Racing to catch up, Julia tore two more sheets of paper from her notebook and wrote "Dark" on one and "Light" on the other. She drew a wobbly-edged grid as the other students moved on to their sewing machines. She was too far behind to ever catch up, but she persevered grimly. Ares had sent her to this godforsaken place with none of the proper materials, but she needed that role and she was going to learn *something* while she was there.

Suddenly a shadow fell over her table. "Is everything okay back here?"

Julia looked up to find Sarah standing on the other side of her table. "I . . . Yes, everything's fine," Julia said. "Please continue."

Sarah looked dubious. "Did you leave your things in your room? You have time to run upstairs and get them."

"No, thank you." The other students had paused in their work to watch. "Please, I don't want to hold up the rest of the class."

"Wasn't there a supply list in the course confirmation packet mailed to your home?"

A supply list. Of course, there must have been a supply list, and it must have been sent to the agency. "There probably was," Julia said, picturing her hands closing around Ares's throat, "but I didn't get it."

"I see," Sarah said, with a puzzled frown that said she didn't see at all.

"I have some extra fabric," said an older woman with a cloud of shockingly bright white hair. "What do you like? Red or blue?"

"Oh, no, that's quite all right," Julia demurred.

The woman was already making her way from the front of the room, a bundle of fabric in her arms. "Nonsense; I always bring plenty." She placed the bundle on Julia's table and held up a piece of kelly green fabric with wide red lines zigzagging across it. "Here's a nice one. Or do you prefer calico?"

"Calico," Julia said quickly, recognizing one of the unfamiliar terms from Ellen's script. The older woman smiled indulgently and handed her a piece of dark blue fabric sprinkled with tiny white flowers.

"Here's something you can use for the light fabric," another woman called out, waving a cream-colored piece over her head like a banner. Sarah supplied her with one of the pizza-cutter tools, and soon everyone had joined in, showering Julia with extra rulers and pins and needles and so much extra fabric she wasn't sure how she'd carry it back upstairs to her room. She felt her face flaming with embarrassment as she accepted their gifts and stammered out her thanks.

"I'm sorry you didn't get the list. There must have been some oversight," Sarah said. "After class, why don't you show me your course list and I'll send into town for the rest of the supplies you'll need."

"Thank you. I'd appreciate that." Julia wished everyone would stop looking at her. Suddenly she couldn't bear for the instructor to think that an experienced quilter would be so ignorant. She lowered her voice. "I'm sorry for the disruption, but I never quilted before."

The white-haired woman overheard, and her eyebrows shot up. "This is your first quilting class? Ever? My goodness, you're ambitious, skipping the basics and going straight to this high-tech stuff."

"Skipping . . ." Julia's voice trailed off, and she looked from the white-haired woman to Sarah. "This isn't a beginner's course?"

"Most new quilters start out in Beginning Piecing," Sarah said. "You've really never quilted before?"

Julia shook her head, thinking *Isn't it obvious?*

"Then . . ." Sarah hesitated. "I don't mean to question your judgment, but why did you sign up for Quick Piecing?"

Julia had never even seen a course description. Ares had signed her up for this course, and suddenly Julia understood why. "Because I need to learn quickly."

The white-haired woman laughed as if Julia had made a joke, but Sarah only smiled kindly. "I think tomorrow morning we should switch you to Diane's Beginning Piecing class, okay?"

"That would be lovely, thank you." Julia wished she could disappear.

On their way to their first activity, Megan confided that she had some misgivings about signing up for the color theory course, but she felt reassured when Donna confessed her own doubts. Their reasons differed, though; Megan feared the class would be dull, while Donna worried that it would be too technical to understand. To their delight, their apprehensions vanished within a few minutes, mostly because their eccentric teacher made the material lively and interesting. Gwen was a stout, red-haired woman who wore a bright blue beaded necklace and a long flowing skirt in a wild print, and her enthusiasm for the subject matter was infectious. "How dare she say such a thing," she had cried when a student timidly mentioned that her elementary school art teacher had insisted that red and purple didn't go together. "Who is she, the color police? Let her make quilts in matchy-matchy colors if she wants, but don't let her prevent you from being more adventurous!"

Her good-humored indignation sent the class into peals of laughter, which turned into murmurs of surprise and delight as Gwen passed out boxes of crayons and sheets of paper. She instructed them in a coloring exercise meant to free their inhibitions and expand their "color sense." Megan colored happily, feeling like a carefree first-grader as she and Donna talked and compared their work.

"As long as we're expanding our color sense, maybe you'll finally give purple a try," Donna said, waving a violet crayon before Megan's eyes.

Megan feigned a horrified shudder. "Get that thing away from me."

"You like blue and you like red. How can you not like purple?"

"It's simply a matter of personal preference. What do you care what colors I use or don't use?"

"I hate to see you limiting yourself."

Megan laughed. "This, from the woman who refuses to use white as a background fabric."

"That's just a habit, not a phobia. And I have good reason. Off-white and cream don't show the dirt as well." Donna gave her a determined look. "I'm going to get you to use purple in a quilt if it's the last thing I do."

Later, after Megan had completed her exercise and was looking around to see what the other quilters had done, she spotted Grace Daniels at a table on the other side of the room. She nudged Donna. "Look. There she is."

Donna's head jerked up, but then she frowned, disappointed. "I thought you meant Julia Merchaud."

"Grace Daniels isn't a big enough celebrity for you?" Megan teased. "Anyway, I don't think Julia Merchaud is really here. Her room is supposedly across the hall from mine, but I haven't seen her."

"Some people say they have."

"Yes, but some people say they've seen extraterrestrials and the Loch Ness Monster. Maybe these Julia Merchaud sightings are like that."

"Sure, Julia Merchaud is the Loch Ness Quilter."

Megan laughed, but her mirth faded as she watched Grace carefully select another crayon, her brow furrowed in concentration. "She seems sad."

"What makes you think so?"

"Everyone else is having fun, but she looks like she's taking the SATs."

"I saw her this morning, in the garden," Donna said. "I thought she wanted to be left alone. Maybe she's worried about her creativity, like she said at the Candlelight."

"She's not talking to anyone."

"Maybe she's shy."

Megan doubted that a famous quilt artist could feel shy among a crowd of admiring quilters, but before she could say so, Gwen announced that class was over. "Let's ask Grace to join us for lunch," Megan suggested as they gathered their things. Donna agreed, but when they looked over at the other side of the room, Grace had already left.

They looked for her outside, where the staff had arranged a picnic buffet on the veranda, but Grace wasn't at any of the tables or standing in line for food. "Tomorrow we'll sit near her in class," Donna said as they joined the queue. "The worst she can do is ignore us, right?"

"She won't. Who would be crazy enough to deny themselves the pleasure of our illustrious company?"

"Julia Merchaud, for one."

They laughed.

"What are you two girls giggling about?" someone behind them in line asked. Megan turned to find a white-haired woman eyeing them with mock suspicion. She wore red tennis shoes and a T-shirt that read "Quiltoholics Anonymous."

Donna laughed and introduced Megan to the woman, Vinnie

from Dayton, Ohio. Megan had remembered her from the Candlelight, and was pleased that Vinnie remembered her.

"Oh, yes, you're the one who won the contest." Vinnie nodded toward the buffet and sighed happily. "Isn't this marvelous? I love a buffet. You can take whatever you want and leave the crap behind."

"Vinnie!" Donna protested.

"Relax, honey, I'm just teasing." Vinnie added a generous helping of baked beans to her plate. "But I'd better not let the staff hear me or I might get expelled." She raised her voice and looked around as if she feared unseen staff members were eavesdropping. "My, this food is so tasty."

"It's too tasty," Megan said. "I'll probably gain fifty pounds this week."

"I don't think you could gain fifty pounds if you tried." Donna's voice had a hint of envy in it. Megan watched as Donna returned the macaroni salad spoon to the bowl without taking any and reached for the tongs in a bowl of tossed salad instead. Donna noticed her scrutiny. "Before you ask, yes, I am trying to slim down."

"For the wedding?" Vinnie asked.

Megan winced. "Don't remind her." Then she shot Donna a sharp look. "Is that really why?"

"I'd happily gain two hundred pounds if I thought it would stop the wedding." Donna's voice was grim. She had reached the end of the line, and she quickly walked off with her plate to an Adirondack chair at the far end of the veranda.

Megan and Vinnie exchanged a look and hurried after her. "Don't you like the young man?" Vinnie asked as they took the empty chairs on either side of Donna.

"I hardly know him. I've seen him and Lindsay together for—I don't know, maybe a total of seven hours over the past two years."

"Maybe once you get to know him better, you'll grow more fond of him," Megan said.

"Maybe." Donna didn't look as if she believed it.

"There's always hope," Vinnie said. "Maybe she'll leave him at the altar."

"That only happens in movies."

"It happened to my grandson."

Megan and Donna stared. "You're kidding," Megan said.

"Well, maybe a little." Vinnie shrugged and nibbled on a piece of fried chicken. "It wasn't exactly at the altar. At least he was spared that indignity. But she did break off their engagement three months before the wedding."

"How awful for him," Donna said.

"Not really. She wasn't good enough for him—as I've told him plenty of times, not that he listens. He deserves better. And he definitely deserved better than to be strung along, only to be jilted after the invitations had been sent out."

Megan murmured her sympathies and refrained from pointing out that they were only getting her grandson's side of the story. In her experience, a woman who left a man usually had a very good reason for doing so. Then, with a pang, she thought of Keith, and his reason for leaving her—a blond Comparative Literature graduate student with no stretch marks and an uncanny ability to ignore Keith's irritating quirks.

Megan said, "If she was going to change her mind anyway, at least she did it before the wedding rather than after."

"He'll find someone else," Donna said.

"Of course he will, with a little help from Nana." Vinnie wiped her lips delicately with her napkin and set her plate aside. "How old is your daughter?" she asked Donna, reaching for the tote bag beside her chair.

"Twenty."

Vinnie took a red plastic photo album from her bag and flipped through the pages, shaking her head with regret. "I was afraid of that. She's too young for my Adam."

"She's too young to get married, period."

"I married at seventeen." Vinnie passed the open album to

Donna. "But that was a different era. This is my grandson. Isn't he a good-looking young man?"

"Very." Donna gave Megan a sidelong look. "He looks close to your age."

Vinnie brightened. "You're single?"

"I am now." Donna held out the album to her, so Megan took it.

"Oh, dear. Divorced?"

"I'm afraid so," Megan said. "Actually, I'm annulled and divorced."

Donna looked bewildered. "How does that work?"

Megan hesitated, surprised by how much admitting his betrayal still hurt her. "When Keith first left me for another woman, a divorce was good enough for them. It was the quickest, easiest way to put me in the past. Later, though, she decided she wanted to get married in the Catholic Church, so he put in for an annulment. According to the Church, our marriage never existed."

"But you have a child," Donna said, aghast.

Vinnie shook her head and clicked her tongue. "It's far too easy to get an annulment these days, if you want my opinion. Not like when I was young. Then, you had to stick around and work on it whether you wanted to or not."

"And too many people spent their lives miserable in unhappy marriages," Megan said. "No, I'm better off single again than married to someone who cheated." *Someone who didn't love me as much as I thought he did,* she added silently. *Who didn't love me as much as I loved him.*

"If only Adam had that attitude," Vinnie said with a sigh.

Then Megan remembered the album, and she glanced down at the photo. What she saw made her gasp.

Vinnie's eyebrows rose. "Goodness, dear, he's handsome, but not *that* handsome."

"I don't believe this. This is the guy from the diner."

Donna's eyes widened. "The apple pie guy?"

As Megan nodded, Vinnie looked from her to Donna and

back, perplexed. Quickly Megan told her the story of their meeting on the road to Elm Creek Manor.

"Did you like him?" Vinnie asked anxiously.

"Well, yes. I mean, I didn't talk to him very long, but he seemed nice."

Vinnie clasped her hands together, delighted. "Your meeting must have been fate! No, something stronger than fate—divine intervention. You live in Ohio, isn't that right? So does Adam."

Megan shot Donna a look of alarm, a look that meant *Save me.* "It might not have been fate."

Donna quickly added, "There are only so many routes to Waterford from Ohio, and not many places to stop to eat along the way. It was just a coincidence."

"I don't believe that," Vinnie said, a stubborn set to her chin. "There are no coincidences. I believe that in life, you meet the people you need to meet, the people who will help you become the person you ought to be."

"Maybe so, but maybe Megan needed to meet your grandson so he could help her find Elm Creek Manor, so she could meet us," Donna said. "Maybe we're the ones she needs to meet."

"I think that's true," Megan said quickly.

"Maybe you need to meet all of us," Vinnie declared, but then she smiled and reached over to pat Megan on the knee. "I think we're going to become quite good friends this week, my dear."

Donna was enjoying her conversation with Megan and Vinnie so much that she was almost late for her appliqué workshop. She rushed in, breathless, and took the first open seat she found, at a table in the back. Donna hated to be late, not because it suggested that she was scatterbrained—which she sometimes feared she was—but because she hated to be rude.

She greeted the few campers she recognized, then took out her supply list and checked her bag to make sure she had remembered everything. She was glad Megan wasn't there to see her; Donna had checked the bag twice before leaving her room and once at lunch, which Megan found hilarious. "Do you think something jumped out of your bag and wandered off while your back was turned?" she had teased.

"It could happen," Donna had retorted. Something had to account for those dozens of rotary cutters and thimbles she had lost over the years.

She put the list away and listened attentively as the teacher introduced herself as Agnes Emberly. A woman slipped into the seat beside her, but Donna pretended not to notice. She had been the recipient of too many annoyed frowns for her own tardiness to feel anything but sympathy for this latecomer.

It wasn't until Agnes passed out pattern sheets and Donna turned to hand them to her table partner that she realized she was sitting next to Julia Merchaud.

She was so surprised that she forgot to let go of the pages when Julia took them. Julia tugged at the pages in vain, and then her famous hazel eyes met Donna's. "I have them, thanks," she said.

Donna released the pages as if they were on fire. "Sorry."

Julia Merchaud nodded in response and turned to the front of the classroom as if she had already forgotten Donna was there. Donna felt like a fool, but she couldn't help staring. It was Julia Merchaud, wasn't it? It had to be. Her long blond hair was pulled back into a French twist, just the way she had worn it the day the oldest Wilson child got married. Donna had seen every episode of *Family Tree* since the premiere. Becca thought it was one of the corniest shows ever created, but Becca had a low opinion of television in general, and Donna had never let her youngest daughter's teasing discourage her from watching.

After a moment, Julia Merchaud gave her a nervous sidelong glance, and Donna quickly snatched her gaze away and pretended she had been studying the pattern sheets. Julia Merchaud was not only at Donna's quilt camp, but at her very table. How could Donna hope to concentrate on Agnes's instructions with a celebrity of Julia Merchaud's stature sitting not three feet away?

Using all her willpower, she forced herself to focus on the front of the classroom, where Agnes was listing the items they would need for the first activity. As Donna withdrew her supplies from her bag, she stole a peek at the other woman, eager to see what fabric a television star used. Expecting to see Hoffman prints with gold-stamped ink or exotic Indonesian batiks packed in a Gucci tote, she was astonished when Julia Merchaud removed a mismatched stack of ordinary calicoes from a paper grocery bag. She placed them on the table, then carefully arranged a pack of needles, a pencil, a small pair of blue-handled scissors, and a spool of thread beside them. Then, in a gesture that seemed both protective and formal, she folded her hands in her lap and turned her attention to the teacher.

Donna couldn't help studying Julia's hands. A ring on her left hand, a large diamond set with pearls, caught the light. A ruby-and-gold tennis bracelet encircled her thin right wrist. The hands themselves seemed strangely out of place, with protruding veins and knobby knuckles. They seemed much older than the rest of her, especially compared to the smooth, faintly lined skin of her face.

At the front of the room, Agnes announced that someone from each table needed to come to the front of the room for a roll of freezer paper. Since she was on the aisle, Donna jumped up. "I'll get it," she said, smiling. Julia gave the barest of nods without looking her way.

The brief errand gave Donna enough time to collect her scattered thoughts. She remembered what she and Megan had promised the previous evening: If they saw Julia Merchaud, they would treat her like any other quilter. *She's just a quilter like any other,* Donna told herself as she returned to her seat, but she couldn't quite believe it. "Here we go," she said brightly, placing the box on the table between them. Julia murmured something that might have been thanks.

Donna had used the freezer paper method for appliqué before; she had tried almost every quilting technique at least once, although she rarely stuck with any one style long enough to truly master it. She had signed up for this course hoping it would help her improve her weakest skill. Following Agnes's instructions, she tore off a sheet of freezer paper, placed it on top of the pattern, and began tracing the first design. Out of the corner of her eye, she watched as Julia imitated her, step by step. Deliberately, Donna slowed her movements and made sure not to block Julia's view of her work. Sure enough, Julia's scrutiny continued as the class went on.

When it came time to sew the appliqué to the background fabric, Donna sensed her neighbor's growing frustration. Summoning up her courage, she whispered, "Do you need some help?" When Julia nodded, Donna went over the steps again, demonstrating each one. When Julia tried again, she managed to complete a shaky but perfectly respectable appliqué stitch. For the first time, Donna saw her smile.

Donna picked up her own needle again, surreptitiously watching Julia's progress. Assured that Julia was doing fine, Donna soon became engrossed in her own work. She had never made an appliqué block as elaborate as a Whig Rose before, but Agnes's instructions were so clear that the pieces seemed to fall into place almost effortlessly.

Class was nearing the end when Julia spoke again. "Excuse me," she murmured. "I don't mean to interrupt you, but you seem to know more about this than I."

"Just a little, maybe," Donna said diplomatically.

"I wondered . . ." Julia hesitated. "Is this the same method as needle-turned appliqué, just using different name?"

"No, they're two different styles. Agnes probably picked freezer paper because many people think it's easier."

"I see." She seemed troubled. "But this technique has been around just as long, I suppose?"

"I don't think so. As far as I know, freezer paper appliqué is fairly modern."

"Oh, dear." Julia set down her needle and sank back into her chair.

"What's wrong?"

"I have to learn needle-turned appliqué."

"Your Whig Rose block will look exactly the same," Donna assured her. "It doesn't matter what technique you use."

"It does matter. I can't believe this. I'm wasting my time. I never should have come."

"Don't say that." Instinctively Donna placed a hand on Julia's shoulder. "I know it can be frustrating sometimes, but you can learn. You just need practice."

"You don't understand." Julia removed a notebook from her paper bag and opened it to the first page. "I have to learn certain quilting techniques for a movie role. But this morning I found out I was in the wrong piecing class, and now I'm in the wrong appliqué class. . . ."

"Don't worry. It'll be all right." Donna patted Julia's shoulder and picked up the notebook. "Let's take a look at this list. Okay. All of these terms have to do with piecing. Are you taking Beginning Piecing?"

"I'm transferring to it tomorrow."

"Then you'll definitely cover the first half of the list. These steps here"—she pointed to the page—"have to do with the actual quilting process itself. Did you sign up for a class on quilting?"

Julia nodded.

"Hand or machine?"

"Hand."

"Then you're all set there, too. The only problem seems to be needle-turned appliqué." As Donna returned the notebook, inspiration struck her. "If you like, I could teach you during free time."

The famous hazel eyes looked guarded. "You would do that for me?"

"Sure. I've never won any blue ribbons for my appliqué, but I can at least give you a crash course in the basics."

"I'd be grateful," Julia said. "Are you sure it's no trouble?"

"Not at all. We can start today after class if you'd like." Then she remembered her plans with Megan. "I'll need to leave a message for one of my friends first, but after that, we can work until supper."

Julia agreed with such gratitude that Donna felt taken aback. Of course she wanted to help a beginning quilter; wouldn't anyone? Julia must not realize how quilters treated each other. Where would Donna have been if no one had been willing to teach her more than twenty years before, when she was pregnant with Lindsay and nearly driven insane by a hormone-induced compulsion to sew a baby quilt?

Then Julia looked hesitant. "I wonder if you would be willing to do something else for me. This might sound foolish, but I don't want anyone to know I'm not already an experienced quilter."

It did sound foolish. Every quilter had to start somewhere. "Why not?"

"It's rather difficult to explain. Would you promise not to tell anyone?"

Donna shrugged. "Sure, okay."

"Would you be willing to sign a confidentiality agreement?"

Donna stared at her. "A what?"

"A confidentiality agreement." Julia smiled and looked apologetic, but also wary. "It's for the lawyers. You know how they are. Everything has to be formal. You'll sign a document promising you won't reveal my, shall we say, inexperience, to anyone."

Donna wondered if most celebrities made a habit of carrying around a folder of confidentiality agreements in their purses. "Don't you think anyone who sees you in class will realize you're a beginner?"

"That would be mere speculation. You have firsthand knowledge." Julia's smile was disarming. "I'd be very grateful."

Resigned but still baffled, Donna nodded. "I'll have to tell my friends something. They'll want to know what we're doing together."

"Tell them you're helping me brush up on my skills. Skills I already have," she added.

Donna didn't know what else to do without rudely revoking her offer, so she agreed.

After class, Julia remained behind while Donna raced upstairs to her room. She hastily scrawled a note: "I'm sorry I'm going to miss Vinnie's show-and-tell session. Please tell her I'm sorry. Something came up. I'll explain when I see you at supper." Then she added, "The presence of the Loch Ness Quilter has been officially confirmed."

She slipped the note under Megan's door and hurried back downstairs to help the famous Julia Merchaud prepare for her movie role.

After supper, Grace returned to her room, intending to go to bed early. Instead, she lay on top of the covers, fully clothed, her fingers interlaced over her abdomen, her eyes closed. She felt a strange sensation of peace settling over her as she listened to the sounds of the old house: the creak of a floorboard, a door closing in the distance. Other noises, soft but distinct, she could not name. An old house like this one probably sheltered its share of ghosts, but if any spirits haunted Elm Creek Manor, Grace was certain they were benevolent.

Her hopes had risen tremendously since that bleak morning in the garden. The forced intimacy she had feared had not surfaced, and she had been allowed to spend the day with a minimum of intrusion upon her solitude. *Solitude* seemed an inappropriate word for it, since she had attended classes and meals surrounded by dozens of other quilters, and yet that was how it had felt, as if she were a stone fixed in a creek bottom, with the water dancing over her and around her and yet leaving her in peace, to move downstream at her own pace. That, she suddenly realized, was what she had been so desperately seeking: a respite from the sense that time was rushing her along too fast, forcing her to break into a stumbling run to keep up.

The creative breakthrough she longed for had not arrived with the suddenness of a thunderclap; she had predicted as much. Even so, she could feel the first stirrings of inspiration within her imagination, like the movement of water beneath the frozen surface of a lake. If she were patient and allowed the stirrings to build, eventually something would surely shatter the ice and allow her to create again. In the meantime, it felt good to be working with fabric, even if she was examining the colors and textures with an unfamiliar detachment, as if regarding them from a great distance or through a blurred lens.

Her mind wandered as she rested. She was picturing herself back in her studio arranging crayons in a three-tiered box when a knock sounded on the door. "Come in," she called, sitting up on the edge of the bed.

Sylvia peered inside. "Did I wake you?"

"No, I was just daydreaming." Grace stood, and as she did, she realized that sometime during the day, the pins and needles sensation in her hand had faded. She had not even noticed.

"The evening activities are about to begin. Would you care to join me?"

"Thanks, but not tonight."

"Are you sure? We're going to play games. It'll be fun."

"I think I'll turn in early instead."

"Then I'll see you in the morning." Sylvia withdrew, but before the door closed completely, she uttered something, not quite under her breath.

"What did you say?" Grace asked.

Sylvia swung the door open again, her expression innocent. "Who, me?"

"Yes, you. What did you call me?"

"I called you a party-pooper. Good night. See you at breakfast."

Grace crossed the room and grabbed the knob before Sylvia could close the door again. "I am not a party-pooper."

"You look like one from here. It must be a trick of the light."

"Is that so?" Grace picked up a light sweater and threw it over her shoulders. "I've forgotten more about having fun than you'll ever know." She marched past Sylvia into the hallway and pulled the door shut behind them.

As they went downstairs, Grace heard laughter and conversation coming from the banquet hall. Inside, the campers had gathered near a long table by the windows and were helping themselves to dessert and coffee. Grace felt a hand squeeze her shoulder, and when she looked over, Sylvia gave her an encouraging wink and left her there on her own.

Seeing that the other quilters were seating themselves, Grace quickly pulled up a chair at a table near the back and watched as Sylvia climbed onto a small riser at the end of the room. She clapped her hands for attention. "If you'll take your seats, we'll get started," she called out. "Four campers to a table, please." She signaled to two staff members, who began distributing sheets of paper and pencils to each table.

"Are you saving these for anyone?" a slender woman in her early thirties asked, placing a hand on the chair at Grace's left. Behind her, the plump woman Grace had seen in the garden that morning smiled tentatively.

"No," Grace said, startled. "Please, go ahead."

"Thanks."

They introduced themselves—Megan from Ohio and Donna from Minnesota. Grace was just about to give them her own name, when a voice sang out, "Save a place for me." A thin, white-haired woman wearing a red straw hat with a plastic daisy in the band hurried to their table. She seated herself and looked over at the dessert table longingly. "Why do they have to start on time? I didn't even get to check out the snacks, and now it's too late."

"Here, Vinnie," Donna said, sliding a plate of brownies and frosted sugar cookies toward her. "I shouldn't be eating this stuff anyway."

Vinnie brightened and raised her eyebrows at Grace. "Do you want anything, honey?" When Grace declined, Vinnie took a bite of a brownie and rolled her eyes to heaven with pleasure.

Party-pooper, Grace could almost hear Sylvia say. "Maybe just one," she said, reaching for the plate.

Donna passed out the pencils the staff member had left on their table. "Please tell me this isn't a quiz."

Grace scanned the list of numbered items. "'How many UFOs do you have?'" she read aloud. "I think it's just a questionnaire."

"'How many paper bags would your stash fill?'" Vinnie read. "That depends. How big are the bags?"

"Do we have to know exactly?" Donna said, her brow creased in worry. "Can we estimate?"

Megan grinned. "I think they expect us to."

"Besides, what are they going to do, go to our houses and check?" Vinnie added.

"What's a UFO?" Grace wondered aloud. Sylvia couldn't possibly mean a flying saucer.

"An Un-Finished Object," Megan said. "Or an Unfinished Fabric Object, whichever you prefer. It's a quilt you've begun but haven't completed yet."

"I thought that was a WIP," Donna said.

"A whip?" Grace asked.

"A Work In Progress."

"When does something shift from being a WIP to a UFO?"

"When you've given up all hope of ever finishing it," Vinnie said.

"By that definition, I don't have any UFOs," Donna said. "I intend to finish every project I've ever started."

"Oh, come on," Megan said. "You don't have any projects you've abandoned? Not even one?"

Donna looked hesitant. "Well . . ."

From the front of the room, Sylvia interrupted by announcing the rules of their first game, which was to fill out the questionnaire "as honestly and completely as you can." There would be prizes for the correct answer to each question. "But I'm not telling you what the correct answers are, so you can't cheat."

The quilters laughed, and Donna raised her hand. "What

about WIPs?" she asked. "Should we include those in our UFO count?"

Sylvia considered. "Yes, go ahead and include any project begun but not yet completed."

"Oh, no," Donna murmured gloomily. "This is going to be embarrassing."

Then Vinnie raised her hand. "For question number two, how big a paper bag are we talking about? Do you mean a grocery or a department store shopping bag?"

Sylvia cast her eyes to heaven. "I see I'm going to have to revise my questionnaire for table number six. A paper grocery sack will do, Vinnie."

Satisfied, Vinnie began filling in her questionnaire with dramatic strokes of her pencil. More cautiously, Grace started hers. How many UFOs? None. Grace preferred to finish one project before beginning another, and she hadn't started anything new in ages. How vast was her fabric stash? That question was more difficult. She pictured the shelves lining her studio wall and the bundles of folded cloth, sorted by color and fiber content, stacked neatly upon them. At least fifty, she decided, and wrote that down. She proceeded through the rest of the questions, from "How many quilts have you finished?" to "How long have you been quilting?" She was filling in the last blank when Sylvia announced that time was up.

"I didn't know there was a time limit," Donna said, dismayed, as a staff member came to their table to collect the papers. "I didn't finish the last three questions."

"Then the best you can hope for is a C-plus," Vinnie said. "So much for the Quilters' Honor Roll."

Donna's eyes widened in alarm before she realized Vinnie was only teasing her.

Next, the staff members placed a sheet of paper facedown on the table in front of each camper. Vinnie gingerly picked up the corner of hers. "No peeking until I say so," Sylvia commanded, and Vinnie quickly snatched her hand back to her lap.

Sylvia went on to describe the rules of the next game. The front side of the papers provided a list of quilt block anagrams, and the quilters at each table would work together to unscramble the design names. The first team to get all the correct answers would win a prize.

"I'm going to be good at this," Vinnie declared. "I do the jumble in the *Dayton Daily News* every day."

Grace was relieved to hear that, because she knew she would be a liability for her team. She hadn't pieced a traditional quilt block since she first learned to quilt. Unless Sylvia had chosen blocks from the eighteen hundreds, in which case Grace's historical textile studies would aid her, she wouldn't be able to contribute much.

"On your marks," Sylvia called from the front of the room. "Get set, go!"

There was an excited scramble as papers were flipped and pencils seized. Grace skimmed the list of twenty anagrams, but nothing came to mind.

"I think I have number three," Donna cried. "'Plane Pipe.' That's Pineapple."

"That's right," Megan said. "Nice work."

As Grace wrote the correct answer on her sheet, she overheard a woman at the adjacent table say, "You guys, the third one is Pineapple." Grace looked up in time to catch the woman's guilty glance before she looked away.

"Well, I never heard of such a thing," Vinnie declared, glaring at the woman.

"Never mind her. Don't let it distract us," Megan urged. "Just keep your voices down from now on."

Murmuring answers across the table, Grace's team worked their way down the list, unscrambling Trip Around the World, Broken Dishes, Hole in the Barn Door, and Feathered Star. Sunbonnet Sue and Grandmother's Fan gave them considerable trouble, but soon they, too, were untangled. Megan and Vinnie quickly proved themselves the strongest members of the team.

Although Donna solved several puzzles, Grace was unable to unscramble a single one. Instead she began giving only half her attention to the paper while scanning the other tables to judge how much progress the other teams were making.

"The team closest to the dessert table seems confident, but intense," she reported. "They might be close to finishing."

"That figures," Vinnie grumbled. "They can reach out and get more fuel anytime they need it."

"Here." Megan passed her the last cookie. "Refuel with this. We're doing fine." It was true; they had completed all but two anagrams.

"I have one," Donna said. "'A pathless totter' is Steps to the Altar. How appropriate."

When Megan nodded in wry agreement, Vinnie gave them a sharp look. "Not necessarily. It depends who's taking those steps."

Only one anagram remained. "'Our nouns be drudgery,'" Grace murmured to herself. Our nouns be drudgery. Something about it tickled a memory in the back of her mind, and suddenly she could picture the answer as clearly as if the letters had rearranged themselves on the page. "Burgoyne Surrounded."

Megan shot her a look. "What did you say?"

"Burgoyne Surrounded."

Donna looked dubious. "Is that a real block?"

"Of course. It's a pattern of squares and rectangles, usually done in two colors. According to tradition, it was named to commemorate British general John Burgoyne's defeat in the Revolutionary War—"

"Skip the history lesson and write," Vinnie cried. Quickly they filled in the last empty line on their papers and waved them in the air. "We're done! Sylvia!"

A groan went up from the other tables, the loudest of all from the group nearest the desserts. Sylvia held up her hands. "Now, now. Don't give up yet. We still have to check their answers." She crossed the room, took Megan's paper, and read the answers aloud. Then she smiled. "We have our winners."

Grace's team cheered and exchanged high-fives. One of the staff members came to their table to award them their prizes: ribbon-tied bundles of fat eighths, hand-dyed in a gradation of rainbow colors. As Grace ran her hand over the soft cloth, she wondered if maybe this fabric would spark the inspiration she so desperately needed. Maybe those fat eighths would become her next quilt.

Sylvia returned to the riser at the front of the room. "While you were working, Sarah and Summer read your questionnaires. The results are in, and we're ready to announce the winners." A young woman with long red hair handed her a sheet of paper. "Which camper has the greatest number of Unfinished Objects? With a grand total of . . ." She read from the sheet silently, then turned to the young woman. "This can't possibly be right, is it?" When the red-haired woman nodded, Sylvia shrugged and turned back to her audience. "With a grand total of one hundred seventeen . . ." A gasp of awe went up from the quilters. "Yes, you heard right, ladies. With a grand total of one hundred seventeen UFOs, Donna Jorgenson!"

Red-faced, Donna rose and went to the front of the room to claim her prize as the campers applauded and laughed. "I'm so embarrassed," she said as she returned to her seat. "As soon as I get home, I'm going to finish some of those quilts."

"At least you won a prize," Vinnie consoled her, leaning over to peer into her closed hand. "What is it?"

Donna handed her a small metal object. Vinnie studied it and nodded in approval before passing it around the table. When Grace received it, she saw that it was a pin with the words "Elm Creek Quilts" encircling a picture of a house and a grove of trees. It seemed familiar somehow, and suddenly she remembered seeing a similar design on a medallion quilt hanging in the manor's foyer.

Sylvia continued. "And now, for the quilter with the least number of UFOs, with a grand total of zero"—this the quilters interrupted with an exclamation of astonishment—"Grace Daniels!"

Her heart heavy, Grace pushed back her chair and went to the front of the room for her prize. Sylvia gave her a sympathetic, almost apologetic smile as she placed a pin identical to Donna's in her palm and closed her fingers around it.

When Grace returned to her table, Megan said, "I was sure I was going to win that one. I only have two UFOs." She shook her head in admiration. "How do you stay so organized?"

Grace's first impulse was to respond with a joke, but she decided to be honest. "It's not organization. It's lack of ideas. I'd do anything to have as many projects in the works as you do, Donna."

"No, you don't want that," Donna said. "All my prize shows is that I have a short attention span."

"At least you both got pins," Vinnie said grumpily. She rapped her fingernails on the table and frowned expectantly at the front of the room.

Sylvia went on to announce the rest of the winners, who claimed their prizes amid praise and teasing. Grace half expected to win a second pin for owning the most fabric, but a woman from New Mexico whose stash filled two entire rooms had them all beat.

Vinnie's fidgeting increased with each new camper who earned a pin. "Don't let it bother you," Megan said. "I'm not going to win anything, either. Besides, we won the group prize."

"I don't mind," Vinnie insisted, her voice falsely innocent. "I can be a good loser."

The other three members of her team exchanged knowing glances as Vinnie hungrily watched three campers, who had taken their first lessons just that morning, approach the riser to receive pins for being the newest quilters.

"And last but not least," Sylvia announced. "For the camper who has quilted the longest, a woman who began quilting at age twelve and has stuck with it through nearly seventy wonderful years—Vinnie Burkholder!"

"Hooray for Vinnie!" someone cried out.

"Vin-nie, Vin-nie," Megan chanted, and soon the whole room had joined in, calling out Vinnie's name in time with their clapping hands. Vinnie sat frozen in her chair, her mouth forming an O. Donna nudged her and motioned for her to stand up. Vinnie started and rose, then brightened and walked to the front of the room waving and bowing graciously to her admirers.

"Vin-nie, Vin-nie," Grace chanted, laughing and clapping her hands as Vinnie accepted her pin from Sylvia and stepped onto the riser beside her, beaming.

As Vinnie returned to her seat, Sylvia Compson looked out over the crowd of quilters. Some chatted with their teammates; others mingled, going from table to table, greeting old friends or making new ones. She watched as her dear friend Grace admired Vinnie's pin; she looked on as women who had been so shy and tentative at Candlelight now threw back their heads and laughed and joked along with the most outgoing of the group. Yes, she thought with satisfaction, the week of camp was off to a fine start, indeed.

Four

V INNIE BEGAN each morning with a conversation with God. *You didn't take away my aches and pains in the night like I asked You to,* she would pray, *but at least You let me see another day, and at my age I ought to be grateful for that.* Then she would thank Him for His many blessings, especially her children and grandchildren, and ask Him to watch over her family and protect them throughout the day.

That morning she added a special request: *Donna and Megan can shout coincidence all they want, but I think I see Your hand at work. If I'm mistaken, please let me know—and make it obvious so I won't miss it. Unless I hear otherwise from You, I'll fit a little match-making into my vacation.*

Satisfied, Vinnie threw off the covers and got up. As she showered and dressed, she thought about Megan and the confidences she had shared with Vinnie and Donna over supper the night before. Megan's ex-husband, Keith, sounded like a scoundrel. Back in Vinnie's day, men hadn't been able to lift a dustcloth to save their lives, and they might have spent one night too many with friends down at the local bar, but at least they had known what a man's obligations were. Nowadays, men seemed to think they could cast off one family and start another, bearing no responsibility for the first wife and the first children. Sometimes the women were just as bad. Vinnie often didn't recognize the world, it had changed so drastically.

But on holidays or other special occasions, when all her children and grandchildren and now even great-grandchildren gathered around her, she would shake off the melancholy of aging and be content. With each graduation or new addition to the family, Vinnie would feel the love of her descendants and admit to herself that she would not trade her presence among them for anything, not even to be reunited with Sam. She'd see him again in God's own good time, and Sam would understand if she lingered. As he had always told her, when you got right down to it, family was all they had, and all that truly mattered.

These days families dispersed to the four winds, mothers and children separated by half a continent or more. She was lucky that her children had stayed relatively close, scattered around the state rather than the entire country. Some of her friends in Meadowbrook Village had children in California or New York or Florida, whom they rarely saw. One woman had never seen her own grandchildren. "Why doesn't that son of yours bring them out for a visit?" Vinnie had demanded.

Airfares were too expensive, she was told, and hotel fees for a family of four were out of the question. Her son would pay for her to visit them, but Vinnie's friend refused. "I'm too old to fly so far," she had said, her face crumpling in grief.

Vinnie had not known what to say, and rarely was she at a loss for words. She was two years older than her friend, but as much as she disliked flying, if a four-hour flight was the only way to get to her family, she would suffer through it. She promised herself right then and there that she would never say she was too old for anything.

Several times since, she had been tempted to chide her friend into getting out of her chair and making that trip, but she held her tongue. Not everyone felt as strongly about family as Vinnie did. Maybe a person needed to grow up without a family to truly appreciate one.

She corrected herself; she *had* had a family—two, in fact, although the second had been more unconventional than the first.

For six years she had been part of a family she supposed other people would consider ordinary: her parents, her elder brother, Frankie, and herself. They lived in a small house in the Hartwell neighborhood of Cincinnati, and Vinnie remembered being happy and content there, until her mother's death changed everything.

Later, Vinnie learned that her mother had succumbed after a long battle with cancer, but at the time, her mother's death seemed as sudden as it was incomprehensible. The funeral passed in a blur of grown-ups with dark clothes and hushed voices. Relatives hugged her and told her that her mother had loved her very much; neighbors dropped off casseroles and told her to be a good girl. Only when the bustle of activity ceased did a chill of realization settle in Vinnie's heart: Her mother wasn't ever coming back, and nothing Vinnie did could make their family whole again.

Her father seemed to wish he had gone away with Mother. He rarely left his chair by the radio, and he seemed not to notice when his children spoke to him. Frankie looked after Vinnie, fixing her cereal and toast three times a day and making sure she brushed her teeth at night. They played quietly in their rooms or in the backyard, avoiding their strangely silent father. Vinnie knew this wasn't normal, but she pretended not to notice.

Then one day, a neighbor spotted them outside, and when she questioned them, something in their hushed voices and guarded manner sent her hurrying inside to her telephone. A few days later, their father's elder sister arrived with a suitcase and a look of determination that reminded Vinnie of how Daddy used to be.

Vinnie was glad to see Aunt Lynn, since in her presence, Daddy remembered to shave and change his clothes. He returned to work. At suppertime they had hot meals; at night they slept in clean sheets scented with lavender. When Vinnie cried at night for her mother, Aunt Lynn came to her in the dark and rocked her until she fell back asleep.

Vinnie didn't know why Aunt Lynn didn't have any children of her own, except that ladies had to have a husband first, and Aunt Lynn didn't. That was one of the things that the other aunts didn't like about her. They also didn't like that she wore lipstick and worked in an office and had turned down two marriage proposals. Vinnie didn't understand why the aunts whispered such things when Aunt Lynn wasn't there; she thought Aunt Lynn was very pretty and nice, and her life sounded terribly exciting.

When she left several weeks later, Vinnie was sorry to see her go. She asked Aunt Lynn to stay, but Aunt Lynn said her boss needed her. "Your Daddy will look after you," she promised, then kissed Vinnie and carried her suitcase outside, where a taxi waited to take her to the railroad station.

As the days passed, it seemed that Aunt Lynn had taken Daddy's restored energy with her. He still went to work and sent the children off to school each morning, but in the evenings he sat alone in his chair by the radio, smoking and listening to music. Vinnie eventually grew accustomed to the gloom, but her memories of happiness grew ever fainter.

She ached for her mother. She ached with the large, constant pain of knowing her mother was gone, and in dozens of small ways when each day brought another sign of how much Vinnie still needed her. The sight of an incomplete Nine Patch block reminded Vinnie that her mother would never finish the quilting lessons that had begun only months before. Each morning Mother had plaited her brown locks into two smooth braids, but the braids her father attempted hung loose, with tufts of hair sticking out here and there, and her bangs grew nearly to her chin. When the popular girl who sat across the aisle at school told her she looked like a sheepdog, Vinnie pretended not to hear her and tried to poke the unruly bangs into the braids. When that failed, she tucked the strands behind her ears. She thought she looked better, but the popular girl snickered. Vinnie's face grew hot with shame, and she whispered, "At least I'm not worst in the class in spelling."

The popular girl's face grew sour, and at once Vinnie knew she should have ignored her. At recess the girl waited until the teacher was out of earshot before calling her a sheepdog again, and before long her friends had joined in, laughing and jeering. Vinnie stood very still, watching the popular girl's sour little mouth blabbering insults, the smug disdain in her eyes, the sunlight gleaming on her two perfect, blond braids—and then something inside Vinnie exploded. She charged into the girl, knocking her to the ground. By the time the teacher ran over and pulled her aside, the popular girl was sobbing, her face red where Vinnie had repeatedly slapped her.

Vinnie was sent home. When her father read the principal's note, he sighed so heavily that Vinnie grew even more ashamed. She stammered out an explanation, but her father seemed not to hear her. Then he said, "Bring me the scissors."

Her heart sank as she found her mother's sewing basket, untouched for so many months, and brought her father the scissors. He sat her down in his chair by the radio, combed out her sloppy braids, and began to trim her bangs. He frowned in concentration as he worked, cutting straight across above her eyes, trimming the uneven edges, then pausing to study his work before cutting again.

"Daddy, that's short enough," Vinnie said, alarmed by the sight of the snipped ends collecting on her lap.

"Be still. I'm trying to make this even."

Vinnie hoped for the best, but when her father finally sat back, satisfied, and sent her to look in the mirror, she discovered a short brown stubble where her bangs had once been.

She felt tears gathering, and tried to hide her face before her father noticed, but his eyes met hers in the mirror. "I can fix it," he said hastily. "If I cut the sides a little shorter, they'll blend in."

"Do you think so?"

"Sure," he said, and steered her back to the chair. Vinnie

clutched her hands together in her lap and closed her eyes, cring-
ing inside with each snip of the scissors. As her head grew lighter,
her stomach grew more queasy. She was afraid to open her eyes,
but when her father told her to, she obeyed.

She looked into the mirror, and a familiar face stared back at
her in horror. Frankie's face. Daddy had cut her hair so that it
looked exactly like Frankie's.

She burst into tears. "I can't go to school like this."

Her father stared at her, an odd, distant expression on his face.
"Your mother is dead, and you're crying over your hair."

Vinnie's tears choked off abruptly. She climbed out of the chair
and went to her room.

The next day she went to school and got into another fight
when the popular girl's cronies teased her for looking like a boy.
The following morning she walked to school with Frankie as
usual, but as soon as he ran off to join his friends, she doubled
back and hid in her bedroom. The school contacted her father
when she had been absent a week. He was instructed to bring her
in for a conference, where the principal lectured them on truancy
while Vinnie stared at the floor and her father repeated assurances
that Vinnie's absences were over.

"I don't know what to do with you," her father said as they
walked home. His voice was flat and hopeless. "Frankie doesn't
give me this kind of trouble. I wish . . ."

He never finished the thought, and Vinnie found herself wondering what exactly he wished.

She was only a little surprised when Aunt Lynn returned the
next week. Her father gave Vinnie a quick hug, so hard it almost
hurt, then took Frankie to the park to play catch.

When they were alone, Aunt Lynn smiled at Vinnie, but her
voice was tentative when she said, "Your father and I thought
maybe you could come to live with me."

Vinnie's heart sank. She liked Aunt Lynn, but this was her
home. "For how long?"

Aunt Lynn shrugged. "We'll see."

"What if I don't want to?" she asked in a small voice.

Aunt Lynn watched her without speaking for a moment, and Vinnie could see the sympathy in her eyes. "Come on. Let's pack your things."

They packed all her clothes and books, and her favorite toys. Vinnie was too numb to cry. She worked slowly, hoping her father would return before she left, but all too soon the last box was filled, and she realized her father would stay out even past Frankie's bedtime to avoid her.

A black car waited at the curb, its back door and trunk open. Aunt Lynn loaded the boxes into the car, motioned for Vinnie to climb into the back seat, then sat beside her and shut the door.

A blond woman in the driver's seat turned around and grinned. "Hiya, Vinnie," she said. "Welcome aboard the Lynn and Lena Express. Hang on to your hat."

Vinnie was too heartsick to reply. She shut her eyes and let Aunt Lynn pull her close as they drove away from the only home she had ever known. She never once looked back.

In the decades that had passed since then, she never forgot how easily a girl could be sent away and ignored as if she had never existed. As she grew older, she realized that age was no protection: Wives could become inconvenient and be put aside as easily as daughters.

Now, with her eighty-second birthday only a day away, she had met a kindhearted woman who deserved better, just as Vinnie herself had deserved better so long ago. Vinnie recognized the grief she saw in Megan's eyes, and the spark of resolve that had not yet been quenched. She remembered what that felt like, and how only the love of two compassionate women had helped her grow from a lonely little girl into a strong, resilient woman. It was long past time she helped another as she had been helped.

If Vinnie had her way—and she usually did—she would see her new friend happy again before another birthday passed.

🌸

Megan saved seats for Donna and Grace in Color Theory, and was pleased when Grace came to sit beside them without waiting to be invited. At the beginning of class, Gwen assigned an exercise, working with paints to explore tints and hues. Each student selected a tube of her favorite color, squeezed a sample onto an artist's palette, and colored the first section of a chart. Next Gwen told them to mix in white paint, one drop at a time, and to fill the chart with the resulting color variations.

Donna tried to convince Megan to use purple, but Megan snatched the blue tube before Donna could hide it. Grace chose red, so Donna took yellow. "Someone at this table has to be daring," she said.

"What's so daring about yellow?" Megan teased.

"For a quilter, yellow is daring," Grace said. "Some quilters refuse to use it at all, and some use so much that it completely overpowers the other colors in the quilt. It's challenging to strike the right balance."

"Besides, it's next to impossible to find the perfect shade of yellow in a fabric store," Donna said. "You want a butter yellow and you have to settle for canary or daffodil."

"Recently I've resorted to dying my own to get the colors I need." Grace frowned at the tip of her paintbrush. "Although to be honest, 'recently' is a relative term. I haven't dyed anything in more than year, or started anything else, for that matter."

"I have the opposite problem," Donna said. "I have so many projects in the works that I won't possibly live long enough to finish them all."

"You should do what my mother does," Megan said. "She keeps each of her works-in-progress in a separate box labeled with the name of one of her friends. If, God forbid, she should pass away unexpectedly, each friend will receive the box with her name on it and think my mother was working on a quilt especially for her. She uses the names of women she doesn't get along with, too. She says it's a great way to make sure she has plenty of guilt-ridden, sobbing mourners at her funeral."

Grace laughed, but Donna shuddered. "That's morbid."

Megan smiled to herself. Donna only thought so because she didn't understand her mother's sense of humor. Megan wished she had inherited more of it and less of her father's somber pragmatism. Maybe then she'd be able to laugh off her failures instead of brooding over them. Maybe then she wouldn't worry about Robby's tendency to embellish the truth beyond recognition and how she could never hope to fully compensate for his father's absence.

"Is your quilter's block because of your daughter?" Donna asked Grace.

Grace hesitated. "Yes . . . well, that's part of it." She added a drop of white paint to her palette and fell silent as she blended the new shade. "I don't know what bothers me most: that she's seeing an older man or that she hasn't told me about him."

Megan thought of her own futile attempts at dating after the divorce. "Maybe she doesn't want to mention him until she knows whether she's serious about him."

"That's exactly the problem. She must be serious about him, because she already introduced him to her son. She's adamant about not letting him meet casual boyfriends." Grace sighed. "I think I've answered my own question. What bothers me most is that she didn't tell me. For all I know, he might be a perfectly wonderful man."

"He probably is," Megan said to reassure her, but Donna shook her head.

"I keep telling myself the same thing about Brandon—my daughter's fiancé," Donna said. "I feel like I'm trying to convince myself that everything is going to be okay, because deep down, I don't really believe it. Does that make any sense?"

Grace nodded emphatically. Megan watched the two women, linked by their similar worries, and thought with some trepidation about her own child. What, if anything, could Megan do to help Robby avoid repeating his parents' dismal mistakes?

Her pragmatism asserted itself. There was no point in worrying about Robby's future relationships now. She'd have time enough to worry when she allowed Robby to begin dating—which she'd be ready to do in about twenty years.

Just then, she heard footsteps behind her and felt a light touch on her shoulder. She looked up to find Sylvia Compson.

"Megan Donohue?"

"Yes?"

"Your mother's on the phone. You may take the call in the parlor, if you'd like some privacy."

"My mom?" Megan pushed back her chair and rose. "Is something wrong?"

"She didn't say so, dear. I'm sure she would have if it were an emergency."

Megan quickly gathered her things and followed Sylvia out of the classroom, finding no comfort in the older woman's sympathetic assurances. Robby. She pictured broken limbs, car accidents, malevolent strangers. By the time they reached the formal parlor in the west wing, Megan's heart was pounding, and she snatched up the phone without remembering to thank her hostess, who quickly departed. "Hello?" she said breathlessly into the phone.

"Honey?"

"Mom? What's wrong? Is Robby okay?"

"He's fine," her mother assured her, then lowered her voice. "I'm so sorry to call you like this, but Robby's upset. He's been crying all morning, and I don't think he'll calm down unless he talks to you."

"Why? What happened?"

"Nothing happened, honey, it's just that . . ." She hesitated. "He's afraid you aren't coming back. I hate to tell you this, but he thinks you've left him like his father did."

"Could you put him on the phone, please?" Megan said, fighting to keep her voice steady.

"Of course."

In another moment, her son's wavering voice said, "Hello?"

"Hi, Robby, it's Mom."

"Mom?" he said. "Where are you? Are you coming home?"

Yes, she almost cried out, Right this minute. I'm on my way. Instead she took a deep breath and said, "I'll be home on Saturday, like I told you before I left, remember?"

"Y-yes." He sniffled, and she could picture him wiping his nose on the back of his hand. "Are you sure you're coming back?"

"Of course I'm sure." She forced humor into her voice. "Did you think I'd get lost or something?"

"Well, you do get kind of lost sometimes, Mom."

She'd walked right into that one. "Not this time. I have a map and everything. Besides, I have to come home. I left all my stuff there."

He mulled that over. "That's true," he admitted.

She kept him on the phone until he was cheerful again, telling her all the fun plans he and his Grandpa were making for the week. She listened and responded with just the right amount of enthusiasm, but inside she was aching and seething, wishing that Keith was there so she could shake him, so she could rage at him, so she could somehow make him see what his silence was doing to their precious child.

Julia sat on her bed looking over her notes from the Beginning Piecing class. The class had covered several of the terms on her list that morning, and the teacher had assured her they would get to the others later that week. For the first time since her plane had touched down in central Pennsylvania, Julia began to feel some hope that this trip wouldn't be a wasted effort, after all.

To her surprise, she had actually enjoyed the lesson. The teacher, a strikingly pretty blond woman in her early forties named Diane, had a dry sense of humor that took some getting used to, but her explanations were clear and simple. The other five students had made templates for a Friendship Star block the previous day, but Diane had helped Julia while the other students cut out their fabric pieces, and before long, Julia had caught up to them. With Diane's class and Donna's private tutorials, Julia might just be able to convince Deneford she had been quilting for decades.

Suddenly a knock sounded on her door. "Megan! Are you decent?" a voice sang out as the door swung open. The white-haired woman stuck her head in the room, and when she spotted Julia, her eyebrows arched in surprise. "My goodness," she said. "You're decent, but you're not Megan."

"No." Startled, Julia rose and smoothed her skirt self-consciously. "I'm afraid you have the wrong room."

"Are you sure?" The woman, whom Julia now recognized as the same quilter from yesterday's disastrous Quick Piecing class, peered around in puzzlement as if she might spy the woman she was looking for hiding in a corner. "I was sure she said first room on the left in the west wing."

"I'm sorry." Julia's surprise was turning to impatience, but, remembering her image, she put on a pleasant expression. "There's no one named Megan staying in this room."

"Oh." The woman frowned, thinking. "Well, I already knocked across the hall, so maybe she went down to lunch already. Are you coming?"

"Well, actually—"

"You're not planning to skip lunch, are you? Someone as thin as you?"

"I'm expecting someone to bring me a tray."

"Are you ill?"

"No, but—"

"Then you can't stay up in your room all alone," the woman protested, and before Julia knew it, she had entered the room and taken Julia's arm. "You'll miss all the fun." Julia was too startled to do anything as the woman began to steer her toward the door and into the hallway. "I'm Vinnie, by the way."

"I don't mean to be rude, but—"

"Tuesday is pasta buffet," Vinnie said. "You pick what shape of pasta you like, what ingredients, and what sauce, and the cook mixes each order in a separate omelet pan. Everyone can have her lunch exactly the way she likes it."

They had reached the stairs, and Julia saw no way to escape without knocking the older woman on her backside. "That sounds delicious," she said instead, her stomach knotting at the thought of a crowd of quilters just waiting for her to slop marinara sauce down the front of her blouse. They passed Sarah on her way upstairs with a covered tray. "I'll be lunching with the other campers today, thank you," Julia said with all the dignity she could muster. In the banquet hall, she resigned herself to being the lunchtime entertainment for the day. Tomorrow, she promised herself, she would remember to lock her door.

The meal itself wasn't as tacky as she expected it to be; the cook prepared her penne with sun-dried tomatoes, fresh basil, and an excellent olive oil she was astonished to see this far from the West Coast. Vinnie ordered a plate of spaghetti and meatballs in a red sauce, then motioned for Julia to follow her to a nearby table where two other women were already seated. One of the women was Donna, who started at their approach.

"These are two of my newest quilting friends, Donna and Grace," Vinnie said, and the two women greeted Julia with silent nods. "Donna and Grace, this is . . ." She looked up at Julia. "My goodness, dear, I didn't even get your name."

"Julia." Was it possible the old biddy didn't recognize her?

"Julia." Vinnie nodded in satisfaction and sat down. "Well, pull up a chair, Julia, before your noodles get cold."

"We can't have that, can we?" Julia said as pleasantly as she could manage, seating herself between Vinnie and Donna.

Just then, another woman joined them. A slender brunette, she was the youngest of the four, but unlike the others, she looked unhappy. "Sorry I'm late," she said, taking a seat between Grace and Vinnie. Then she bounded to her feet again. "Oh. I forgot my food."

"What's wrong with Megan?" Vinnie asked as the harried young woman headed for the pasta bar.

"She received a phone call in the middle of Color Theory class," Grace said. "I hope it wasn't bad news."

When Megan returned, her eyes met Julia's, and she nearly dropped her plate. "Oh my goodness, I didn't even see you there."

Vinnie reached for Megan's hand in a grandmotherly gesture that completely escaped the younger woman's notice. "Megan, this is Julia."

"Yes, I know. Julia Merchaud." She fumbled for her chair and sat down, still staring at Julia.

"You've met?"

"Well, no, but everyone knows Julia Merchaud."

Vinnie turned to her. "Is that so?"

Before Julia could reply, Donna said, "You're kidding, right? You've never heard of Julia Merchaud?"

"No." Vinnie looked from Donna to Julia and back. "Well, why should I have heard of her? She's probably never heard of me. Are you another famous quilter, like Grace?"

"She's famous, but she's not a quilter," Megan said.

"She most certainly is too a quilter," Donna said hastily, stealing a quick glance at Julia. "You're sure you've never heard of her? Julia Merchaud, Grandma Wilson from *Family Tree*? On television?"

Vinnie gave Julia a guilty smile. "I'm sorry, dear. I suppose I'm not watching the right channels. What day is your show on? I'll be sure to watch for you."

"It's been canceled," Julia managed. Eight years in the same role, one that earned her four Emmys and a Golden Globe, and someone from her core demographic didn't even recognize her.

"It was a great show, though," Megan ventured.

"It was my favorite," Donna said. "I wrote a letter to the network and complained when it was canceled, but no one ever wrote back."

Julia's annoyance ebbed, no match for Donna's admiration. "That's typical of the networks," she said, stabbing a piece of pasta with her fork. "They pay more attention to advertisers than viewers."

"That's a shame," Vinnie said. "Well, dear, if Donna and Megan here are any indication, you have loyal fans who won't rest until they see you on another show soon."

"Do you have any other projects pending?" Grace inquired.

"I do have one that's rather important. That's why I came to quilt camp—to brush up on my skills. My agent insisted, unfortunately. I'd planned on a week at my favorite spa." Julia sighed. She could be receiving a massage at that very moment. Instead her fingertips were sore with needle pricks, and she kept finding stray bits of thread all over her clothes. "I'll be playing a quilter in a feature film that begins shooting in a few months."

"How wonderful," Vinnie exclaimed. "A movie about quilters. It'll be a hit; I'm sure of it."

Warming to her subject, Julia divulged some details about the plot, and about how Ellen, whom she generously described as a "promising new voice in filmmaking," had based the story on her great-grandmother's diaries. As the four women hung on her every word, Julia forgot that she had not desired their company in the first place.

"That sounds so exciting," Donna said wistfully. "All I've ever done with my life is keep house and raise kids."

"That's all?" Grace said. "That's everything. There's no more important job in the world than raising your children. No job is more difficult, either."

"Or more rewarding," Vinnie said. "I raised four children and don't regret for a moment any of the sacrifices I made for them. I don't know how mothers these days can bear to leave their children in day care while they go off to work."

Megan gave her a wan look. "It isn't easy."

"Your situation is different," Vinnie said. "It's not your fault that husband of yours left. I'm sure you'd stay home if you could."

Grace laughed. "My husband left me, too, but even if he hadn't, I still would have kept up with my career. Yes, motherhood is my most important calling, but I would have gone crazy if I hadn't had some other outlet."

"I would have gone crazy if I hadn't stayed home," Donna said. "I wouldn't have been any use to an employer, anyway, on the phone all day checking in on the girls, staring out the windows fretting about what milestones I was missing."

"Every family is different," Megan said. "My son is loved and well cared for, and that's what matters most."

"Hear, hear," Vinnie said, raising her coffee cup and clinking it against Megan's.

"I like to think I set a good example for my daughter by being a mother and also pursuing my artistic career," Grace said. "She grew up assuming that there are many possibilities for women."

Megan nodded, looking hopeful for the first time since she had sat down. Then suddenly, her face fell. "Leaving my son for work is one thing—that's a necessity—but I'm never going to leave him for a vacation again."

"Let me guess. This is your first time away from your son overnight?" Grace asked, and Megan nodded. "He'll be all right. When you come home, that will reassure him, and your next trip away will be much easier."

"I don't think I could leave him another time," Megan said.

"You have to," Vinnie cried. "Next year, during my birthday week. You are coming back to camp next summer, aren't you?"

Megan looked dubious, as if she hadn't planned on it but liked the idea.

Donna said, "You should, Meg. It will be good for Robby—and for you."

"You have to come back, too," Grace told Donna. "I have to hear how that wedding works out."

"I guess that means you've already decided you'll be here," Megan said to Grace.

Grace let out a small, self-conscious laugh. "I suppose it does."

"By that time you'll have a new work-in-progress to show us," Vinnie declared. When Grace winced, Vinnie added, "Have a little faith in yourself. A whole year to begin one quilt. A lot can happen in a year."

Julia looked around the table, an observer rather than a participant. Only moments ago she had been the center of attention, but now the others seemed to have forgotten she was there—and not one had thought to ask her if she would return the next year. Why should they? They knew her trip was all business, no pleasure. No doubt they assumed she had better things to do—which she did, but it would have been nice if at least one of them had included her, if only to be polite.

Julia wondered what she was doing there, a childless woman among mothers whose shared experiences forged a bond between them she would never understand. They looked toward the future, each of them, because their love for their sons and daughters gave them a fierce and passionate stake in it. Julia's parents were dead; her link to the past was broken and her link to the future never forged.

She had always believed her work made her immortal, but watching these women, who had neither fame nor fortune to compare to hers, she realized that they, and not she, would live on forever. Her work would one day be forgotten, and all memory of her would one day disintegrate with the videotape that had captured her image, but part of these women would always live in their descendants' memories, in their very flesh and blood and bone.

Her work was nothing. What had she ever done to truly affect the life of another human being for the better? Throughout her career she had clawed and scratched and scrambled over competitors and colleagues alike to get where she was today, and for what?

Julia felt herself adrift in time, barren and alone.

In appliqué class after lunch, Julia still held the needle guardedly, but Donna was pleased to see that her pupil was making progress.

Even so, Julia spoke so little during class that Donna worried that Vinnie had truly offended her. "Don't mind Vinnie," Donna apologized later, after they had begun their private needle-turn class in Sylvia Compson's formal parlor. "She's probably asleep by prime time."

"Hmm? Oh, that. I had forgotten."

Donna wasn't quite sure if she believed her. "About that confidentiality agreement . . . since you told the others about the movie at lunch, does that mean I can talk about it now?"

Julia sighed. "I suppose so."

"Does it really matter how recently you've learned to quilt?" Donna ventured. "What's important is how well you quilt when they're filming, right?"

Julia set down the leaf appliqué she was stitching to her Whig Rose block. "Yes, I suppose you're right. Except for my pride, of course. My agent—my former agent—told the producer I already knew how to quilt. He won't be pleased to learn we deceived him."

"What do you mean, 'we'?" Your agent lied, but you didn't. If the producer does learn the truth, you can just tell him your agent made a mistake."

"He's not a very gullible person."

"Maybe not, but you're a very good actress."

"That's true." Julia smiled briefly and picked up her block again. "If he hears the truth from me first, I won't have to worry about one of these other campers running to the tabloids and telling them what a terrible quilter I am."

"You're not a terrible quilter," Donna chided her, then hesitated. "Do you really think one of the other campers would do such a thing?"

"I'm no longer surprised by what anyone will do, for the right price."

Julia spoke airily, as if accustomed to betrayals. Donna felt a sudden surge of sympathy for her. It must be difficult going through life suspecting everyone, guarding your words and your actions. Quilters aren't like that, she wanted to say, but uncertainty held her back. For all she knew, campers were taking notes and snapping photos of Julia with hidden cameras. Julia's paranoia was rubbing off on her. "I don't think you have anything to worry about," she said, her loyalty to her fellow quilters outweighing her desire to appear agreeable.

"I have much to worry about. You have no idea how important this role is to my career. Now that the series is over, if something doesn't go right for me soon, I'll be lucky if I can get a spot in an antacid commercial." She shrugged and flashed Donna what was probably meant as a nonchalant grin, but the pain beneath it was obvious.

"You can't mean that," Donna said. "You've won five Emmys. You must have directors begging you to star in their shows."

"Four Emmys," Julia said. "And a Golden Globe. But that doesn't matter much when you're my age. How often do feature films star a woman, and I mean really star, as the main character and not just someone's girlfriend or wife? And how many women over forty do you see in any roles at all?" She shook her head and began stabbing her quilt block with her needle in quick, emphatic motions. "In Hollywood's version of America, women over forty have all but vanished."

Donna barked out a laugh. "It's not just Hollywood. We haven't disappeared, but we might as well be invisible for all the respect your average wife and mother receives in our society. At least you have your career. People have to respect you."

"For being an entertainer?" Julia said. "For reciting lines someone else wrote? What's the merit in that? What exactly have I contributed to the world?"

Their eyes met briefly, and for a moment Donna was struck with the unsettling sensation that Julia Merchaud envied her. "Your work is important," she said. "You present stories and situations that teach, that make people think."

Julia brushed that off with a wave of her hand. "Please. 'Next, on a very special *Family Tree*, Grandma Wilson cures cancer and feeds the hungry.'"

"I'm serious," Donna insisted. "Your work can be positive or negative, but if people watch it, it will influence them. My daughter studies drama, and she would tell you the same thing." Donna suddenly lost her enthusiasm. "Or at least she used to study drama."

They worked on in silence, but Donna's thoughts churned. Who was she to be making impassioned speeches, as if she had cornered the market on confidence and self-worth? She had spent far too much of her time apologizing for being a stay-at-home mom, all the while secretly consoling herself with the assurance that she was doing what was best for her children. But now, despite all her love and encouragement, her eldest was dropping out of college to get married, just as Donna herself had done. Maybe Grace was right: If a mother worked outside the home, she proved to her daughters that there were other possibilities for women.

She felt overcome with heartsickness. She couldn't bear the thought that she had set her own sights too low, and had thereby influenced her daughters to do the same.

Lindsay used to study drama. Soon, Donna would say that her daughter used to be a promising student at the University of Minnesota, that she used to be active in college organizations, that she used to have a future bright with promise and possibilities. Too much of her daughter's life was shifting into the past tense with this impending marriage, and Donna couldn't accept that.

And why should she accept it, without first trying to persuade her daughter to take another path? In hindsight, she should have stepped in earlier, when Lindsay moved into Brandon's apartment at the beginning of the summer. She had not protested then because she didn't want to appear out of touch or old-fashioned. Well, she was old-fashioned, and although Lindsay might prefer that Donna accept every one of her daughter's choices without question, Donna would do so no longer.

She couldn't simply order Lindsay not to marry Brandon or postpone the wedding; young women who thought they were in love rarely listened to logic or common sense. Instead, Donna would focus on Lindsay's education. Surely she could find a way to convince Lindsay that furthering her education would be best for her—and by extension, for her marriage—in the long run.

Lindsay had to finish school. Donna couldn't let Brandon become Lindsay's whole life.

Five

VINNIE WOKE Wednesday morning with a sense of triumph. She had made it to her eighty-second birthday.

She said her morning prayers quickly, eager to start the day. Before she left her room, she studied her face in the mirror and practiced looking surprised. If Sylvia and her staff discovered she anticipated their annual surprise parties, they might stop having them.

At breakfast, Vinnie graciously collected birthday greetings and a few ribbon-tied fat quarters from well-wishers she had met during previous years' camp sessions. "When's the party?" several whispered when no one on the staff could overhear, forcing Vinnie to feign innocence. Keeping up the pretense of surprise was part of the fun.

Vinnie loved celebrating her birthday and was impatient with people who refused to acknowledge their own. What was so shameful in living another year? It was considerably better than the alternative. Vinnie never missed an opportunity to have fun, especially when other people wanted to show their affection for her. She had learned that from Aunt Lynn and her aunt's friend, Lena.

Lena was the blond woman who had driven Vinnie from her home to Aunt Lynn's small house in Dayton so many years ago. She had tried to engage Vinnie in conversation as they drove, but Vinnie was too numb to respond. Her father had sent her away—and although he had not explained why, she knew. If she had only been good, he would have kept her, as he had kept Frankie.

As the weeks passed, Vinnie's shock and grief lessened but never quite left her. A chasm of grief and loneliness seemed to separate her from the other girls at her new school, and she still felt like a stranger in Aunt Lynn's home. Her new teacher was kind, and encouraged the other children to include her in their play, but Vinnie usually wandered off to be alone and think.

She had to find a way to persuade her father to let her come home. She wrote to him often, telling him how good she had been and how she never got into trouble at school anymore. She told him that Aunt Lynn had taught her to clean and sew, and how she would do all the chores, hers and Frankie's both, if he would just let her come home.

He responded to her first letter, writing that he was pleased she was being a good girl and he was sure she wouldn't give Aunt Lynn any trouble. Frankie wrote frequently, reporting on the neighbor's new puppy and a trip to the zoo with Daddy, but Daddy rarely sent letters, and never once did he respond to Vinnie's questions about when she might return home.

One day, after many months, Aunt Lynn asked Vinnie how she would like to celebrate her upcoming eighth birthday.

"I want to go to the zoo with my daddy," Vinnie said, remembering Frankie's letter.

Aunt Lynn and Lena exchanged a look. "How about if we take you instead?" Aunt Lynn asked. "Your dad might not be able to go."

Vinnie felt her eyes welling up with tears. She didn't care about the zoo; all she wanted was to see her father. "If he can't take me, I don't want to go."

"Would you like to do something else?" Lena asked.

"I don't want to have a birthday at all."

"We have to celebrate your birthday," Aunt Lynn said.

"We didn't last year." Last year, so soon after her mother had died, no one in the family could have imagined celebrating. Talk of her birthday called back all that grief and loneliness, which were never far away.

Without another word, she left the room rather than cry in front of Aunt Lynn and Lena. She doubted they would ask her father about the zoo; even if they did, he would refuse, if he bothered to reply at all.

Aunt Lynn and Lena said no more about her birthday, so she assumed they had forgotten about it, as she wished she could. Then one Saturday morning, Aunt Lynn and Lena bounded into her room and threw back the curtains. "Get up, sleepyhead," Aunt Lynn sang out.

Lena sat on Vinnie's bed and bounced up and down on the mattress, grinning. "Come on. You don't want to sleep in on your birthday!"

"I thought I wasn't having a birthday this year," Vinnie said, sitting up and blinking in the light.

"We decided to celebrate anyway," Aunt Lynn said. "In fact, we're celebrating twice as much. You missed two birthdays, so we have to make up for lost time. Otherwise we'll have to celebrate three times as much on your next birthday, and that might be too much for us old spinsters." Aunt Lynn and Lena looked at each other and laughed.

"Well, get up," Lena admonished. "The Pot-Luck Pals will be here soon."

Vinnie needed no further enticement. She flung back the covers and scrambled to get ready.

Vinnie hadn't made any friends of her own in the neighborhood yet, but the Pot-Luck Pals were the kind she hoped to have someday. Aunt Lynn and Lena's friends came over twice a month for a pot-luck supper and wild games of gin rummy that lasted long after Vinnie had been sent to bed. Some of the ladies were married, but most were single women in their late twenties and early thirties, like Aunt Lynn and Lena. They were shopgirls and secretaries and schoolteachers, and they were unlike any grown-up women Vinnie had ever known.

Not long after breakfast, the Pot-Luck Pals began to arrive, each bearing a covered dish and two colorfully wrapped gifts. "Happy seventh birthday," Margaret said, kissing Vinnie on one cheek. "And happy eighth," she said, kissing the other. Carla, the oldest, put a funny paper hat on Vinnie's head and placed an identical one on her own dark curls; her sister, Ethel Mae, picked up Vinnie and spun her around for good luck, seven times for her seventh year, and eight more times for the eighth. Afterward, she collapsed on the sofa and said, "If I keep this up, I won't need any of Lynn's punch!"

Never had the Pals filled the little house with so much warmth and laughter. They laughed and joked and played party games; they turned on the radio and danced themselves breathless. At noon they had a pot-luck lunch, one of the best the Pals had ever prepared, and then Vinnie opened her presents. She blew out candles on two birthday cakes and drank lemonade until she thought she would burst. The party grew louder and happier as the Pals indulged in more of Aunt Lynn's famous punch, the kind Aunt Lynn told her she'd be allowed to have on her eighteenth birthday and not an hour before. When Aunt Lynn wasn't watching, Ethel Mae let Vinnie have a taste from her cup; it burned going down, and Vinnie couldn't imagine why the Pals liked it.

The party lasted all day, until one by one the Pals went home, leaving the house a whirlwind of dirty dishes and party favors. Vinnie was exhausted, but happier than she had been in years. She helped Aunt Lynn and Lena begin to clean up the mess, but before long the three of them collapsed on the sofa, Aunt Lynn and Lena leaning against each other, Vinnie's head resting in Aunt Lynn's lap.

"Look at that grin," Lena said, nudging Aunt Lynn and nodding down at Vinnie. "I didn't think the kid knew how to smile like that."

Vinnie's smile broadened even as her eyelids drooped with sleep.

"I wonder what she wished for when she blew out her candles," Aunt Lynn said, her voice sounding far away.

"Don't make her tell, or the wish won't come true."

As Vinnie drifted off to sleep, she held her secrets close to her heart. As the last candle on the first cake had flickered out, Vinnie had wished that she would never forget that day as long as she lived. Over the candles on the second cake, she had made not a wish, but a promise: One day, she would be as carefree and confident as Aunt Lynn, Lena, and the other Pot-Luck Pals. No one would ever again believe she didn't know how to smile.

She kept her promise so well that people who knew her later probably never imagined that Vinnie had ever been anything but happy. Her birthday wish came true, as well, although some years—the birthdays when Sam was overseas, the time all four kids came down with the chicken pox, the first lonely birthdays as a widow—Vinnie found it more difficult to celebrate. If not for that brochure about the first Elm Creek Quilt Camp, she might have let her promise slip away, and a fine show of appreciation for Aunt Lynn and Lena that would have been. She filled out the form and sent it in over the protests of her children, who had planned to throw her a party. "You don't want to spend your birthday alone," her daughter said.

"I won't be alone," Vinnie replied firmly. "I'll be with other quilters."

The moment Vinnie stepped on the grounds of Elm Creek Manor, she knew she had made the right decision. That evening, at the Candlelight welcoming ceremony, she told the other campers why she had come, and was warmed by their sympathy. On the morning of her birthday, Sylvia Compson, a widow herself, hosted a delightful birthday breakfast. As she blew out the candle on her blueberry muffin, Vinnie made another wish and a promise: a promise that she would come back to Elm Creek

Manor each year to celebrate her birthday as long as she was able, and a wish that she would always find herself among friends. She kept that promise, and every year Sylvia and her staff rewarded her with a suprise birthday party.

This year they made her wait in suspense all day, so long that Vinnie began to worry that perhaps they had forgotten. But when she entered the banquet hall for supper, the lights were out and the curtains drawn. And when the lights suddenly came on—

"Surprise!" the campers shouted, showering her in confetti. They blew noisemakers and broke into a chorus of "Happy Birthday" while she stood in the doorway reveling in the attention. Almost too late, she remembered to open her eyes wide and let her jaw drop.

"My goodness," she exclaimed. "You should know better than to scare an old lady so." Everyone laughed, because no one could imagine considering Vinnie an old lady, a fact that pleased Vinnie beyond measure.

Dinner was wonderful—stuffed pork chops, her favorite, though she couldn't imagine how Sylvia had known that. The quilt campers were delightful company, just as they were every year, and this time there were two celebrities present. Julia Merchaud hugged her and gave her a lovely pin as a gift, which told Vinnie, to her relief, that the television star had forgiven her.

As the guest of honor, Vinnie sat at a special table with Sylvia and two other co-founders of Elm Creek Quilts, but she insisted that her newest quilt buddies join them. Everyone applauded when Sarah wheeled out a birthday cake large enough for all the campers to share.

As she blew out the candles, Vinnie glanced at Megan, smiled secretly to herself, and made a wish.

After breakfast Thursday morning, Grace retreated to the formal parlor with a box full of photographs Sylvia had provided. All that week in photo transfer class, Grace had managed to avoid any actual hands-on work by observing the other quilters as they practiced the various techniques. Sylvia must have told the instructor, an auburn-haired young woman named Summer, to permit Grace to proceed at her own pace, for although Summer urged the other students forward, she left Grace alone, merely checking now and then to see if she was enjoying herself or if she had any questions. Grace, who would have balked if she were pushed, appreciated Summer's patience. Best of all, it had paid off. Grace now felt ready to do something she hadn't done in over eighteen months: begin a new project.

First, however, she would need a photo. Class members who had registered in advance had brought pictures from home, but aside from a few wallet-sized snapshots of Joshua and Justine, Grace had none. When she explained her dilemma to Sylvia, she suggested Grace choose a photo from a previous session of quilt camp. Alone in the parlor, Grace curled up on an overstuffed sofa and began sorting through the box. Many of the photos were candid shots taken during classes; in others, campers posed in various locations around the estate, their arms around each other, smiling happily for the camera.

Grace held one photo thoughtfully, studying the smiling women. She, too, had made friends that week at camp, something she had never expected. She had Sylvia to thank for that. Just that morning at breakfast, she and Donna had had a long heart-to-heart about their daughters. How refreshing it had been to commiserate about the trials of motherhood as if those were the only problems on her mind. She had even managed to forget about the other problems for a little while.

Grace set the photo aside. Although today's project would be merely an exercise in which any photo would do, she wanted a more meaningful image than a group of strangers. What a shame she couldn't use one of Megan's photos. During the evening festivities she was rarely without her camera, but of course, her film wasn't developed yet. Megan had offered to get multiple prints and send them each a set after they returned home, but Grace needed something now.

She took out another handful of photos and thumbed through them. A frontal view of Elm Creek Manor would be perfect, if she could find one. It was hard to believe that someone as organized as Sylvia would store her photos so haphazardly. Grace would have expected them to be neatly mounted in scrapbooks in chronological order according to subject.

She paused at a picture of Sylvia and the rest of the Elm Creek Quilts staff sitting on the front veranda. She thought it must have been taken in autumn, judging by the fallen leaves scattered in the foreground.

"Are you having any luck with those?"

Grace looked up to find Sylvia standing in the doorway. "I just found one of you and your staff," she said, showing Sylvia the photo. "I'm surprised at you. What do you call your filing system? Random or chaos?"

"Don't blame me. Those are Sarah's photos, not mine." Sylvia sat beside her to get a better look at the photo. "Hmm. Oh yes, I remember that one. Camp had ended for the season weeks earlier, and we were just about to leave on a road trip to the International Quilt Festival in Houston. That was the year I had my stroke." She settled back against the sofa cushions. "It's funny how I mark time these days—before Elm Creek Quilts and after, before my stroke and after."

Grace nodded, uneasy, wondering if Sylvia had guessed more than she let on. She knew exactly what Sylvia meant. She had her own demarcation, the time when she thought she was merely overtired or stressed out, and the bleak, sterile months that followed the doctor's diagnosis.

But Sylvia continued. "I was thinking, after your classes today, perhaps you'd like to join me in searching for those old Civil War quilts I told you about? If my sister didn't sell them, they could be up in the attic. I know the exact trunk they would be in, but we might have to move some boxes around before we unearth it."

Grace wanted to see those quilts so badly she almost agreed—but then she thought of all those flights of stairs, of the strain from moving boxes, and knew she wouldn't make it. She'd been pushing her luck all week, and although she longed to spend a leisurely afternoon exploring the manor's hidden treasures, she couldn't risk another exacerbation. "I can't."

"Why not?" Sylvia asked. "Don't you have free time this afternoon?"

"Yes, but I'm afraid attics aren't good places for me."

"We don't have any bats that I know of," Sylvia said. "Are you allergic to dust?"

Grace nodded, but her conscience stung from the lie.

Sylvia sighed and rose. "I thought you'd jump at the chance to find those old quilts."

"I would like to see them." Grace hated to see Sylvia so disappointed, so puzzled by her ostensible lack of interest. "If I had brought my medication, I'd be up there in a second, believe me."

"I understand. I can hardly take a breath around cats, myself. Perhaps I can drag Matthew up to the attic today to shift some clutter. If I find the quilts, I'll bring them down to you."

Grace thanked her, and with a promise to see her later, Sylvia left. Grace set the photo of the Elm Creek Quilters aside and returned to the box. She hated keeping secrets from a trusted friend and she hated lies, but she hated pity even more. Justine had said she was too proud, and maybe Justine was right, but it was her life, and she was determined to live it on her terms as long as she was able.

Just then, her fingertips brushed another photo, jostling it loose from the box. As the picture fell to the floor, she glimpsed a patch of cheerful red, in the midst of which, to her surprise, was Vinnie. She sat in the gazebo in the north gardens, a red straw hat perched jauntily on her white curls. Draped over her lap was a cheerful Ohio Star quilt in bright rainbow colors. Vinnie's mouth was slightly open, and she had a mischievous look in her eye as if she had been interrupted while telling a joke.

Grace couldn't help smiling. It was hard to believe that spirited woman had just turned eighty-two. If Grace had half her energy, she'd probably whip out a dozen quilts a year.

Suddenly Grace had an idea. She would use this picture for Summer's photo transfer workshop. After the photo's image was reproduced on fabric, Grace would frame the portrait in Ohio Star blocks pieced from the hand-dyed fat eighths she had won Monday night. She could machine quilt the finished design and make a small wallhanging, which she would present to Vinnie as a belated birthday gift.

With a newfound thrill of anticipation, Grace returned the other photos to the box and hurried off to class. Granted, this quilt wouldn't be museum quality or win praise from art critics, but at least she would be creating again.

The more Julia learned about quilting, the more she realized a week's worth of classes wouldn't be enough to enable her to pass herself off as a master quilter. She had never known how much work was involved in making a quilt, from piecing the top to stitching the three layers together. What once seemed a simple, even mundane bed covering now took on a new meaning as a true work of art. She felt a new respect for those who managed to finish even one full-size quilt in one lifetime, though only weeks before she would have dismissed them as pitiable women with nothing better to do than waste their time on tedious hobbies.

She had finished her Friendship Star block and was well on her way to completing the Whig Rose when Megan suggested she try other patterns, enough to sew a small sampler. Julia knew she would need to practice her skills after camp ended, but when she thought of all the work involved in sewing an entire quilt, even a wallhanging, she grew discouraged. "Don't think about the entire quilt," Megan said. "Just take it one block at a time."

"Sounds like a twelve-step program," Julia said, but she agreed to try. Megan suggested other patterns that would teach her various quilting techniques: the Drunkard's Path for learning to piece curves, the Stamp Basket for setting in pieces, and a few others. Donna, Grace, and Vinnie contributed ideas of their own, and by Thursday afternoon they had helped her design a sampler of nine blocks arranged in a three-by-three grid, separated by strips of fabric Vinnie called sashing.

"The studio should hire you four as consultants," Julia teased them.

Grace laughed, but Donna asked in earnest, "Do you think they would?"

"Don't be silly," Vinnie admonished. "How will Julia keep her secret if we're hovering around telling her what to do?"

They all knew Julia's predicament by now, and while they didn't quite believe that her career could be in jeopardy, they were eager to teach her all she needed to know for the role. Instead of one tutor, Julia found herself with four. Sometimes she wondered exactly what they hoped to gain from helping her, but eventually she decided to accept their assistance for what it appeared to be, kindness and generosity. Since she desperately needed them, she didn't have much choice.

She would have practiced late into the night if left to herself, but the others insisted she join them for the evening program. Her fingertips were so sore from hand-quilting that her pace had slowed considerably, so with more relief than reluctance, she agreed to meet them in the ballroom.

When she arrived, she saw that some of the classroom partitions had been removed to make room for several rows of chairs in front of a raised dais at the far end of the room. "What's all this?" she asked her new acquaintances as the rows began to fill with excited, chattering quilters. The news that the Campers' Talent

Show was about to begin made her wish she had stayed in her room. The last thing she wanted was to endure a hapless amateur hour when she had so much work to do.

Vinnie must have sensed her reluctance, for she pushed Julia into a folding chair. "You're not leaving," she said. "Not until you give me your professional opinion of my acting. Your honest opinion, mind you."

Julia smiled at her weakly and hoped that Vinnie would be remarkably good, but if it came down to telling the truth or hurting the feelings of someone whose help she needed, she would lie.

The show was rather informal. Instead of waiting backstage, the performers sat in the audience. When one act ended, Sylvia Compson announced the next by calling the soloist or group to the front of the room. Several of the acts were skits, which, based upon the laughter from the audience, she assumed were supposed to be humorous. Since even the solemn Grace smiled, Julia decided that quilters must have inside jokes she simply didn't understand.

Some of the performers were surprisingly good. One woman gave a dramatic monologue from Shakespeare; afterward Julia overheard that she was a professor of English literature at Brown. Vinnie and Donna nearly brought down the house with their rendition of "Who's on First." Even Julia had to laugh when Vinnie brandished a yellow plastic whiffle ball bat and shrieked, "I'll break your arm if you say 'Who's on first!'" The audience roared with laughter so long that Donna grew flustered and forgot her next line. When Vinnie prompted her loudly enough to be heard in the back row, the laughter erupted again.

When the performers returned to their seats amid a shower of applause, Vinnie whispered to Julia, "Well?"

"I can honestly say that was the most original Abbott and Costello impersonation I've ever witnessed," Julia said.

Vinnie looked pleased, but Donna said, "She's just being nice. I stunk up the place."

They laughed as Sylvia called the next performer to the stage. "Megan, dear, it's your turn. Megan Donohue, everyone."

As Megan went to the front of the room, two staff members wheeled a baby grand piano to the front of the stage. Megan flashed the audience a quick smile before she sat down at the bench and tested the keys.

"I should have done that instead," Vinnie whispered. "I can play 'Heart and Soul' with my eyes closed."

Donna stifled a giggle, then jumped in her seat as Megan's hands suddenly crashed onto the keyboard in a resounding chord. To Julia's astonishment, the aerospace engineer from Ohio was playing Chopin's *Fantasy Impromptu* in C-sharp minor—and playing it well. Remarkably well, in fact. Soon Julia forgot herself and listened as breathlessly as the rest of the audience as the music flowed from the piano and washed over them. When the final notes died away, there was a moment of stunned silence before the listeners applauded wildly.

Megan returned to her seat, her cheeks flushed, pausing to accept congratulations as she went. "I bet you're glad you stuck to comedy," Donna teased Vinnie. Julia could tell from her proud expression that she had long known of Megan's gift.

When Megan finally was able to sit down, Julia leaned over and said, "You play wonderfully." Megan flashed her a quick, embarrassed smile and said nothing, but she looked pleased.

"Does anyone else wish to entertain us?" Sylvia called out from the front of the room. "Grace?"

Grace looked alarmed. "Not me."

"Julia? How about you?"

To Julia it seemed as if everyone in the room suddenly turned in their seats to look at her. "Well . . ." Their eyes were so eager and expectant that she was at a loss for words.

"Oh, come on, dear. Surely you can't have stage fright."

Julia wavered. "I didn't prepare anything."

"Give me a break, honey," Vinnie said, nudging her. Before Julia could protest, Donna and Megan had pulled her to her feet. The campers burst into cheers. Julia couldn't help basking in the admiration as she went to the dais and seated herself at the piano.

She warmed up with a few chords, then said, "Here's a song I'm sure you all know. It suits this week very well, I think." *Corny, but true,* she thought, especially for herself.

Julia had chosen "Climb Every Mountain" from *The Sound of Music.* She chose it not only because she thought it would appeal to this particular audience, but also because it was her standard musical audition song. She had rehearsed and performed it more times than she could count, and knew the phrasing and emphasis by heart. As a pianist she fell far short of Megan, but the tune was simple enough that she could play it flawlessly. Her voice sounded rich and full, and as she held the final note, she saw with satisfaction that her listeners were entranced.

As she rose and bowed to thunderous applause, Julia felt a contentment in her heart she hadn't sensed in years. It had been far too long since she had performed for the sheer joy of it.

"You sure gave them a thrill," Vinnie said over the cheers of the other campers when Julia returned to her seat. Julia glowed, delighting in their response. She lived for the stage, for the admiration and appreciation that only an audience could provide. *Family Tree* was over and she might never have another series, but her fans had not forgotten her. They still loved her.

Sylvia stood on the dais trying to quiet the audience. "Thank you to all our performers," she said. "And now, if you'll mark your ballots, we'll select our winner."

Julia felt a jolt. "Winner?"

"That's right," Vinnie said, handing her a stack of blue slips of paper and a handful of golf pencils. "The winner gets a prize. Donna, if we win, do you think we'll each get a prize or will we have to split one?"

"We don't have to worry," Donna said.

Vinnie laughed, then raised her eyebrows at Julia. "Well, go on, honey. Take one and pass the rest down. Unless you're planning to stuff the ballot box?"

Julia took one ballot and passed the rest on to Grace. She stole a glance at Megan, who was writing on her slip of paper, apparently unconcerned. Except for Julia herself, no one else had received such enthusiastic applause, and Julia never would have participated if she had known a winner would be selected. She was a professional; it was inappropriate for her to snatch a prize away from an amateur in an amateur competition. What if Julia won instead of Megan? Then she had a horrible thought: What if she *didn't* win?

Quickly Julia scribbled her own name and handed the slip of paper to the staff member passing through the center aisle. Her heart pounded as Sylvia and her staff tallied the votes at the front of the room.

"Your attention, please," Sylvia finally said, and the quilters fell silent. "I'm pleased to announce that by an overwhelming margin, the winner of the Campers' Talent Show is—Julia Merchaud!"

Numb with relief, Julia went to the dais to receive her prize, acknowledging the audience's applause as graciously as she could manage.

"Congratulations," Grace said when Julia returned to her seat. She nodded in response.

"What did you win?" Vinnie asked.

Only then did Julia inspect her prize. Sylvia had given her an Elm Creek Quilts pin identical to those her friends had won on games night.

"Now we all have one," Vinnie exclaimed, then caught herself. "Oh. Except for you, Megan."

Megan shrugged. "We still have one more day of classes. Maybe I'll have better luck tomorrow." She smiled at Julia. "Congratulations."

Suddenly Julia was stung by shame. "You deserve this more than I do."

"What are you talking about? You won, fair and square."

"But I only won because . . ." Because she was more popular, because she was famous, because the campers had been so thrilled to see a star perform live that they failed to see the merit of Megan's performance. "I never should have entered."

She tried to give Megan the pin, but Megan merely laughed off the gesture, as if she weren't the least disturbed by the unfairness of the competition. Her refusal to become resentful only made Julia feel worse, and that unsettled her. After all, she had trampled over her competitors as long as she had been in Hollywood. More than once, she had stolen other actresses' roles through conniving and manipulation. She had destroyed rivals' careers by anonymously revealing their addictions to the media and had alienated more than one co-star with her insistence on top billing. Many times Julia had deserved to lose, then reveled when she managed through luck or subterfuge to come out on top. But now, as the quilters bid each other good night and went off to their rooms, she felt oddly empty. Where was that familiar sense of triumph after a victory?

Clutching the pin in her fist, she went upstairs to sleep so she wouldn't have to think about it anymore.

❧

On Friday morning, Vinnie waited, watching the clock, until she couldn't wait any longer. She dialed Adam's number and hoped she wouldn't wake him.

"Hello?" he said groggily after the fifth ring.

"Good morning, honey," she said brightly. "Did I wake you?"

"Nana?" In the background she heard bedsprings creak. "Is something wrong?"

"No, dear, I just wanted to be sure you're planning to pick me up from quilt camp tomorrow."

"Of course," he said through a yawn. "I'll be there around eleven."

"Could you make it any earlier?" Vinnie glanced at the door as if someone might overhear. "Around ten, maybe?"

"I thought camp wasn't over that early."

"It's not."

"Don't you have that special farewell breakfast? Why do you want to leave early?"

"I don't want to leave early," she said impatiently. "Goodness, Adam, can't you just do as you're told? Be here by ten or I'll—just be here by ten."

She hung up the phone before he could ask any more questions. That young man had a way of sneaking the truth out of her.

🌿

Friday passed so swiftly that before Megan knew it, her last full day of quilt camp was over. That evening, a comedy improv group comprised of students from nearby Waterford College put on an entertaining show, but the campers' laughter was not as joyous as it would have been earlier in the week or even a day before. Already Megan felt nostalgic for camp, which was too soon coming to an end. She missed Robby, but part of her wished that she could stay at the elegant manor for another week of quilting and fun with her new friends.

After the show, Sylvia announced that the final breakfast would be served on the cornerstone patio, where they had held the Candlelight ceremony. "We'll have one last good chat before you leave," she said. "Bring something for show-and-tell."

Julia looked dubious. "Show-and-tell?" she said in an undertone as the campers left the room and headed up the stairs. "As in grammar school?"

"Don't be such a wet blanket," Vinnie teased. "You're never too old for show-and-tell."

Megan suppressed a smile. She wondered how long it had been since someone had dared to tease the great Julia Merchaud.

Megan bid the others good night and went to her room to pack, but within a few minutes, she began to feel lonely. She set her suitcase aside and went down the hallway to Donna's room, but before she could knock on the door, it opened. "I was just about to come to your room," Donna exclaimed. "Come on in."

"I can't believe camp is over already," Megan said, dropping dejectedly into a chair. "I feel like we just got here."

Donna agreed, then settled in on the bed across from Megan.

They talked for a while about how much the week had meant to them, then began to gossip about some of the other members of their Internet quilting newsgroup. They were in near hysterics recalling a flame war about off-topic posts when a knock sounded on the door. Grace poked her head in and demanded to know what was so funny. By the time Megan finished recounting the tale, their threefold laughter elicited yet another knock.

"Come in," they shouted together.

Vinnie peeked in. When she saw them, her face brightened. "Ooh, a party," she exclaimed, and quickly ducked back outside again. In a moment she returned with a grocery bag. "We can't have a party without refreshments."

"You brought all this from home?" Megan said, eyeing the tins of homemade cookies, the bags of popcorn, and the jars of nuts.

"I thought I might get hungry on the drive."

"Where were you driving from, Alaska?" Donna asked, helping herself to a few chocolate chip cookies.

"Ohio, wise guy," Vinnie said, taking a jar of cashews for herself. "You know, all we're missing are a few Chippendales dancers and this could be a real party."

Just then someone knocked on the door.

"Vinnie, you didn't," Grace exclaimed.

Vinnie's face went nearly as white as her hair. "Oh, my goodness. I didn't mean it." Her look of genuine shock set the others laughing even harder than before. When Donna finally managed to greet the unknown visitor, Julia opened the door warily. She stood for a moment taking in the scene of half-hysterical quilters, a quilt block and needle in her hand.

"I was hoping you could help me with this," she said to Donna. "Maybe I'll see you in the morning." She started to shut the door, but Donna jumped to her feet and pulled her inside. When Julia stammered something about making an early night of it, the others drowned out her protests. Reluctantly, she perched on the bed and showed them the Whig Rose block that was giving her so much trouble. Calming themselves for her sake, each inspected the block and offered suggestions for improving her appliqué stitch. When Julia was ready to begin, Grace sat beside her on the bed and watched as Julia put their ideas into practice.

They chatted as Julia worked, alternating between comical and serious topics. They talked about the families and problems they had left behind at home and would be returning to the next day. Somehow, knowing she would probably never see these women again pained Megan, yet it freed her to be more open than she ordinarily would have been. As she told them about Keith, for the first time Megan didn't feel that she had to apologize for not being stronger, for not already filling up—with work and friends and new love—the hole he had left in her life. She was so grateful for her friends' acceptance that she wished they had had this talk earlier, so that she would have had more time to savor their friendship before they parted. But she also sensed, as the night turned into early morning, that a special closeness bound them, something almost magical. Perhaps they couldn't have talked this way on any other night.

Donna's alarm clock announced that morning had arrived all too soon. She was not a night owl by any stretch of the imagination and knew she would suffer all day for her late night. She simply couldn't have closed down the impromptu party, though, and since no one had volunteered to be the first to leave, the festivities had stretched on into the early morning hours. Even after she was alone, Donna couldn't drop off to sleep right away. Her thoughts and her heart were too full.

She met the others on the cornerstone patio for breakfast. The day promised to be warm and sunny, but Donna's mood was dark. She missed her family, but camp had been so much more special than she had expected, and she couldn't bear to see it end. She wondered if she would ever again have a week full of such perfect moments.

After breakfast, the campers gathered in a circle as they had the first night of camp, this time for show-and-tell. Each quilter showed something she had made that week and shared her favorite memory of Elm Creek Manor. Even the beginning quilters proudly displayed their handiwork. Julia held up her Friendship Star block, and seemed genuinely pleased when the other campers praised her piecing skills. When Sylvia prompted her to name her favorite memory, she hesitated before looking right at Donna and saying, "The kindness of other quilters who were so willing to share their knowledge. I can honestly say it's been a long time since I've experienced such generosity."

Donna was surprised and pleased to know that Julia had appreciated her simple lessons so much, but she couldn't help feeling sorry for Julia and wondering why someone so successful apparently had so little kindness in her life.

Vinnie showed off a half-finished Double Pinwheel quilt top she had worked on in her Quick Piecing classes, and declared that her favorite memory was her surprise birthday party. "That's what you said last year," Sylvia said, her eyes glinting with merriment, "and the year before. It's time for you to come up with something new."

Vinnie pursed her lips and thought, then said that if Sylvia wouldn't let her use her real favorite memory, she would have to go with the food. "It was especially good this year," she protested when everyone laughed.

For her turn, Megan held up an exquisite Feathered Star miniature quilt, only fourteen inches square. When the other quilters marveled at the precision of her piecing, Megan passed the quilt around the circle. "When you see it up close you'll spot the mistakes," she said, but everyone declared that they couldn't find a single one. When she held the quilt, Donna couldn't find even the smallest tip of a triangle out of place or truncated, and she shook her head and announced that Megan was being too critical of herself.

"She should win a prize for being the toughest judge of her

own work," Vinnie hinted to Sylvia. "Maybe one of those Elm Creek Quilts pins." But Sylvia merely laughed.

Donna had brought two items to show: the Whig Rose block she had completed in the appliqué workshop and the color gradations chart she had made in Color Theory. She was especially proud of the latter, since her color choices tended to be conservative, and the chart had inspired her to be more daring. "My favorite memory is easy," she said. "Meeting all my wonderful new friends."

Grace went last, and, remembering her confession during the Candlelight ceremony, everyone waited with anxious expectation to see what she would show them. To Donna's surprise, she held up not a small block or an exercise from Color Theory, but a small quilt bordered with Ohio Star blocks. In the center was a photo-transfer block of Vinnie sitting in the garden with a quilt on her lap. "Thanks to Summer and Sylvia—in fact, thanks to all of you, for your encouragement—I finally broke through my quilter's block. Happy birthday, Vinnie."

"For me?" Vinnie's eyes shone as she took the quilt. "Why, it's lovely. Ohio Star blocks, and I'm from Ohio!"

"That's why I chose them."

"Oh, my." Vinnie was speechless for a moment as she held the quilt up to admire it, then hugged it to her chest. "I'll treasure it always."

"What about your favorite memory?" another quilter prompted.

Grace smiled at Vinnie admiring her gift. "I think this is it."

Everyone laughed, but a little sadly, because now every quilter had taken her turn. The week of camp was over.

Donna was reluctant to leave, so she lingered on the cornerstone patio with her friends as the other campers exchanged hugs and tearful good-byes. She and Megan would keep in touch, of course, but what of the others? She would never know if Grace would continue to triumph over her quilter's block or if Julia would convince her producer that she was an expert quilter. She would never know if Vinnie would find her grandson a new girlfriend. In turn, they would never know if she had convinced Lindsay to stay in school, and when the wedding came and she needed their support, they would be miles away, scattered around the country when she needed them most.

"I'm going to miss you," Donna said, embracing each of them in turn. "Without you, I don't think I ever would have found the courage to face Lindsay. I wish . . . I wish we could all be there to help each other with all the problems waiting back home."

She looked around the circle of friends and knew at once that each felt the same way.

"A few days ago we all said we were coming back next year," Donna said. "Let's promise each other right now that we will, that we won't let anything stand in the way."

The others nodded, Julia a bit hesitantly, as if she wasn't sure Donna meant her, too. "A year is a long time," she said. "We don't know where we'll be in a year."

"I know where I'll be," Vinnie declared. "I'll be right here celebrating my eighty-third birthday and congratulating myself on finding my grandson a new sweetheart."

She succeeded in making them laugh, and Grace added, "Well, then, I'll be here showing you all my latest projects."

Julia gave them a small smile. "And I suppose I'll be here telling you how filming went."

"Oh, you must," Vinnie exclaimed. "I have to know how everything turns out. That goes for all of you—I can't bear thinking that I might not know how everything turns out. Donna's daughter's wedding, Megan and little Robby—"

Megan looked resolute. "By this time next year, I promise I'll have done everything humanly possible to bring Keith back into his life."

"We won't have to face our problems alone," Grace said. "We'll be with each other in spirit."

"We'll keep in touch," Megan said. "Whenever we need encouragement, we can write, or call, or E-mail. Are the rest of you on the Internet?"

Grace nodded, but Julia shook her head and Vinnie said, "Heavens, no."

"You have to get online," Megan insisted. "It's the best way to stay in touch."

Donna, usually the most optimistic of the group, felt her spirits drop. "People always say they'll keep in touch, but they usually don't."

"We'll be different," Vinnie said stoutly.

Donna wished she could believe her. They might leave Elm Creek Manor with the best of intentions, but as the weeks passed and they fell into the patterns of ordinary life, they might forget how special—how magical—the week they had spent together had been. If they failed to nurture it, their friendship might become nothing more than a fond memory, something to reflect upon and cherish when leafing through an old scrapbook rather than something vibrant and alive.

"We need a symbol, something to remind us of our promise," she heard herself say.

"I have a wonderful idea," Vinnie said. "Let's make a challenge quilt."

"A what?" Julia asked.

"A challenge quilt. We'll take a piece of fabric and divide it into equal shares. We'll each piece a block from it, and next year, we'll meet at camp and sew them into a quilt."

"The challenge comes from being required to use a particular fabric rather than being free to choose whatever you like," Grace told Julia. "But sometimes there are other restrictions. Should we have any?"

"How about this," Megan said. "We can't start working on our block until we take steps to solve our problems. That will keep us from procrastinating."

On our quilt blocks or on solving our problems? Donna wondered. She knew which project she'd rather face.

"All right, then," Julia said. "As soon as the first day of filming is over, if I haven't been fired, I'll start piecing my block."

Vinnie clasped her hands, delighted. "Then I'll start mine the first time I ask Adam if he's heard from Natalie and he says, 'Natalie who?'"

They all laughed, and Donna felt her spirits rising. For the first time, she felt that even though they would be scattered cross-country, they would remain close friends.

"Cross-country," she murmured, then added in a louder voice, "That's what we are, the Cross-Country Quilters."

"A name makes it official," Vinnie declared. "How can we fail?"

After they had finished packing, the Cross-Country Quilters gathered in the parking lot for a final good-bye. When Megan's car was loaded up and they were waiting outside the manor for Vinnie's grandson and Julia's limousine—in which she had invited Donna to join her for the drive to the airport—Vinnie brought out her bag of quilting supplies. "We still need to choose a fabric," she said. "Who will do the honors?"

"I'll pick," Donna said eagerly. She dug around in the bag and laughed. "How about this?" She pulled out a print of black-and-white cows grazing in a meadow.

Julia looked alarmed, and Megan said, "No way."

Donna pouted, but she returned the fabric to the bag and tried again. "How about this?"

This time she held up a blue-and-red paisley print. Megan liked it, but there was only a fat quarter. "Do you think there's enough for all five of us?"

"You can't reject everything I pick," Donna complained. "We'll be here all day."

Vinnie glanced at her watch, then frowned at the empty road. "I might be here all day regardless if my grandson doesn't get a move on. I told him to be here at ten."

"Why so early?" Megan said.

Vinnie's eyes widened in innocence. "No reason."

Megan knew Vinnie well enough to be suspicious of her attempts at innocence, but she shrugged and turned to Donna. "Okay, I'll cooperate. Whatever fabric you show us next, I'll agree to it."

"You might regret that," Grace warned, but it was too late. Donna's eyes lit up, and she plunged both hands into the bag. A few moments later, she pulled out a yard of fabric and held it over her head.

"I have it," she shouted in triumph. "This is the one!"

Megan stifled a groan of dismay. It was a beautiful print of autumn leaves on a cloth of excellent quality, expertly designed, and highlighted with silver embossing. The leaves were burgundy, loden green, a rich beige—and purple.

Even Julia laughed out loud.

Megan knew when she was beaten. "All right," she said. "We can go with the cows."

"Absolutely not." Donna put the rest of the fabric away. "I'm not going to miss this chance to force you to use purple."

"There might not be enough," Megan tried to argue, but Vinnie would have none of that.

"There's an entire yard," she said, taking the fabric from Donna. "I have more at home, so we'll divide this into fat quarters for the four of you."

When each had her fat quarter of fabric, it was time to go. They exchanged addresses and phone numbers, and Megan made one last entreaty to Julia and Vinnie to get E-mail addresses. Grace already had one through the museum where she worked as a curator, although she rarely used it. "You'll use it more now," Donna promised.

Just then a long black limousine crossed the bridge over Elm Creek and circled the parking lot. "There's my ride," Julia said with regret.

Megan, too, was reluctant to leave, but now that the time had come, she was eager to get on the road. She had a long drive ahead, and she hoped to be back to her parents' house in time for a homecoming supper. Just as she was about to bid the others good-bye, Vinnie grabbed her arm. "There's my grandson," she exclaimed. "Don't you girls leave until I have a chance to introduce you."

Suddenly Megan felt an urge to sprint to her car, but Vinnie held fast. She threw Donna a helpless look as an older model compact car pulled into the parking lot. Megan glimpsed a familiar face through the windshield, and sure enough, when the car parked in front of them, the man she had met at the diner stepped out. "I'm sorry I'm late, Nana," he said, bending to kiss her. He picked up her suitcase, smiling. "Did you have a good time?" Just then he glanced at Megan, and utter astonishment came over his face. "Hey. It's you. The woman—"

"From the diner." Suddenly nervous, Megan forced herself to smile and extend her hand. "Megan Donohue."

Quickly he set down Vinnie's suitcase and shook Megan's hand. "I see you made it to Waterford okay."

"Yes, thanks to your directions."

Vinnie patted his arm proudly. "Adam's a teacher. He's very good at explaining things."

Adam looked embarrassed. "But not very good at being on time. Sorry I'm late, Nana. There was construction on the turnpike."

"That's all right," Vinnie said graciously. She introduced the other Cross-Country Quilters. Adam's startled expression returned when she named Julia.

"You must have had quite a week," he said to Vinnie. His gaze rested on Megan again, and he smiled warmly.

"I'll tell you all about it on the drive home," Vinnie promised, then beamed at her friends. "Drive safely, ladies. I'll see you next year."

"Drive safely," Megan echoed, and the others joined in.

Vinnie took her grandson's arm and let him help her into the car. As they drove away, Vinnie gave them a jaunty wave and a cheerful, satisfied smile. Her eyes met Megan's, and suddenly Megan knew as clearly as if she had spoken that Vinnie intended to be the first of the Cross-Country Quilters to complete her block.

Six

PAUL AND BECCA had kept the house fairly tidy during Donna's absence, but for two intelligent and capable people, they otherwise seemed to have no idea how to manage a household. On Tuesday the kitchen sink had sprung a leak, and Paul had to phone Lindsay for the name of their usual plumber. When it came time to pay him, Paul had forgotten where Donna kept the checkbook and had to race to the nearest ATM for cash. The next day Becca had attempted a load of laundry, but had turned all the socks and underwear a delicate shade of pink. When Donna's car pulled into the driveway, her husband and daughter ran outside to meet her. Donna soon discovered the reason for their joy and relief, and she wondered if her family had missed her or just the cook and maid services she usually performed. That evening, though, after Paul took her out to eat and Becca asked her to demonstrate how to run the washing machine properly, Donna relented. After all, it was nice to have all her hard work noticed and appreciated. She decided to leave them on their own more often, to provide them with more opportunities to fend for themselves—and to remind them not to take her too much for granted.

By the next day, Donna had restored the household to its usual order. She had invited Lindsay and Brandon for Sunday dinner, and as she roasted a chicken and tossed the salad, she resolved to look for the best in him, and not to become a stereotypical mother-in-law if she could possibly avoid it.

When she heard Lindsay's car, Donna wiped off her hands on a towel and went to the window, where Paul had already pulled back the curtain and was peering outside. "She's alone," he said, relief in his voice.

Donna felt the same way, but she said, "We have to start getting to know him sometime."

"I already started, and I know as much as I need to."

"Paul," Donna gently admonished him. At the restaurant the previous night, he had told her unhappily of the unfavorable impression Brandon had made on him when the two families met during Donna's absence. Brandon bossed Lindsay around, telling her what entrée to order and advising her to go without dessert so she would look better in the wedding pictures. Brandon's mother was a meek and silent woman, but his father more than made up the difference. Obnoxious, Paul called him—Paul, who never insulted anyone unless he truly deserved it.

"There must be some good in him or Lindsay wouldn't love him," Donna told her husband. "We might have to look hard to find it, but it must be there."

Paul nodded to show he agreed with her logic, but he looked doubtful.

Lindsay entered then and greeted her mother with a warm hug. "Couldn't Brandon make it?" Donna asked.

"He had some studying to do."

"Before classes even start?" Paul asked, a little sharply. College had been a sensitive topic with him ever since Lindsay's announcement.

Lindsay shrugged. "He's busy," she said, which didn't really an-

swer the question. She left her purse on the counter and began to
set the table. What a pair she and Paul were, Donna thought as
she assisted Lindsay. They were glad Brandon hadn't come and yet
were slighted that he hadn't bothered to show up. If Brandon suspected any of this, he'd wonder just what kind of family he was
marrying into.

During supper, Donna told her family amusing stories about
her week at quilt camp. Even Becca was thrilled to hear that she
had befriended the famous Julia Merchaud. Still, although Lindsay smiled and joined the conversation, she seemed distant and reserved, as if her thoughts were elsewhere.

After the meal, Lindsay helped Donna clean up, although that
was traditionally Becca's chore. They chatted about trivial subjects,
Donna wondering all the while what her daughter really wanted
to discuss. Only after the last plate was placed in the dishwasher
did Lindsay tentatively ask if Donna had a moment to talk about
the wedding.

Donna's heart flip-flopped, but she dried her hands on a dish-
towel and tried to appear calm. "Sure, honey. What did you want
to talk about?"

"I've been looking through bridal magazines to get ideas for
my gown." Lindsay hesitated. "I tried on some at a bridal shop
near school, but they're much more expensive than I thought they
would be."

Donna's heart went out to her, and she felt a stab of regret picturing Lindsay shopping for a gown alone. She had always imagined they would choose together, but it was her own fault. No
wonder Lindsay hadn't invited her along, after the way she had reacted to the announcement of the engagement. "Don't worry about
the expense," she said. "Your dad and I will pay for your gown."

"I know. But . . . well, until I get a full-time job, I don't feel
right about spending so much money on something I'm going to
wear only once. Do you think you could make me a dress? I'm not
asking just to save money."

"Oh, honey." Donna reached out and tucked a loose strand of

blond hair behind her daughter's ear. "I'd love to make a wedding gown for you." Then inspiration struck. "Or would you like to wear mine? I could take it in to fit you—"

"Oh, Mom, that would be perfect," Lindsay gasped. "Your gown is so beautiful. That's what I wanted all along, but I was afraid . . ."

Her voice broke off so abruptly that Donna knew she had finally touched on what had been troubling her all evening. "You were afraid of what?"

Lindsay's cheeks flushed. "I was afraid that you would say no, because—because you don't like Brandon."

"Lindsay, sweetie . . ." Too overcome to speak, Donna took Lindsay in her arms and hugged her tightly. Whenever she had thought of her daughters' wedding days, she had imagined planning every detail with joy, sharing a special closeness as the day approached, watching them dance with their father at the reception. She had never intended to ruin what should be one of the happiest times in Lindsay's life.

Blinking back tears, she held Lindsay at arm's length so she could look her daughter in the eye. "If I told you I didn't wish you'd wait a few years, I'd be lying," she said. "But it's not that I don't like Brandon. I don't know him well enough to dislike him."

Lindsay gave her a wan smile. "Great."

"I'm not saying this right. What I mean is, I wish I knew him better, and I wish you'd consider waiting until you finish college. Lindsay, even before you were born your father and I promised ourselves you would receive a good education. I think it means even more to me than to your dad, since I didn't finish college myself. You seemed so happy with the university, I'm just surprised you'd give that up."

"I told you what Brandon said."

"I remember, but I don't think he's thought this through. Maybe he'd like you to be out of school now, but what about later? What if he loses his job or becomes ill, and you need to support the family?"

Lindsay shook her head. "He would hate that. I don't think he would let me."

Donna winced. "'Let you?' He's going to be your husband, not your keeper."

"I didn't mean it that way. It's just . . . I think it would hurt his pride if I had to support us."

"Well, God willing he'll never be sick or lose his job, but it's best to be prepared, and you'd be able to get a much better job with a college degree. And what about when you want to buy a home, or when your own children are ready to start college? You might want to work for the extra income."

Donna could sense her daughter's conflicted emotions, and see from her expression that she was torn between logic and loyalty. "I hadn't thought of that," Lindsay admitted.

Donna doubted that Brandon had, either. "Besides, what else are you going to do all year? You can't plan a wedding all day long, and you don't have a full-time job. What if you can't find one right away?"

"I don't know." Lindsay hesitated. "I couldn't just sit around the apartment all day."

Donna knew she had to take a chance before Lindsay could talk herself out of it. "I'll make a deal with you. Go back to school and finish your degree, and you won't hear a word of complaint from me about the wedding from this moment forward. Unless, of course, you pick an awful dress for the bridesmaids just to infuriate your sister."

Lindsay allowed a small smile. "Really?"

Donna hugged her. "I promise." It wouldn't be easy, but she would have her jaws wired shut if it would keep Lindsay in school. "Now, you have to promise me you'll keep your part of the bargain."

After a pause, Lindsay took a deep breath and said, "I promise." Silently Donna rejoiced in her victory and kissed her daughter on the cheek. Lindsay clung to her for a moment before pulling away. "I'm not sure how I'm going to tell Brandon."

"Just tell him."

"It won't be that easy. He's very sensitive."

Donna thought that Brandon struck her as one of the least sensitive young men she'd every met. And when had Lindsay ever been too anxious to speak her mind? Instead of saying so, she reasoned, "What's good for you is good for your marriage. Explain it to him logically, just as we've discussed. I'm sure he'll agree that you've made the right decision."

Lindsay looked dubious, but then she relaxed. "You're right," she said, and for a moment she sounded like the old Lindsay. "I'll tell him tonight. Registration doesn't end for a few more days, so I shouldn't lose any of the classes I signed up for last spring."

Donna was so pleased she didn't trust herself to speak. She stroked Lindsay's hair. "Come on," she said. "Let's have you try on that gown."

As they went upstairs, Donna remembered the promise she had made to herself and the other Cross-Country Quilters only a day before. Would she be the first to begin her Challenge Quilt block?

An anxious thought came to her then: Surely it couldn't be this easy. But as Lindsay modeled the wedding gown and chattered happily about the upcoming semester, Donna forced the lingering worries from her mind. Lindsay would be returning to college, and that was all Donna could fairly ask, for now.

❧

Megan's work had piled up during her absence, but instead of griping about how the other engineers on her team hadn't picked up the slack, she was guiltily relieved to be too busy to spare Keith much thought. By Saturday, though, she knew she had to stop procrastinating. She warmed up by sending Donna an E-mail and writing letters to Vinnie, Grace, and Julia, then steeled herself and began a letter to Keith.

Her first two drafts went straight into the trash. They were too accusing and shrill, and she knew she wouldn't get anywhere with him if she put him on the defensive. After two more failed attempts, she considered phoning him instead, but her stomach twisted at the thought of hearing his voice again. It had to be a letter, or nothing.

She took a break to do the laundry and fix Robby his lunch, then forced herself to swallow her pride and try again. She imagined she was writing to a colleague, and this time she managed to strike a cordial, professional tone free of whining and neediness. She couldn't bear it if he thought she was begging for his attention, although in a way she was—not for herself, but for their son.

It was difficult to invite him to visit Robby, because she knew it would hurt her to the core to see him again. She prayed he'd have the decency to leave his new wife, Gina, at home. She reminded him that school would be starting soon, and Labor Day weekend would be perfect for Robby's schedule as well as his own.

She mailed the letter and tried to put it out of her mind for a while. The annual bustle of activity that heralded the new school year provided a much-needed distraction, but when a week passed with no reply, she began to grow anxious. Then, two days later, an envelope arrived. Inside Megan found a check for two hundred dollars filled out in loopy, girlish handwriting. The memo read "Back-to-school clothes." There was no letter.

Fuming, Megan was tempted to tear up the check. She had asked for Keith's time, not his money. But then practicality set in; she could hardly complain about his sporadic-at-best child support payments and then refuse to accept the money he did manage to send. But why hadn't Keith sent so much as a sentence in response to her request? Maybe his new wife had intercepted Megan's letter, and Keith knew nothing of either Megan's request or the check. It was difficult to imagine Keith willingly sending Megan money, after the way he had fought for the house and the car in the divorce proceedings. He had won the car but lost the house, and ever since, his reluctance to send his child support payments clearly indicated he still held a grudge.

After a day of indecision, Megan sent another letter. Labor

Day was fast approaching, she told Keith, and she would need a definite answer one way or the other. If traveling to Ohio would be too inconvenient, Robby could come to Oregon. Megan swallowed hard as she wrote the lines; she was reluctant to send Robby on a plane by himself, but she would, if there were no other way.

Labor Day came and went, and Robby started the third grade without a visit or even so much as a phone call from his father. Megan was furious and heartbroken for his sake, and her only consolation was that she had kept the proposed visit secret, just in case it didn't work out.

Two weeks into September, another envelope came, bringing Megan a letter from Gina. "Dear Megan," she had written, "I hope Robby's school year is off to a good start. I'm sorry the Labor Day visit didn't work out. Keith would have come, but I'm expecting a baby and he is saving up all his vacation days for after we deliver. Maybe next summer, Robby can stay with us for a week or so and meet his new brother or sister. All the best, Gina."

They were expecting a baby. Gina was carrying the second child Megan longed for and would never have. And Keith, who had gone back to work the day after Robby was born and had not changed a single dirty diaper in his life, now planned, with this new child, to make up for all the attention he had withheld from his firstborn.

Or was he? A thought struck her then: Keith had national holidays off, so Labor Day weekend wouldn't have cost him any vacation days. And something about Gina's letter was strangely familiar, too. Megan recognized in Gina's strained apologies the same excuses she herself had made for Keith for so many years.

Gina was expecting, and it was while Megan was carrying Robby that Keith had first turned away from her. Surely Gina would remember that.

As Megan threw the letter away, she wished her former rival luck. Unless Keith had truly changed, she would need it.

If not for the lifeline her upcoming role in *A Patchwork Life* provided, Julia thought the new fall television schedule might have driven her to drink or to her plastic surgeon's office for another face lift. She couldn't believe the cheap vulgarity that passed itself off as comedy these days, and as for the dramas, she had never witnessed such self-indulgent whining in all her life. She could click from channel to channel all day long and see nothing but beautiful twenty-somethings bemoaning the trivia of their empty lives. It sickened her almost to the point of throwing her flat-screen, high-definition television into the swimming pool, but it had been one of the few possessions she had argued out of her third husband's clutches during the divorce proceedings, and, knowing how much he had treasured it, she intended to hold on to her trophy until its wires fused together.

Occasionally an especially inane scene would have Julia seething. Her assistant had long ago adopted the policy of leaving the room whenever Julia turned on the television, so Julia had no one to complain to except the actors on the screen. Not only was that unsatisfying, it made Julia feel uncomfortably like some elderly eccentric who had lost touch with reality. She had enough insecurities about her age without adding that one to the list.

Eventually she abandoned her critique of the fall television season and resumed practicing her quilting. After her return from quilt camp, she had sent her assistant out in search of the supplies she would need to perfect her skills. Since most of her quilting scenes involved hand-quilting, Julia set her pieced and appliqué blocks aside. At camp, one of the Elm Creek instructors had traced a pineapple motif on a piece of unbleached muslin for her; now Julia placed it on top of cotton batting and another piece of muslin and held the layers snugly together in a lap hoop. With a short needle called a "between" and a piece of cotton quilting thread, Julia worked the needle through the layers along the traced line until the picture began to emerge from the smooth muslin. As the weeks passed, the rocking motions of hand-quilting became more familiar until her work acquired a soothing rhythm. Often she would sit outside on the patio of her hilltop estate in Malibu, quilting and enjoying the fragrances of orange trees and flamevine as a gentle breeze tinkled wind chimes overhead. As her stitches became smaller and more even with practice, she wished she could show the Cross-Country Quilters how much progress she had made.

Already quilt camp and the Cross-Country Quilters had taken on an air of unreality, like something out of a vivid dream only dimly remembered. It was hard to imagine herself confiding in a group of women who were, after all, little more than strangers, especially considering how fiercely she usually guarded her privacy. Still, Julia found herself missing Elm Creek Manor and wishing for a dose of Vinnie's sharp humor, Donna's optimistic kindness, and the encouragement and companionship of the whole group—especially after Ares would phone with updates on the movie, reawakening Julia's fears that she wouldn't be able to quilt convincingly enough and the director would denounce her as a fraud.

Julia had expected the Cross-Country Quilters to write, especially Donna and Megan, who were avid E-mail correspondents, but the weeks passed without a word. She even took to sorting her own mail, but after a few days she returned the task to her assistant. Perhaps they were waiting to hear from her first, but somehow Julia couldn't bring herself to initiate the correspondence. Or perhaps they weren't as close as Julia had thought. Maybe they had only exchanged addresses to be polite. It had been so long since she'd had a friend that she was unfamiliar with the etiquette of such things.

At the end of September, Julia and Ares went to the first of several script meetings. On the way to the studio, Ares filled her in on the rest of the cast. The good news was that the role of Young Sadie had been given to Samantha Key, a virtually unknown actress with only a few bit parts to her credit. She couldn't afford to play the diva, not with Deneford, so Julia needn't fear she'd try to expand her role at Julia's expense. Julia had never heard of

Cameron Miller, who would play her youngest son, but Noah McCleod, the eldest Henderson boy, had a reputation for being talented, professional, and down-to-earth. She had worked frequently with child actors on *Family Tree,* and Julia was confident she'd get along fine with the two young men.

She was less pleased to hear that Rick Rowen had won the role of Augustus. She had worked with him only once, when they had cohosted a holiday special three years before, but he had been an arrogant man then, and rumor had it he had become even worse after *People* magazine named him one of its Fifty Most Beautiful People. Only a month ago, his latest movie, an action film set in South America, had premiered at number one and held steady, which meant that he was no doubt being buried in offers for which he could name his salary. Given his elevated circumstances, Julia wondered why he had accepted a small role in a serious drama, and decided that he must have signed the contract before his fortunes rose. Working with him was sure to be excruciating. Fortunately, Augustus would be dead by the second reel.

When she and Ares arrived at Deneford's conference room, Julia realized at once that they would not be reading from the script, as indicated by the agenda faxed to her the previous day. The sheer number of agents in the room told her they were in for some negotiations first, and as much as she disliked Ares, she was suddenly glad that he had accompanied her. Rick looked bored and cocky, Samantha gazed listlessly at the table, but their agents radiated caffeinated energy. They eyed Julia with carnivorous eagerness as she entered, and only then did she note that the children and their ubiquitous mothers were not present, which suggested they were in for a brawl.

Deneford sat at the head of the table. In her younger years Julia would have seated herself at his right hand, the better to make suggestive eye contact and accidentally brush her leg against his beneath the table throughout the meeting, but in this light she knew distance would be more flattering. She chose the chair directly across from Deneford at the foot of the table, where she would be sure to catch his eye now and then. Ares took a seat at her left hand; to her right sat Ellen Henderson.

When Julia greeted her, Ellen whispered bleakly, "Did you hear? I'm out as director."

"I know, dear," Julia said sympathetically, and it struck her that she sounded exactly like Vinnie.

"This was supposed to be my breakthrough project."

"It still can be. You're still the writer. You'll receive plenty of recognition for that."

Just then, Deneford spoke. "Since we're all here, let's get started." He turned to Rick's agent, a young man with dark, slicked-back hair who looked vaguely familiar. "Jim, since you have the most to say, I'll let you begin."

"Rick isn't happy with the script," Jim said. "His talents aren't being fully utilized."

Talents? Julia thought scathingly.

Deneford shrugged. "He liked the script just fine when he first read it."

"That was before *Jungle Vengeance*." Jim looked around the table as if to enlist the others' support, which surely he knew was a wasted effort. "Let's be honest here. Does it really make sense to kill off your male lead so early in the picture?"

"But that's how it really happened," Ellen interjected.

Jim gave her a withering look, then ignored her. "A lot of people are going to consider this a Rick Rowen film. They're going to see it because they want to see Rick Rowen. Do we really want to disappoint them?"

Ares said, "You're kidding, right? This is a Julia Merchaud film."

You'd better believe it, Julia thought.

"That's funny, I thought it was a Stephen Deneford film," Deneford said dryly. "Okay, Jim, you've made your point. And I agree with you to a certain extent. The last two thirds of the story—"

"Turn it into a chick movie," Rick interrupted. Samantha

stirred long enough to give him a sidelong look, but then her gaze reverted to the tabletop. "I don't do chick movies."

"Chick movie?" Ellen bristled. "This is a movie about women—strong, intelligent women going about the difficult business of living in nearly impossible circumstances."

Rick shrugged, puzzled. "Right. A chick movie."

Jim leaned toward Deneford as if they were alone in the room. "We both know Rick Rowen's presence in this picture guarantees a huge opening weekend—if word of mouth is good. It won't be if his fans don't get to see enough of him."

"Now I'm barely making a cameo appearance," Rick complained. He flipped through the script, shaking his head. "It should be Augustus, not Sadie, who keeps the farm from going up in flames. He should be the one to scare off the claim jumpers. I mean, come on, who's going to believe a woman did all that?"

In a cold and steady voice, Ellen said, "That's how it really happened."

"How it really happened doesn't matter," Deneford said. "What matters is that it's believable."

"You mean as believable as one man saving a legion of Green Berets from the entire Colombian army?"

"That could happen," Rick shot back.

Ellen snorted disgustedly and sat back in her chair, folding her arms.

"I fail to see what's so unbelievable about a woman performing heroic acts," Julia said. "Especially to protect her children. Women were widowed all the time on the frontier. They could hardly afford to wait around for a man to rescue them."

Ellen shot her a grateful look. Julia gave her a small nod in return, her conscience pricking her. She had spoken up to protect her role, not the integrity of Ellen's script. The scene where Sadie faced down the unscrupulous cattle ranchers with nothing more than an unloaded rifle and a pitchfork contained one of the film's best monologues. Julia wasn't about to let Rick Rowen get it instead.

Jim's attention was still on Deneford. "Given Rick's draw,

would it really be such a bad idea to steer the picture in a more action-adventure-type direction?"

Deneford stroked his chin, thinking.

Encouraged, Jim pressed ahead. "It would be like *Little House on the Prairie* meets *Die Hard*."

Suddenly Samantha spoke up. "I like *Little House on the Prairie*."

Everyone stared at her for a moment before her agent jumped in. "If Samantha likes it, I have no argument with expanding Rick's part."

"Hold on just a second," Ares said, without needing any prompting from Julia. "I'm not about to let Julia's best scenes go to Rowen. We're ready to walk away right now."

Julia felt a flash of panic as he shoved his chair away from the table, but to her relief, Deneford held up his hands. "Julia won't have to sacrifice any of her screen time. We'll just cut out some of the domestic scenes and add new material for Rick."

"Domestic scenes?" Ellen echoed sharply.

"Not all of them. In fact, since Augustus will be sticking around, we'll probably need a few love scenes between him and Sadie." He looked at Jim. "Any problems with that?"

Jim glanced at Rick, who grinned. "No problems," Jim said, than glanced at Julia. "Um, which Sadie are we talking about?"

"Julia."

Jim made a barely perceptible wince and glanced at Julia once again. "I'll have to speak to my client." As he bent his mouth close to Rick's ear, Julia pictured herself leaping across the table to claw his eyes out. She knew what he was whispering into the young actor's ear—would he be willing to do love scenes with, to put it politely, an actress of Julia's maturity? How dare he, and right in front of her. It took all her strength of will to keep her expression serene.

When Jim straightened, Rick grinned. "I'm cool with that," he said, leering at Julia. "When I was a kid I used to dream about doing it with the mom from *Home Sweet Home*."

"How charming," Julia muttered, as disgusted as she was surprised that someone his age remembered her first series.

"Fine. Augustus lives, Augustus and Sadie have a roll or two in the hay, maybe literally, everyone's happy." Deneford raised his eyebrows at Ellen. "Can you make those changes without delaying our production schedule?"

Ellen looked faintly ill.

"If you can't do it, say the word and I'll get a team of studio writers—"

"I'll do it," Ellen said quickly. She slumped back in her chair in disbelief.

After a brief discussion of the production schedule, the meeting broke up. Julia and Ares went out to the parking lot, where Ellen caught up to them and asked to speak with Julia privately.

"I can't believe they want so many changes," Ellen said. "I've never written by committee before. Is this typical?"

"That's part of the business." Julia patted her on the arm and smiled. She was in a good mood, since the meeting had worked out largely in her favor. She hadn't lost a moment of screen time, and although Rick disgusted her, a few love scenes with a popular young actor couldn't hurt her image. "I'm afraid you'll just have to get used to it."

Ellen looked dubious. "I'm afraid they're going to ruin my movie."

It's Deneford's movie now, Julia almost said, but she decided to be kind. "Nonsense. You're a gifted writer. I'm sure the revisions will be just as wonderful as the original."

"If you say so, I'll believe you. I feel like you're the only person who shares my vision about this project. You're the only one who cares about my great-grandmother's history as much as I do."

Julia forced herself to keep her smile in place. "Of course I do." She patted Ellen on the arm again and hurried off to her car before the conversation could make her even more uncomfortable.

Grace returned home from the doctor's office in a gray fog of depression. Her condition was unchanged—no better, no worse. She was lucky, according to the doctor, especially after she told him about the minor exacerbations she had experienced at quilt camp. "No exacerbation can be considered minor," he reminded her for what must have been the thousandth time. "You need to take it easy. Stress can aggravate MS."

MS. He tossed off the initials so casually, as if her life weren't at stake. Grace knew he was not trying to be unkind; he was so used to treating multiple sclerosis patients that he had learned to be matter-of-fact with the disease, while she still treated it warily, like an enemy who had moved into her home, someone she could not ignore but must address with cautious respect.

For nearly eight years Grace had experienced strange symptoms—tingling in her hands and feet, pain in her eyes and problems with her vision, and slight uncoordination. The symptoms would flare up unexpectedly, then completely disappear. So much time elapsed between occurrences that she attributed the odd sensations to stress, fatigue, poor circulation, and overwork, and in fact, the first few doctors she consulted had made the same diagnosis. Not until a frightening incident four years before had Grace, at Justine's insistence, pursued a more aggressive search for answers.

She had been driving to the deYoung Museum to study some new acquisitions when suddenly her hands felt as if they were being pricked by hundreds of needles. Her hands gripped the steering wheel clumsily, and, suddenly alarmed, she set a turn signal and pulled over to the shoulder of the freeway. When she tried to ease off the gas and apply the brake, her right foot was numb and unresponsive. Grace used all her force of will to command her sluggish foot to move—and it did, but too late to prevent the car from slamming into the guard rail.

Although the car sustained substantial damage in the accident, she was physically uninjured but emotionally traumatized. Her little difficulties, as she had called them, had never affected her so strongly before. What if she had been on a road with no guard rail? What if she had struck another car and injured its occupants? She could not trust herself to drive again until she knew for certain what was wrong with her.

She consulted one doctor after another. Some found nothing wrong with her; others suggested she try antidepressants. Grace, who knew her emotional state was a symptom and not the cause of her physical problems, persisted. She underwent blood tests and CT scans, none of which yielded any conclusive answers. Finally a practitioner of alternative medicine provided some help. She suggested that Grace was suffering from some autoimmune response to toxins in her environment. Purging her home and her diet of harmful chemicals, combined with daily meditation, might help her manage her symptoms.

At first Grace was skeptical, but to her grateful surprise, the prescription seemed to work. At least she certainly felt healthier, more relaxed and at peace. She even began driving confidently again. But three months into her treatment, Grace's symptoms returned with such force that she went to the emergency room, certain she was having a stroke. That was where she was referred to Dr. Steiner, who took a clinical history, ordered an MRI and a spinal tap, and determined she had MS.

She had been seeing him ever since, as well as participating in clinical trials and learning all she could about the disease. At first she retained some confidence, because it seemed that her disease followed a relapsing-remitting course, which meant that she could expect some or even complete recovery between attacks. But as the months dragged with no new advances in treatment, no miraculous remissions or sudden leaps forward in the medical understanding of MS, her faith began to ebb. Dr. Steiner had never tried to conceal her prognosis, and she knew she was looking at a future of possible incapacitation, the abandonment of all the activities she cherished, and total dependence—the one thing she simply could not bear.

Grace had told Justine and her immediate family, but had

sworn them to secrecy. Not even her closest friends suspected what she was going through, and that was exactly how Grace wanted it. She would not have anyone treating her any differently than they always had.

"Eventually they'll know something's wrong," Justine had told her. She meant that eventually the disease would progress so far that Grace would no longer be able to conceal it. A wheelchair was a difficult contrivance to ignore.

"So that's when I'll tell them," Grace had said, and refused to discuss the subject further. Justine insisted that the support of her friends was what she needed most, but what Grace wanted most was her old life back. She wanted a sense of normalcy and ordinariness; she wanted the same blissful ignorance of the future most people enjoyed.

She prayed for guidance, for serenity, for a miracle, but her sewing machine gathered dust and her fabric stash permanent creases from being left folded in the same positions for so long.

Since returning from Sylvia's nearly eight weeks before, Grace had tried to maintain her resolve to work through her creative block. She thought of how Sylvia had worked through the impairment brought on by a stroke, and knew she had to keep trying. She went to her studio and sat on a stool, propping her elbows up on a work table and studying the shelves full of fabric. No matter how low she felt, the colors never failed to lift her spirits.

After a while, she took out the fat quarter of the autumn leaf print Vinnie had given her. According to the loose rules the Cross-Country Quilters had established, she couldn't begin sewing her block yet, but she could choose some suitable complementary fabrics. She spent a quiet hour searching through her inventory, comparing the colors in the fat quarter to the many shades in her collection. She had chosen a rich burgundy cotton with a visual suede texture and a purple floral print with striking blue highlights when someone buzzed her loft from the front door. When, a moment later, the elevator sounded, she knew her visitor was Justine, who had a key.

Grace left the material on a work table and went to meet her daughter at the loft door. To her delight, Joshua was with her.

"How did it go?" Justine asked after Grace had greeted her visitors with hugs and kisses.

Grace shrugged. "Same as before."

Justine's tense expression eased. "That's good news, at least."

"I'd hardly call it that."

"It's better than hearing that you've gotten worse."

Grace felt a flash of annoyance. "Little pitchers," she said, tilting her head toward Joshua, who was playing with blocks on the floor.

Justine gave her a look that said she was being ridiculous. "You don't like to talk about it, but you should."

"I'll talk about what I please, when I please."

"You'd feel better if you were more open and honest about this. Not just with me, but with yourself."

"The way you've been open and honest with me?" Grace shot back.

Justine stared at her. "What are you talking about?"

"Nothing. Never mind." She leaned over to pick up a block that had tumbled away from Joshua's pile and returned it to him.

"No, you brought it up. Something's obviously bothering you. Let's air it out."

Grace took a deep breath. "I know you're seeing someone."

Justine's eyebrows rose. "What?"

"I know you're seeing someone, and I know . . ." She glanced at Joshua and lowered her voice. "I know it's serious."

"Mom, you couldn't be more wrong."

"Don't give me that. Sondra saw you together at a restaurant back in July. Joshua was with you."

Justine set her jaw. "Your friends are spying on me?"

"That's hardly fair. Sondra happened to see you, and she asked me who the man was, and of course I had to tell her I didn't know, since you didn't have the decency to tell me on your own."

"Mom—"

"And what's worse than being the last to know about these important developments in your life—and Joshua's life, I might add—is that your new boyfriend is my age."

"Mom, you have it all wrong."

"I most certainly do not. Sondra told me he's old enough to be your father."

"That's because he *is* my father."

"What?"

"The man Sondra saw us with is my father."

Grace stared at her as the words slowly sank in. "Oh my God."

"I didn't tell you because I thought you'd be upset." Justine sighed. "Which, judging by the way you're staring at me, you obviously are."

"What does he want?"

"What does he want? He wants to see his daughter. He wants to get to know his grandson. He'd even like to see you, if you're willing. I told him you probably wouldn't be, but he said—"

"You're right. I don't want to see him." Grace squeezed her hands together to keep them from trembling. Gabriel, back in their lives after so many years. "I don't understand. How did he find you? Or did you go looking for him?"

"He came to the legal aid clinic one day while I was working."

"Is he in some kind of trouble?"

"He wasn't coming for himself. One of his students was being abused by her live-in boyfriend, and he was investigating resources to recommend to her."

So Gabriel was teaching again. "He couldn't have recognized you." The last time he had seen Justine was when she was four.

"No, but I recognized him from your pictures, and when he gave me his name, I knew."

Grace felt her face grow hot. Those pictures, that one album she had saved and had assumed was safely hidden in her closet. When had Justine seen it? "You should have told me you had met with him."

"I didn't want to upset you."

Grace closed her eyes, nodded, and tried to still her churning thoughts. His abrupt departure twenty years before had torn out her heart, and it had taken her a long time to recover. For all intents and purposes, he had been dead to them. And now he had returned.

Grace steeled herself and spoke the question she dreaded to ask. "Are you going to see him again?"

She knew what the answer would be even before Justine nodded.

Autumn was Vinnie's favorite time of year. By mid-October, the days were still pleasantly warm but the evenings took on a slight chill—"good quilting weather," Vinnie called it.

In her last letter, Donna had written that nearly all the leaves were off the trees in her backyard and that she wouldn't be surprised if it snowed by Halloween. Vinnie figured that was normal for northern Minnesota, although it seemed to her a bit early to be thinking about snow. No doubt Julia was still basking in the southern California sunshine; Vinnie couldn't say for certain, since Julia had not responded to a single one of her letters. Since Vinnie had heard from the other Cross-Country Quilters several times already, she was beginning to suspect that maybe her letters were getting lost amid the piles of fan mail Julia probably received each day. Undaunted, Vinnie wrote another letter, but this time she decorated the outside of the envelope with little quilt blocks drawn in colored pen. As an extra measure, in the return address, she wrote her name as "Lavinia Burkholder, AKA Vinnie from Quilt Camp." There. If that didn't get through to Julia, Vinnie didn't know what would.

Writing letters was a habit she had picked up while living with Aunt Lynn—where, Vinnie reflected, she had also acquired the habit of writing letters without expecting a response. She had written three or four letters to her father for every one he sent her.

Frankie had written more frequently; she had learned more about her father from her brother's letters than from his own. She grew accustomed to her father's indifference, which was made easier to accept by the love Aunt Lynn and Lena showered upon her.

But although Vinnie felt secure and content in her new life with Aunt Lynn, she had learned to expect change.

She was too absorbed in school and her friends to pay much attention to the news of the stock market crash, but the trouble forecast by adults' worried expressions and hushed conversations was soon confirmed. Aunt Lynn explained that they might face difficult times ahead, but Vinnie shouldn't worry because Aunt Lynn had a secure job in a government office. Vinnie believed her aunt, but she soon realized that other families on their block were not as fortunate as they. Even the Pot-Luck Pals seemed to have to work harder to be cheerful, and they brought smaller covered dishes to their twice-monthly gatherings.

For months Vinnie had overheard Aunt Lynn and Lena discussing the possibility of Lena's losing her job at the factory where she worked as a secretary. She sounded confident that the boss couldn't manage without her, but one night, long after Vinnie was supposed to be asleep, sounds came through the wall that separated her bedroom from Aunt Lynn's. She could have sworn she heard Lena weeping.

The next morning, Lena and Aunt Lynn met her at the breakfast table with somber expressions and bad news. As it turned out, Lena hadn't been fired after all. The company had gone bankrupt and the entire factory shut down, which meant that all the employees—including Lena and her boss—were out of work. Until she found another job, Lena could no longer afford her room in the boarding house across town. Aunt Lynn hesitated before asking Vinnie if she would mind if Lena came to live with them.

"It's fine with me," Vinnie said, surprised that they would need to ask her. Lena spent the night so often that it was almost as if she lived there already. "Do you want my room?"

Aunt Lynn and Lena exchanged a quick look. "No, honey. Lena will stay with me," Aunt Lynn said. "That's very nice of you to offer, but you need a quiet place to do your homework."

That seemed reasonable to Vinnie, so the following weekend, Lena moved in. For the first few days her presence made the house seem festive, but before long Vinnie began to wish she could do more to help. Aunt Lynn went to work every day and took all the extra hours her employer would spare, while Lena took care of the home. Although they never complained, at least not in front of her, Vinnie knew both women were tired from overwork and worried about money. Once Vinnie asked Aunt Lynn if she should quit school and find a job.

"Your job is to go to school," Aunt Lynn said. "You help us by doing well with your studies."

"And keeping your room picked up," Lena added, tweaking her nose.

Vinnie wasn't satisfied. She wanted to contribute something to the household, enough so that Aunt Lynn would relax and be cheerful the way she used to, enough so that Lena would crack jokes and smile again.

Since she knew of no other way to contribute, Vinnie devoted herself to her schoolwork. She often stayed after class for extra help, which her teachers were willing to provide, pleased to have such a diligent pupil. One afternoon, as she worked through some long division problems on the blackboard, Miss Kelley leaned over her desk to check her work and caught her dress on a rough edge.

Vinnie heard fabric tear. "Oh, no," Miss Kelley groaned, bending over to free her hem. As her teacher examined it, Vinnie glimpsed a three-inch-long tear in the fabric. "Of all the days to rip my dress."

"You can sew it when you go home," Vinnie said.

"That's the problem. I'm not going home. I'm going straight to my fiancé's parents' house for supper. I can see his mother's smirk already. Wouldn't she just love to catch me walking around with a hole in my dress!"

"Why would she love that?"

Miss Kelley caught herself. "Never you mind," she said sternly, then added, "When you have a mother-in-law, you'll understand."

"If you have a needle and thread, I could sew it for you," Vinnie offered. At first Miss Kelley demurred, but when Vinnie insisted, she retrieved a needle and thread from her purse. Vinnie studied the tear. It was a simple rip right along the grain of the fabric, and soon Miss Kelley's dress was mended, the seam almost invisible.

Miss Kelley, much relieved, offered to pay her, but Vinnie grew embarrassed and refused. "I hate to sew," Miss Kelley said. "Won't you take something for saving me the trouble?"

"You don't take anything for helping me with my math."

Vinnie had never spoken so boldly to a teacher before, and she felt her face growing red-hot. She expected Miss Kelley to scold her, but instead she looked thoughtful. "If this had been your job, would you have allowed me to pay you?"

Uncertain, Vinnie could only nod.

"Then do you suppose if I brought you some other mending, I could hire you to complete it? As long as your aunt agrees, of course."

Vinnie promised to ask, and she ran home, her spirits soaring.

Aunt Lynn seemed dubious at first. "Will you have enough time for your schoolwork?"

"How much mending could one teacher have?" Lena said, giving Vinnie a wink. "The kid looks like she'll pop if you say no, Lynn."

At that Aunt Lynn laughed and agreed that Vinnie could try it for a while, but if her grades suffered, she would have to stop. The next day Vinnie raced to school with the news and returned home with a bag full of stockings that needed darning. When she finished, Miss Kelley paid her five cents for each pair. Vinnie triumphantly presented the money to her aunt.

Soon other teachers learned of the arrangement, and within a month Vinnie had added two other teachers to her list. Then Mr.

Borchard from English class became a client; a bachelor, he soon had recommended her to several of his unmarried friends. Before long Vinnie had sewing projects every night and was making more money than she had ever dreamed possible.

But her success kept her up late and away from her books. When her term report card showed a slight dip in her grades, Aunt Lynn worried that she was spending too much time working. "I can do both," Vinnie insisted. She knew her earnings made a difference to the family and couldn't bear to quit, not until Lena found work. Eventually Aunt Lynn agreed to let her continue, but no more than one hour on school days and four on the weekends.

Dismayed, Vinnie nodded and carried her sewing basket into the other room so Aunt Lynn wouldn't see how upset she was. On Aunt Lynn's schedule, she wouldn't have enough time for more than two or three clients. Blinking back tears, she set herself to work, determined to finish as much as she could.

After a while, Lena sat on the sofa beside her and watched her hemming a skirt. "That looks difficult."

Vinnie didn't feel like talking. "It's not."

"I haven't sewed since high school home ec. Would you show me?"

Her heart still heavy, Vinnie demonstrated the stitches. Lena caught on quickly and asked for a scrap of fabric so she could practice.

All that week and the next Vinnie taught Lena what she knew. Lena practiced, sometimes on scraps, sometimes on the clients' garments under Vinnie's close scrutiny. Then one afternoon Vinnie returned from school to discover that Lena had finished reattaching three loose collars and hemming two suits.

Lena was obviously proud of herself, but her voice was hesitant when she said, "What do you say you and I become partners, kid?"

Delighted, Vinnie agreed. The next day Lena dusted off Aunt Lynn's sewing machine and set about teaching herself how to use it. She visited the library and checked out books on sewing and dressmaking and tailoring. Together she and Vinnie were able to take on more work for more money. Before long, Lena's skills surpassed Vinnie's own, and she made plans to expand their business into making custom-made garments. One of the Pot-Luck Pals printed up advertisements, which Lena distributed around the city. She modeled her creations at Dayton's fine boutiques, whose clientele had thrived despite the Depression. With her striking blond good looks and professional manner, she impressed the boutique owners as well as their customers, and soon Lena began receiving regular orders for everything from casual attire to gowns. Within a year Lena's enterprise had become so successful that her earnings equaled her previous salary.

Looking back, Vinnie marveled how Aunt Lynn and Lena had managed to see their little family through the Depression unscathed. Even now she admired Lena for transforming loss into opportunity, and she was proud of herself for her role in it.

Sometimes all people needed was a little nudge in the right direction, and they would go far. Vinnie picked up the phone and dialed Adam's number. Her grandson could use a little nudge right about now.

A few days later, Megan received a letter from Vinnie:

Dear Megan,

I was tickled to get your last letter. I'm sorry to hear your ex is being such a louse. But don't worry. I know you'll figure out something and you'll get to make your quilt block yet.

Do you and Robby have any plans for Halloween? I hope not, because I'd like to invite you for a visit. Meadowbrook Village has a Halloween party and trick-or-treating every year, and I would be honored to have you two as my guests. My grandson, Adam, is coming too, but since he's a little old for trick-or-treating, I thought it would be much more fun if you brought Robby.

If you don't wear a costume, you'll be the only person there who doesn't. I'm going as Raggedy Ann.

Hope to see you soon!

Love from your quilt buddy,
Vinnie

Megan considered the letter thoughtfully. Vinnie's invitation was an answer to a prayer. The boy next door, who had been Robby's playmate until a year ago, was having a Halloween party, too, and Jason had invited all the boys in the class—except Robby. Jason's mother spotted Megan raking leaves in the backyard, came outside, and made an awkward apology over the fence. "You know how kids are," she said, shrugging and trying to smile.

Yes, I know, Megan thought. She knew how kids were. She knew they needed to be taught that kindness mattered more than popularity, and that they ought to include the outcast even if they preferred not to, simply because it was right, because inviting every boy but one was cruel. Megan couldn't bear the thought of Robby watching out the windows as the other boys' parents dropped them off next door for a night of wild Halloween fun.

She wouldn't have hesitated to accept Vinnie's invitation—except for Adam. Vinnie had to be the least subtle matchmaker in the history of romance, and Megan cringed when she pictured Adam's embarrassment when Vinnie nudged them together, beaming and dropping hints. Then again, he would have to be a total idiot not to see what his grandmother was doing, and since he was still willing to attend, he must not mind all that much.

He had been rather nice at the diner.

"Robby," she called out, returning the letter to its envelope. "Do you want to go to a Halloween party?"

Seven

G RACE HOPED to channel her anger into the creation of a new quilt so that at least some good would come of her argument with Justine. In the past she had been able to work out her frustrations by slicing through fabric and pounding the pedal on her sewing machine, but like so much of her pre-MS life, that ability, too, had apparently been lost. Thwarted, she flung her rotary cutter aside, switched on her computer, and vented her frustrations in an E-mail to Donna and Megan instead.

TO: Megan.Donohue@rocketec.com,
    quiltmom@USAonline.com
FROM: Grace Daniels <danielsg@deyoung.org>
DATE: 9:27 AM 18 Oct
SUBJECT: May I start my quilt block now?

I wish I were asking because I've broken through my quilter's
block, but unfortunately, that's not so. However, I have made

progress on the other aspect of my challenge . . . if you can call it progress. It turns out my daughter isn't dating an older man after all. The man my friend saw with Justine and Joshua was her father.

Should I be happy that Justine wasn't keeping a boyfriend secret from me, or outraged that she's been in contact with my ex-husband of twenty years and didn't see fit to tell me? It's not much of a consolation that I'm halfway to fulfilling my promise to the Cross-Country Quilters. What do you think: Although I haven't started a new quilt yet, am I allowed to begin working on my Challenge Quilt block?

Donna must have been online, because she wrote back almost immediately:

TO: Grace Daniels <danielsg@deyoung.org>
FROM: Donna Jorgenson <quiltmom@USAonline.com>
DATE: 18 Oct 11:35 AM CDT
SUBJECT: Re: May I start my quilt block now?
CC: Megan.Donohue@rocketec.com

Good grief. I don't know whether to congratulate you or not. At least Justine wasn't hiding a secret romance from you, but it sounds like you have a bigger problem on your hands. Have you talked to the Ex yet?

As for the Challenge Quilt, I don't think you should be allowed to start until you have at least a plan for a new project. Sorry, but the motivation will be good for you. Good luck.

Megan didn't respond until later that afternoon, and when she did, Grace could almost feel the computer screen steaming from her indignation:

TO: Grace Daniels ‹danielsg@deyoung.org›
FROM: Megan.Donohue@rocketec.com
DATE: 2:00 PM 10/18
SUBJECT: Re: May I start my quilt block now?
CC: quiltmom@USAonline.com

So where's he been all this time? Did he only just remember
he had a daughter?

Grace wondered about that herself, but in order to get an answer, she would have to talk to Gabriel, and she was not ready to
do that. She doubted she'd ever be. Twice Justine had invited
Grace to join them for outings with Joshua, but Grace had refused. She had nothing to say to Gabriel that silence wouldn't
communicate just as well.

"Don't you even want him to apologize?" Justine persisted.

Grace wanted that very much, but she wasn't willing to admit
it. "How do you know he will?"

"I just know."

Grace let out a scoffing laugh and shook her head. "I think I
know him better than you do. He was never good at regret."

"He's changed. Give him a chance."

"I've given him more than twenty years' worth of chances,"
Grace said. "In all that time, did he ever come to see you? Did he
ever send so much as a letter to let us know he was still alive?"

Justine watched her in silence for a long moment. "If you talk
to him, he'll explain."

"I don't need his explanations now. Anything he could say
would be too little, too late."

After that, Justine did not mention him for weeks. Grace tried
to put him out of her mind, as she had done so well for so long,
but her anger smoldered. She knew Justine was seeing him every
week and that Joshua called him Grandpa, as if Gabriel had been
there all along, as if he hadn't abandoned his family as easily as
sloughing off soiled clothing.

As the weeks passed, it became clear Gabriel intended to remain a part of Justine's life. Just that morning, Justine had asked her if they could invite him to Thanksgiving dinner. The request left Grace speechless. "Thanksgiving is for family," she finally managed to say.

"He's family. He doesn't have anyone else."

"That's his own fault."

"Mom—"

"You know I'm supposed to minimize the stress in my life. Believe me, inviting him to your aunt's for Thanksgiving will not help."

"Don't use your MS as an excuse."

Anger and humiliation surged so intensely that tears came to her eyes. "I told you, do not mention that in front of Joshua," she gritted out, her voice shaking.

"He's my father, Mom," Justine pleaded. "He's Joshua's grandfather. Don't shut him out."

Grace couldn't believe what she was hearing. Since when was Gabriel's estrangement her fault? "You are a disloyal and ungrateful child."

"You're jealous and holding a grudge."

Her words stung. "He left us, Justine. Did you forget that?"

"He says you kicked him out."

"Only to force him to get help," Grace snapped. "Did he tell you that part? His drinking was destroying our family."

"He's sober now, Mom. He's been sober for ten years."

"Then he should have contacted us ten years ago."

"Why bother, for this kind of welcome?" Justine scooped up Joshua and stormed out.

Grace and Justine had often disagreed and sometimes even argued, but never before had they fought with such fury. Alone in her loft, Grace tried meditating to calm herself, but her thoughts were churning too strongly. The truth was, she *was* jealous. Grace had been there for Justine and Joshua all their lives, and now Gabriel could waltz in, the prodigal father, and Justine was willing for him to step right back into the family as if he had never left, as if she cared nothing for her mother's pain. Gabriel had done nothing to earn such a welcome, and Grace couldn't bear it.

If Justine knew the whole story, she would never attribute Grace's feelings to something as simple as holding a grudge.

She and Gabriel had met as students at Berkeley, in a time of turmoil and hope, when their unjust society seemed more malleable than at any time in history. An art history major, Grace had noticed the tall, strikingly handsome man in several of her classes, but had never spoken to him, although campus was not yet so integrated that most African-American students did not have at least a nodding acquaintance. It wasn't until her junior year—while both were part of a group picketing against a local chain restaurant that had repeatedly demonstrated racism against black students and faculty—that he approached her and introduced himself. They struck up a friendship based on mutual interests and attraction, which soon blossomed into romance.

After graduation, Gabriel entered graduate school with the goal of becoming a professor of history. Grace turned down other, more lucrative opportunities and accepted a position at an art museum on campus in order to remain near him. They married a year later.

Gabriel had always drunk at parties and other social gatherings, no more than anyone else and less than most, and since he didn't care for marijuana, it never occurred to Grace that he might have a problem. Only after they began living together did she realize how much, and how often, he drank. At first it was merely a few beers after classes had ended for the day, and possibly another as he unwound before bed. Then he began drinking at lunchtime, joking that he needed the fortification to deal with the class of brainless freshmen whose papers he was obligated to grade as a part of his teaching assistantship. When Grace expressed her concern that his graduate advisor would probably disapprove, Gabriel retorted, "He disapproves of everything I do anyway. The only way I could please him would be if I turned white overnight."

When his professors evaluated him at the end of the semester, his advisor called him in to talk. Gabriel came home in a rage. Somehow—Gabriel insisted he had no idea how—he had developed a reputation as argumentative, undisciplined, and unreliable. No one in the department questioned his intellect and passion, his advisor explained, but they needed him to make a more obvious commitment to the profession if he wished to continue in the program. Gabriel blamed his advisor for blackballing him. Grace blamed the alcohol.

When she realized she was pregnant, she doubled her efforts to get him to stop drinking, but he turned his anger on her instead. Somehow he managed to scrape his way through school, earning his master's in history when Justine was a year old. To Grace's relieved astonishment, he was accepted into the Ph.D. program. Now, she told herself, he would have no choice but to give up the drinking and concentrate on his work and family. Instead, the increased pressures of the more rigorous academic program augmented his need for drink, and he left school after three months.

He found a job teaching history at a local high school, and for a while, the bitter disappointment of losing his long-held dream shocked him into sobriety. For two years he limited his drinking to the home, and would drink only in the evenings, when he would play with Justine for a little while after supper and then settle in front of the television set, sipping one drink after another until he passed out. In the mornings he would get up, shave, and head to work on time, so Grace decided to count her blessings. She loved him deeply, and learned to accept that he was not the husband she had once thought he would be.

Then one day, the principal of his school phoned her at work and told her in a stiff voice that Gabriel had fallen ill and needed to be picked up immediately. Grace arrived to find him in an empty classroom, nearly unconscious and reeking of alcohol. The principal said nothing as he helped her walk her husband to the car, but his anger was unmistakable. Grace was so ashamed she could barely look at him.

The principal expedited the paperwork, and when Gabriel was fired a few days later, he blamed a racist school board for his dismissal.

"It's always someone else's fault, isn't it?" Grace shot back. "It's never you. It's never your drinking."

He glared at her balefully and rolled over onto his side on the sofa. In another moment, he was snoring.

Gabriel didn't even attempt to look for a new job. Sometimes he left in the mornings before Grace took Justine to the sitter's and went to her own work, but he was always home by the time she returned, passed out on the sofa. They hardly spoke anymore, and Grace was afraid to leave Justine alone with him. Gabriel stopped coming to their bedroom at night, which was more of a relief than she ever would have thought possible. His loving touch had long since given way to awkward gropings in the dark, resulting in failure most of the time, and leaving her angry and confused even when they didn't. She felt desperately alone but was too loyal to talk about the situation with anyone, not even her sisters, whose disapproving expressions suggested they knew something was wrong but respected Grace's pride too much to confront her.

Then something happened to shake Grace from her complacency.

One night she woke to the acrid stench of burning. Her heart pounding, she scrambled from bed to find the living room in flames.

"Gabriel," she screamed at the motionless lump on the sofa. Choking on smoke, she stumbled to his side and shook him, screaming his name over and over until she managed to rouse him. She helped him stagger outside and let him fall uncomprehending on the front lawn. Her heart racing with fear, she turned back inside, only to find that the fire had spread. The hallway to the room where Justine lay sleeping was impassable.

Frantic, Grace ran outside and raced around the backyard to Justine's window. Her eyes burned and streamed tears; her ears were full of the menacing roar of the fire as it consumed her home.

She struggled to open the window, but it wouldn't budge. She searched around blindly until she stumbled upon a lawn chair. Without a thought, she lifted it over her head and smashed it through the glass.

She didn't remember climbing past the broken shards and hauling Justine to safety, only sitting on the front lawn with her daughter in her arms and a neighbor's blanket over her shoulders. She stared at the house unblinking as the firefighters struggled to extinguish the blaze. Justine sobbed and buried her face in Grace's shoulder.

When the house was nothing more than a smoldering ruin, a paramedic came to inspect Grace's injuries. Still dazed, at first Grace refused to let go of Justine, but eventually was persuaded to allow a neighbor to take her. She stared at the embers of her life as the paramedic examined her. "We'll have to take her to the hospital to remove the glass," she overheard him say. Only then did she feel the sharp stinging in her hands and legs and feel the wet slickness of her own blood on her skin.

Helen, one of her elder sisters, took them in. A few days later, Grace learned that the blaze had started when Gabriel fell asleep holding a lit cigarette. He dropped it and set fire to the drapes. In a way, they had been fortunate. If the cigarette had fallen on the sofa, the investigators said, the foam cushions would have burned much more rapidly than the drapes, almost certainly killing Gabriel and possibly the rest of the family. They were lucky.

"Lucky," Gabriel mumbled, and left Helen's house for a drink.

Under Helen's watchful eye, Grace could no longer maintain the facade of a happy family. She crumbled and tearfully confessed the pain of the past few years. Helen listened without judgment until Grace was spent. Then she said, "If he had killed your baby last night, that would have been his fault. If he kills her tomorrow, it will be yours."

When Gabriel returned, drunk and stumbling, the house was closed to him. Helen went outside only long enough to tell him to find another place to spend the night. She handed him a letter

Grace had written, a painful message of love and resolve in which she told him he could come home to his wife and daughter when he was sober, and not a day before.

Gabriel tried to change her mind, but with Helen to support her, Grace held fast. She had forgotten what it was like to wake up in the morning not dreading the day, how peaceful it was to be able to walk from the hallway to the kitchen without averting her gaze to avoid seeing her husband passed out in the living room. When Justine asked for her daddy, Grace told her he was away but he would be coming home to them soon. She thought she was telling the truth.

🍂

The Thursday before Halloween, Robby picked two of the best pumpkins from his grandmother's garden, one for him to carve and one for Megan. When they reached home, Robby's description of his carving strategy abruptly broke off. "What's that?" he asked, pointing to the front porch.

Megan glimpsed a brown box by the door as she as she pulled into the garage. "Looks like someone sent us a package."

Robby was out of the car and racing around to the front door almost before she turned off the engine. Carrying the pumpkins, she entered the house through the garage, unlocking the front door for Robby on her way. He met her in the kitchen with the parcel in his hands. "It's for me," he exclaimed, showing her his name printed in block letters with a black marker above their address. "Look. It's from Oregon. It's from Dad."

"That's great," Megan said, hiding her astonishment. Robby set the box on the table and tore into it, tossing packing materials aside. Then, suddenly, he froze, and his smile faded.

"What's wrong?" Megan asked. She peered into the box to find gingerbread and sugar cookies cut into the shapes of ghosts, pumpkins, and black cats, beautifully decorated with frosting. They were carefully packaged and unbroken, and seemed to be arranged several layers deep.

"Dad didn't make these," Robby said flatly. "*She* sent them."

"You don't know that. Maybe Dad bought them in a bakery." Megan indicated an orange envelope. "There's a card. See what it says."

Reluctantly, Robby opened the envelope and read the card, which he promptly threw back into the box. "They're from her," he said again, sliding down from his chair.

"Robby . . ." she began, but he left the kitchen with his mouth set in a sullen line. In another moment she heard the door to his room slam shut. Her heart sinking, Megan picked up the card. It had a picture of a haunted house on the front and a simple rhyming poem inside. The signature, in Gina's handwriting, said, "With love from Dad and Gina."

Megan sank into the chair Robby had vacated, the card in her hand, wondering what to do. If only Keith had taken the thirty seconds required to sign the card himself. It would have been far better for Gina to send nothing than to go to such trouble to send a present Keith obviously had nothing to do with. Sighing, she returned the card to its envelope, placed it on top of the cookies, and discarded the scattered wrapping. Then she took a gingerbread ghost down the hall and knocked on the door to Robby's room.

When he didn't respond, she said, "May I come in?"

"I'm busy." His voice was muffled through the door, but she could hear the tears in it.

"Oh. Okay." Megan thought for a moment. "Well, I'm going to start supper. It might be a while. Do you want a cookie to tide you over?"

"I'm not allowed to eat sweets before meals."

"Just this once we can make an exception."

"I don't want any stupid cookies."

"Do you mind if I have one?"

A pause. "I don't care."

"Okay, then." Megan took a bite of the ghost's head. "Mmm. This is delicious."

"You can have them."

"I can't eat them all myself. I'll get sick." She took another bite. "Maybe you'll want some after supper."

"I don't want anything *she* makes."

Megan waited for him to say something more, but when he didn't, she decided to leave him alone. "I'll be in the kitchen," she said, hoping he would join her there to talk. She waited, but he didn't leave his room until she called him for supper, and then he took his seat and ate without a word. His eyes were red-rimmed, and as soon as he had finished eating, he returned to his room without clearing his dishes, a chore that had become such a habit that he sometimes automatically rose to clear his place at restaurants.

After straightening the kitchen, Megan tried again. She knocked on his door and asked if he wanted to carve pumpkins. "No," he said through the door.

"But you planned your design and everything."

"I don't feel like it."

Megan covered the kitchen table with newspapers in case he changed his mind, but he only left his room once, to go to the bathroom and brush his teeth, and then it was his bedtime.

The next morning, Megan taped the box of cookies shut and placed it by his backpack and the bag holding his Batman costume. When he saw the box, he gave her an odd look. "Why is this here?"

"I thought you could share the cookies with your class."

"They won't want them."

"Not want cookies? You're kidding, right?" Megan made sure his jacket was zipped, then put on her own coat and opened the door to the garage. "Come on, let's go. We'll be late." Sullen, Robby picked up the bag and backpack, leaving the cookie box for her to carry.

As they drove to school, Megan reminded Robby that she was leaving work early so she could pick him up right after the class parties ended. "If there are any cookies left, bring them," she said. "We can take them to Vinnie's."

Robby perked up at the reminder of the party, enough so that he submitted willingly to a hug and kiss. "I'll see you later," she called as he shut the door. He waved good-bye with the tips of his fingers, his left arm wrapped around the box of cookies.

Throughout the day, Megan found herself thinking about Robby and wondering how his day was going. She doubted she would be able to persuade him to send Gina and Keith a thank-you note for the cookies. Most likely she would end up sending an acknowledgment herself. She wondered if this would be the way of things for the rest of their lives, Keith and Robby communicating by proxy through her and Gina.

Robby's school ended classes for the day after lunch, when the students gathered in the gymnasium for a Halloween parade. When Robby was in kindergarten, Megan had joined the other adoring parents with camcorders in the bleachers, searching the long line of costumed children for her son, and grinning with delight when she spotted him marching proudly with his friends. Afterward, the students held parties in their separate classrooms. Megan pictured Robby distributing the cookies Gina had so lovingly made, and hoped the other students wouldn't reject them as they had most of Robby's other offers of friendship.

The school parking lot was reserved for faculty and staff, so Megan parked on a side street a few blocks away and walked to school, self-conscious in her costume. Because of the trouble with the cookies, she had postponed the decision until that morning, when she put together an empire-waist dress, elbow-length gloves, and other period accessories and decided she was Elizabeth Bennett. Throughout the day, however, she began to have an uncomfortable suspicion that not even fans of *Pride and Prejudice* would be able to identify her, even with her hair up. Only then, when it had been far too late to change her mind, did it occur to her that whatever she wore would make a lasting impression on Adam.

She still wasn't sure what impression she wanted to make. As nice as Adam had seemed, Megan had mixed feelings about Vinnie's matchmaking. She had grown accustomed to being alone, and in many ways, although she wasn't as happy as the happily married people she knew, she was much more content than those tangled in fractious relationships. The thought of enduring all the heartache of falling in love and breaking up and starting over with someone else in a unrelenting cycle of searching and hoping made her weary. She didn't think she should put herself—or Robby—through that again.

Robby was waiting for her on the playground, as they had arranged. Other children played nearby, but he sat alone on a swing in his Batman costume, scuffling his feet in the gravel. Megan spotted his backpack and the bag with his school clothes on the ground not far away.

He looked up when Megan called his name, smiled, and got off the swing. "Where's the box?" Megan asked him. "Are all the cookies gone?" At that, Robby's face fell, and he turned his back on her to pick up his backpack. "What is it? What happened?" She pictured him shyly offering the other children the cookies, and some bully shoving them back in his face. "Didn't the other kids want the cookies?"

"No."

"Why not?"

"They got broken."

"Got broken?" Megan echoed. "How?"

Robby shrugged.

"You must know how."

Robby said nothing, his eyes downcast. "They broke on my way to school."

"But I let you off right in front of the building."

"I dropped the box."

Megan watched him, waiting for more. Gina had padded those cookies with so much plastic wrap and paper that Robby could have dropped the box off the roof of the school and the cookies might have survived unscathed. "What did you do with the box?"

"Threw it away."

"Show me."

"But they're only crumbs now."

"Show me."

Reluctantly, Robby led her toward a garbage can on the edge of the playground. He stopped a few feet away and pointed. With her thumb and first finger, Megan gingerly moved aside wadded-up brown paper lunch bags, school assignments on lined paper, and crumbled candy wrappers until she uncovered the box. She stooped down, placed it on the ground, and lifted the lid. Inside it was just as Robby had said: Each cookie had been pulverized into crumbs until their original shapes were completely obliterated. Some of the crumbs had been compressed into piles, and in these she found the impression of the sole of a shoe.

She took a deep breath and rose, returning the box to the garbage can. "Who did this?"

Robby shrugged.

"One of the other kids?" She recalled the name of the sixth-grade terror who had stolen his lunchbox the previous month. "Was it Kenny?"

He shook his head.

Megan was quiet for a moment. "Did you do it?"

Robby held perfectly still, which told her all she needed to know.

"Let's go." She took his clothing bag in one hand and placed the other arm around his shoulders, and led him back to the car.

The drive to Dayton took more than twenty minutes, and Megan used the time to tell Robby, as she did every day, some of the interesting things that had happened at work. Eventually, perhaps because of the familiarity of the routine, he relaxed and told her about the school parade and his class party. He didn't mention the cookies, and neither did she. She didn't have the heart to scold him for destroying Gina's present; in fact, she thought she might have done the same in his place.

They arrived at Meadowbrook Village Retirement Community to find a high-rise apartment building surrounded by several one-story condos, four units to a building. They were set back into a woods, giving them an air of privacy despite their closeness. Vinnie's condo was the farthest from the parking lot, as Megan and Robby discovered as they walked from building to building searching for the right number.

Vinnie answered the door dressed in a blue-and-white-checked dress and a red yarn wig. Two bright red circles were painted on her thin cheeks. "Come in, come in," she said, ushering them inside. She hugged Megan. "Hello, dear. I've missed you."

"I missed you, too," Megan said, surprised by how much. Suddenly she felt a wave of nostalgia for camp—for the freedom and friendship and peace it had brought her. She wished all the other Elm Creek Quilters lived close enough so that they, too, could have come to the party.

Vinnie turned to Robby. "You must be Robby. I'm Vinnie, but you can call me Nana. I don't know anyone your age who doesn't call me Nana."

"Nice to meet you," Robby said, shaking her hand. If he was startled to be conversing with an eighty-two-year-old dressed as a Raggedy Ann doll, he hid it well.

"Let's see. What are you supposed to be? Now, don't tell me. Let me guess." Vinnie put her hands on his shoulders and spun him around slowly, inspecting his costume. "Are you one of those rangers, one of those Power Rangers?"

"You're a few years behind the times," Megan said. "They're not in anymore."

"I'm Batman."

"Oh, of course!" Vinnie shook her head helplessly. "I'm afraid I don't keep up with my superheroes as well as I should. If your mother had dressed as Robin I would have known right away." Her eyes went to Megan. "What exactly are you?"

"I'm almost afraid to let you guess."

"Are you Betsy Ross? No, you'd be carrying a flag. Are you a suffragette?"

"No, I'd be carrying a picket sign."

"Or a ballot box." Vinnie studied her for a moment longer, then sighed. "I'm afraid you'll have to tell me."

"Elizabeth Bennett, from *Pride and Prejudice*?" Megan had a feeling she'd be repeating that line many times that night.

"Of course," Vinnie said, but she still looked puzzled. At that moment, a buzzer sounded somewhere out of sight, just as the doorbell rang. "Oops, my brownies are done. Will you get the door?" Vinnie asked as she hurried off down the hallway. "It's probably Adam."

"Sure." To her annoyance, Megan felt a flutter of nervousness at the prospect of seeing him again. She hung back and let Robby open the door. On the doorstep stood the same brown-haired man from camp and the diner, almost unrecognizable in a fifteenth- or sixteenth-century-style cape, leggings, and plumed hat. In one hand he carried a telescope; with the other, he doffed his plumed hat, and smiled.

He looked endearingly ridiculous, and Megan suppressed a smile. "Adam? Is that you?"

"At your service." He replaced the hat and came inside. "Hello there," he greeted Robby. "Hey, don't I know you? You look familiar." He frowned. "You resemble—but no, that couldn't be it."

Robby was interested. "Who?"

"Well, I was going to say you look like the famous millionaire Bruce Wayne, but anyone can see you're Batman." Adam shook his hand. "It's an honor to meet you. I admire your work."

Robby grinned and took off his mask.

Aghast, Adam flung up an arm to shield his eyes. "Don't do that! You'll give away your secret identity."

"I'm not really Batman," Robby explained. "This is just my Halloween costume. I'm Robby Donohue."

"Of course." Adam smacked his forehead with his palm. "Halloween. I forgot."

Robby grinned, recognizing that Adam was pretending but going along with the joke. "Who are you?" he asked.

"Guess."

Megan saw Robby's gaze travel from the plumed hat to the leggings to the telescope. "Christopher Columbus?"

"Not a bad guess, but that's not it." He raised his eyebrows at Megan. "Care to try?"

She had been about to guess Christopher Columbus, too, but she noticed the deliberate way he held his telescope and said, "This is a long shot, but how about Copernicus?"

"Very good," he said, impressed. "Wrong, but close. I'm Galileo. Most of my students thought I was supposed to be one of the Three Musketeers."

Robby's face screwed up in puzzlement. "Wouldn't you need a sword or something?"

"Exactly. That's what I told them. Can you imagine a musketeer whacking people with a telescope? He wouldn't get very far that way."

Robby laughed, then tugged at Megan's hand. "Mom's turn. Guess who she is. No one else knew." He looked up at his mother. "Can I give him a hint?"

"No hints," Adam said. He studied Megan's costume, looking her up and down until she felt her cheeks growing warm. "Are you Jane Austen?"

Megan's jaw nearly dropped. "I can't believe it."

"Am I right?"

"No, but that's the closest anyone's come all day. I'm supposed to be Elizabeth Bennett." With a self-conscious laugh, she twirled around in her long dress. "I guess I should have chosen something less obscure."

"No, you look beautiful."

Robby grinned up at her, nodding so that Megan grew flustered and quickly changed the subject. "Do all the teachers dress up at your school?"

"Not all," Adam said with a shrug, and Megan guessed that only those with a sense of humor did. She wondered what he was like as a teacher. She suspected he was one of those whom the students liked, even when he graded tough and pushed them to work harder than they ever had before.

Vinnie joined them then, purse in hand. She hugged her grandson and raised her cheek for him to kiss. Then she declared that they had better get over to the clubhouse for the party before all the food was gone, and she shooed them outside.

The clubhouse was in the lobby of the high-rise, and it had been decorated with black and orange streamers, jack-o'-lanterns, and cardboard cutouts of black cats and ghosts. The other residents and their children had already gathered there and had seated themselves at tables covered with orange-and-white-checked tablecloths. Costumed grandchildren darted among the tables, and Robby looked after them longingly as Vinnie led her guests through the refreshment line and to an unoccupied table. Robby hastily ate one cookie, claimed to be full, and ran off to join several young vampires, princesses, and Jedi Masters in a game of tag.

Megan kept one eye on Robby while chatting with Vinnie and Adam. Vinnie found frequent excuses to leave them alone while she hurried off to greet one friend or another. Megan smiled, watching her travel among clusters of friends, just as she had every day at quilt camp.

"Why are you smiling?" Adam asked.

"I enjoy watching Vinnie have a good time."

"So do I." They both watched as Vinnie and two other women burst into laughter at some joke. "After my grandfather died a few years ago, I wondered if I'd ever see her like this again."

"I'm sorry," Megan said, turning to face him. "I knew Vinnie had lost her husband, but I had no idea how recently."

"That's why she moved here. She couldn't stand being alone in the house they had shared for so long." Adam's eyes were on his grandmother. "They married young, right before my grandfather was sent overseas in World War Two. Each was the other's first love."

"It's hard to lose your first love," Megan said, thinking of

Keith. Then she remembered what Vinnie had told her about Adam, and said, "Oh, I'm sorry."

"About what?"

"Vinnie told me about your . . . situation. About your fiancée."

"Oh." Adam let out a wry laugh. "I guess I should have expected that. I imagine everyone at camp knows?"

Megan nodded apologetically. "I didn't mean to dredge up unhappy memories."

"It's okay, really. Besides, Natalie wasn't my first love."

"She wasn't?"

"No. Before her I was in love with a beautiful brown-eyed girl named Michelle. She was the love of my life. Of course, we were only in the fifth grade at the time, so our relationship consisted mostly of holding hands at school roller-skating parties and claiming to hate each other."

Megan couldn't help smiling. "How did it end?"

"She left me for a sixth-grader with a moped."

Megan laughed. Just then Robby ran over to grab another cookie and to ask Adam to be his partner in the three-legged race. Adam good-naturedly agreed, and Robby led him off.

Vinnie returned then, and took her seat with a happy sigh. "Sorry I left you alone for so long. I trust my grandson is behaving himself?" Without waiting for an answer, she patted Megan on the hand and said, "Now, catch me up on all the latest news. Have you heard from that ex-husband of yours?"

Except for the Halloween present Gina had sent on his behalf, she hadn't, so Megan had little progress to report on her quest to involve him in Robby's life. "I think the Challenge Quilt will be one block short," she said.

"Nonsense. You're trying, and that's all we expect you to do. The rest is up to Keith," Vinnie said. "Have you heard from any of the others recently?"

Vinnie knew about Donna's success in getting Lindsay to return to college, but Grace owed her a letter and so she had not yet heard about the true identity of Justine's older man. Vinnie listened, wide-eyed, as Megan filled her in. Afterward, she lamented, "Such interesting news, and I'm the last to know. Why didn't Grace tell me?"

"If you were online, she would have," Megan said, although Vinnie had often declared that she and computers didn't get along and that she had no intention of setting fingers to keyboard in this lifetime. Now, however, she looked undecided, and said she'd think about it.

"Did Julia ever get an E-mail address?" Vinnie asked.

"If she did, I don't know it. I don't think she's much of a letter writer."

"I've written to her five times, and all I get back are these silly form letters and autographed pictures. The same letter, the same photo, each time."

Megan laughed. "I bet that's the same letter and photo I received. I only tried once, though."

"Did you notice the return address? It was some agency in Burbank. I don't remember the name offhand, but I know it was wasn't the mailing address she gave us."

Megan hadn't noticed. "Do you think she isn't getting our mail? Maybe she just doesn't want to write back."

"Nonsense. She enjoyed herself at camp with us, I'm sure of it. And I don't think she has so many friends that she can afford to ignore the four of us."

"What makes you think she doesn't have friends?"

Vinnie shrugged. "Instinct, I suppose. The way she hung around the outside of our circle and never seemed quite comfortable with us, as if she expected us to send her away at any moment. I think our Julia is a bit lost, the poor girl."

Megan pondered this in silence. Via E-mail, she and Donna had decided that Julia's silence was intentional, that the Hollywood superstar had forgotten them as soon as her plane left Pennsylvania. Now she felt ashamed of their assumptions. "What should we do?"

"I suppose we'll have to wait to hear from her," Vinnie said. "But if she thinks we're ignoring her, we might be waiting a long time."

Just then, a young woman wearing a Meadowbrook Village name tag stepped to the front of the room and announced that it was time to award prizes for the best costumes. Robby and Adam returned to the table, discussing strategies for the rest of the games. They had come in third from last in the three-legged race, but were determined to stage a comeback. As prizes were announced in two divisions, one for the residents and one for the children, Megan watched Robby and smiled to herself. His eyes lit up as he and Adam whispered their plans, and he had looked so delighted as he played with the other kids. She wished he could have that joy every day of his life, the pleasure and security of knowing he was liked and wanted. He deserved that much, after what his father had put him through.

Vinnie and Robby won prizes for their costumes—Vinnie for Prettiest, and Robby for Most Heroic. In fact, Megan realized, every resident and child was awarded something, which meant that near the end of the list, some of the categories became rather far-fetched, such as Most Scientific and Biggest Mask. Vinnie's prize was a gift certificate to the residents' holiday craft sale, which would be held in December, and Robby, like all the children, won a small plastic jack-o'-lantern filled with candy.

It was near Robby's bedtime by the time the party began to wind down, but since it was a Friday and Robby didn't have school the next day, Megan agreed to Robby's request to stay until the end. Afterward, Vinnie invited them back to her condo for coffee—or hot chocolate, in Robby's case—and some of the brownies she had baked. At first Megan begged off, citing the drive back to Monroe and the piles of treats Robby had eaten already. "I only had two cookies and a popcorn ball," Robby protested. "That's hardly anything. I'm starving."

"You wouldn't send a starving child home without one more

treat, would you?" Vinnie asked. She and Robby looked up at Megan with expressions of mournful hope, so similar that she had to laugh.

"All right," she said. "One small brownie, and you'll drink milk instead of hot chocolate."

Robby let out a cheer and slipped his hand into hers. As they left the clubhouse, though, his jubilance seemed to fade. Megan hoped it was only because he was growing tired, and not that he had suddenly remembered Jason's party, which was likely just finishing.

Back at the apartment, Vinnie and Adam went to the kitchen to fix coffee while Megan helped Robby hang up his coat. He was unusually quiet considering his recent excitement, so Megan took her time, waiting for him to speak.

"Mom?" he finally said. "Why did the kids here at the party like me and the kids at school don't?"

Megan felt a pang of sadness. "I don't know why the kids at school act the way they do, honey." She knelt beside him and brushed his hair out of his eyes. "But it's not your fault. The kids here liked you, right? So do the kids from soccer. That proves that you're a likable, fun kid, someone any sensible person would want for a friend."

He looked at her, unbelieving. "*Am* I fun?"

"Of course you are," she exclaimed. "You're the most fun of any kid I know. You were fun even before you were born."

Robby frowned, dubious. "How could I be fun before I was born?"

Megan rocked back on her heels. "When I was pregnant with you, we used to play games."

"Uh-*uh.*"

"It's true. I called one of them the Kicking Game. You would kick and I would push back, gently, just like this." She touched him softly on the stomach. "And you would kick back, and I'd push back, and we go back and forth just like that. And sometimes your dad would rest his head on my stomach and talk to

you, and once you kicked him right in the nose!" Robby grinned.
"It didn't hurt, of course. You were so little."

"What else did I do?"

"Well, sometimes I would lie on my back and place my hand
flat on my stomach, like this, and you would press up against it."
She remembered thinking at the time that it felt like her baby was
curling up in her palm for comfort. "You had a sense of humor,
too. Sometimes I would try to let other people feel you moving
around. As soon as you starting kicking, I would call for everyone
to come running, but as soon as someone else put their hand on
my belly, you would hold still. As soon as they lifted their hand,
you would kick. So I'd say, 'The baby's moving! Come back!' but
when they did—"

"I held still?"

"Oh, so you remember now?" She tickled him under the chin
until he laughed. "Everyone thought I was making it up, you little
goof. You made your mom look pretty silly."

"Sorry," Robby said, but he didn't look sorry. He looked delighted.

"You were fun then, and you're fun now." Megan hugged him
tightly and made a silent promise that she would figure out something, some way to get the kids at school to give him a chance.

"Let's go see Vinnie before she thinks we got lost," she said.
She released him and rose, only to find Adam standing at the end
of the hall, watching them. Her heart thumped, and she wondered how much he had overheard.

"Nana wants to know if you'd like regular or decaf." Adam's
voice was quiet, and he reached out to ruffle Robby's hair as the
boy passed him in search of Vinnie.

"Either one is fine with me."

"Robby's having trouble in school?"

Megan shrugged and felt tears pricking her eyes again. "You
know how kids are. They have a pack mentality, and unfortunately, Robby's the one they decided to pick on."

"But he's such a great kid."

"I know that. Of course, I'm biased." She tried to laugh. "Don't worry about it. It's no big deal."

Adam came closer, studying her. "It seems like a big deal to you. And to Robby."

Suddenly weary, Megan dropped the pretense. "It is. It's breaking my heart. And it doesn't help that his father . . ." She broke off. She didn't want to talk about Keith, not to Adam. "If only I could figure out some way to help him."

"Have you spoken with his teachers?"

"No." Megan remembered then that he was a teacher, and felt a stirring of hope. Maybe Adam had known other children like Robby, and would know how to help him.

"His teacher might be able to give you more information. Tell you things Robby won't."

Megan was taken aback. "Robby tells me everything."

"No third-grade boy tells his mother everything." Adam smiled sympathetically. "Trust me. I used to be one. He knows you hurt when he hurts, and he might be trying to protect you."

It had never occurred to Megan that Robby might worry about her feelings. "I'll talk to his teacher," she said.

"Good." He placed a hand on her shoulder. "Come on. Nana's dying to show you some of her quilts."

They joined Vinnie and Robby in the living room, where they enjoyed their dessert and talked about the party. Though at first he seemed too wound up to rest, Robby soon fell asleep on the sofa, his head in his mother's lap. Megan stroked his hair as she, Vinnie, and Adam spoke softly so as not to wake him. Later Vinnie brought out several of her quilt projects for Megan and Adam to admire, then mentioned casually, "Adam is a quilter, too, you know."

Megan looked at him in surprise. "No kidding?" She had never met a man who quilted.

"I've made two quilts," Adam admitted, embarrassed. "They weren't very good."

"Of course they were," Vinnie protested. "If you stuck with it, you could be very good. Not as good as I am, but still, not too bad."

"They were for school," Adam explained. "We were working on tessellations in geometry class, and I had my students piece quilt blocks that used tessellating shapes."

"He likes to use examples from real life," Vinnie added. "Otherwise his students pester him with 'When are we ever going to need to know this?' every time he teaches them something new."

"Some still say that," Adam said. "But now they also ask, 'When am I ever going to make a quilt?'"

Vinnie laughed so loudly that Robby stirred. Megan glanced at her watch and couldn't believe how much time had passed. With regret, she told Vinnie she had to get Robby home. She helped Adam carry the dishes to the kitchen, then collected Robby's treats and woke him. "It's time to go home, sweetheart," she murmured in his ear. He nodded sleepily and said good-bye to Vinnie. When he called her Nana, Vinnie broke into broad grin and hugged him. She hugged Megan, too, and whispered that she hoped they'd see each other again soon.

Adam walked her to the car, a half-asleep Robby between them. They helped him into the front passenger seat, then Megan went around to her side. "Well," she said. "It was nice seeing you." She extended her hand.

"It was nice seeing you, too." He held her hand for a moment before releasing it. "If I can think of some way to help Robby, I'll let you know."

"Thanks."

"I could call you. . . ." He hesitated. "Or maybe you'd rather have me tell my grandmother, and have her call you?"

"You can call. Vinnie has my number."

Adam smiled. "Great. I'll get it from her."

Megan nodded, trying to keep her teeth from chattering in the late October chill that had settled in after nightfall. Adam noticed and said, "I guess you'd better go." Megan nodded again and got into the car. Adam shut the door for her, then stood on the sidewalk and watched as they drove away.

Robby woke in time to wave good-bye. "I like Adam and Nana," he told her.

"So do I."

"I think Adam likes you."

Megan felt a jolt. How would Robby feel if Adam did? How would she feel? Keeping her voice casual, she asked, "Why do you say that?"

"He said you were beautiful."

"I think he was talking about my costume."

"No, I remember. He said, 'You look beautiful.'"

Megan didn't know what to say. "He was probably just being nice."

"Whatever you say, Mom," Robby said in such a world-weary tone that she had to laugh. She reached over and tousled his hair as he grinned and tried to duck away.

As Robby dropped off to sleep again, Megan thought about Adam. It had been a long time since anyone but her parents had told her she looked beautiful. She wondered if he meant it. He seemed sincere enough, and if he had been trying to flatter her, he could have done better than that. Keith knew how to lay on the charm, and lay it on thick. Within ten minutes of conversation, he could have any woman feeling as if she were the most remarkable person in the universe. Unfortunately, Keith would make every woman in the room feel that way, even when his wife was watching.

How had Keith changed from the loving husband who played the Kicking Game with his unborn son to the sort of man who chafed under the yoke of marital fidelity? Or had he always had a wandering eye? Was her sense of judgment so impaired that she had overlooked such a significant flaw, or had she deliberately ignored it, hoping he would change?

She supposed she would never know for certain—but she would never make that mistake again.

Nana was waiting for Adam just inside the door. "Well?"

"Well what?"

"What did you think?"

Adam feigned ignorance. "About what?"

"Don't torment me. About Megan. What did you think of her?"

"She seems like a very lovely woman."

"And pretty."

He had noticed. "That, too." He bent forward to kiss his grandmother on the cheek, careful to avoid the red Raggedy Ann circle she had painted there. "I have to get going. Thanks for the party. I had a good time."

She scowled at him. "That's all you're going to tell me?"

"That's all," he said, cheerful but firm. Anything he told Nana would be reported back to Megan, and probably half the residents of Meadowbrook Village.

"Well, take her phone number, at least," she said grumpily, handing him an index card with Megan's name and phone number, as well as her postal and E-mail addresses.

"Thanks, Nana."

"Will you at least tell me if you like her?" Nana pleaded as he left.

"I like her," he said. "Good night." He kissed her again and shut the door.

As he drove home to Cincinnati, Adam admitted to himself that he'd had a much better time than he had expected. He had come to the party mostly to appease his grandmother, and only partly because the green-eyed woman from the diner intrigued him. He liked the way she had agreed to share the apple pie with him, as if she were a decent, down-to-earth person and expected him to be one, too. In Megan's place, Natalie would have given him a cold, withering glare and written him off as a lunatic. Natalie had certain ideas of what was proper and what was not, and splitting desserts with strangers would definitely fall into the latter category. After years of trying to please Natalie and soothe her unpredictable temper, Megan's willingness to take a chance had been refreshing.

Should he call her? He wasn't sure Megan wanted that. She had been friendly enough, but there had been a reluctance about her, as if she were afraid of bruising herself. Considering what Nana had told him about her ex-husband, Adam wasn't surprised. He was resuming dating rather gingerly himself, and he and Natalie had been together only five years. How much more difficult it must be for Megan, who had married this man and had a child with him, only to be betrayed. At least Natalie hadn't been dishonest with him; she had always been perfectly clear about what she wanted, and equally clear about her displeasure when he failed to deliver.

The breakup had been coming for months. In hindsight, he supposed he knew Natalie was going to leave him long before she did.

They had met at a wedding. One of Adam's cousins was the bride; Natalie was a friend of the groom. He was first attracted to her dark-haired beauty, and later, her unpredictability and passion for life drew him in deeper. When they were together she made him feel that like her, he, too, was exciting and passionate. Even years later, when infatuation grew into love and he thought they understood each other as well as any two separate people could, he still wasn't sure why Natalie had been interested in him at the start. She said his personality, especially his kindness and honesty, had drawn her to him, but he wondered about that, since those had been the very things that had later driven her away.

He had been teaching in the parochial school system for several years by then and had always been open about his plans to remain in the profession. Natalie had recently been hired as an assistant to the associate buyer for an upscale department store chain whose flagship store was in downtown Cincinnati, but her ambitions aimed higher. She had a six-year plan to become the principal buyer for the entire chain, and a ten-year plan to be named a vice president.

Before he met Natalie, Adam had spent weekday evenings quietly at home, grading papers and planning the next day's lessons. An eventful night might involve attending one of the school sporting events or chaperoning a dance. Natalie, meanwhile, took business associates out for drinks, hosted dinner parties, or attended social events where she would be likely to brush shoulders with the "right people," as she called them. To please her, and because he loved her and wanted to be with her, Adam became her willing escort. He was proud of her beauty, and the ease with which she could charm even the most reserved or withdrawn. If the conversations at these gatherings tended toward the trivial, the irrelevant, the shallow, he could ignore that for her sake. As Natalie said, such socializing was important for her career, and if rising in her company would make her happy, Adam wanted to help in any way he could.

He knew his friends thought them an unlikely pair. In the past Adam had always dated women who had chosen the helping professions, women with a strong sense of social justice and commitment to social change—women more like himself. Natalie's beauty they understood well enough, but not her craving for material signs of status and wealth. Still, they were his friends and accepted his choices, and always treated Natalie courteously enough. They did not know how Natalie picked them apart behind their backs, criticizing their clothing, their cars, what she called their appalling lack of ambition. Only Adam's former college roommate, a gentle man who had become a Benedictine monk, cautioned him against rushing into a lifetime commitment. "Don't lose sight of who you really are," John advised, and said nothing more on the subject.

But John's words stayed with Adam, and he began to reflect on what he became when he was with Natalie. He felt as if he were playing a role to please her, setting aside everything that truly mattered to him. He didn't like what that said about him, especially since compartmentalizing his life like that contradicted every value he tried to instill in his students.

They had been engaged nearly eight months by then, and had already completed pre-Cana premarital counseling. Natalie and her mother had whirled about in a frenzy of wedding preparations, leaving Adam feeling more like a spectator than one of the principal participants. But it was not embarrassment or anxiety that kept him from suggesting they reconsider or at least postpone the ceremony. He still loved Natalie, although he knew they weren't right for each other, and he couldn't bear to lose her. Besides, he had asked her to marry him, and he was a man of his word.

He supposed he ought to be grateful that Natalie had acted more decisively than he had. She had spared them both a world of pain and recriminations.

He hoped Natalie would be happy. He figured she would; she knew how to get what she wanted. He was less certain of himself.

He missed Natalie the most at times like these, when he was pulling into the driveway of his darkened house. He had left the porch light off to signal his absence to trick-or-treaters, but the house looked so lonely and forlorn he wished he had left it on. Once he had thought that Natalie would live there with him, an assumption that in hindsight seemed ridiculous, since his was a small, older home, and never had been much to her liking. It occurred to him then that at that moment, Megan might also be arriving home with no warm welcome waiting from someone she loved. But she had Robby. He was glad for her that she was not alone.

When he went to the kitchen to check his messages, he noticed that his answering machine was flashing a steady pattern of two blinks. His first, foolish thought was that Megan had called, but as he pressed the play button he remembered that he had not given her his number.

He listened to two hang-up calls, then shook his head and re-wound the tape. Nana, he guessed. She loathed answering machines almost as much as computers, and refused to leave messages for him. She had probably called as he was en route to her home to make sure he wouldn't be late, as he had been when he had picked her up at Elm Creek Manor.

Suddenly cheerful, Adam carried the newspaper into the living room and settled down to read. Nana was something else. Even from miles away, she had welcomed him home.

Julia was enjoying her day off, so when the phone rang, she groaned, turned the page of her magazine, and allowed her assistant to pick up in the other room. She did a few deep-breathing exercises to ward off a tension headache, which in the past few weeks had become a nearly daily occurrence. Perhaps it was an overstatement to say she was enjoying her day off when in truth, relief was her strongest emotion. Filming had not been going well, and Julia needed this day away from the set to relax. Today she wanted to do no work at all, unless reading a copy of *Quilter's Newsletter Magazine* counted as research for the role of Sadie.

Since the first script meeting, there had been a decidedly negative atmosphere on the set. Julia now realized she had taken the collegial feeling of the *Family Tree* cast and crew for granted. Deneford was a stubborn tyrant of a director; Samantha, as Young Sadie, seemed to have misplaced her brain most days; and Rick was a preening peacock. Aside from Julia herself, the only members of the cast who were behaving themselves were the extras and the two young boys playing her sons. Worse than the actors, if less noticeable, was Ellen, who moped around the studio in a state of perpetual gloom, muttering about the script changes Deneford continued to demand of her. To Julia's consternation, and for reasons she couldn't fathom, Ellen had selected her as her special confidante, which meant that Julia was privy to every minute detail of her despair, delivered in tearful monologues as Ellen paced around in Julia's trailer. Yesterday she had spent the better part of an hour bemoaning the title change.

"*Prairie Vengeance?*" she had cried in disbelief. "There's no vengeance in this movie. What is Deneford thinking?"

Patiently, Julia reminded her what the director had said at the morning meeting. "He's trying to capitalize on the success of *Jungle Vengeance.* Rick Rowen's agent is thinking about having him do an entire *Vengeance* series."

"This film doesn't belong in that series," Ellen said. "Can't you see what they're doing? They're turning this picture into a vehicle for Rick, and that takes away the focus from Sadie. This story is supposed to be about Sadie."

Julia did feel a twinge of apprehension at that. She had heard rumors that Rick's name would be appearing above the title, which she wouldn't mind, as long as hers preceded his. Lately, though, she had heard other rumors that Rick's name would appear there alone. She wondered if her name would be placed below the title, or worse yet, buried somewhere after Samantha's.

But she shook off her doubts and said, "You have to expect these things. A film is a collaborative effort, but the director's vision has priority. We all have to adapt for the greater good of the final project."

"But we're getting so far from my great-grandmother's diaries."

"You're young, Ellen. You have to pay your dues. Just cooperate and don't make any enemies, and when *Prairie Vengeance* is a success, you'll have much more control over your later projects."

Ellen accepted this, as she did all of Julia's advice, with resignation about the way things were and gratitude that Julia took the time to explain them. Julia had to admit Ellen's behavior was rather flattering. Although Ellen was only a writer and not an actress, Julia almost felt as if Ellen were her protégé. In fact, it was better that Ellen was only a writer, as Julia had always been suspicious of the young starlets nipping at her heels, begging for advice, no doubt longing for the day when they could steal her roles and send her tumbling into the netherworld of rare guest appearances on sitcoms. Ellen, on the other hand, was obviously no threat, so Julia could afford to be generous.

But not today. She snuggled back into the sofa cushions and tried to lose herself in an article about the Smithsonian Institution's collection of antique quilts. Today she simply did not feel like discussing the capricious nature of the movie industry with Ellen, or with anyone else, for that matter.

Her assistant entered the room, the cordless phone in her hand. "Miss Merchaud, there's an urgent call for you."

"From whom?" *Please,* she thought, *don't say Ellen.*

"It's Miss Henderson again, ma'am."

Julia let her head fall back against the pillow. "Did you tell her I'm home?"

Reluctantly, her assistant nodded.

Sighing impatiently, Julia sat up. "Lucy, you and I need to have a serious talk." Lucy gulped, handed her the phone, and hurried from the room.

Julia took a moment to compose herself before putting the phone to her ear. "Ellen, dear. What a lovely surprise."

"Miss Merchaud?" Ellen's voice was so quiet the bustle in the background nearly drowned her out. Where was she calling from, the runway at LAX?

"Yes, it's me."

"There's a problem."

Naturally. "Would you mind speaking up?" she said, a little sharply.

"I can't. I'm on the set, and . . ." Ellen fell silent, and when she spoke again, her voice was an anxious whisper. "I can't talk now, but you need to get down here right away."

"They aren't filming any of my scenes today," Julia reminded her.

"Not yet they aren't," Ellen said darkly. "Just get down here. Please." With that, she hung up.

Uneasy, Julia turned off the phone and set it aside. Not yet they aren't? What was that cryptic remark supposed to mean?

Whatever it was, it couldn't be good, Julia decided as she hurried to her bedroom to change.

She had given her driver the day off, so after telling Lucy she was going out for a while, she drove her Porsche as fast as she could down PCH to the studio. Fortunately, traffic was relatively light, so not quite forty minutes later, she was driving through the front gates and parking behind the sound stage reserved for *Prairie Vengeance*'s indoor shots. According to the production schedule, Deneford planned to shoot several of Samantha's and Rick's scenes that day, including a love scene Deneford had added to the original script. As she slipped inside the darkened building, Julia wondered if that was what Ellen was so worked up about. If so, Julia would finally give her the dressing down she deserved. Neophyte or not, she ought to know better than to drag Julia all the way down there merely to vent.

But when Julia reached the set for the interior of the farmhouse to find Samantha dressed as Sadie and sitting at the quilting frame as she recited her lines, Julia's breath caught in her throat. Those were Julia's lines; that was the quilt Sadie made to raise money to purchase seed wheat after their last crop was lost to a grasshopper plague.

"What is going on here?" she shrilled.

"Cut," Deneford called out sharply. He looked around to glare at whoever had been foolish enough to ruin his shot, but when his eyes fell on Julia, his anger was immediately replaced by a mask of bland nonchalance. "Julia," he said, rising to greet her. "What brings you in today?"

"Why is she doing my scene?"

Deneford placed his hands on her shoulders in an attempt to calm her. "Julia, let's go to my office and talk."

Julia wouldn't budge. "I asked you a question," she said, raising her voice and not caring who heard her. In the corner of her eye, she saw Ellen emerge from the shadows, her expression a mix of indignation and triumph. If not for her, Julia would have shown up on Monday completely unaware of Deneford's duplicity, and as for that conniving little Samantha . . .

"We're just rehearsing," Deneford said soothingly. "Just to see how it plays."

"What good does it do to rehearse my scenes without me? Unless they aren't my scenes anymore."

"Okay. Look. I'm sorry you had to find out this way, but we're shifting some of your scenes to Young Sadie. Just a few of the quilting scenes, nothing major."

"Nothing major?" Julia gaped at him. The quilting scenes were among the most important in the entire film. "Do you mind telling me why?"

"To be honest—"

"I certainly wish you would be."

"To be honest, the quilting close-ups look more realistic when Samantha does them. Frankly, Julia, I know you say you're an experienced quilter, but Samantha's better. It's that simple."

"I like quilting," Samantha said dreamily. Sure enough, as Julia watched, Samantha deftly worked the needle through the three layers held fast in the quilt frame, as swiftly as any of the teachers at Elm Creek Quilt Camp. Julia was too far away to see, but with a sinking heart, she suspected Samantha's stitches were similarly tiny and perfect. "My grandma taught me when I was just a little girl."

You're still a little girl, Julia almost retorted, but realized just in time that emphasizing the difference in their ages probably wouldn't help her much.

Deneford took Julia by the arm and steered her toward the exit. "It's only three scenes," he said as they walked through the darkened hallway. "The material we've added with you and Rick together will more than make up the difference, and the new material is better. Trust me."

That was the last thing Julia intended to do. "Which three scenes?" she asked, thinking. *Please, not the quilting bee.*

"This one, and the scene after the neighbor's barn burns down, and the quilting bee."

Silently, Julia swore. "I want the quilting bee," she said, her voice shaking. She hated to beg, but that scene was *hers*. She needed it. "You know as well as I that Samantha has the emotional depth of a potted cactus. She can't handle the dramatic shifts of that scene."

"She did fine when we shot it this morning."

Julia went cold. "This morning?" The quilting bee scene called for more than thirty minor characters and extras. To coordinate such a shoot required advance planning, hardly the spur-of-the-moment decision Deneford had implied only moments before. "That was no rehearsal back there, was it?"

"It was a rehearsal; Samantha needed one. But to answer your next question, yes, we will be filming that scene with her in the role of Sadie."

Julia forced air through her constricted throat. "I see." Another breath. "Then let me shoot the scene, too. You choose the superior performance. That's fair, don't you think?"

"No."

Julia stared at him. "What do you mean, no? Just no? You're not even—"

"Julia, why are you doing this to yourself?" He seemed genuinely puzzled. "Why make this more difficult than it has to be?"

Her thoughts in a whirl, Julia couldn't respond. When Deneford opened the door, she blinked in the bright sunlight and stepped outside. "We'll talk on Monday," he called after her, but she didn't acknowledge him. The door fell heavily shut behind her, and she walked to her car, numb.

She heard the door open and shut again, and then footsteps on the pavement. "Miss Merchaud," Ellen called out. Julia stopped and turned around, her movements mechanical. "What did he say? Did he change his mind?"

"He's going to use Samantha."

"That ignorant hack!"

"He's no hack." Julia's voice sounded wooden to her ears. "He has an Oscar and four Emmys. Or is it five? I don't remember—"

Ellen seized her shoulders. "Miss Merchaud, we can't let him ruin our movie."

"It isn't our movie," Julia said, Ellen's touch drawing her back to awareness. "You sold him your script. He owns it now. Whatever he wants to do, he can do."

Ellen looked close to tears. "I wish I'd never sent him a single page."

"At least you'll still receive credit for the screenplay."

"I don't know if I want it."

Suddenly Julia's own voice echoed in her thoughts: *A film is a collaborative effort,* she had told Ellen, *but the director's vision has priority. We all have to adapt for the greater good of the final project.* The memory taunted her, and she thought she might be ill.

She closed her eyes to still her churning stomach. *Breathe,* she ordered herself. When she opened her eyes again, Ellen was staring at her, worried. "Are you all right?"

Instead of answering, Julia said, "He'll know someone tipped me off. You better get back in there or he'll figure out it was you."

Ellen laughed bitterly. "He barely even notices when I'm there. I don't think he'll notice that I'm gone."

"I'm serious, Ellen. He could have you barred from the set."

Ellen looked taken aback. "He can't. It's my movie."

"It isn't your movie," Julia said, each word clear and emphatic. "It's his movie. Accept that, and make the best of it."

Ellen stared at her for a moment, then swallowed and nodded. She turned and hurried back into the building. Only after she was gone did Julia realize she had forgotten to thank Ellen for the warning.

As she drove home, her thoughts gradually became more clear. She would fight. It was a slim chance, but there might be something in her contract prohibiting this. The first thing she would do was call Ares and get him searching for a loophole.

But when she called, his assistant said he would be in meetings all day and wouldn't be available until tomorrow. "He has to check in sometime," she snapped, thinking of how Maury would interrupt a meeting, any meeting, to take her emergency calls. "Have him call me then." She slammed down the phone without waiting for a reply, and then, since Deneford and Ares were out of range, she kicked over a copper vase full of dried decorative grasses and sent it clattering across the gleaming hardwood floor. Now what was she supposed to do?

Suddenly inspiration struck. "Lucy, there's a mess in the parlor," she called out as she raced to her study. Samantha had replaced Julia because she was a better quilter. Well, that was a situation Julia could remedy. She yanked open her desk drawer and took out her folder of quilt camp notes. Near the bottom was the sheet of paper with Donna Jorgenson's address and phone number.

Julia sat down and rested her hands on her desk to compose herself. Very well. None of the Cross-Country Quilters had seen fit to contact her, and her injured pride had prevented her from reaching out to them. But now she needed Donna's help, and could wait no longer.

The phone rang twice before a girl's voice answered, "Hello?"

"Yes. May I speak with Mrs. Donna Jorgenson?"

"Hold on, please." There was a hollow sound, as if the mouthpiece had been covered, and then a muffled, "Mom, it's for you."

A moment later, a familiar voice said pleasantly, "Hello?"

"Donna?"

"Yes?"

"It's me. Julia." For a panicky moment she wondered if Donna would remember her. "From quilt camp."

"Julia?" Donna cried, delighted. "I can't believe it. It's so nice to hear from you. Where have you been? We all thought you fell off the face of the earth."

Was that so? "You could have written," Julia said, petulant.

"Are you kidding? We did! I wrote twice, Grace and Megan each wrote once, and Vinnie—well, gosh, she must be on her eighth or ninth letter by now. All we get back are these form letters and autographed pictures. Don't get me wrong; we're glad to get them, but honestly, how many identical photos do we need?" She laughed.

For the second time that day, Julia felt as if she had tumbled into a separate reality from the one she usually inhabited. "You wrote to me? At my home?"

"Well, I'm not sure. It's the address you gave us at camp. I assumed it was your home." Donna read off the address for Julia's home, not a digit out of place.

"I don't understand this."

"Neither did we, especially since that's not the address on the envelopes you sent us."

Donna recited a second address, but Julia only needed to hear the first word to realize what had happened. "That bastard."

"What? Who?"

"My agent." Somehow he'd arranged to have her mail routed to his office, and suddenly she understood who his accomplice must have been. "And my assistant. She gave him my personal mail."

"Why?"

"I don't know, but I'm going to find out, and then I'm going to fire her."

"Fire her?" Donna sounded horrified. "I'm sure there must be a logical explanation—"

"For stealing my mail?" Didn't Donna understand? All those weeks of feeling neglected and forgotten, and Lucy—with specific instructions to notify her the minute a letter from the Cross-Country Quilters arrived— "I have to fire her."

"Can't you just tell her not to do it again?" Donna begged. "Give her another chance. You're too nice a person to fire someone this close to the holidays."

Donna was wrong. Julia was not a nice person, and she was feeling especially not nice at the moment. But something in Donna's voice nagged at her, until, against her better judgment, she reluctantly said, "I'll get her side of the story first. I'm not promising anything, but I'll give her a chance to explain." And if Julia didn't like what Lucy had to say, *then* she'd fire her.

"I'm sure you'll be glad you did."

Julia doubted it, but she had bigger problems on her mind. "Donna, the reason I'm calling—"

"Yes?"

Donna's voice sounded so warm, so full of concern, that Julia's pride evaporated. "I need your help."

Eight

EGAN HAD been too busy to check her E-mail all day, so it wasn't until she was about to go home that she finally had a chance to download her messages. Several were waiting, including an exchange between Grace and Donna that had begun the day before, when Donna had written to announce that Julia was alive but facing problems with her agent and her director, not the least of which was having her personal mail misdirected. Today Grace responded:

TO: Megan.Donohue@rocketec.com,
    quiltmom@USAonline.com
FROM: Grace Daniels ‹danielsg@deyoung.org›
DATE: 8:14 AM PT 9 Nov
SUBJECT: Re: News from Julia

I'm glad she didn't forget us. Someone should tell Vinnie before she buries southern California beneath an avalanche of mail. We really have to get those two online.

Any thoughts on how we can help Julia with the movie problems?

Donna had written back:

We could fly down there and give her director a few good pokes with our needles.

Within minutes, Grace had answered:

I wish we could. I'd love to get out of town. You aren't going to believe this, but I agreed to let Gabriel come to Thanksgiving dinner. My sisters think I'm crazy, but Joshua dotes on his grandfather, and I didn't want to ruin the holiday for him.

Donna answered that she didn't envy Grace, but she didn't expect her own holiday to be much better. Lindsay and Brandon were coming for Thanksgiving dinner, which meant that Donna intended to put on a production worthy of Martha Stewart. "I have to make up for all these months of pretending the engagement would just go away if I ignored it," she wrote. "Lindsay sounds so stressed out lately, and I'm sure it's my fault. I have to stop acting like an evil mother-in-law before Brandon runs screaming for the hills."

Megan smiled and wrote:

Donna, honey, you are not an evil anything. But tell the truth, would you really mind if Brandon ran away?

She waited a few minutes just in case Donna was online and would respond quickly. When she checked her E-mail, a message downloaded:

TO: Megan.Donohue@rocketec.com
FROM: wagnera@rogerbacon.k12.oh.edu
DATE: 5:43 PM 9 Nov
SUBJECT: Checking in

So, how did the meeting go?

Megan felt a stirring of pleasure at the sight of the familiar address. Since Halloween, she and Adam had begun corresponding
by E-mail, and she usually heard from him several times a week.
They exchanged small talk, mostly, details about their work and
their plans for the weekends. Megan had discovered that Adam's
quirky sense of humor was just as amusing via E-mail, although
she found herself thinking she would have preferred to hear his
voice. Especially now, since the meeting he referred to had felt
more like an ambush than a parent-teacher conference.

When Megan had entered the classroom, she was surprised to
see the teacher was not alone. The man with her introduced himself as the school counselor. "I'm glad we're finally able to meet,"
he said, shaking her hand.

"Finally?" Megan said. The teacher and counselor exchanged a
look, and then it came out: In the past few months, they had sent
Robby home with three requests for a teacher-parent conference.

"Why didn't you mail them?" Megan managed to ask. "Why
didn't you phone me at work or at home?"

They explained that they would have, eventually, but unfortunately three postponements weren't unusual in these situations.

"And what kind of situation is that, exactly?" Megan asked.

Minor disciplinary problems, of course. If it had been something egregious, they hastened to assure her, she would have been
contacted immediately.

Megan sat numbly as they explained. Robby was a bright and
imaginative boy, but quieter than the others and somewhat withdrawn. Usually. Other times, he would tell wild, outlandish tales,
and when the other students teased him, he lashed out. He had

trouble controlling his anger, and sometimes he would have out-bursts with no apparent provocation. That was why they sus-pected some trouble at home.

They paused then, waiting for her to speak, and their scrutiny made Megan feel powerless and fearful. The look in their eyes sug-gested they had already decided she must be an unfit mother and were only looking for the evidence to support their conclusion. "Robby doesn't do anything like this at home," she stammered, just as she remembered Gina's cookies. "I mean, the usual child-hood disobedience, testing authority and such, but nothing like what you've described."

"That's not unusual," the counselor said. "What about Robby's father? He couldn't come today?"

"He lives in Oregon. We're divorced."

"I see." The counselor nodded and made some notes on a pad. "Does Robby have much contact with his father?"

"Very little since he moved away at the beginning of the sum-mer. Before then, they saw each other maybe once a month." Megan inhaled deeply to still the pounding of her heart. "My for-mer husband wasn't very good about keeping to the scheduled vis-itation agreement."

"Robby often tells stories about his father," the teacher said. "One week he's a secret service agent, the next he's a fighter pi-lot—"

"It seems likely his behavior problems are related to his father's absence," the counselor broke in. "Don't you agree, Mrs. Dono-hue?"

"I . . . yes, that seems likely." Megan could have told them that years ago. She counted to three silently before asking if they had any suggestions for how to help Robby. They recommended pro-fessional counseling to help him deal with his emotions, especially his anger at his father.

The teacher and counselor had seemed satisfied as she left, as if they had discharged their duties appropriately and now were free to turn their thoughts to other matters. They probably had no idea they had tapped into the deep spring of anxiety that welled up in the heart of every mother, that despite all her love and her best efforts she had failed her child. If she wanted to absolve herself of responsibility, she could shift the blame to Keith, but that would neither ease her conscience nor help her son. She was the custodial parent; she should have done more, somehow, to compensate for Keith's neglect.

Even now, after the initial shock of Robby's deceptions had dulled, just thinking of it threatened to bring on tears of frustration, so she kept her reply to Adam vague:

It was not especially helpful. I'll write more tomorrow.

Almost immediately, Adam responded:

Would you like to talk about it in person instead?

Megan's hands froze on the keyboard. She pictured him jumping into his car and racing to comfort her. It was an unexpectedly reassuring image, and for some reason that bothered her. She took a deep breath and wrote:

What did you have in mind?

Adam replied:

Dinner? There's a great Italian restaurant halfway between your place and mine. We could meet there Friday night at seven.

Megan's pulse quickened. He must mean just the two of them, because they could hardly discuss Robby with him present. She felt a strange mixture of pleasure and discomfort at the thought. A

Halloween party at Vinnie's was one thing, dinner alone quite another. She wasn't sure she was ready for that.

She glanced at the calendar to see if she was free, already knowing she was, and suddenly she thought of Gina and the baby she
was expecting. Keith had moved on with his life long ago, but
Megan had been stuck in the same place for years, wavering, uncertain. After all this time, if she were not yet ready to resume dating, it was because she had decided she preferred to be alone for
the rest of her life. Besides, this might not even be considered a
date. Adam knew she was Vinnie's friend, and since he worked
with children, his intentions were probably only professional.

She clenched and unclenched her hands to warm them and
typed:

Send me the directions. If my parents can watch Robby, I'd
like to come.

She clicked the mouse on Send before she could change her
mind.

November 11

Dear Vinnie,

*A thousand apologies for not writing to you sooner. You
are such a darling to send me ten letters although I never
wrote back! I can't imagine what you thought of me. I do
have an excuse: My agent told my assistant to forward him
all my fan mail because he didn't want it to "distract" me.
Can you imagine? I was more distracted by wondering why
I hadn't heard from any of my camp friends. Now the misunderstanding is all sorted out, or so I'm told, so if you write
to me again, I should receive your letter just fine.*

*The movie is not going well, unfortunately. The male
star is a spoiled brat, and the girl who plays Young Sadie is
as dizzy as the day is long. She also happens to be a talented*

quilter, which means that my director has shifted some of my scenes to her. I've been practicing until my fingertips bleed, but I don't know if I'll improve enough to hold on to my role. Keep your fingers crossed for me.

I haven't made much progress on the sampler quilt you and the others designed for me at camp because I've been practicing my hand-quilting instead. I did begin another Friendship Star block with your autumn leaf fabric, my small contribution to the Challenge Quilt. Now I feel as if I shouldn't be allowed to finish it until shooting ends, because I might be completely squeezed out of this picture if things don't turn around for me soon.

I hope all is well in Ohio.

Sincerely,
Julia

November 14

Dear Julia,

Testing, testing . . . This letter is for Julia Merchaud. If you are Julia's assistant or agent, stop reading and give this letter to Julia right away! I mean it, Nosy!

There. If you're still reading, you must be Julia. My goodness, it was nice to hear from you. I'm sorry the movie isn't going as well as you hoped. Chin up, honey. I've been watching old episodes of Family Tree *on Lifetime, and you're a wonderful actress. I didn't know you were the mother from* Home Sweet Home, *too! I used to watch that show all the time, and now I'm enjoying it again on Nick at Night. If I had put two and two together, I would have recognized you right away when we first met at lunch at camp. (I hope you've forgiven me for that.) Anyway, I can't imagine that any director with a brain in his head would let you get away, so keep practicing quilting, and I'm sure everything will work out fine. I can't wait to see the movie. I know it will be a big hit, because every quilter in America will go to see it. I'll be first in line in Dayton.*

I started my block for the Challenge Quilt, too, but I don't know if I should have. You know my challenge was to find a new girlfriend for my grandson. Well, after much thought, I decided that Adam and Megan would make a charming couple. I invited them and Megan's son, Robby, here for a Halloween party, and they seemed to hit it off, but now neither one will talk about the other, and it's driving me crazy. If Megan mentions him, would you please tell me? Even if she makes you promise not to? A grandmother has a right to know.

Well, that's enough for now. Keep me posted on the movie. I want to have time to pick out my outfit for Oscar night.

Your quilting buddy,
Vinnie

PS: This is some of my famous peanut-butter fudge. Share some with that sourpuss director of yours. It might sweeten him up.

PPS: Why did you pine away at the mailbox all these months instead of writing to us first?

Megan drove through a chilly drizzle to the restaurant, wondering if she'd made a mistake. As soon as she stepped inside, though, and the warm fragrances of fresh bread, olive oil, basil, and garlic enveloped her, she felt some of her nervousness disappear. It vanished completely when she saw Adam waiting. He wore a sport coat, which made her glad she had worn her favorite casual dress instead of slacks.

"What, no plumed hat this time?" she teased.

"Not today," he said, smiling. "You look very nice."

Megan thanked him. The hostess approached then and

showed them to a small, candlelit table in a secluded section of the restaurant. They chatted as they studied the menus, but while Adam seemed perfectly comfortable, Megan felt her earlier nervousness resurfacing. Silently she scolded herself to stop acting as if she were on a job interview and relax. What was the worst that could happen? They could have a miserable evening and might decide never to see each other again. She'd survived far worse.

It wasn't exactly the power of positive thinking, but somehow that realization put her at ease. By the time their salads were served, she felt as if she were enjoying a pleasant evening with a good friend. She liked the way Adam's eyes lit up when he talked about teaching, and the stories he told about his students soon had her laughing. She wished her son had a teacher like him.

Eventually the conversation turned to Robby, and Megan told Adam about the miserable conference. When she finished, Adam winced. "I hope you don't judge the entire teaching profession by those two."

"Of course I don't. But tell me, am I wrong to think they should have made more of an effort to contact me earlier?"

"In their place, I would have tried." He hesitated. "Did you ask Robby about the notes they sent home?"

"As soon as I got home. At first he said he lost them, but after I reminded him that he should have at least told me about them, I couldn't get another word out of him." She still couldn't believe her sweet son had lied to her. "I told him how important it was for us to be honest, and that no matter what, I would always love him. I don't know if he believed me or not."

Adam reached across the table and took her hand. "I'm sure he knows that. Anyone who sees the two of you together knows that."

"Then why did he lie to me?"

"To keep from getting in trouble. Because he didn't want you to talk to his teacher. There could be many reasons."

Adam's hand was warm and comforting around hers. "I did take their advice. Robby will begin seeing a counselor next week.

If nothing else, I think that will help him deal with his anger about his father."

Adam nodded, thoughtful, and then said carefully, "Is there any chance you might be able to get Keith more involved?"

"I don't know." Megan pulled her hand away and toyed with her fork, remembering their phone conversation. When she finally reached Keith, after three evenings of leaving unanswered messages, he had listened in silence as she described the situation and asked for his help.

"If you had let me have custody," Keith had said in a flat voice when she finished, "he wouldn't be in so much trouble now."

"You never asked for full custody." Megan said, taken aback. "I offered you joint custody. You said visiting on the weekends was enough."

"Well, what do you expect me to do now?"

"Can you come for a visit? Can he visit you, for Thanksgiving break, maybe?"

"Do you know what a pain it would be to try to get an airline ticket now?" Keith complained, "Look. I can't do this right now. Gina's baby is giving her terrible morning sickness. I can only concentrate on one crisis at time."

"Keith—"

"I'll call him. Okay? I'll call him soon." With that, Keith had hung up.

Gina's baby, Megan had thought as she replaced the receiver. Not *their* baby, or even *the* baby. Gina's. Keith would never learn.

Now, Megan looked across the table at Adam and tried to smile. "I don't think he's going to be much help. At least Robby has his grandfather. He's very busy, but they still spend quite a bit of time together."

"Have you thought about Big Brothers?"

"I looked into it, but there isn't a chapter in our town."

"I used to be a Big Brother," Adam said. "Just until last January, in fact, when my little brother moved out of state. I was going to sign up for a new one, but—"

When Adam didn't continue, Megan said, "But what?"

Adam looked sheepish. "But Natalie didn't want me to. She thought, with the wedding coming up and everything . . ."

Megan nodded. "I see." She was beginning to piece together a rather unflattering portrait of Natalie, and she wondered why anyone as nice as Adam would have chosen someone so unlike himself. "I suppose she thought you would be too busy."

Adam's face hardened. "Only too busy for the things that matter." Just as swiftly, the shadow passed, and he smiled again. "What do you think about me being Robby's Big Brother? I mean, not officially, through the organization, just informally."

The suggestion was so totally unexpected that Megan didn't know what to say. "Well—"

Adam held up his palms. "I have no ulterior motives, I swear," he said. "You can check me out if you want. All teachers at my school are investigated before they're hired, and I'm sure Big Brothers would be willing to provide an evaluation."

"It's not that," Megan said. "I . . . I just . . ." She studied him quizzically. "Would you really want to?"

"Sure. Robby's a great kid. We had a ball at the Halloween party." He took her hand again. "How about this: The three of us can go out together, and if we're getting along well and you agree, I'll ask Robby if he wants to do something the next weekend. If he says no, we'll forget the whole thing."

Megan considered the idea. As difficult as it was to admit it, she couldn't be everything to Robby, and a good friend, someone outside of the family, could become the confidant he needed. She had watched Robby and Adam together at the Halloween party, and had reflected on how well they got along. They could try it, she decided. If it didn't work out, she would call it off.

"If you're sure," Megan said. "Yes. Let's see what we can do."

Adam squeezed her hand, smiling. "It'll work out. You'll see."

Something in her heart told Megan she could believe him.

The Saturday before Thanksgiving, Donna was in the basement excavating her cartons of holiday decorations. This year, since Brandon would be coming for dinner, Donna intended to outdo herself. She knew she had a cornucopia basket down there somewhere, and with a bit of cleaning and some embellishment, it would make a lovely centerpiece. The night before, she had completed one of her longtime UFOs, a table runner for the sideboard, in the Pine Burr pattern. The new decorations and her best table linens would show Brandon the Jorgensons were eager to welcome him into the family.

She had spent the morning poring over her favorite cookbook and leafing through the recipes she had collected from her online quilting buddies over the past several months. When she suggested to Becca and Paul that they try a completely different menu this Thanksgiving, they exchanged unhappy glances.

Surprised, Donna said, "After all these years of teasing me for serving the same thing every Thanksgiving, when I finally suggest a change, you're turning me down?"

Becca fidgeted and said, "The regular stuff is nice." Paul only nodded, but Donna understood their unspoken plea: When so much about their family was changing, the comfort of familiar traditions was more important than ever. So Donna agreed to keep the menu the same—that would be easier, anyway—and settled for the new table runner and centerpiece to accompany their traditional table decoration, a pair of brass candlesticks that had once belonged to Paul's mother.

She found the cornucopia basket and dug it out of its box. She was eager to see Lindsay, who for weeks had been too busy to come home. As for Brandon, he was so abrupt on the phone whenever he called for Lindsay that Donna feared he had detected—and resented—her misgivings about the wedding. She intended to make it up to him over the holiday, for Lindsay's sake.

The phone sounded faintly from upstairs. Donna blew dust off the basket and listened, but when Becca didn't shout for her, she decided the call was for someone else. She had thought it might be Julia, who in the past few weeks had taken to calling almost every other day for quilting advice. It wasn't easy to continue their lessons over the phone, but from what Julia said, if she didn't improve soon, she could lose her movie role altogether. Donna didn't understand why any director in his right mind would cut an actress as talented and popular as Julia, but as Lindsay had told her, acting was a difficult, uncertain profession. Donna was glad Lindsay had chosen to pursue directing rather than acting—although it remained to be seen whether she would continue to pursue any career after graduation.

At least Lindsay was involved in the university's fall production; she had almost bowed out, but after persistent pleading from her friends in drama club and at least two professors, she had agreed to direct again. She was enjoying herself so much that Donna was certain she'd participate in the spring semester play, too. Donna would volunteer to handle the details of the wedding preparations if Lindsay thought she would be too busy to do both.

Just then, Donna heard footsteps coming down the basement stairs. "Mom?" Becca said. "That was Lindsay on the phone."

"Oh, good." Donna carefully maneuvered through the stacks of cartons, the cornucopia in her hands. "Did you two have a nice chat?"

"Not really." As Donna continued toward the stairs, Becca added, "Don't bother. She already hung up."

Donna halted. "Already?" She hesitated, surprised and a little hurt. "She didn't want to talk to me?"

"She said she was too busy, and not to call her back, because she's going out." Becca winced as if she'd rather not say anything more. "Mom, I have some bad news."

"What?"

"They're not coming for Thanksgiving."

"You mean only Lindsay is coming?"

"No, I mean they're both not coming."

Donna felt a weariness come over her. "Oh." She sat down heavily on a stack of dusty boxes. "Are they going to Brandon's parents' home instead?"

"I think they're staying at the apartment."

"Why?"

Becca shrugged, and only then did Donna see the anger in her face. "Lindsay says Brandon has a major project due before the end of the semester, and she has to work on the play."

"Can't they come just for the day?"

"Brandon says it's too far to drive."

"But it's only an hour there and an hour back."

"That's what I said. Lindsay never thought it was too long before." Becca's gaze was beseeching. "Mom, do you think you can talk her out of it?"

"I can try," Donna said, but somehow she knew she wouldn't succeed.

Sure enough, when she went upstairs and dialed Lindsay's number, the phone rang and rang. Becca leaned on the kitchen counter, watching her mother expectantly. The answering machine eventually picked up, and Donna forced herself to leave a cheerful message.

"She won't come," Becca said. "I hate Brandon."

"Becca—"

"I mean it, Mom. I know this is his fault. Lindsay never missed Thanksgiving before, not because of a play, not for anything." Scowling, she stormed out of the kitchen, adding, "I'd never let some guy control me like that."

"He's not some guy. He's her fiancé, and . . ." Abruptly Donna fell silent, stopped short by Becca's last words, unable to defend him. Brandon did seem somewhat domineering, and even Paul had called him bossy. But Lindsay was a strong person, too, and surely she would never do anything she didn't want to do simply because Brandon said so.

Perhaps Donna, Paul, and Becca had to accept the possibility that Lindsay preferred to be alone with Brandon. As much as it hurt Donna to think that her daughter didn't want to spend the holiday with the family, she couldn't ignore that this was, in a sense, the couple's first Thanksgiving together. Surely they wouldn't need to be alone every holiday, but maybe this first one was special. Besides, Christmas wasn't too far away, and it would come after the play and the semester had ended. Surely Lindsay would come home for Christmas, with or without Brandon.

Just then Donna realized she still held the dusty cornucopia. She studied it for a few moments, turning it over and over in her hands, then carried it back downstairs and packed it away.

On Thanksgiving Grace drove for the first time in four months, as a favor to her sister. Helen usually took Mother to holiday church services, but on Tuesday she had phoned and begged Grace to take her instead. Helen's son needed to be picked up from college on Wednesday, and although Helen's husband had intended to make the trip, at the last minute he could not get the day off from work. Driving all day would put Helen so far behind schedule that she'd need all of Wednesday night and Thursday morning to get ready for the more than forty relatives who would gather at her home to celebrate Thanksgiving.

"You wouldn't be in this mess if you'd let us each bring something," Grace teased. Helen was notoriously finicky about the holidays and insisted on preparing the entire meal herself.

"Thanks for volunteering. You can make the rolls," Helen countered, then hung up before Grace could protest.

So on Wednesday, Grace baked two kinds of rolls, sourdough and rye, then made a pumpkin pie for good measure, until the whole loft was filled with the spicy fragrances of baking. On Thursday she packed the rolls and the pie carefully in two baskets, summoned up her courage, and went to her building's underground garage. She expected to find cobwebs clinging to the rearview mirror and an engine choked with dust, but the car looked no different than the last time she had driven it, and it started up immediately as if that had been only days ago. At first Grace felt uncomfortable and nervous behind the wheel, but soon she relaxed. Traffic was light, the day was bright and sunny, and she had been feeling well for weeks, so well that she had even begun sketching a new quilt. If not for the occasional pins-and-needles sensations in her hands, she could almost believe the doctor had misdiagnosed her.

"Don't get overconfident," Dr. Steiner cautioned her at her last visit, when she told him how remarkably healthy she felt. "You still need to take it easy. If you overdo, you could have a relapse."

Grace knew he was right, but his warning only slightly diminished her optimism. Spontaneous remissions occurred in other, even more serious diseases; there was no reason why she couldn't hope for one in her case. "Hope never hurt anyone," she told the doctor, and he agreed, but said that while she was hoping, she should err on the side of caution and be sure to take care of herself.

Dr. Steiner's warnings were never far from her thoughts, but it was a sign of just how good she felt that she was driving that day. The doctor had never forbidden her to drive; that prohibition had been her own, borne of the fear that had haunted her since her accident. Even if she had felt only half as well, however, she still might have agreed. Mother had to get to church, and Grace couldn't picture convincing Helen that her fears about driving were realistic. And Grace couldn't ask Justine to drive them, because for all Grace knew, Gabriel might be with her.

Mother still lived in the home where Grace and her sisters had grown up. She was waiting in the front room, neatly attired in a wine-red suit and a pillbox hat with a short veil that did not quite reach her eyes.

"There's my baby girl," she said when Grace entered, and hugged her. Then she held Grace at arm's length for inspection. "You look well."

"I feel great. Never better."

Mother nodded, satisfied, and picked up her purse from the credenza near the door. She also retrieved a covered casserole dish and gestured to two plastic pie carriers beside it. "Will you take those for me?"

"I hope one of these is your sweet potato pie," Grace said as they left the house.

"Of course. It wouldn't be Thanksgiving without it. The other one is apple, and this is my green bean casserole. Helen said to bring just the pies, but you know your sister. She won't ever admit when she needs help." She gave Grace a sidelong glance as Grace helped her into the car. "Must run in the family."

"It skipped Mary, then," Grace replied, ignoring the obvious reference to her own stubborn independence, and shut her mother's door.

"Mary's more like your grandmother," Mother conceded when Grace entered the car on the driver's side. "She'd rather ask for help than try something on her own."

"I'm going to tell her you said that."

"Go right ahead. She knows it's true."

Grace laughed and started the car. As they drove to church, Mother updated Grace on all the news from the neighborhood—who had died, who had moved away, who had gotten married, and who had welcomed new babies into their families. Several of Mother's friends had asked about Grace, and Grace grew tense until her mother assured her that no one knew of her MS. "They're just being friendly," her mother said. Grace had never known her mother to lie, but she couldn't help wondering if Mother had inadvertently let clues fall, not only by what she told her friends, but by what she didn't say.

The church was full, as it usually was on Thanksgiving, mostly with older couples Mother's age, some accompanied by grandchildren. Grace listened to the preacher's words of forgiveness and gratitude and reflected ruefully on how well they applied to her that day, as if the preacher knew about her impending reunion with Gabriel and had written the sermon especially for her. In the spirit of the day, she promised herself that she would be civil to him.

Afterward, as Grace and her mother drove to Helen's home, Grace said, "Did Helen tell you Gabriel will be joining us?"

"Yes, she did, although I think she wishes he wasn't," Mother said. "She wouldn't have allowed it, except that I told her if you didn't object, neither should we. That's very Christian of you, Grace, to allow him to come. Forgiveness is never easy, and he's done much to be forgiven for."

Grace was silent. "I don't know if I've forgiven him," she finally admitted. "Justine grew up without a father, and nothing he does now can change that. I don't know if I can ever forgive him for that."

Mother patted her on the arm. "You're willing to try. That's a step in the right direction."

Her voice was reassuring and kind, so Grace didn't have the heart to tell her she had only reluctantly allowed Justine to invite Gabriel, and then only because she didn't want to ruin Joshua's holiday. That, and because she couldn't bear to let Justine think she was keeping him away out of jealousy.

When they reached Helen's home, the driveway was already full of cars and others were parked along the street in front of the house. When they opened the front door, they were greeted by hugs from aunts and uncles and cousins, as well as the delicious aromas of roasting turkey, dressing, and other tempting dishes. Grace and her mother brought their contributions to the meal into the kitchen. Before she could slip away to search for Justine, Helen tossed her an apron and put her to work. Sometime later Justine entered, carrying Joshua on her hip. "Tell Grandma 'Happy Thanksgiving,'" she coached as she held him out for Grace to take. Joshua obediently obliged as best he could, and Grace laughed and hugged him.

"You're my good boy," she said, kissing him on the top of the head. She set him down, and as he toddled off to the living room in search of his cousins, her eyes met Justine's. "Is he here?"

"He's in the other room. Last I saw him, he was talking to Uncle Steve. I think I'll join them."

Justine left, and Grace was about to resume mashing the potatoes when Helen took the masher from her and said, "You might as well get it over with." She gave Grace a knowing look and tilted her head in the direction Justine had taken.

Grace nodded and untied her apron. Helen was right; it would be better to face Gabriel for the first time now rather than across the supper table. She went into the crowded family room, stopping to chat or exchange hugs as she worked her way across the room. She spotted her mother and Justine in the crowd, but Gabriel was not with either of them.

In the living room, Gabriel was seated on the sofa beside Grace's sister Mary, with Joshua on his lap. His back was to her, so only Mary saw Grace enter. "Um, I just remembered," she said, rising. "I told Helen I'd help set the table."

Gabriel must have seen Mary's gaze wander, for he turned and spotted her. "Grace. Hi." He set Joshua down in Mary's place and stood. He smiled, hesitantly, and extended his hand.

She had to force herself to shake it. "Hello, Gabriel." Her voice sounded calm and even, which astonished her. Somehow, after so much time, she had expected not to recognize him. He was thinner, and the mustache was gone, and there was a slump to his shoulders that she had not seen before, but except for the gray in his hair, little else about him had changed.

He flashed a nervous smile. "You're looking well."

"Thank you." Only then did she realize that one by one, the other family members had slipped out of the room, except for Joshua, who sat quietly playing with an Oscar the Grouch doll. Grace picked up her grandson and sat down on the sofa, placing him in her lap. "I see you've met Joshua."

Gabriel took that as his cue to sit beside her. "Yes, we're getting to be good friends. Aren't we, Josh?" In reply, Joshua grinned up at his grandfather.

What a shame you missed his first two years, Grace thought. What a shame he had missed most of Justine's life. Justine had been just as beautiful a child. "So, are you back in town for good, or just passing through?"

"My passing through days are over, Grace," he said quietly, as if she had rebuked him. "I'm working as an adjunct professor at the city college."

"That's right. Justine said you were teaching again."

"Just nights. During the days I work as a drug and alcohol abuse counselor."

Her eyebrows shot up. "Really."

"You're thinking, 'Physician, heal thyself.' I've been sober for ten years."

It angered her that he assumed he still knew her well enough to guess her thoughts. It flustered her that he had guessed correctly. "I'm happy for you."

"It wasn't easy, but I made it." He reached out and stroked Joshua's head. "Not soon enough, I'm afraid. I missed out on so much."

More than you'll ever know, Grace wanted to snap at him, but she was too angry to speak.

"I wish that I could make it up to you." He rested his elbows on his knees, unable to meet her eyes. "I can't say I know what you went through, but I can imagine. I'm sorry I wasn't there for you, Grace. For Justine. I wish things had been different. I can't change them now, but I would if I could. I'm sorry."

She watched him, speechless. Ever since he had come back into Justine's life, Grace had hungered for his apology, but now that she had it, she felt empty.

Gabriel looked up, his eyes pleading. "I don't expect you to forgive me, and I don't expect to pick up where we left off—"

Grace laughed, once, loud and sharp. She hadn't meant to, but it escaped before she could restrain it. Pain flickered in his eyes, and he turned away again. "I'm sorry," Grace said. "But what you said was . . . unexpected."

"All I meant was, I'd like to be a part of your life again. We have a history. We have a child and a grandchild. If you're willing, I'd like us to be friends."

"I don't see how that's possible," Grace said, just as Helen called everyone in for supper. She picked up Joshua and carried him into the dining room without sparing Gabriel another glance.

Helen's dining room wasn't large, but somehow all forty-two members of the family, four generations from Mother, the eldest, to Joshua, the youngest child, crowded into the room. Justine came to Grace and took Joshua, giving her a questioning look that Grace pretended not to see. "Mother's going to say the blessing," Helen called out over the din of voices, which immediately quieted. The family members joined hands and bowed their heads as Mother began to speak.

Even in her anger, Grace enjoyed the meal. Helen was easily the best cook among them, and the others' contributions were nearly as delicious. Gabriel spoke to Grace only once, to compliment her on the rolls. Grace thanked him but did nothing to prolong the conversation.

When the meal was nearly over, Mother suggested, as she did every year, that everyone at the table tell the others what they were especially thankful for that year. "I'll begin," she said. "I'm thankful that once again we've all gathered together to celebrate this special day. It does my heart good to have my whole family around me." Then, with a quick glance at Grace, she added, "I'm also especially thankful that we all continue to enjoy good health, especially Grace."

There were murmurs of assent, and Grace felt her face growing hot. Mother knew she wished to keep her illness secret from all but family. Had she forgotten Gabriel was there?

The others expressed similar sentiments, and she herself said something about the blessings of Justine and Joshua, but she was distracted, waiting with faint dread for what Gabriel would say. He didn't disappoint. "I'm grateful to be alive," he said, and received affirming nods in response. "I'm also deeply thankful that Grace and Justine have given me the opportunity to earn their forgiveness."

Grace couldn't bring herself to look at him.

After dessert, Gabriel caught her alone in the family room. "I meant what I said," he said without preamble, in a quiet voice so no one would overhear. "Please give me a chance to earn your forgiveness. Don't put this off. We don't have a lot of time."

She felt as if an electric shock had shot through her, freezing her to the marrow. She stared at him. "What did you say?"

He looked back at her, and this time she knew what he was thinking.

"You know, don't you?"

He hesitated, then nodded.

Grace felt all the blood rush to her head. "I have to . . ." She struggled to stand, and brushed off Gabriel's hands when he tried to assist. He knew. Justine had told him, Justine or someone else. "I have to go."

"Grace . . ."

Blinded by tears, she stumbled into the hallway and fumbled in the closet for her coat and purse. She threw the coat over her shoulders and raced to her car, blocking out the alarmed voices calling after her, calling out her name. He knew. He knew, and she could not bear for him to know.

Adam was enjoying his Thanksgiving break so much that not even the stack of geometry tests that needed grading could dampen his spirits. On Thursday his family had gathered at his mom's house for their annual feast, and he had spent the day eating, playing football in the backyard with his cousins and brothers, and watching games on television. Whenever she had been able to catch him alone, Nana had pestered him about Megan, and he teased her by refusing to answer her questions. He didn't tell her about their E-mail exchanges, which he had come to expect and anticipate every day, or the night they had dined out together, or their upcoming meeting on Saturday, when he, Megan, and Robby planned to have lunch and see a movie. Nana was so annoyed at him that she forbade him to have any of her apple pie, which she knew was his favorite, but at the end of the day she relented and sent him home with the two pieces that somehow had been left over.

The next day, Adam graded half of the tests and began writing his final exams, went to the gym, and worked around the house a bit, relaxing, but watching the clock in anticipation of the next day. He was tempted to call Megan, but not wanting to interrupt her holiday, he settled for sending her an E-mail message telling her he was looking forward to seeing her and Robby. When he checked his E-mail that evening, she had not yet responded. He was disappointed, but told himself she was probably at her parents', where she didn't have access to a computer.

On Saturday, they met at noon in a restaurant in Monroe. Megan had offered to meet him halfway, as they had before, but Adam wanted to spare her the drive. Robby seemed delighted to see Adam again, but when Adam asked him about school, Robby withdrew. Quickly Adam dropped the subject and asked him about video games instead. His familiarity with some of the games, though only slight, pleased Robby greatly. "Mom doesn't like video games," Robby told him sorrowfully, and Megan laughed.

After the movie, Megan suggested they go to an orchard on the outskirts of town for apple cider and cinnamon doughnuts. As they finished eating, Megan asked Robby to pick them a few apples to take home. When Robby ran off, Megan turned to Adam and said, "He seems to like you."

"I like him."

"Are you still interested in the arrangement we discussed earlier?"

Adam smiled at her sudden formality. "Of course."

"It wouldn't be a burden?"

"Not at all. In fact, it would give me an excuse to have some fun every once in a while."

Megan smiled then, and Adam realized he had been waiting all day for her to smile at him alone. "Okay, then. We'll see if Robby's willing."

When Robby returned with a basket full of apples, Adam asked him if he liked football. Robby winced and said, "Watching, not playing."

"How come?"

Robby glanced at Megan before answering. "The other kids in my class are bigger than me, and I get crunched a lot. I like kicking, though. I'm good at that. And I don't get tackled so much."

"Really? How good are you?"

Proudly Robby recited his statistics, which were remarkably good for a kid his age. "I'd like to see that," Adam said. "Would you show me? Maybe we could get together next weekend and practice."

Robby looked pleased. "That would be fun." He looked up at Megan. "Can we, Mom?"

"I have some things to do, but why don't the two of you go?" She glanced at Adam. "If that's all right with you?"

They arranged that next Saturday afternoon Adam would pick up Robby at Megan's place and they would kick the football around at the local middle school for a few hours. Then, to Adam's disappointment, Megan said it was time to go.

She paid for the apples, and as they walked to the parking lot, Megan allowed Robby to run ahead to the car. "Thank you," she said, offering Adam her hand to shake. "I appreciate this."

"It's my pleasure," Adam said, and meant it.

Megan rewarded him with another smile, and as she got into her car, she called out, "I'll see you online."

Adam waved good-bye and watched them drive off before getting into his own car. The memory of her smile lingered as he drove home. He liked Megan. He liked her quiet gentleness that would unexpectedly break into humor; he liked the way she was with Robby, the way she patiently listened to him and thoughtfully considered what he said. He liked the way her face lit up with love when she hugged her son close, and he found himself wishing she would look at him with such fondness.

When he returned home, there was a message on the answering machine, and for a moment Adam hoped it was Megan calling to talk, and feared it was Megan canceling their plans for next Saturday. He never would have expected the voice that played back on the tape, a voice he knew so well but had not heard in so many months.

"Adam, it's me," Natalie said. "Are you there? Please pick up." A lengthy pause. "Come on, I know you're mad at me, but don't play games, okay? Not today." Another pause, and then a sigh. "Okay, I guess you're not home. I was just calling . . . well, I was just calling to see how you're doing. And to wish you a happy Thanksgiving." Another pause, and then she quickly added, "You don't have to call me back. I'm not home anyway. I'm in Aspen. It's great here. You'd love it. Well, anyway, I hope you had a good holiday." She hung up.

Stunned, Adam stood staring at the answering machine before playing the message again. It was not his imagination; Natalie sounded lonely. Sad, too. He sat down heavily on a kitchen stool and wondered what had prompted her to call, from her skiing vacation, no less. Could she have changed her mind? The thought, which once he would have greeted with relief and joy, now made him uncomfortable. As much as their breakup had wounded him, he knew now that they were not well suited for each other, just as Natalie herself had said when she returned the engagement ring. He hoped she wasn't thinking about . . .

He shook off the thoughts. Of course she wasn't thinking about getting back together. She was just calling to wish him a happy Thanksgiving. Maybe she had started to feel some remorse over the way she had treated him, but he was positive she felt nothing more than that. Not Natalie.

He rewound the tape and went into the second bedroom he used as an office to finish checking the geometry tests. By the time he went to bed, he had almost forgotten Natalie had called.

The next morning, he fixed himself some breakfast and read the paper before getting ready for church. He usually skipped the Sunday business section, but a prominent headline caught his eye: "Lindsor's stock down amid rumors of buyout."

Lindsor's—the department store Natalie worked for. Adam read the article, dismayed to learn how declining sales had hurt the store, but had made it a more attractive purchase for a large chain. Spokespeople acknowledged that representatives of the two stores were in contact, but would neither confirm nor deny that an offer had been made. Regarding the rumors that some stores would be closed and others consolidated—resulting in hundreds of layoffs—they had no comment.

Adam shook his head in regret, thinking of Natalie. The weeks between Thanksgiving and Christmas were usually her favorites, frantically busy with sales and social gatherings. The frenzy burned out some of her colleagues, but the stress and excitement suited her, and she was in her element. This stress was different, though, and it pained him to think of her wondering if the job she had fought so hard for was in jeopardy.

No doubt that explained the odd tone in her voice; surely she would have known of the situation before it made headlines. Should he call her to offer some sympathy, to give her a chance to vent? He considered it before remembering that she was out of town. He couldn't reach her if he wanted to, and somehow that filled him with relief. They had promised each other they would be friends, but she couldn't expect more from him than that.

Nine

WITH A SIGH, Vinnie set aside the letter Donna had enclosed in her Christmas card. She wished she could drop everything and fly off to Minnesota to comfort her friend. Not only had Lindsay canceled her plans to visit her family for Thanksgiving, but she hardly talked to her mother anymore, not even on the phone. "I feel like she's pulling away from us," Donna had written. "I suppose this is natural, considering she's going to be married in a few months, but it makes me heartsick."

Vinnie wanted to write back with words of encouragement, but could find nothing encouraging in the little she knew of this young man Brandon. Vinnie didn't consider Lindsay's withdrawal at all natural; in her experience, weddings brought families together rather than wedging them apart. Even Natalie had warmed to her new in-laws and Adam's extended family in the months leading up to the expected ceremony, and that engagement had been a disaster from the beginning. Vinnie had never met Lindsay, but the young woman's behavior seemed odd, even troubling, and her fiancé's was worse.

Vinnie didn't want to stir up trouble by alarming Donna with warnings that might be unfounded, but she suspected Donna's worries had merit. Donna was a kind, generous, and loving woman, not the sort to cling jealously to her daughter rather than allow her to make a new life with the man she loved. Even now, she continued to give Brandon the benefit of the doubt, long after others—Vinnie included—would have become suspicious enough to confront him, or at least to speak to her daughter.

Donna would have to approach Lindsay with much more tact than Vinnie herself could have mustered, but keeping silent any longer wouldn't do Donna's nerves any good, and if it turned out there was some reason why Lindsay and Brandon shouldn't marry, the sooner they found out, the better. She had learned that from Adam and Natalie.

Vinnie knew her Cross-Country Quilter friends wondered why she was so eager to see Adam married, or even dating, so soon after the breakup of his engagement. They thought she innocently believed that once married, everyone lived happily ever after. But they misunderstood her. She had learned from her own parents that happy marriages could end too soon in grief; her own marriage had taught her that even happy unions had ups and downs, and that each day required a renewed commitment to make it work. But from Aunt Lynn and Lena she had learned that love and companionship were essential for any other kind of happiness.

Vinnie had married young, at seventeen. She had known Sam for less than a year, but had known almost from the start that she loved him, and that he was the only man she would ever love.

They met at a dance on a Friday evening in early June. Vinnie was dating another young man at the time, but the passing years had faded her memories of a time she felt affection for any man other than Sam, so that sometimes, even when she concentrated, she could hardly picture his face. Sam, too, had a girlfriend, and they were very close to getting pinned. They might have married one day if Sam's girlfriend had not caught a bad cold on the same weekend Vinnie's boyfriend was out of town visiting relatives, and if their respective groups of friends had not cajoled them into going to the dance anyway.

Vinnie had seen Sam before, since his girlfriend attended her school and Sam had occasionally escorted her to school functions. What Vinnie didn't know until later was that Sam had seen her before, too, and thought she had a wonderful laugh and the most beautiful face he'd ever seen—an observation he kept to himself rather than share with his girlfriend.

When Sam saw Vinnie at the dance, he had to wait through several songs until she was free. Then he quickly stepped in and invited her to dance. His girlfriend didn't like to swing dance, so he wasn't as polished as some of the other young men, but Vinnie was an excellent dancer and made up for any of his shortcomings. He liked the way her eyes lit up with fun as they danced, and so he stayed by her side for the next dance, and the next, and before either of them realized it, they had spent the entire evening together.

Vinnie had enjoyed dancing with the tall, handsome man with the slow smile and the easy manner, but since he was three years older than she and was dating a senior from her own school, she didn't expect to dance with him again after that night. She certainly didn't expect to run into him the next day at the library, where she studied every Saturday afternoon with her friends. When he asked her to go out with him, at first she was too startled to reply. For one quick, guilty moment she thought of her boyfriend, but she accepted.

When one date led to another and they began to go steady, the senior girls at her school rallied around their scorned, heartbroken friend and made life difficult for Vinnie. Their eyes narrowed as Vinnie passed them in the hallways, and the whispers followed her wherever she went. Tramp, they called her, assuming that she must agree to all sorts of sinful things in the dark with Sam. Only that could have turned his head, when he had been so faithful for three years. Three years Sam and his girlfriend had been together, and yet he had broken off the relationship within a week of meeting Vinnie. A week!

Vinnie let her own boyfriend down more gently, and he took it bravely, which made Vinnie feel worse. But only for a little while—she was young, after all, and she was in love, and all that mattered was Sam and herself and the future they had begun to talk about, first tentatively, and as time passed, with greater assurance and hope.

Then the whole world erupted in war, and the United States was drawn into it. Sam, at twenty, was eligible for the draft, and for the first time since meeting him, Vinnie feared all their hopes and plans had been in vain. She cried when he asked her to marry him, because she knew his haste came from an all too plausible concern that if they did not marry soon, they might never have the chance. Aunt Lynn gave her blessing, but cried a little over Vinnie's leaving school. She also urged Vinnie to ask her father to give her away, because although she rarely saw him, he was, after all, the only father she had. Vinnie's instinct was to retort that he had given her away a long time ago, but because Aunt Lynn wanted it, she agreed.

Within weeks Lena had whipped up a wedding dress and Aunt Lynn had planned a modest celebration. Her father escorted Vinnie down the aisle and gave her hand to Sam, then exacted a tearful promise that Sam look after his little girl. Vinnie wasn't sure what astonished her more, her father's emotion or his belief that he was relinquishing the role of her protector to Sam. If anyone ought to do that, it was Aunt Lynn, and her aunt would assume Vinnie planned to take care of herself.

But Vinnie was too joyful to dwell on the unhappiness of the past, or the way her father had failed her. She danced with her father at the reception, but saved most of her dances for Sam, who had improved so much since that first swing dance they had shared that Friday night in spring, and who had since become her partner in so many greater things.

As the hour grew late, her father kissed her good-bye and tried, in his own stumbling way, to apologize. "I never wanted to send you away when your mother died," he said. "Boys I understood, but I didn't know how to look after a little girl."

Suddenly she saw him not as her father, but a man regretting his mistakes, a man who had made unfortunate choices at a time when his reason was clouded by grief. He had not meant to hurt her, and ultimately, he hadn't, because everything had worked out for the best. She embraced him, and in her heart, she forgave him.

Several weeks passed before Sam was called up. She feigned bravery for his sake and pretended to believe him when he promised her he would return. He survived the Normandy campaign when many of his friends did not, but Vinnie ached for him, wondering how long his luck would last. She prayed, alone in their apartment, and her days grew darker and more bleak as the war dragged on.

It was Lena who urged her to return to high school. At first Vinnie demurred, believing that as a married woman her place was at home, but then she began to long for her books and her friends, anything to ease the loneliness and fear of waiting. The school board rejected her application for readmittance, saying that married women were not permitted to attend classes with the unmarried girls.

But Lena, who knew something of how it felt to have one's last hope snuffed out, refused to allow Vinnie to give up. She stormed into a school board meeting and demanded that Vinnie be permitted to return. She cited Vinnie's excellent academic record and argued that their obstinance was not only unreasonable and unfair, but also unpatriotic, considering that Vinnie's husband was risking his life for his country. "You make a mockery of all the women fighting on the home front," she accused them, and said she'd see that the whole city learned of it.

They relented, and Vinnie resumed classes the next quarter. By the time Sam returned safely home from the war, she had her diploma and a job at the local library, a job she willingly gave up when their first son came along a year later. Two more sons followed, and then, at last, a daughter.

She loved all her children deeply, and knew that a mother shouldn't have favorites, but she couldn't help herself. This precious girl child, the last of her babies, was the child of her own heart. Vinnie was fierce in her determination that her daughter would never know the grief and loneliness she had known. She would protect her daughter as best she could, as long as she could, and would lavish upon her all the love and attention she herself had longed for as a motherless—and fatherless—girl. She would love her daughter and all her children as her aunt had taught her to love.

She named her daughter Lynn, and when her daughter married and bore a son and named him Adam after Vinnie's own father, Vinnie extended her vow of protection to him. She wanted Adam to be happy, to know the blessing of love as his parents and grandparents had, and to be spared the loneliness that had been the burden of the great-grandfather whose name he bore.

For she knew Adam was much like herself, unable to completely enjoy his life unless someone shared it with him. She had learned well in her eighty-two years that she could not guarantee her own happiness, much less that of someone else, but she would do what she could to care for the people she loved.

Even when that meant meddling, she told herself with a laugh. Especially when that meant encouraging them down paths their hearts had already chosen to follow.

The exacerbation struck when Grace was Christmas shopping. First she couldn't feel her hand on the escalator rail, and then her legs went out from under her. If not for the man three steps below, who caught her before she could tumble to the first floor, she might have broken her neck in the fall.

Hours later, after Dr. Steiner had examined her, the pins-and-needles sensations in her hands had not yet faded, and this time they were also in her feet. She tried to walk, but could only manage a sort of slow shuffle. Her mind, too, felt numb, as it had ever since the doctor had told her she might not have a complete recovery this time, and that she might have to resort to a wheelchair sooner than they had hoped.

When Justine arrived, her mouth tight with worry, Grace couldn't bring herself to repeat the doctor's bleak report, so Dr. Steiner took Justine into the hallway and explained. When she returned, Grace saw resolution in her eyes, but she also saw that her daughter was pushing a wheelchair.

"You're allowed to go," Justine said, and patted the back of the chair. "Come on. I'll help you."

Grace turned her face to the wall. "I'm not leaving in that."

"Then you're not leaving at all. Hospital regulations. You have to be wheeled out of here. I can do it, or I can get an orderly. Your choice."

At any other time Grace would have smiled to hear her own stubbornness echoed in her daughter's voice. Today she blinked back tears and allowed Justine to assist her into the wheelchair. She felt trapped and exposed as Justine wheeled her to the front desk to take care of her discharge forms and arrange to rent a wheelchair. She tried to stand, but Justine put a firm hand on her shoulder and gently held her back.

"Where's Joshua?" Grace remembered to ask as Justine drove her home.

"He's being watched," Justine said shortly, and Grace knew this meant he was with his grandfather. Grace had forbidden Justine to mention Gabriel ever since the day after Thanksgiving, when Justine admitted that she had told him about the MS.

"You promised to tell no one outside the family," Grace had shrilled into the phone. After her abrupt departure from Helen's house, Justine had been phoning Grace's loft all evening, leaving one message after another as Grace listened in on the answering machine. Grace eventually picked up only because Justine declared that if she didn't, Justine would assume she was injured and couldn't reach the phone, and would summon the police. "How could you have told him?"

"I needed to talk to someone. Can't you see that you're not the only one hurting?"

"You could have talked to your cousins. You could have talked to me."

"I can't talk to you, Mom. You won't talk about it."

Grace hung up before Justine would know she was crying. She turned off the ringer to the phone, turned down the volume on the answering machine, and went to bed, where she lay awake for hours, her thoughts in turmoil. Gabriel knew. Was that why he had been so eager to see her again, to apologize before it was too late to obtain absolution?

He was twenty years too late, Grace had told herself. Her MS had nothing to do with that.

Even with the rented wheelchair, Justine struggled to maneuver Grace from the underground parking lot to her third-floor loft. In the elevator, Justine slid the metal gate shut and reached for the lever, but then she pulled her hand away and said, "You do it." Grace didn't like the new bossiness in her daughter's voice, but she obeyed—or tried to. From her seat in the wheelchair, she couldn't reach the controls to operate the elevator.

"You'll have to do it," Grace said, her face burning.

"Who manages this building?" Justine asked. "Don't they know we have wheelchair accessibility laws in this state?"

"This building was grandfathered out." Grace wondered how she remembered that. It had never mattered to her before.

When they reached the third floor, Justine urged Grace to open the gate herself. With some difficulty Grace managed, but when Justine told her to wheel herself off the elevator, she found that the elevator had stopped just below the floor of her loft, the gap just wide enough to block forward motion. Justine had to tip the chair onto its rear wheels and give it a good shove to lift her over the barrier. Justine then pushed her into the kitchen and asked her to reach the sink, which she couldn't; then it was on to the bathroom, to the quilt studio, to the bed, with Justine growing more determined, and Grace ever more humiliated.

"All right, you've made your point," she said when she couldn't bear any more. "I'm helpless in this chair. Do you think I don't know that?"

Justine's face softened. "That's not what I've been trying to say at all." She gestured around the roomy loft. "It's this place, not you. You live in a converted warehouse. It won't meet your needs anymore."

At last Grace understood. "I'm not moving."

"Mom—"

"I mean it. I'm not leaving my home." Abruptly she pushed herself away from her daughter. Didn't Justine know her at all? Wasn't it enough that she had to sacrifice her pride, her art, her livelihood, that Justine wanted her to give up her home as well?

Justine followed, and for more than an hour argued the merits of moving to a newer, more convenient apartment, but Grace refused to listen. Over the next few days, Justine persisted, bringing her brochures for attractive condos and even scheduling an appointment with a real estate agent, but Grace rebuffed every attempt to persuade her. She had lost too much of the old Grace to abandon the quirky loft and its eclectic neighborhood for some shiny new condo with smooth floors and no personality. The loft held too many memories, and she would not part with them.

By that time Grace had recovered enough to forgo the wheelchair, and on her follow-up visit to the hospital, she returned it and canceled the rest of the rental contract. She waited for Justine to tell her she had made a mistake, but Justine didn't, nor did she say anything more about leaving her home.

The next day, Grace was in her studio sketching the central motif for a new pictorial quilt when the buzzer sounded. Usually interruptions of her work frustrated her, but today she was glad for the excuse to take a break. This new quilt, a thematic interpretation of the twenty-third Psalm, had been begun in a burst of inspiration that had since dissipated, like the seven other quilts she had tried to design since returning from Elm Creek Quilt Camp. She was almost tempted to make something using a pattern from a magazine just so she could finally begin her block for the Challenge Quilt—and have something positive to tell the Cross-Country Quilters when they asked about her progress.

Since she wasn't getting anywhere with her quilt, she gladly buzzed back, and soon heard the elevator rising to the third floor. She expected Justine or Sondra or another friend, and so she could only stand there in shocked amazement when Gabriel pushed back the gate.

"Morning, Grace," he said, hesitating in the elevator. On the floor beside him Grace saw a large toolbox, and behind him was a stack of assorted pieces of wood and metal. "May I come in?"

"What do you want?"

"I want to talk to you about this place."

"I'm not leaving."

"I know. Justine told me." Gabriel stepped out of the elevator and slowly turned around, scanning the loft. Then his eyes met hers. "Want to show me the kitchen?"

"Why?"

"Because that's where I'll start. Then the bathroom, the bedroom, and your studio. I might not get it all done today."

Grace stared at him, exasperated. "What are you talking about?"

In response, Gabriel began unloading the elevator. When she didn't move, he walked past her and found the kitchen on his own. Grace followed, only to find him measuring the height of the countertops and the width of the aisles. "What are you doing?" Grace asked, although she was beginning to suspect.

"I'm retrofitting your loft."

"The whole building was retrofitted for earthquake safety years ago."

"Not for an earthquake; in case you need that chair again."

Grace felt hot anger rise in her chest. "So Justine told you about that, too?"

Without a word, Gabriel stepped past her and returned to the elevator for some tools and two-by-fours, and before she knew it, he had set himself to work.

"I didn't ask for your help," Grace snapped.

Gabriel snorted, but never paused. "If I waited for you to ask . . ." He shook his head.

"Did Justine put you up to this?"

At that Gabriel looked up. "No, this was my idea, and frankly, I don't think Justine will approve. She wants you to move, and if I adapt the loft, you won't need to. So do you want me to keep working or not?"

His directness startled the anger right out of her. "What do you know about retrofitting a loft?" she said, disguising her confusion with scorn.

"I'm a licensed carpenter. I've been working as a contractor for more than eight years."

Grace didn't know what to think. "Well, aren't you full of surprises," she managed to say. Gabriel made no reply, but continued working as she stood there trying to make sense of him, wondering what to do. She didn't want to talk to him, and she felt foolish standing there watching him, so eventually she returned to her studio to complete her sketch. But she could not focus her thoughts knowing he was in the other room, so instead she toyed with her colored pencil and listened to the sounds of hammer, drill, and saw.

After two hours of this, she shoved herself away from the drafting table and went to the kitchen. Gabriel had begun widening the aisle by removing part of the countertop and was now partially hidden, his head and shoulders inside a lower cupboard. "What are you doing?" Grace asked.

"Adjusting the shelves so you can reach them from a seated position with a grabber. I thought you could move your plates and cups down here, and put some of the lighter things in the top cupboards."

Grace admitted to herself that wasn't a bad idea, but she wouldn't say so. "You don't have to do this, you know."

"I know."

Grace held back an exasperated sigh and glanced at the clock. "I was going to fix myself some lunch. Do you want something?"

Gabriel came out from the cupboard, an electric screwdriver in his hand. "I would. Thanks."

As Gabriel washed up, Grace heated some leftover bean soup and made ham sandwiches. A distant memory came to her, of standing at the kitchen counter of the home that had burned, fixing him sandwiches to eat during his breaks between classes. She pushed the thought aside and set the kitchen table, clearing away some of Gabriel's scattered tools. She started eating without him, but he joined her a few moments later, his hands and face clean, his hair combed.

"Delicious," he said, tasting the soup. "You always were a great cook."

She refused to allow his flattery to move her. "I do appreciate what you're doing."

"You're welcome." Gabriel savored a bite of his sandwich. "I know what it's like to lose a home. I've lost several. I wouldn't want that to happen to you."

To happen to me again, Grace almost corrected him, thinking of the fire, but she managed to hold it back. "What made you take up carpentry?"

"When I started to get sober, a man from my AA group was looking for someone to help in his contracting business. He offered me a chance to learn and to make some money at the same time. I was living in a shelter at the time and wanted to get a room somewhere, so I took him up on it. He said if I showed up drunk, that would be my last day of work. He was a good motivator."

"You lived in a shelter?"

"I've lived in several." Gabriel gave her an indecipherable look. "What did you think I did after I left you?"

"I . . . I assumed you stayed with friends or family."

"I did, for a while, but eventually I used up my last favor. I traveled around, stayed in LA for a while, but when my money ran out, I ended up on the streets."

He said it matter-of-factly, but Grace was transfixed with horror. In all of her frantic and lonely wondering about him, about where he was and what he was doing, she had never imagined him homeless—a homeless alcoholic on some filthy city street. "How did you ever . . ." But then she could say no more.

"How did I get back?" Gabriel prompted. Grace nodded. He sighed and sat back in his chair. "I hit rock bottom, as they say, after some long, ugly years I've been blessed with a selective memory about. The short version is that I went to a mission one day hoping for a hot meal, and stumbled into an AA meeting. I thought it was a joke, at first, but eventually it started to sink in that I wasn't a lost cause. As soon as I believed that, I wanted to get better. I had a lot of setbacks, but I made it. I've been sober for ten years, and each day, I have to remind myself where I'll end up if I take another drink." He shrugged and resumed eating with a nonchalance she knew to be false, from the way he couldn't look her in the eye.

Softly she said, "I'm sorry that happened to you."

Gabriel looked up, and his eyes were full of pain. "I'm sorry this happened to you." He closed his hand over hers, where it rested on the table, and said, "No one deserves a disease like this, Grace, least of all you. When I think of all I must have put you through, it kills me. I want you to know, I let you down then, but I won't now. I'm here, and I'm going to help you in every way I can. If you let me."

His hand was warm and strong around hers, but it was not the soft scholar's hand she remembered. She thought then of how easy it would be to allow herself to accept his help, not only in retrofitting the loft so that she could keep her home, but in all the other ways she would need assistance in the future. She knew her prognosis; she knew the ultimate course of her disease; she knew that the independence she had fought so hard to win would, in the years to come, grow ever more difficult to keep. Every time she held off relying on her daughter or his sisters or her friends was a triumph; every bit of dependence she acquiesced was like losing a piece of her soul. But with Gabriel it would be different. With Gabriel it wouldn't be a matter of accepting charity because she was an invalid. Gabriel owed her.

How tempting it would be to let him take care of her, and to lie to herself when she said it was merely his penance for leaving her and Justine. It frightened her how easily she could imagine it.

She pulled her hand away. "Thanks, but my family is here for me. Adapting the loft is help enough."

He nodded, but she sensed his disappointment and prayed that he would never know how hard it had been to refuse his offer, and how essential it had been that she do so.

A week after their dinner together, Adam came to Megan's house to pick up Robby. He came inside and chatted with her, but only for as long as it took Robby to tie his shoes, throw on the coat Megan insisted he wear, snatch up his football, and race out the door. "We'll be back in a few hours," Adam said, grinning as Robby shouted for him to hurry.

When Megan shut the door, the house fell silent, and it occurred to her that she had a few hours to herself for the first time in ages. It had been so long since she had last had free time that for a moment she was at a loss for what to do. She considered reading some technical papers she had brought home from work, but decided to brave the malls and go Christmas shopping instead.

Ordinarily Megan disliked shopping because she invariably had to cram two hours' worth into twenty minutes between leaving work and rushing off to pick up Robby from his grandparents'. On this outing, she browsed through the stores at a leisurely pace, listening to Christmas carols, and soon found she was enjoying herself. After selecting gifts for her parents and picking up a few things from Robby's list, she stopped by her local quilt shop, where she purchased a few fat quarters in Christmas prints to send to Donna. Afterward she stopped by her favorite bookstore and treated herself to a novel, which she began to read in the coffee shop over hot chocolate and shortbread, and continued later at home, as she soaked in a hot bath. She hadn't felt so relaxed since quilt camp.

As the afternoon waned, an unexpected loneliness crept into the quiet house, so she started the beef barley vegetable soup that she planned to have for supper with the whole wheat bread she'd purchased at the bakery next door to the quilt shop. As the soup simmered, she sat at the kitchen table and read, glancing out the window at nearly every car that passed. When Adam's car finally pulled into the driveway, she marked her place in the book and went to meet them at the door.

"Did you have fun?" she asked Robby as they came inside, red-cheeked and grinning. She hugged her son and took his football so he could unzip his jacket.

"I made a field goal from the ten-yard line," Robby said.

"Did you?" Megan said, impressed. "That's a record, isn't it?"

"For me it is." Robby grinned up at Adam. "Adam showed me a better way to kick to make it go farther."

"He didn't need much coaching from me," Adam said. "He's a natural."

"Adam says he thinks I could make the middle school team when I'm older, if I practice."

"Oh, he did, did he?" Megan gave Adam a sidelong look, picturing enormous linebackers lumbering forward to crush her child. "Well, we'll see."

"That's what she says when she means something's too dangerous," Robby said to Adam. "She thinks I'm still a baby."

"That's not true," Megan protested as they laughed. "'We'll see' means I'll think about it."

"Can Adam stay for supper? Please, Mom?"

Megan smiled, glad to be able to repay Adam for giving her the luxury of an entire afternoon to herself. "If he'd like to, he's more than welcome. We're having beef barley vegetable soup."

"Not from a can," Robby added. "Mom says that has too much sodium and preservatives."

"Homemade soup?" Adam began to remove his coat. "You don't have to ask me twice."

The soup was flavorful, the crusty bread warmed in the oven and light, perfect for a crisp early December day. Robby and Adam soon had her laughing with stories of their afternoon outdoors. She enjoyed herself so much that she was glad Robby had invited Adam to stay, and she wished she had thought of it herself. After supper, Robby helped Megan clear the table, and to her amusement, Adam began rinsing off bowls and stacking them in the dishwasher. He looked up from his work to see her stifling a laugh, and he grinned sheepishly. "It's a habit," he said, shaking water off his hands and stepping back from the sink. "Sorry."

"No, no, that's quite all right," she said, and began to help. They chatted as they worked, and when Robby was out of earshot, Megan thanked Adam for spending the day with him.

"No need to thank me. I had a great time," Adam said, but Megan wished she could do something more to show him how much she appreciated the way he had befriended her son. She wondered if he had any idea how her heart swelled with gladness to see Robby so happy.

The next Saturday, Adam and Robby went to the Books & Company bookstore in Dayton to meet J. K. Rowling, who was signing copies of the latest Harry Potter book. Megan enjoyed another relaxing afternoon on her own, finishing her Christmas shopping and working on her quilt block for the Challenge Quilt. Although she hadn't completely accomplished her goal, Vinnie had reminded her that she was only required to try, and she had certainly done that. Keith had phoned Robby on Thanksgiving; Robby's counselor said he was making progress, and he hadn't had an outburst at school since the Halloween cookie fiasco; and he was getting along wonderfully with Adam. Until recently, Megan had feared she'd never be able to complete her block without breaking the rules of the challenge, but recently, with Adam's help, she had begun to feel hope.

She began by selecting fabrics for her block, and soon found a clear, rich blue floral print that complemented Vinnie's autumn leaf fabric so well that she had to admit that maybe purple wasn't so bad after all. Choosing a pattern proved to be much more difficult. The one-patch styles Megan preferred didn't suit a sampler quilt, so she didn't have a store of favorite blocks to call upon. She paged through several of her quilting books for ideas, but none of the designs or block names fit as a symbol of her accomplishment. As she finished looking through the third book, she realized that it had grown dark outside. She had lost track of time, but apparently so had Adam and Robby, for they had not yet returned.

She put her books away and hurried downstairs to start supper, but despite her late start, by the time Adam's car pulled into the driveway, she had been keeping the meal warm in the oven for a good half hour. Relieved, she went to the door to greet them.

Adam began apologizing before she could even say hello. "The event went on longer than I expected," he said. "I should have called. I didn't think of it until we were on our way home."

Robby was glowing with excitement. "We had to wait in line for hours," he exclaimed, delighted rather than annoyed, as Megan herself might have been. "There were thousands of kids there." Megan and Adam looked at him skeptically, and he quickly amended that to, "Maybe one thousand."

"I'd say at least eight hundred," Adam added, and with a single look to Megan over Robby's head, he conveyed what it had been like to wait in line among so many excited kids and their beleaguered parents all afternoon.

Megan suppressed a laugh and said, "Supper's ready if you're hungry. Adam, will you stay?"

Adam agreed, and in a few moments they were sitting around

the table, eating and listening as Robby told them what questions the audience had asked and how the author had responded. Robby reverently showed Megan the autograph on the title page. He raced off to read his book as soon as he finished eating, but Megan and Adam lingered, talking about work and the upcoming holiday.

Together they cleaned up the kitchen, and then continued their conversation over coffee. Before she knew it, hours had passed, and it was Robby's bedtime. Adam, who seemed as surprised by the late hour as she, hugged Robby and wished him good night. Megan walked Adam to the door and watched out the window as he drove away. Then she went upstairs to make sure Robby brushed his teeth.

When Megan arrived at work Monday morning, she sent Adam an E-mail note telling him that she had hardly seen Robby all weekend, so engrossed was he in his book. Adam wrote back before noon, and they sent messages back and forth throughout that day and the next. By Wednesday she expected to find a note from him whenever she checked her E-mail, which she found herself doing more frequently than usual. On Thursday, Adam suggested that the three of them go out for pizza after he and Robby went to the movies that weekend. Pleased, Megan agreed, and the rest of the week dragged as she waited for Saturday afternoon.

But on Saturday morning, Adam phoned. "Megan, it's Adam," he said, his voice so weak and hoarse that Megan didn't recognize it. "I hate to do this, but I'm going to have to cancel. I think I have the flu."

"You sound terrible."

"I feel terrible. Will you tell Robby I'm sorry?"

"Of course. He'll understand." She understood, too, and sympathized, but she couldn't help feeling disappointed. "I hope you feel better soon. Get plenty of rest and drink lots of fluids, okay?"

He coughed and groaned. "Not if it means getting off the sofa."

"I mean it. You have to take care of yourself."

"Okay, doctor," he said wearily. "I'll try."

She wouldn't hang up until he promised he'd take her advice, but his promise came so halfheartedly that she doubted he'd keep it. Her hand still on the receiver, she considered calling him back, but then an idea came to her, and she phoned her mother instead.

Robby was in his room reading the last few chapters of his Harry Potter book. "I have some bad news," she said, and waited for him to set down his book. "Adam has the flu. He can't come today." Before he could get too disappointed, she quickly added, "But I called your grandma and grandpa, and they're going to take you to the movie instead."

Robby brightened, but then he looked puzzled. "Aren't you coming?"

"No," Megan said, embarrassed. "I'm going to make sure Adam's all right."

Robby agreed that this was a good idea. Vinnie had given her Adam's address months earlier, and Megan obtained directions to his house from an Internet mapping site. Before long she had dropped off Robby at her parents' house and was on her way to Cincinnati.

Adam's house was a red-brick colonial with black shutters on a quiet street in the northern part of the city. Megan parked in the driveway and hesitated before knocking on the front door, wondering if she had made a mistake by coming there. She considered jumping back in the car and driving home, but Adam might have seen her from the window, and she didn't know what she would tell Robby when he asked how his friend was doing, so she shoved her worries aside and knocked.

She waited, but there was no answer. She knocked again, louder, and then rang the doorbell. Finally she heard someone fumbling with a lock, and the door swung open to reveal Adam, unshaven and pale in gray sweatpants and a long-sleeved T-shirt. He looked even worse than he had sounded on the phone.

"Oh, no," Megan said, appalled. "I should have let you sleep."

Somehow Adam managed a bleary-eyed smile. "Megan," he

said, and he sounded glad to see her. "Didn't you see the quarantine sign?"

"I'm sorry I got you up."

"No, no, that's okay." He opened the door wider. "Come in, if you aren't afraid of the plague."

Megan entered the foyer, her face growing warm. "I thought I'd check in on you to make sure you don't need anything." She looked past him into the living room, where she saw a pillow and a quilt on the sofa, but nothing, not even an empty water glass on the end table, to indicate he had followed her directions. She folded her arms and regarded him with stern amusement. "Have you been taking fluids?"

"I was just going to get myself a glass of orange juice."

"A likely story." She spun him around and gave him a gentle push in the direction of the sofa. "Go lie down. I'll bring you some."

Adam nodded meekly and shuffled off, and as Megan found the kitchen, she heard him groan as he returned to the sofa. She opened the refrigerator door and sighed at what she found there—or rather, what she didn't find. There was a half-empty gallon bottle of milk, some condiments, two Chinese takeout containers—no orange juice, and nothing she could use to make him something nutritious to eat. "Don't you buy groceries?" she called to him, and received a weak apology in return.

Megan found a tea bag in a cupboard, but no kettle, so she boiled water in a saucepan and poured it into a mug. As the tea steeped, she took inventory of the kitchen and made a shopping list. When the tea was ready, she carried it to him and said, "I'm going to run to the grocery store. Is there anything you need?"

"A new set of lungs and some sinuses would be nice." He took a drink of the tea. "Thank you. This is great."

"I'll be back soon."

"Wait," he called after her. "The front door locks automatically. There's a spare key in the drawer of that table in the entry."

"I found it," Megan called back after a brief search. "Drink your tea and try to rest. I'll be back soon."

She tucked the key into her purse and drove to a grocery store she had passed on her way to the house, where she bought more milk, some tea and honey, a quart of orange juice, crackers, and the ingredients for chicken noodle soup. When she returned to Adam's home, she let herself in with the key as quietly as possible, left the grocery bags in the kitchen, and tiptoed into the living room to check on him. He was asleep, the empty mug on the floor beside the sofa.

Megan decided sleep was probably better for him than a glass of orange juice, so she carried the mug into the kitchen and left Adam alone while she prepared the soup. She checked in on him from time to time while the soup simmered, but with the exception of a few fits of coughing, he slept peacefully. She remembered seeing a newspaper on the front porch and went outside for it, then pulled up a stool and read it at the kitchen counter, pausing every so often to check the pot on the stove. Just as she decided the soup was finished, the phone rang, startling her with its abrupt shattering of the silence.

She snatched up the receiver, hoping the noise hadn't woken Adam. "Hello, Wagner residence." There was a pause, and then a dial tone.

As Megan hung up, she heard Adam call to her from the other room. When she joined him, he was sitting up weakly. "Who was it?"

"A wrong number, I guess. They hung up. Was it all right that I answered? I was hoping you'd sleep through it, but maybe I confused them."

"That's fine, thanks. I've been getting a lot of hang-up calls lately, mostly on my answering machine. I think something's wrong with my line." He paused. "What is that wonderful smell?"

"Chicken noodle soup. Are you hungry?"

"I didn't think I would be, but I am." He started to get up, but

Megan ordered him to stay where he was, and she brought him a bowl of soup, some crackers, and a cup of tea. When she returned with soup and tea for herself, Adam had settled back against the sofa cushions, eyes closed. At first she thought he had fallen asleep again, but then he opened his eyes and said, "This is without a doubt the best soup I've ever tasted."

Pleased, Megan settled herself on the floor beside him. "Thanks. It's my mother's recipe."

"I don't think I'll ever be able to eat soup from a can again."

"That's my mission in life, to remind people of how food tastes when it's not made in a factory."

He laughed, but the laugh turned into a cough, and he fumbled for the box of tissues on the end table. "How's Robby doing?" he asked when he was able to talk again.

"He's almost finished with the book you bought him last weekend. Which reminds me, I need to pay you back for that."

"You're kidding, right?" He nodded at his bowl, now nearly empty. "After all this?"

"How about if I leave you the leftovers, and we'll call it even?"

Adam agreed, then finished his soup and set the bowl on the end table. Still weak, he lay down on the sofa again, then watched her as she finished her meal and placed her empty bowl beside his. "Do you want any more?" she asked.

"Not now." His eyes were still red-rimmed, but he looked more comfortable and rested. "How do you do it?"

"How do I do what?"

"How do you do everything you do so well? You're a rocket scientist, a real one, you're a wonderful mother, you're beautiful, and you make homemade soup. It's hard to believe you're real."

"I think we should take your temperature. You're delirious."

"I mean it." He watched her so steadily that she wanted to look away, but found herself unable to. "I would really like to kiss you right now, but I don't want to give you the plague."

Megan's heart jumped, but she said lightly, "I don't think you have the plague."

"Whatever it is, it's killing me, because otherwise I could be kissing you." He considered. "Of course, without this fever, I probably wouldn't have started this conversation."

"Probably not," Megan said gently.

"I still wish I could kiss you, though."

Her eyes locked on his, Megan slowly kissed her fingertips and pressed them to his cheek. He raised his hand and held it over hers, then clasped it and brought it to his lips and then to his heart. Then, slowly, his eyes closed, and he fell asleep again.

Megan eased her hand free, then returned to the kitchen, where she stored the leftovers and washed their dishes. When she finished, she poured Adam a glass of orange juice, placed it on the end table, and sat down on the sofa beside him. She woke him by touching him lightly on the shoulder and telling him she had to go.

"I wish you could stay," he murmured.

"So do I," she said. "But Robby's waiting."

"Would you tell him I'll see him next week?"

"Are you sure? So close to Christmas?"

"Of course."

"I'll tell him." She squeezed his shoulder and stood up.

"Megan—"

"Yes?"

"Thanks for everything. The soup, the company—everything."

Megan smiled at him. "It was my pleasure."

Outside, night had fallen, and light flakes of snow were drifting down and dancing in the winter wind. She closed her eyes and raised her face to the darkened sky, feeling snow crystals fall like kisses, cool and gentle upon her skin. She almost laughed out loud. "Snow crystals," she whispered, knowing at once what block she would create to represent the changes she wanted to make, and was making, in her life. Snow like a soft quilt blanketing the earth, clean, fresh, and new, as hopeful as a mother's dreams for her child.

Donna's first thought when she woke Christmas morning was that Lindsay was coming home. Her heart light, she threw off the covers and hurried to shower and dress. Lindsay was coming home, and they'd have an old-fashioned family Christmas as they always did, Brandon or no Brandon.

She sang carols as she made blueberry pancakes for breakfast, anticipating the day with great joy. She had spent Christmas Eve baking, and the whole house still smelled of gingerbread and apple pie. The tree in the living room was beautifully decorated and surrounded by colorfully wrapped gifts, snow was falling outside, and the day promised to be festive and fun, full of love and laughter with the people she loved most.

Paul and Becca came downstairs for breakfast, smiling and teasing each other. Paul liked to pretend that Becca still believed in Santa Claus, and Becca went along with it to amuse him. "I think I heard reindeer on the roof last night," he said, and Becca bounced up and down in her chair as if she were six rather than sixteen. Donna laughed, enjoying their closeness, and told herself that Lindsay's presence was all she needed to make the day complete. She brushed aside any worry that Lindsay would cancel as she had at Thanksgiving. Lindsay would be there; Donna refused to believe otherwise.

But when the phone rang and Becca answered, her heart began to pound. She prayed it was her brother calling from California to wish them a happy holiday, but when Becca told her flatly that Lindsay was on the line, she steeled herself for the worst. "Merry Christmas, honey," she said with forced cheerfulness. "I thought you'd be on the road by now."

"Merry Christmas, Mom." Lindsay's voice sounded strained. "I thought we would have left by now, too, but we're running late."

"You're still coming, aren't you?"

"Of course. I wouldn't miss Christmas. What time were you planning to have dinner?"

"Around two."

"Okay. We'll be there by one thirty."

"But we were going to open presents first."

"Can we do that after?" Donna heard a low voice speaking in the background, and a hollowness while Lindsay covered the mouthpiece and murmured a response. "It won't take long, will it?"

Donna's throat tightened. "Tell Brandon it will take as long as it takes. It's Christmas, and I'm not rushing through it to please anyone."

Lindsay was silent for a moment. "Okay. We'll be there at one thirty. Bye, Mom. See you soon." She hung up.

"Is she canceling again?" Paul asked.

"No. She'll be here."

Becca looked relieved, but Paul merely nodded grimly.

Donna pretended that nothing was wrong and went about fixing Christmas dinner. *They're only delayed,* she chided herself. Anyone could be delayed driving in Minnesota in December. She was overreacting. But Paul and Becca also seemed ill at ease, for instead of returning to the family room to watch Christmas parades on television, Paul put carols on the CD player, and they stayed in the kitchen, assisting her when she asked, and talking about some of their favorite Christmases of the past.

At a quarter before two, Brandon's car pulled into the driveway. "They're here," Becca called out, running to the front door to meet her sister. Lindsay entered, shaking snow from her blond hair, carrying gifts in one arm and hugging Becca with the other. Paul went to greet her, too, but Donna hung back in the kitchen, listening to the reunion in the foyer with uncertain relief. Because of Lindsay's phone call, she had expected Brandon to be in one of his bad moods, the kind he always seemed to be in whenever Donna phoned her daughter. She dreaded that he would be unpleasant and ruin the holiday.

But when Lindsay led Brandon into the kitchen, he was smiling, and after Lindsay hugged her, Brandon did as well. "Merry Christmas," he said cheerfully. "Thanks for having us. Everything smells great." His enthusiasm was so unexpected that Donna could just barely manage to stammer a Christmas greeting in reply. She caught Paul's eye, and he shrugged, clearly as surprised as she was.

Brandon asked Becca to show him to the Christmas tree so he could leave some gifts beneath it. Lindsay watched them go, then turned to give her mother another hug. "I'm sorry we're late."

"It's all right," Donna said, and now that Lindsay was there, it was. She held her daughter at arm's length and looked her up and down. "Goodness, honey, you're getting so thin."

Lindsay rolled her eyes, smiling. "No, I'm not. You say that every time I visit."

Donna let it go, but Lindsay did look thinner, and she had always been slim. Her face looked tired, too, as if she'd been ill or had slept poorly. "You need a good home-cooked meal," she said, wishing that Lindsay would be spending the night in her old bedroom so Donna could see to it she had a hearty breakfast, too.

The turkey was ready, so Donna and her daughters quickly set the dining room table with the good china and served the meal. Her family praised her cooking, as they always did, declaring this Christmas feast the best yet. For his part, Brandon said her turkey was perfect and her stuffing the best he had ever tasted. Pleased in spite of herself, Donna thanked him, and gradually, as he joined in the dinner conversation as pleasantly as she could have wished, her apprehensions ebbed away. She had to admit that Brandon was handsome and charming, and she understood why her daughter was attracted to him. The worst she could say was that he tended to interrupt when others were speaking, but she could hardly condemn Brandon for something Paul had done to her at least twice daily throughout their nearly twenty-five years of marriage.

After supper, Donna, Lindsay, and Becca cleaned up the mess while Paul and Brandon went into the family room to watch the last quarter of a football game. From the kitchen Donna heard them talking and, every so often, laughing out loud. "They seem to get along well," Donna remarked to Lindsay, who glanced toward the family room and nodded in a distracted way as she wiped off the countertop.

When they finished tidying the kitchen, Donna and her daughters joined Paul and Brandon in the family room to exchange presents. Lindsay explained their tradition to Brandon: The youngest person would give a present to the second youngest, who would unwrap the gift and then give a gift to the next oldest. When the oldest person had received and opened a gift, he would give a gift to the youngest. The pattern would repeat, each person giving a gift to the youngest person they had not yet given a gift to, until all the gifts were distributed.

Brandon shook his head and grinned. "Sounds more complicated than necessary."

"It's a tradition from my side of the family," Paul said.

"Which explains why it's so confusing," Becca added. "And why I always have to be last."

Everyone laughed, but Donna defended her husband, saying, "It's better than what we did in my family. Everyone just tore into the packages at the same time. Wrapping paper flew everywhere, and you could never see what everyone else had received. This way it lasts longer."

With the same grin, Brandon said, "That could be either good or bad, though, couldn't it?"

"Here, Becca," Lindsay said quickly. "I'm younger than Brandon. I'll start."

Becca handed her a box wrapped in red-and-white-striped paper, and for the next half hour, they opened presents one by one, with Paul's system creating occasional but easily remedied confusions, since Lindsay and Brandon had already exchanged gifts. Donna had not expected a present from Brandon, and thought that, at the most, Lindsay would include his name on her gifts, but Brandon had brought presents for everyone. To Paul he gave a computerized day planner; for Becca, he had brought a cashmere sweater set that made her squeal with delight; Donna received an elegant gold watch, set with a diamond chip.

"Brandon, this is too much," Donna exclaimed, admiring the watch. She and Paul had given him a nice sweater and a medical text on CD-ROM that Lindsay had said he wanted, and until that moment, she had considered them suitable gifts. Now she realized Brandon's family must celebrate Christmas on a much more lavish scale than the Jorgensons did, and she wondered if he would think them cheap. He seemed pleased by their appreciation of his gifts, however, so she decided not to fuss about it, and to make it up to him on his birthday.

After the last present had been unwrapped and admired, they were sitting around the Christmas tree chatting when suddenly Brandon slapped his thighs, smiled at Lindsay, and said, "Well, honey? Should we hit the road?"

"Already?" Donna protested. Brandon smiled amiably, but Lindsay looked uncomfortable. "You haven't even had dessert yet."

"Thanks, but we don't want dessert." Brandon stacked up his gifts and rose, then turned to Lindsay. "Are you ready?"

Lindsay hastened to gather her boxes. "Thanks for everything," she said, her voice apologetic. "Dinner was great, Mom."

"Dessert will be great, too," Becca said. "Mom made apple pie especially for you. Don't go yet. It's not even dark outside."

Lindsay hesitated, and glanced at Brandon, who smiled regretfully and shook his head. "I'm afraid we can't," he said. "My parents are expecting us, and it's a long drive. We're going to have dessert there." He headed for the front door. "Come on, honey. Let's go."

"At least let me pack you some gingerbread cookies," Donna said, her face growing hot. She realized with alarm that she was on the verge of bursting into tears. *It's been a nice afternoon,* she scolded herself. *Don't ruin it with a tantrum.* She hurried into the kitchen and filled a cookie tin with gingerbread men, then filled a second for Brandon's parents. By the time she joined the family in the foyer, Brandon had already left to carry their presents out to the car.

Donna hugged her daughter tightly. "I wish you didn't have to go so soon."

Lindsay clung to her, burying her face in her mother's shoulder as she used to when she was a little girl. "I'm sorry. I want to stay."

Suddenly Donna felt awful for making her daughter feel guilty. "It's all right," she said briskly, releasing Lindsay and forcing herself to smile. "I have to share you with your future in-laws. I'm sure they want to see their son as much as we want to see you."

Wordlessly Lindsay nodded and took the cookies, then gave her father and sister quick hugs before hurrying outside to the car, her coat still unfastened.

As they drove away, Donna shut the door against the winter cold.

They returned to the family room, their spirits greatly subdued. Before long Becca excused herself to go to her room to try on her new Christmas clothes, and Paul turned on the television to watch the rest of the football game. Or perhaps it was another game. Donna didn't know and she didn't much care.

She retreated to her quilt room to page through the pattern books Lindsay had given her, but before long she pushed them aside and switched on the computer. She sent Christmas greetings to Megan and Grace, and hoped they were having a happier holiday than she was. After shutting down the computer, she went to her sewing machine to work on the block she had begun for the Challenge Quilt. She had chosen the Hen and Chicks pattern as a teasing reminder of how she played the mother hen to her two girls, and how she had henpecked Lindsay into returning to the university. It had been easier to poke fun at herself then, when she thought everything would be fine as long as Lindsay continued her education. Lindsay was back in school now and doing well, but Donna felt worse than ever. Brandon was charming, but there was something else beneath the charm, something that troubled her.

"Mom?"

Donna started and turned around in her chair. Becca stood in the doorway, her expression unhappy. "Yes, honey?"

"Something's bothering me," Becca said. "First Brandon said they didn't want dessert, but then he said they were going to have dessert at his parents' house."

Donna hadn't noticed, but even now, this seemed insignificant compared to some of his other behaviors. "I suppose when he said they didn't want dessert, he meant that they didn't want it here, because they were going to eat at his parents' later."

"I thought of that, but I wanted to know for sure." Becca hesitated. "So I checked."

"You checked?"

"I called their apartment."

"Becca, you didn't."

"I couldn't help it. I was worried." She crossed the room and sat down on the floor to put her head in her mother's lap. "They were home. Lindsay answered, but when she found out it was me, she said she couldn't talk and hung up. Mom, there wasn't enough time for them to do anything but go straight home."

Donna stroked her daughter's hair. "Maybe they stopped home to pick up something on their way."

Becca pushed herself away from her mother. "Why are you always making excuses for him? Can't you see what a jerk he is? He lied to us, and Lindsay turns into a little mouse around him! Am I the only one in this family with a clue?"

"Okay, honey," Donna soothed, holding out her arms. Becca scowled at her stubbornly for a moment before allowing herself to be pulled into a hug. "I'm not as clueless as you think. I agree that Brandon . . ." She struggled to find the right words, but her feelings were so jumbled that she failed. "He does seem a bit domineering."

"A bit?"

"Well, the holidays are stressful, and you know what Lindsay says about medical school. He's under a lot of pressure. Maybe he was just having a bad day."

"All his days are bad."

"We don't know that. We don't see him every day, not the way Lindsay does. She knows him better than we do, and she wouldn't settle for anything less than a good, kind man who treated her well, would she?"

"Maybe she's confused," Becca persisted. "People do stupid things when they're in love. Remember that time in seventh grade when I called John Richardson's house fifteen times in one day and hung up as soon as someone answered the phone?"

"I thought you said it was only those two times your father caught you on the phone."

"That's what I told him, but it was really more like fifteen."

Donna laughed and hugged her. "Okay, you're right. People do foolish things when they're in love, but Lindsay is sensible, and agreeing to marry someone isn't in the same league as prank phone calls."

"They weren't prank calls. I just got too nervous to stay on the line."

"Either way." Donna sighed. "Honey, maybe Brandon isn't the man we would have picked for Lindsay, but it's not up to us. What's important is that Lindsay is happy. If they love each other, we'll only ruin things if we don't welcome him into our family."

Becca looked her straight in the eye. "Do *you* think Lindsay is happy?"

"I hope she is," Donna said carefully. "I can't believe she would marry him if she didn't believe she and Brandon would be happy together. That's not what I taught you girls."

"Maybe Lindsay didn't learn as well as you think she did."

The doubts that had nagged Donna for months now erupted in a frenzy of warning. Yes, this was what she feared, this was what she was afraid to face, that somehow she had failed to teach Lindsay something intrinsic to her future happiness. She thought back to when the girls were young, and she would overhear them swearing or discover one picking on the other. "What are you doing?" she would scold, astonished anew to discover that her angelic little girls could be vulgar or spiteful. "You didn't learn that in this house. In this house, people are kind to each other."

She longed to take Lindsay in her arms and ask her why she let her fiancé determine when she could visit her family and for how long, why she let him intimidate her into covering up his lie, why she hung up on her sister rather than let Brandon know they were speaking. *You didn't learn that in this house*—but Lindsay had learned it somewhere, and Donna was at a loss, uncertain what to do about it, how to teach her daughter at this late date something she should have been learning all her life.

Suddenly grief welled up in her throat. She wished she had the words to reassure Becca, but she couldn't even reassure herself. For months the Cross-Country Quilters had been encouraging her to trust her instincts, but her feelings were so muddled that she hadn't known what to say. Now she realized she couldn't let another day pass without speaking frankly to Lindsay. She knew she risked offending and possibly alienating her daughter by voicing doubts about the man she loved, but surely Lindsay would understand. Surely when Donna asked her if this is what was she truly wanted, and reminded her that it was not too late to back out, Lindsay would know that she was speaking from the heart, as a mother who wanted only what was best for her child.

She picked up the phone beside the computer. "Are you calling her?" Becca asked.

Donna nodded and listened to the phone ringing, once, twice, a third time—and then, finally, her daughter's voice. "Hello?"

"Lindsay, it's Mom."

"Oh." Lindsay's voice lowered to a whisper. "What is it?"

"Why are you whispering?"

"I'm not," Lindsay said, and her voice returned to a normal volume, almost. "Is something wrong?"

That's what Donna wanted to know. "Sweetheart, I need to ask you something and I want you to give me an honest answer." She steeled herself. "Are you sure you want to go through with this marriage? Are you sure you and Brandon will be happy together?"

On the other end of the line, there was only silence.

Donna quickly added, "Because if you want to call it off, it's not too late. We would all support you."

Donna waited for Lindsay's indignant reply: *How could you ask such a thing?* she might say, or *Why in the world wouldn't I want to marry Brandon? I love him.* But Lindsay said nothing. Donna heard her breathing; if not for that, she would have thought the line had gone dead.

When Lindsay finally spoke, she said, "I can't. I couldn't do that to him."

"What about you? What about what this is doing to you?"

"Mom, I can't talk right now."

"When can you talk about it? Let's go out to lunch tomorrow, honey, okay? We can—"

"I have to go," Lindsay whispered. "I'm sorry." And with that, she hung up.

Slowly Donna replaced the receiver and met Becca's hopeful gaze. She shook her head. Becca sighed and lay her head in her mother's lap again. Donna stroked her hair in silence, wondering what to do.

Eventually Becca said, "Since Lindsay doesn't seem even close to changing her mind, I guess I ought to tell you what she asked me today."

"What's that?"

"She wanted to know if you've started her wedding quilt yet."

Donna's breath caught in her throat. "Oh, dear." Her own daughter's wedding was a mere six months away, and Donna hadn't sewn a stitch of her bridal quilt. Not only that, although she had made many others for her nieces and nephews, it had never occurred to her to make one for Lindsay and Brandon.

"I didn't think you'd started it yet, so I thought I ought to warn you she's hoping for one."

"Thank you, honey."

In response, Becca hugged her, rose, and told Donna she'd be in her room. Donna nodded absently and watched her leave. Lindsay wanted a wedding quilt made by her mother's hands. Lindsay knew what a wedding quilt symbolized—enduring love, patience, commitment—and she would not ask for one lightly. She would not hope for one if she had any uncertainties about marrying Brandon.

Alone in her quilt room, Donna put away the pieces to the Hen and Chicks block, which now seemed inappropriately whimsical. She went to the bookshelf and took down one of her best-loved pattern books and began paging through it, searching for inspiration for the wedding quilt that she had somehow forgotten to begin, that she had not allowed herself to remember would be expected. She tried to find a pattern that would celebrate a lasting union between Lindsay and Brandon, but every block reminded her of her daughter, of Lindsay alone, the way she used to be—joyful and confident and self-assured, and not the apologetic, silent ghost of herself who had come home that Christmas day. She searched through one book, and then another, until all the books were scattered about her on the floor like windblown leaves, but she could find no way to stitch together the lives of her daughter and the man she had agreed to marry, no pattern beautiful, harmonious, and whole that had Brandon in it.

For weeks, Adam had been following the grim story of Lindsor's department store in the newspaper, wondering what its gloomy prospects meant for Natalie. He knew she would be feeling threatened, angry, and frustrated—so he was not surprised when she called him a few days after Christmas and asked if he were free New Year's Eve, and if he wanted to get together.

He wasn't free, and told her so; as much as he sympathized with her plight, he didn't intend to cancel his plans with Megan to spend the evening consoling Natalie. She persisted, and since he did care about her and wanted to reassure her that whatever happened at

Lindsor's she would find a way to land on her feet, he agreed to meet her for dinner the first Friday evening after New Year's Day.

She picked their favorite French restaurant downtown, which pained him, as he had asked her to marry him there and hadn't returned since she broke off their engagement. He was waiting at their table when she arrived twenty minutes late, apologizing for a crisis at work that had delayed her. He rose to pull back her chair and breathed in her perfume as she seated herself. The fragrance, exotic and yet so subtle that he had almost forgotten it, flooded him with memories, none of them particularly pleasant. As he returned to his own seat, wishing he had never come, he reminded himself that he was the one who had suggested they remain friends, and that right then Natalie needed a friend.

"You would not believe what a fiery pit of hell work has become," she said, shaking her head in disgust and opening the menu. Her eyes snapped with anger, which somehow enhanced her beauty. He suddenly realized she was wearing her red silk dress. It had always been one of his favorites, off the shoulder and clinging to her curves in a way that was undeniably alluring. It wasn't the sort of dress she wore to work, so she must have changed before meeting him.

"I've read about the takeover," he said, refusing to second-guess Natalie's intentions. She enjoyed the challenge of charming people; naturally she would choose a dress she knew he liked. "Do you think it's a possibility?"

"It's not only a possibility, it's happening." She paused as the waiter arrived to take their order, then added, "Whatever you see in the news is at least a week out of date. Lindsor's has already accepted their offer."

"I'm sorry," Adam said, with genuine regret. "How will this affect you?"

She shook her head and took a drink of wine. "I don't know. It's too soon to say." Suddenly she looked tearful. "They're going to close stores and cut jobs, and not just on the lower end. They're consolidating upper management, but they haven't told us yet who goes and who stays. The office has been a nightmare—everyone scrambling to prove how essential they are to the corporation and accusing everyone else of being dead weight. People I trusted, people I thought were my friends—they're just like everyone else, backstabbing and conniving."

Adam thought Natalie more than capable of holding her own in such a situation, and told her so, but she shook her head. "It's different there now. I can't make alliances, and can't make compromises, not when everyone knows the person you help today could be the one who has your job tomorrow."

"You'll be fine," Adam assured her. "Think of all you've accomplished there. They can't afford to lose you."

"That's what I keep telling myself, but in the meantime, I've been working on my résumé." She smiled and reached across the table for his hand. "All that socializing you always made fun of might finally pay off. The CEO and CFO like me, and that might just give me an edge."

"It couldn't hurt." Out of habit, he ran his thumb over her knuckles as he held her hand.

"I could have used your help New Year's Eve," she scolded him gently. "I attended a function and ran into the presidents of two other chains. It would have been wonderful if you had been there to charm their wives in case I'll be asking them for a job in a few weeks."

"I had other plans," Adam said, and didn't elaborate. Megan had invited him to her house, where they and Robby had some kind of delicious beef wrapped in a pastry crust for supper. Afterward they watched videos, and when Robby fell asleep on the floor in his sleeping bag, Megan snuggled up beside Adam on the sofa and they held each other. At midnight, they kissed, and it was the most gentle, warm, and loving kiss he could remember ever receiving. Then they woke Robby to wish him a happy new year, and Megan put him to bed. Adam hoped she would ask him to stay the night, but he didn't expect it, not so soon and not with her son in the house. She didn't, but she did kiss him in a way that

that made him hope that the night they could stay together wouldn't be too far off.

Suddenly Adam realized Natalie's hand was still in his, and abruptly, he released it. The waiter arrived then with their entrees, and as they began eating, Natalie asked him how school was going. He reminded her he was still on break and told her how the semester had gone, keeping it brief, because he knew lengthy narratives about his students bored her. To his surprise, she listened as if she were interested, and even prompted him for more details about a student she remembered from the previous year.

"You seem to be doing well," she said when he had finished, and gave him a wan smile. "I think you're doing better than I am."

"Our careers are too different to compare—"

"I wasn't talking about work. I was talking, you know, just in general."

Adam wasn't sure what she meant, but something in her expression made him uncomfortable. "You're going to be fine."

"I hope you're right." She drained the last of her wine and set down the glass, her slender fingers grasping the stem, her gaze lowered. "Adam, I've been thinking. I've had a lot of time to think about my future, and about us, and about how it ended."

In a flash of insight, he realized where she was going, and he urgently wanted her to say no more. "Natalie—"

"No, please, let me finish. I've been thinking that I made the biggest mistake of my life in letting you go. I had a good thing, and I threw it away." She hesitated. "You don't have to answer now, but please think about it. I know I hurt you, but I also know you're the kind of man who forgives. I was wondering if you thought you could ever forgive me, and if maybe we could try again."

Adam couldn't believe what he was hearing. Once he would have rejoiced to hear Natalie speak those words, but that was months ago. "Of course I forgive you," he said. "And I hope you forgive me. But you were right to break it off. It wouldn't have worked. You were just the first of us to realize it."

"But I think I was wrong." She smiled at him, her eyes warm

with encouragement and wistful hope. "What do you say? Shall we start over?"

"Natalie, are you sure . . ." He chose his words carefully. "Are you sure you'd be saying this if not for the troubles at work?"

She sat back in her chair, stung. "How could you say such a thing?" Her eyes were bright with tears.

He felt horrible. "I'm sorry. It's just that you're upset and anxious—and maybe that's why you think we ought to try again. In hindsight, especially compared to how awful things are at Lindsor's these days, maybe our relationship seems better than it really was."

"I know how good it was," she said stubbornly. "I know you loved me once, and I think you still do. Why can't we try again? Is it because you think I'll break up with you? I promise you, I swear to you I won't."

"I can't."

"Why not? There isn't someone else, is there?" She stared at him in disbelief. "Oh, my God. There is, isn't there?"

He took a deep breath. "Yes, I'm seeing someone."

"Oh my God." Natalie raised her wine glass to her lips, forgetting it was empty. "Is she the one who answered the phone at your house?"

"What?"

"Who is she?"

"You've never met."

"Is it serious?"

He hated hurting her, but he had to be honest. "I think it might be."

Natalie was incredulous, close to tears. "Do you love her?"

He had not yet asked himself that question, but now, confronted with it, he found he knew the answer. "Yes, I think I do."

"I can't believe this." A tear slipped down her cheek, and angrily, she whisked it away with a fingertip, careful not to smudge her mascara. "Well, you must not have loved me very much if you could fall for someone else so soon."

Her words stung. "That was an ugly thing to say. You know I loved you."

"Apparently not as much as I thought," she said with a brittle laugh. "Is she prettier than me? Wait, don't answer that. I don't want to know."

"Natalie—"

"Just tell me one thing, though, would you? How long have you two been seeing each other? Were you seeing her while we were still engaged? Did it start before or after we broke up?"

"After." Adam fought to keep his irritation under control. As difficult as Natalie had been sometimes, he never would have considered betraying her. "Months after."

"Then you couldn't have been with her for very long, a few months at most. What's that compared to the years we've shared?"

"This isn't something we can negotiate." Adam kept his voice low in an attempt to prevent hers from rising even higher.

Her tears were falling freely now, and she made no attempt to conceal them. "You love her," she said. "Tell me something else. Why her? Why her, and not me?"

"Let's not do this, please."

"No, really, I want to know." She folded her hands on the table and regarded him with cool, businesslike interest, but her tears betrayed her. "Maybe this will help me in the future."

Adam didn't see how, but he was willing to do anything to help her stop crying. "She's a good person. I think you'd like her—"

"Oh, *please*. Give me some specifics."

"What do you want me to say? She's smart, she's kind, she's a wonderful mother—"

"So that's what this is all about. It's always kids with you, isn't it?" Suddenly she softened. "Look, I'm willing to consider it, okay? Maybe having kids wouldn't be so bad. I might be willing to compromise on that point."

"You shouldn't compromise on having kids," Adam said, incredulous. "I never wanted you to have them for me. If you don't want them for yourself, you shouldn't have them." Suddenly he felt exhausted, drained by her anger and the effort it took to try to avoid hurting her when hurt was inevitable. "I don't know what else to tell you. I'm sorry. I hate hurting you, but I can't try again, knowing how it will turn out."

"You don't know how it will turn out."

"I do know."

"You can't. I'm different now. Things won't end the same."

But Adam was different, too, and he realized then that Natalie would never see that. "I'm sorry," he said, at a loss, knowing nothing he said would comfort her or convince her he was right.

Natalie took a deep breath, and then another, staring at the table. "All right." Her voice was hollow. "I can accept this. You're punishing me. I suppose I deserve that, after breaking off the engagement."

"That's not it." Frustration gave his voice an edge. "I care about you, I really do, but it just won't work."

"Because of her."

"Not only because of her."

Natalie sniffed scornfully, then fell silent, one graceful hand toying listlessly with her wine glass.

"I'm sorry," Adam said again, helpless.

"You can stop saying that." She took another deep breath, and then, much calmer, she met his gaze and said, "Can we at least still be friends, or will that upset your girlfriend?"

"Of course we can be friends," he said, ignoring the snide emphasis she had given the last word, unwilling to start a new argument. "I hope we'll always be friends."

She nodded and looked away. "Well." She gathered her purse and coat and cleared her throat. "If you don't mind, I think I'll be going. I'm not very hungry, and I have a lot of work to do this weekend."

Adam rose with her, but she hurried away from the table before he could say good-bye.

He sank heavily into his chair, wondering if he could have possibly made a worse mess of things. He pictured Natalie's tears and silently berated himself for causing them.

Disgusted with himself, he signaled the waiter for the check, eager to be away from there.

Ten

TO: Donna Jorgenson ‹quiltmom@USAonline.com›
FROM: Megan.Donohue@rocketec.com
DATE: 11:34 AM 1/4
SUBJECT: Re: Happy New Year!

I haven't been avoiding your questions! Yes, I did have a date
for New Year's Eve, and yes, you guessed right, but I wish you
would stop calling him the Apple Pie Guy.

TO: Grace Daniels ‹danielsg@deyoung.org›
FROM: Donna Jorgenson ‹quiltmom@USAonline.com›
DATE: 4 Jan 12:35 PM CDT
SUBJECT: We were right. . . .

It's true, Megan and Adam are dating!

TO: Donna Jorgenson ‹quiltmom@USAonline.com›
FROM: Grace Daniels ‹danielsg@deyoung.org›
DATE: 1:26 PM PT 4 Jan
SUBJECT: Re:We were right . . .

I can see Vinnie celebrating already. She's going to finish her
Challenge Quilt block first. I wonder if I'll ever be allowed to
start mine.

TO: Donna Jorgenson ‹quiltmom@USAonline.com›
FROM: Megan.Donohue@rocketec.com
DATE: 4:57 PM 1/4
SUBJECT: Re: Happy New Year!

About my earlier message . . . Don't tell Vinnie, all right?
Adam and I have been seeing each other, but Robby is almost always with us so I'm not sure how serious this is. You
know how I've been disappointed before, and I refuse to set
myself up for another fall.

Megan stopped, read over her message, and hit the Delete key
until most of the words had been erased, leaving only:

About my earlier message . . . Don't tell Vinnie, all right?

She added, "Thanks" and sent the message off through cyber-
space.

When Donna received it, she bit her lip and thanked heaven
Vinnie didn't have E-mail and that the mail carrier had not yet arrived to pick up the letter waiting in Donna's mailbox. Donna
hurried outside to retrieve it, then returned to the computer, wondering if she should confess. There was no need, she decided.
Megan had said not to tell Vinnie, not that she couldn't tell *anyone*. And it wouldn't be fair to tell Grace without also telling Julia.

January 8th

Dear Vinnie,

*Just a quick note for now—I promise I'll send you a
longer letter soon. Thank you for the pumpkin bread but
please don't send me any more sweets or I'll burst the seams
on my Sadie costumes. A pox on whoever invented the corset!*

*I have delightful news. I have it on very good authority
(Donna) that Megan and Adam are seeing each other. Now,
you have to promise me you'll keep this to yourself. Donna
told me not to tell you, but I remembered what you said
about a grandmother's right to know, and I couldn't bear to
keep you out of the loop. I hate it when people keep secrets
from me. It makes me feel so unpopular.*

I'm sending some California sunshine your way.

Your quilting buddy,
Julia

*PS: Remember, not a word to Donna! She'll never forgive
me, and you wouldn't deprive me of my quilt tutor, would
you?*

Vinnie whooped with delight and danced around her living
room, waving the letter over her head and cheering with such sustained enthusiasm that her next-door neighbor grew alarmed and
called the Meadowbrook Village emergency line. Thus was Vinnie
forced to spend a good hour of her afternoon having her vital
signs checked and explaining to a concerned nursing staff that she
had not lost her marbles, and if they didn't mind terribly much,
she had important quilting to get back to.

Donna was in her quilt room when the phone call came that
changed her life.

"May I speak with Lindsay Jorgenson, please?" the woman
asked.

Her voice was pleasant and professional, but Donna didn't recognize it. A telemarketer, she decided. Everyone else knew to call Lindsay at school. "No, I'm sorry, she's not here."

"Is this her mother?"

"Yes. May I help you with something?"

"Oh, dear. I hope I didn't get you out of bed."

"I beg your pardon?" Donna asked, confused. "Who is this, please?"

"I'm Alicia Solomon, one of Lindsay's professors. Last night Lindsay left a message on my answering machine about your illness."

"My illness?"

"I hope it's nothing serious. Lindsay sounded so upset on the phone that I was worried. Is there anything I can do?"

"N-no," Donna stammered. "Actually I'm . . . feeling much better, thank you."

"I'm relieved to hear that. When Lindsay said she had to go home to take care of you—well, the entire department was concerned. She's quite a favorite around here."

"Yes . . . well, thank you."

"Please let her know she can make up the exam in my class whenever she comes back to campus. I'm sure her other professors will be willing to make arrangements for anything else she's missed."

"Oh, of course. I'll let her know."

"Thank you. Do you know when she might be returning? I'm also the faculty advisor of the drama society, and I'm wondering about the play. We just started this semester's production. We should be able to manage without our director for a few days, but if she'll be away longer—"

"She won't," Donna broke in, eager to get off the phone. "I'll have her contact you, okay?"

"I'd appreciate that. Thanks very much," the professor said. "It was nice chatting with you. I hope you're feeling better soon."

"Thank you. Me, too," Donna said, and hung up. Her heart racing, she hurried downstairs where Becca was lying in front of the television doing her homework. "Becca, do you know if Lindsay cuts classes? Would she tell you if she did?"

Becca looked up from her Spanish textbook, eyebrows raised. "You're kidding, right? Lindsay, cutting classes? Teacher's pet Lindsay?" Then she must have detected the alarm in her mother's expression, for suddenly her manner changed. "What's wrong? Who was that on the phone?"

"One of her professors."

Becca looked uneasy, but she said, "College isn't like high school. Everyone skips a class now and then. Lindsay told me so."

"But Lindsay skipped an exam." Sick at heart, Donna went to the kitchen to phone her. Becca jumped up from the floor and followed. "I think she's also skipped rehearsals. She told her professor she had to come home because I'm ill."

"Lindsay wouldn't miss a test unless she was sick," Becca said. "And that's a perfectly good excuse, so she wouldn't lie about it."

That was exactly what Donna thought. Her hands trembling, she dialed Lindsay's number. The phone rang four times before the answering machine picked up. They had changed the outgoing message; instead of Lindsay's voice, Brandon spoke in her ear, cordial yet somehow cool. "Honey, this is Mom," Donna said after the beep. "Please call me back as soon as you get this message." She hung up and glanced at the clock. Five minutes after four.

"Mom?" Becca asked in a small voice. "Is something wrong?"

"I don't know, sweetheart." She picked up the phone again and dialed Paul's cell phone number. He had told her that morning he planned to be out of the office all day, inspecting a site for an insurance claim. The phone rang only once before a recorded message announced that he was out of range. "I'm sure everything's okay," Donna assured her visibly stricken younger daughter, wishing she felt as confident as she sounded. "Lindsay must have decided to play hooky today."

"Lindsay doesn't play hooky."

Donna checked the clock, hesitated, and dialed Lindsay's number a second time, only to reach the answering machine again. Donna left another message, then hung up the phone. She wished she could talk to Paul; she wished she knew what to do. She wished the university wasn't so far away.

Donna grabbed her purse off the counter. "I'm driving down there to check on her."

"Don't go by yourself. Wait for Dad."

"He won't be home for two hours."

"Then let me come with you."

Donna was about to refuse, but when she saw the urgency in her daughter's eyes, she nodded. Donna scribbled a hasty note to Paul as Becca grabbed their coats; within five minutes, they were on the road to the Twin Cities.

The mid-January afternoon was overcast and bitterly cold, but the freeways had been cleared since the last snowfall, and only a few icy flurries blew in the wind. Never had Donna traveled from Silver Pines to the university so quickly, nor with such fear and trepidation. When they pulled into the parking lot of Lindsay's apartment building nearly an hour later, Becca pointed and said, "There's her car. I don't see Brandon's."

Nodding, Donna parked nearby. They hurried up the side-walk, where Donna looked up at the third floor and saw a light on in one of Lindsay's windows. Becca reached the front entrance first and pressed the buzzer for her sister's apartment. A moment later, the speaker beside the door crackled with Lindsay's voice, barely audible as she asked who was there.

"It's us, honey," Donna said into the intercom. "Mom and Becca." She glanced up and saw a shadow move toward the living room curtains, then away.

"What are you doing here?"

"Professor Solomon called for you at home. You weren't answering your phone, so we came to see if anything was the matter."

Silence.

Donna buzzed again. "Honey, are you still there? Will you let us in?"

"You shouldn't have come."

Before Donna could reply, Becca put her face close to the intercom and said, "Lindsay, would you let us in, please?"

There was another silence, and then, like a sob, came Lindsay's voice. "All right." The door buzzed and clicked. Becca seized the handle and yanked it open, then raced ahead of her mother upstairs, taking the steps two at a time.

Donna reached Lindsay's front door just as Becca finished knocking. Donna heard a bolt slide back, and then the door opened a crack, enough to glimpse part of Lindsay's face but nothing of the room within.

"Please," Lindsay said, her voice oddly muffled. "Please go away before Brandon gets back."

At those words, a surge of rage filled Donna and she shoved the door open. Lindsay quickly turned her back and began to walk away, but Donna took her by the shoulders and spun her around. Behind her, Becca gasped.

Lindsay's lower lip was split and swollen, her right eye a mass of fresh bruises.

"Dear God," Donna breathed.

"I'm okay." Lindsay tried to turn away, and her hand trembled as she lifted it to brush her bangs over her face. "I'm okay."

"You most certainly are not," Donna snapped with pain and angry grief. "Did Brandon do this to you?"

Lindsay froze—then suddenly she dropped her guard. She nodded and sank into a chair, burying her swollen face in her hands.

"Becca, lock the door," Donna ordered. She marched into the bedroom and searched until she found Lindsay's steamer trunk and suitcases. Flinging open the closet, she put Lindsay's clothing, hangers and all, into the first bag, then started with the chest of drawers. Anger, blinding and white-hot, propelled her through the room. *This is not happening,* she thought as she snatched up Lindsay's belongings. *Not to my daughter.*

"I have her books," Becca said, clutching Lindsay's backpack. She was crying.

Donna snapped the first suitcase shut and gave Becca her car keys. "Put this in the car," she said. "Hurry back." Becca did as she was told, wearing the backpack and lugging the suitcase with both hands.

"Mom, don't," Lindsay begged. "Please."

"If there's anything you want from the other room, you'd better get it," Donna said, fighting to choke back her sobs. "I don't know what's yours and what's his."

"I can't leave."

"You can and you will. Today. Now."

"I can't do this to him."

"You can't do this to *him*?" Donna whirled to face her. "Did I raise you to be a punching bag? It won't get any better, Lindsay. If it's like this now, it won't get any better once you're married."

Lindsay's voice broke. "He loves me."

"This is not love," Donna said. "You know that." She had to. "You know this is not love. Where did you learn that Brandon— that *anyone* can hit you? Did your father ever lay a hand on me? Did we ever hit you?"

Lindsay shook her head, tears streaming down her lovely face, made ugly by Brandon's fists. "I don't . . ." She gulped air. "I don't . . . know what he'll do . . . if he comes home and finds me gone—"

"He won't do anything. He'll never get close enough to you to do anything." Donna went to her and held her tightly. "You have to get out of this now. It will never be any easier."

Lindsay clung to her, weeping. Donna sat down on the bed and held her, murmuring to her and rocking her back and forth— but her heart leaped into her throat when the front door slammed. Lindsay stiffened. "It's only me," Becca called, and Lindsay went limp in her mother's arms again.

"Come on." Donna pulled Lindsay to her feet and gestured toward the trunk, which Lindsay began to fill with her possessions, first dazedly, and then with gradually increasing haste. Lindsay carried the second suitcase out to the car, then returned to help her mother with the trunk. As they were maneuvering it down the staircase, Becca remembered the computer. While Donna started the car, shivering with cold and apprehension, her daughters raced back upstairs. It seemed forever until they hurried back out to the car again, Lindsay carrying the computer, Becca, the monitor.

"We had to leave the printer," Becca gasped, breathless from exertion as she climbed into the back seat.

"Forget it," Donna said. Urgency had stolen over her as the afternoon sky turned to dusk, and she expected to see the headlights of Brandon's car as he tore around the corner, at any moment. As frightened as she was, she knew Brandon was fortunate she had not seen him that night. She wanted to leave before he returned; she wanted to stay and tear his heart out as he had torn hers. She was no hen pecking haplessly after her chicks; she was a mother bear, her blood raging hot with fierce love, her overwhelming instinct to lay her teeth and claws into anything that dared hurt her cubs.

She reached over and squeezed Lindsay's hand, then raced toward home with her most precious cargo.

⁂

"Did she call the police?" Adam asked. Robby had long since gone to bed, and Megan and Adam were sitting in front of the fire Adam had built to ward off the cold from a spell of frigid temperatures that had descended that last week of January.

"I don't think so." Megan stretched and settled back against him, enjoying the comfort of his arms and the warmth of his breath on her cheek. "She says Lindsay refuses to say anything against him. Donna probably thinks it's enough that she was able to convince Lindsay not to accept his phone calls."

"While Lindsay's at home that might be fine, but what about when she goes back to school?"

"She's on special leave, so that won't be until August." Megan remembered how relieved and happy Donna had been when Lindsay agreed to return to school. Now, only a semester later,

Lindsay had been compelled to withdraw, and for reasons none of them ever could have predicted. "Maybe they think it will all blow over by then."

"I hope they're right," Adam said, but he sounded doubtful. He kissed Megan and added, "I'd better go."

"Already?"

He stroked her arm. "Unless you want me to stay."

Megan knew he meant stay the entire night, but she couldn't agree to it, not with Robby there. Robby might not mind finding Adam at the breakfast table the next morning—in fact, he would probably be pleased—but Megan wasn't comfortable with such casual overnight arrangements. She didn't want to make an implicit promise to either of them, and for her, allowing Adam to stay the night implied an understanding, a commitment. Although Megan was confident and hopeful that they were headed in that direction, she was content to wait. They had all been through too much heartache not to proceed carefully now, and they were happy, so she felt no urgency to hasten into anything before she and Adam were both certain the time was right.

So she shook her head and said, "I'm sorry."

"Don't apologize," he said, and kissed her. "I understand."

He did understand, and he accepted her feelings and her right to them without judgment or complaint, which was one of the reasons she loved him.

She went with him to the door, and as he was putting on his coat, she said, "Oh, I've been meaning to give you your key back. I accidentally left it in my purse that day you were sick."

"Keep it."

"Are you sure?"

"Of course." Adam smiled and touched her face. "I'll see you next week."

After one last embrace, Adam went outside into the cold. He waved before getting into the car; Megan waved back before shutting the door against the bitter night air. She shook her head and smiled at herself for being so pleased that he wanted her to have his key. He lived far enough away that she would never be in the neighborhood and able to drop by unannounced, so she would probably never use the key unless Adam locked himself out. But somehow it touched her, as if in giving her his key he meant to show how much he trusted her, and how he expected them to be together for the long term.

The next morning when Megan checked her E-mail, she found a message that Adam had sent the night before:

TO: Megan.Donohue@rocketec.com
FROM: wagnera@rogerbacon.k12.oh.edu.
DATE: 12:43 AM 23 January
SUBJECT: Missing you

When I came home I thought of how much nice it would be if we were together. Now that you have the key, every morning when I wake up, I'll open my eyes hoping to find you here.

I love you, Megan.

Megan wanted to write back that she loved him, too, but she had never told him so before, and the first time she said those words to him, she wanted it to be in person.

January passed with bitter cold and heavy snows and no end to Brandon's phone calls. Lindsay flinched whenever the phone rang, and refused to read her E-mail unless Donna or Becca downloaded it first and deleted Brandon's messages. Or so she said—twice Donna had entered Lindsay's room only to find her seated at the computer, her face wet with tears. She would jump in her seat at her mother's approach, and quickly shut down the computer before Donna could see what she was doing. It made Donna sick at heart to think that Lindsay was still in contact with the man who had treated her so brutally, and it troubled her even more when Lindsay would not say for certain whether she had broken off the engagement.

This infuriated Paul, and he implored Lindsay to press charges against Brandon for striking her. "If he had been a stranger on the street," he stormed when he and Donna were alone, "there wouldn't be any question of protecting him like this."

Donna tried to soothe him by emphasizing that at least they had separated the couple and Lindsay was safe in their home. Privately she thought that Lindsay's refusal to go to the police was only in part to protect Brandon, and partially to protect herself. For weeks Lindsay had drifted about the house gingerly, as if she thought she might shatter from the impact of a stray thought or harsh word. The young woman who had been so willing to forgo her education the previous summer now seemed to consider her decision to withdraw from the semester as evidence that she had failed her parents and herself. It didn't matter that Paul and Donna supported her choice. Lindsay had retreated into a world of her own, and Donna feared the old Lindsay might be lost to them forever.

But as the days passed, Lindsay gradually lost the haunted look in her eyes, and by the end of February she had resumed some of her usual interests. She went out with old high school friends who had remained in town; she visited the public library often to check out books on stagecraft and filmmaking. She rented videos of stage plays, which she and Donna would watch together and discuss. Each day brought a new, positive change in Lindsay's behavior, and only infrequently did Donna hear her crying in her room.

Then one gray morning, when Donna and Lindsay were alone in the house, Donna heard a car pull into the driveway. There was no mistaking the car, or the young man who jumped out of it and strode purposefully toward the house.

Donna hurried to the door, glancing up the stairs to Lindsay's bedroom and praying that she had been too engrossed in her reading to have heard the car. The doorbell rang, and before she could respond, a fist pounded on the door. "Lindsay," she heard Brandon shout. "Lindsay, it's me. Let me in."

"She doesn't want to see you," Donna shouted back.

A pause, and then, louder, "Lindsay, it's Brandon."

Donna checked to be sure the chain was fastened before opening the door a crack. "I said, she doesn't want to see you."

Brandon glared at her, his face pale with outrage. "Then let me hear it from her."

Donna heard Lindsay's door open and the faint creak of her footfall on the stairs. "I'm going to shut this door," Donna said, "and you're going to get in your car and drive away. If you don't, I'll call the police."

To her shock, instead of backing off, Brandon shoved the door, straining at the chain. "I know she's in there. Lindsay," he shouted. "We're supposed to get married in a few months. Talk to me."

"If you have something to say to my daughter, you can say it to me." Donna glanced over her shoulder to find that Lindsay had not descended past the top step.

"I need to talk to her alone."

"That," Donna said fiercely, "is one thing I will never allow."

Brandon swore and gave the door another hard shove before stepping back and raking his fingers through his hair. "You can't keep me away from her. We love each other. We won't let you come between us."

"She isn't coming back to you, Brandon."

"That's her choice, not yours," he shot back. "And she'll choose me."

"Stay away from Lindsay," Donna's voice was clear and emphatic and trembling with anger. She closed the door. "Stay away from my family."

"She'll choose me, and do you know why?" Brandon shouted through the door. "Because she doesn't have anything else, and she knows it. You hear me? She knows it!"

Donna carefully locked the door and forced herself to walk

away, back to the kitchen, where she watched through the curtains as Brandon paced around the front porch for a while, until he threw up his hands in frustration, stormed back to his car, and sped off.

Valentine's Day fell on a Sunday that year, but Adam invited Megan out for the preceding Saturday night instead. After spending the afternoon ice skating with Robby, Adam hurried home for a quick shower and a change of clothes, then returned with roses and a box of chocolates for Megan. She laughed but seemed pleased, and Adam saw as if for the first time how beautiful she was, not just because she had dressed up for the occasion, but because when she was happy, she glowed with an inner light. He was drawn to her anew each time he glimpsed it, and it made him never want to leave her side.

When they took Robby to her parents' house, Megan invited him in to meet them. They were down-to-earth, pleasant people, and Adam saw in them the source of Megan's common sense and good humor. He liked them, and to his relief, they seemed to like him.

The evening went as perfectly as Adam could have wished. The restaurant was romantic, the food delicious, and Megan such lovely company that for long moments he could do nothing more than marvel at how lucky he was, and how blessed by the circumstances that had brought them together. Afterward Megan invited him home, as he had hoped she would; when he kissed her and told her he loved her and she returned the sentiment, he was so overcome with happiness that he held her close and wished he never had to let her go.

He longed to spend the night rather than return to the loneliness of his empty house, but Megan gently reminded him that her parents were expecting them to pick up Robby. "He could have stayed overnight," she said, chiding herself. "But I didn't plan . . . this."

He kissed her and said, "Some of the best things in life don't happen according to plan." She smiled at him then in a way that left him overcome with desire, but her family was waiting. After retrieving Robby and seeing the two safely to the door, Adam kissed Megan one last time, then drove home alone.

In the morning he woke from dreams of Megan to early sunlight spilling in through the windows. Something had roused him, and as the sleepy cloudiness left him, he heard it again: a rapping on the front door. Groggy, he padded to the door wearing only his pajama bottoms. Fumbling with the lock, he opened the door—and found Natalie standing on the front porch, smiling at him.

"Natalie," he said, suddenly conscious of the cold. "What are you doing here?"

She held up a paper bag from a coffee shop they used to frequent together. "I brought breakfast. Bagels and cappuccino." Then she brought out a hand from behind her back and held out a single red rose. "Happy Valentine's Day."

He didn't take it. "Natalie—"

"Those pajamas have a top, you know," she said, eyeing his attire. "I should know. I bought them for you." She tossed her hair over her shoulder. "So are you going to let me in or what?"

"Sure." He held the door open for her, and she entered. Yawning, he indicated the kitchen and said, "I'll get dressed and be there in a minute."

Natalie laughed. "Don't bother if you're comfortable. I've seen you in far less than that."

Instead of answering, Adam went to his bedroom and threw on a pair of jeans and a sweatshirt. By the time he returned to the kitchen, Natalie had set the table for two and had placed the rose in a bud vase she had once bought him. She smiled when she saw him and began unpacking the bag. "Hungry?" she asked.

Adam nodded and sat down. "You should have called."

"Why? Do you have company?"

"No, but I might have." He didn't intend for the words to come out so sharply, but Natalie took no offense. Instead she served him his cappuccino, and he wasn't surprised to find that she had remembered exactly how he liked it. Resigned, he helped himself to a bagel. "You should have called."

She just laughed at him and changed the subject. She looked bright and fresh and pretty, not at all as she had the last time they were together. If she remembered how angry and hurt she had been that night, she gave no sign as she asked about his family and updated him on the ever-worsening situation at Lindsor's.

She was well into a description of the most recent layoff scare when the doorbell rang. "Aren't you popular," she said, irritated by the interruption.

With a sudden surge of anxiety, Adam went to answer the door.

It was Megan, smiling and carrying a paper bag.

"Happy Valentine's Day," she said, kissing him. "I was going to use my key, but I saw the car in the driveway and figured you had company...." Her gaze traveled past him and her voice trailed off.

He didn't need to look to know Natalie had joined them in the foyer.

"Hi, I'm Natalie," Natalie said, stepping forward to shake her hand. "And you are?"

"Megan." As she shifted the bag to shake Natalie's hand, Megan met Adam's gaze with pained confusion. "Megan Donohue."

"What's in the bag?"

"Oh." Megan looked down distractedly. "Groceries. I thought I would make breakfast."

Natalie smiled indulgently. "How sweet of you, but we've already eaten."

"Natalie came over just this morning," Adam broke in. "I wasn't expecting her. She surprised me." He heard himself babbling, and how he made the truth seem false. "Do you want to come in?"

"No—no, thanks. I'd better get home." She wouldn't look at him. Abruptly she turned and headed for her car.

Adam followed her outside. "Megan, she just showed up about a half hour before you did. Uninvited."

"Uh-huh." She fumbled the key in the lock.

"It's true."

"Fine, it's true." She opened the door and placed the bag inside.

"If you believe me, why are you acting like this?"

"Acting like what? I'm not acting like anything."

Adam put his hands on her shoulders and turned her to face him. "Megan, I wasn't with her last night. I was with you."

"I know." Finally she looked at him, and her gaze was cool and steady. "It's this morning I'm concerned about."

He couldn't believe the coldness in her expression. He remembered then how Keith had betrayed her, and felt a tremor of something close to fear, fear of losing her. "I wouldn't lie to you. You know that."

She nodded, but said, "I have to go."

"Megan . . ."

But she climbed into the car and shut the door. He stood shivering in the driveway, and watched her drive off.

He walked back to the house. Natalie was waiting in the foyer. "Isn't she going to stay for breakfast?"

"Stop it, Natalie."

"I didn't know she was coming over," she protested. "But what's the problem? It's just a misunderstanding. You'll sort it out."

Adam wasn't so sure. "You should leave now."

"Don't take this out on me—"

"Just go." He returned to the kitchen without looking back, and called Megan's house.

He waited all day, but she didn't return the message he left on her answering machine, nor did she respond to his E-mail notes. After school the following afternoon, he hurried home to check his answering machine, but if Megan had phoned, she had not left a message.

He tried her number again, and hung up as soon as the machine picked up. Later that evening he phoned again, and this time, Robby answered.

"Hi," Robby greeted him happily. "Guess what? I got an A on my spelling test today."

"That's great. Congratulations." Adam was about to ask for Megan when he heard her voice in the background.

"It's Adam," Robby told her, then paused. "Oh. Okay. Adam, my mom wants to talk to you."

"Megan?" Adam waited, eager to hear her voice. "Are you there?"

Her voice was soft, nearly a whisper. "Yes."

"Are you still angry?"

"No."

Relief washed over him. "Can I come over tonight so we can talk?"

There was a long pause. "I don't think that would be a good idea."

"But Megan . . ."

"I also don't think you should see Robby anymore."

"Megan, please don't do this."

"Good-bye, Adam." He heard a gentle click, then the line went dead.

Days later, Megan reflected on what Vinnie had said at quilt camp, that there were no coincidences, that in life you meet the people you need to meet. Perhaps that was true, but as Donna had added, perhaps the reason one needed to meet someone wasn't what one thought. Perhaps she and Adam had been destined to meet, but not because they were meant to spend the rest of their lives together. Adam might have come into her life to prove to her that she could find love again—although not with him.

She accepted the situation sadly, because she had no other choice. She only wished she could explain things in a way Robby could accept and understand. She couldn't tell him what had really happened that morning at Adam's house, but although it would have been simple to say that Adam was too busy to be Robby's friend anymore, somehow she couldn't bear to say something so untrue. So she simply told Robby Adam couldn't come over anymore, and when Robby asked why, she fell back on the phrase she had promised herself never to utter as a parent: "Because I said so."

Julia couldn't think of any place she would less rather be than Kansas in late February, except for the more specific hell of the *Prairie Vengeance* location shoot in Kansas in late February.

A knock sounded on her trailer door. "Five minutes, Miss Merchaud," someone called. With a sigh, Julia rose, checked her hair and makeup, and drew on her parka. They must have finished shoveling off the cabin, a task that wouldn't be necessary if the weather would cooperate, or if production hadn't been delayed so long. The scene scheduled to shoot that day was supposed to take place in September. Since even in this part of the country a six-inch-thick blanket of snow didn't suit September, the cabin and grounds standing in as the Hendersons' homestead had to be cleared off. Ellen grumbled that if they had used her original script, they would have been able to film these scenes on schedule, which would have meant last October at the latest. Privately Julia agreed with her, but she worried that the young woman was growing careless. At first she had had enough sense to keep her complaints to herself when Deneford was around, but as the script changes accumulated, she had abandoned her sense of discretion. Julia had warned her to be cautious, since Deneford could ruin her movie career, but Ellen had said, "I almost don't care anymore."

"Wait until you're sure you don't care anymore, and then you can gripe to your heart's content," Julia had retorted, and Ellen contritely pledged to try.

Someone had shoveled a narrow path from the door of Julia's trailer to the cabin, where the crew was busily preparing for the shoot. The cast, barely recognizable in their thick coats, sipped coffee from foam cups or paged through their scripts. Julia spotted Noah McCleod, the actor playing her eldest son—and the only member of the cast she was in any mood to speak to that morning—sitting in a chair reading a book.

He smiled as she approached. "Do you know much about geometry?"

"Not much," Julia admitted. "Although a friend of mine has a grandson who teaches it. Unfortunately, he's in Ohio, so he won't be much help. Where's your tutor?"

"In the trailer with the flu."

"Delightful." No doubt they would all catch it soon. Suddenly she had a hopeful thought: If she fell ill, she might have to go to the hospital. "Where's Cameron?"

Noah shrugged. "In the wardrobe trailer, last time I saw him."

"Again?" The actor who played her youngest son seemed to grow half an inch every day, much to the chagrin of the wardrobe mistress.

Deneford joined them. "Are you two ready?" Without waiting for an answer, he said, "Julia, you'll be at the quilt frame with your friends. Noah, when you and Cam run up to tell her about the rattlesnake, I want to see real fear. Okay? Can you do that?"

"Sure, I'll just think about my geometry homework," Noah said good-naturedly, and set his book aside. "See you soon, Ma."

Julia smiled. "Very well, son." The extras had already removed their coats and sat shivering around the quilt frame in front of the cabin. Julia kept her parka on until the last minute, taking her place just before the shot.

She sat down, greeted the extras cordially, and slipped her thimble on the first finger of her right hand. Closing her eyes, she summoned up her character and called up memories of warm autumn days. When she opened her eyes again, she could almost forget the cold.

"Action," Deneford ordered, and the scene began. Sadie and her fellow settler women worked on the quilt, discussing the ominous news that cattle ranchers planned to buy up their town.

Out of the corner of her eye, Julia spotted a grimace from the cinematographer, who made a gesture of disgust as he spoke to Deneford. "Cut," Deneford called out. "Take a break. A short break." Shivering, the extras scrambled into their coats.

"A break, already?" Ellen groused, arriving to hand Julia her coat.

Julia thanked her and was about to suggest they get some coffee when Deneford called her over. "Don't let them change the lines," Ellen hissed. Julia gave her a look that said, *As if I have a choice.*

She joined the two men, who had withdrawn somewhat from the others. "Yes?" she asked.

"We have a small problem," Deneford said. "It seems that your hands . . ." He looked to the cinematographer. "How did you put it?"

"They're too old."

Stung, Julia fought off the instinct to hide her hands behind her back. "I beg your pardon?"

"They look too old," the cinematographer said. "When I move in close enough to follow your quilting, the camera picks up every wrinkle and vein. When I pull back far enough for your hands to look Sadie's age, I can't tell what you're doing."

"Well, what do you suggest I do about it?" she asked crisply.

Deneford and the cinematographer exchanged a look. "Is there anything you can do to make your hands seem younger?" Deneford asked. "Could you wear gloves? Not those winter gloves. You know the type I mean. Kid gloves, I think they're called."

"I can't quilt with gloves on."

The cinematographer shook his head and said to Deneford, "We aren't going to find a local hand model who knows how to quilt."

"We don't need a hand model," Julia snapped. "My hands are

perfectly appropriate for my character. Sadie was a frontier farm wife. She worked with her hands from dawn until dusk in every season. She would have had weathered hands."

"There's weathered, and there's aged," the cinematographer remarked. Julia glared at him.

Deneford intervened. "All right. We'll go ahead and film it as is. If I don't like the dailies, we'll think of an alternative."

Julia gave them a sharp nod, not trusting herself to speak. She stormed back to her place and practiced her relaxation breathing. Silently she cursed the cinematographer. Her ability to quilt had won her that role, and in another moment Deneford might decide to put Samantha Key and her Young Sadie hands in Julia's place.

She calmed herself in time for the second take, which went perfectly. Always the dictatorial perfectionist, Deneford called for a third and fourth without giving the women around the quilt frame time to slip into their coats and warm themselves. Julia contented herself with dreaming up horrible accidents that might befall him this far from civilization.

Finally Deneford was ready to move on. "Okay, kids, rattlesnake time," he said to Noah, then looked around and asked, "Where's Cameron?"

Noah shrugged. "Try the wardrobe trailer."

"Again?" He raised his voice. "Everyone be back here in fifteen." With murmurs of relief, the cast and most of the crew headed for their trailers. Deneford strode off toward the wardrobe trailer, the assistant director at his heels.

Julia waited until they were out of sight before hurrying off to her trailer, unwilling to let them see how they had alarmed her. So her hands looked too old for close-ups. Very well. She'd find a new pair of hands, and not those of Samantha Key, who had already taken over too many of Julia's scenes. And she didn't want some hand model with fantasies of becoming an actress, either. She needed someone who would be content with this small, uncredited role and wouldn't dream of stealing Julia's part, someone who would stand by her and believe in her despite her flaws, despite her aged hands and her mediocre quilting and her failures of the past.

She needed a friend.

◦⋟◦

Julia's cell phone transmitted her voice with perfect clarity, but Donna still wasn't sure she understood what her friend had said. "You want me to be a what?"

"A stunt quilter," Julia repeated. "You'll sit in for me during all my close-up quilting shots, although I'm afraid only your hands will be on film."

"That's fine," Donna said, with a tremor of excitement mixed with stage fright. "I don't think I'd want any more of me to show. I won't have to speak any lines, will I?"

"No, just quilt."

"Well, I can certainly do that."

"Please, Donna, say yes. You'll be paid the standard rate, and I'll cover your travel and housing expenses personally. I'm afraid the accommodations aren't exactly luxurious out here on location, but when we return to California—"

"You mean I'll get to go to Hollywood?"

Julia laughed. "Sure, we can visit Hollywood if you'd like. When we're done with the location filming, we'll have more scenes at the studio to shoot. I'd love it if you'd stay with me in my home in Malibu until the movie's finished." Her voice turned wistful. "It would almost be like quilt camp again. Except for the climate, at least while we're on location. I'm a bit embarrassed asking you to come to Kansas at this time of year."

"Oh, that's no problem. I wouldn't mind some milder weather for a change." Donna's thoughts were racing with the possibilities. "I'll do it under one condition. Let me bring Lindsay. Give her a job, too."

"Your daughter?" Julia asked. "But I only need one stunt quilter."

"That's all right. She doesn't quilt. But she is a drama major at the University of Minnesota, and she's performed in and directed many plays. I know that's not the same as movies, but she's very bright and she's a hard worker, and there must be something she can do."

Julia paused. "And this would get her away from Brandon."

"Exactly." Distance would provide Lindsay with safety and perspective, and working on a movie would remind her of her talents, her interests. *I'm all she has, and she knows it,* Brandon had said, and those words had haunted Donna ever since. If there were any chance Lindsay truly believed that, Donna needed to prove him wrong.

"I'm sure we can find something for her," Julia said. "We always need gofers and assistants. I'll look into it. In the meantime, may I take the liberty of making your airline reservations?"

"As long as you reserve two seats."

"I'll do that," Julia promised. "And Donna—it'll be so good to see you again."

After they hung up, Donna stood lost in thought for a moment. She probably should have discussed this with Paul and Becca first, but Paul would understand the urgency of seizing this opportunity, and he and Becca would get along fine without her for a while. They would be glad to if it meant helping Lindsay.

She went upstairs to Lindsay's room, hopeful and yet anxious. Lindsay might refuse to go. Since Brandon's visit she had lost the ground she had gained earlier in the month, and spent most of her time alone in her room. Once she told them Brandon had written to her, suggesting they attend couples' counseling. "We could sort out our problems now, so we won't have to postpone the wedding," she had said wistfully. Paul had overheard, and had become outraged, more angry than Donna had ever seen him. She, too, could not understand how Lindsay could even consider marrying Brandon after all that had happened, and the way Lindsay clung to the hope that he would change bewildered Donna. She and Paul had begged her to break off the engagement, and Paul had even declared that he forbade her to marry him, but Lindsay still wore the engagement ring Brandon had given her the previous summer.

But now Donna had a chance to change all that. She took a deep breath, knocked on Lindsay's door, and softly called her name. She received a muted, "Come in," in response, and entered the room. Lindsay was lying on the bed, holding a pillow to her chest and gazing at the ceiling.

"Honey?" Donna said. "There's something I'd like to discuss with you."

She told her daughter about Julia's phone call and the troubles she had been facing with the movie ever since accepting the role. At first Donna wasn't sure her daughter was paying attention, but as she narrated the twists and turns of Julia's misery on the set, she detected a flicker of interest in Lindsay's eyes. Eventually Lindsay sat up and began to react to Donna's story, by turns laughing and shaking her head in disbelief.

"What is she going to do?" Lindsay asked when Donna concluded. "Do you think she'll lose the part?"

"That's where we come in. Julia offered me a job. She wants me to be her stunt quilter."

"A stunt quilter?" Lindsay laughed. "That's wonderful! You're going to be a star."

"Well, I don't know about that. Only my hands are going to be on film." Donna bit her lip, feigning the uncertainty that was so close to the nervousness she already felt. "That's if I take the job."

"If? Why wouldn't you want to? It sounds like so much fun."

"I don't know." Donna shrugged. "It would be hard to be away from the family for so long."

"I think we can manage, Mom."

"It's not that. I'll get lonely. So I told Julia I'd only take the part if you came with me."

Lindsay started. "Why did you tell her that?"

"Because I want you to be there." Donna sat down on the edge of Lindsay's bed and took her hand. "When I told her you were available, she asked if you would come work on the set, too. You'd be an intern, or an assistant, something like that. You'd get to work behind the scenes of a real movie. Just think of what a great experience this would be."

Lindsay looked tired. "I don't think I can do it."

"Why not?"

"I just don't think I can." She lay down again and closed her eyes.

"A year ago you would have done it."

"A year ago." Lindsay's voice was faint. "A year ago I was a different person."

Watching her, a spark of resolve kindled in Donna's heart. "Come here." She stood up and, still holding Lindsay's hand, pulled her to her feet. "I want to show you something."

She led Lindsay to the quilt room, where she opened her closet and brought out a pile of quilt blocks, all different patterns, some traditional, some of her own invention. Each had spoken to her heart as she assembled it, whispering messages of hope and faith and encouragement she alone understood.

"I tried to make you a wedding quilt," Donna said as she spread out the blocks on the table. "I couldn't do it. When I thought of you and Brandon together, not a single pattern came to my mind. But when I thought of you, Lindsay, just you, the ideas kept coming, one after another. The quilt blocks just spilled out of me." She picked up one, an appliqué block of the traditional symbol of the theater, the masks of comedy and tragedy. "I made this one first, and then this"—she picked up a second block—"to accompany it. The names of all the plays you've ever worked on are embroidered on it."

She handed the blocks to her daughter, who traced the outline of the masks with a finger. "This one I made from your high school basketball uniform," she continued, holding up a Weathervane block. "Do you remember? You were a guard, and in your senior year your teammates chose you as captain."

"I was only second string."

"Yes, and they chose you anyway, even though you weren't the best player, because of who you are. Because of your character and your kindness. Because of what you contributed to that team when you encouraged the other girls to do their best."

Donna passed her another block, a photo transfer made of a snapshot from Lindsay's first day of kindergarten. "Remember this?"

Lindsay let out a small laugh and bit her lip.

"I was so proud of you that day," Donna said. "I hated to see my baby grow up, but I loved your confidence. Remember when that other little girl at the bus stop wouldn't stop crying because she was scared to go to school? You held her hand and promised you would be her friend, and you would sit with her on the bus and play with her every day."

"Her name was Molly."

"That's right. I had forgotten." Donna held up a blue-and-white LeMoyne Star block. "Do you recognize these fabrics?"

Lindsay touched it. "The blue—it's from my prom dress."

"And the white is from the hem of your graduation gown. This one—I call it the Golden Gopher block. Remember that T-shirt you wore constantly your freshman year?"

Lindsay smiled and nodded, tears shining in her eyes. "I washed it so much that it shrank to half its size. I thought you threw it out."

"I saved it." She had saved it, and two years later cut out the emblem and appliquéd it onto a quilt block so Lindsay could keep it forever. Donna waved her hand over the table and watched as Lindsay took in all the blocks, all the patchwork memories Donna had created to celebrate her life. "Look at all you've accomplished," she implored. "Think of all the people who care about you and have always cared about you. You are a wonderful, talented, beautiful, and loving young woman, Lindsay. You deserve to be happy. You deserve to be cherished." She reached out and brushed away her daughter's tears, then cupped Lindsay's cheek in her hand. "Please don't ever let anyone convince you otherwise."

Lindsay threw her arms around her mother and wept. Donna patted her on the back and murmured to her soothingly. Lindsay cried until she cried herself out, then she pulled away, brushed the tears from her eyes with the back of her hand—and then, slowly but with resolve, she removed the engagement ring.

She placed it on the table with the quilt blocks. The she turned to her mother, who embraced her and held her tightly, as if she could pass strength from her arms to her daughter's heart, so that Lindsay would forever be protected by her love.

Eleven

WINTER GAVE WAY to the first signs of spring, and on the Kansas set of *Prairie Vengeance,* Lindsay blossomed. She started out as the assistant to an assistant, but before long she had proven herself to be capable and smart. She was promoted once, and then again, until she was named a production assistant. Even Deneford took notice of her, after some subtle hints from Julia, and he told Lindsay if she wanted work during the summer, he could get her an internship at the studio.

For her part, Donna didn't see herself becoming a professional stunt quilter anytime soon, but she enjoyed working with the other extras and seeing what went on behind the scenes. Deneford's behavior quickly confirmed that Julia had not exaggerated in her stories about him. It heartened Donna to see Lindsay stand up to his blustering, and moving confidently about the set as if she had been the production assistant for dozens of films.

Before leaving for Kansas, Lindsay had phoned Brandon to break off the engagement. Paul later reported that Brandon showed up as scheduled to pick up the ring, but when he learned Lindsay wasn't there, he refused to take it. "Why should I," he told Paul, "when I'll be giving it back when she changes her mind?" Back then Lindsay had been distressed by his refusal to accept her decision, but by the time the cast and crew were closing down the Kansas set, her determination had strengthened. While Donna and Julia flew to California, Lindsay went home to Minnesota. She arranged to meet Brandon at a restaurant adjacent to campus, one popular with professors and students from the medical school. There she handed him the ring and told him in no uncertain terms that they were finished. Since they were in a public place, and Brandon was intelligent enough to realize what losing his temper in front of his colleagues could mean to his career, he contented himself with shoving the ring in his pocket and snapping, "Fine. You were never good enough for me, anyway." Lindsay merely stood up, went to her car, and drove home to visit her father and sister before catching a plane to LAX.

Julia, Donna, and Lindsay spent the days working on the set; in the evening they relaxed by the pool or saw the sights of southern California. Some nights Julia and Donna would work on their blocks for the Challenge Quilt. They spoke fondly of their friends from camp, and looked forward to the day they would meet again at Elm Creek Manor.

Then Donna was struck by a delightful idea: Why wait until August? Why not meet at the American Quilter's Society show in April?

Megan was the first to promise she would be there, and each evening when she left work, she crossed off a day on her calendar with relief. The passage of one more day brought her one day closer to seeing her friends, to getting over Adam, to helping Robby accept the loss of Adam's friendship. Robby still saw his counselor every week, but lately he had been making no progress, and in some ways was worse off than before. The low point came when he had to serve an in-school suspension for tearing up the poster another student had made for science class. Megan tried to talk to him, both alone and with the counselor, but only succeeded in making Robby feel miserable. "I'm sorry I'm so bad, Mom," he said one night as she tucked him in, breaking her heart. She hugged him and told him she loved him and always would, no matter what. He drifted off to sleep, and she went into the other room and cried.

Megan needed a break, and the trip to Paducah, Kentucky, to see her friends would be a balm for her wounded spirit. She only hoped they wouldn't talk about the blocks they were supposed to make for the Challenge Quilt. She had chosen her pattern, inspired by the gentle snowfall outside Adam's house, and selected the fabrics, but as Robby's newfound happiness faded, so did her eagerness to complete the block. Now the pieces sat on her sewing machine, and she did not know when she might take them up again.

Vinnie might have found herself in a similar situation, except that she had finished her block the day Julia's letter arrived, revealing the secret romance between Adam and Megan. She wondered grumpily if she ought to remove the stitches now that everything had ended so badly. Not that Adam had bothered to tell her it was over; instead he merely showed up at his mother's birthday party hand in hand with Natalie. "We're not getting married," he assured Vinnie privately, when he finally stopped ignoring the glares she had been shooting him all afternoon. "We're just seeing how things go." Vinnie thought he ought to see how things would go with Megan instead, and told him so. A shadow of sadness crossed his face, and he replied, "That's not up to me." Vinnie didn't know what to make of that, but since she suspected Adam wasn't happy with this turn of events, she was willing to travel much farther than Paducah to get the opportunity to talk some sense into Megan.

When Grace learned that the others planned to be there, she abandoned her hopes that the plans would fall through and forced herself to decide whether she would join them. Throughout February she had been plagued by exacerbations, and only by the last

week of March had she recovered enough to walk unsteadily about
the loft Gabriel had renovated for her, instead of relying on the
wheelchair. She had no idea whether her symptoms would improve or worsen by mid-April, but she knew she couldn't bear to
have her friends see her in her current condition.

But since it was her practice to attend the AQS show every
year, eventually she agreed to meet the others in the lobby of the
convention center on Friday afternoon of the quilt show. If she
were still symptomatic, the quilt show would be large enough that
she could avoid the Cross-Country Quilters. But by then she
might be feeling fine, and, she hoped, she might have a new quilt
started. By then she might have something more than false starts
and abandoned sketches to show for the months she had struggled
to keep the promises she had made at Elm Creek Manor.

On a Wednesday afternoon in mid-April, Vinnie rode a chartered
tour bus from Dayton to Paducah with a few quilters from Meadowbrook Village and many others from throughout the city. She
wore her favorite quilted vest and a red hat studded with pins
from all the quilting events she had attended throughout the
years. The Elm Creek Quilts pin was displayed proudly in front,
and she missed no opportunity to tell the other passengers how
she had won it.

Some of the women slept on the drive, but not Vinnie. She introduced herself to all the quilters in the nearby seats and chatted
happily, thrilled to be attending another American Quilter's Society show. The best of the best entered their quilts in this competition, and although Vinnie considered herself an above-average
quilter, the masterpieces displayed at this show humbled her—
and humbling Vinnie was not easy. In addition to the more than
four hundred quilts entered in the competition at the Executive
Inn Convention Center, there were classes taught by renowned
master quilters from around the world, lectures, award banquets,
fashion shows, and the nearby Museum of the American Quilter's

Society, where the Best of Show quilts from previous years were displayed. Then there was perhaps Vinnie's favorite venue aside from the quilts themselves: a merchants' mall where hundreds of vendors set up booths selling every sort of fabric, pattern, and quilt notion imaginable. Each time she attended the show, Vinnie resolved to stick to a budget, but within a day the dazzling display of wares would prove to be too much for her willpower, and she would invariably exceed her allotment for the entire weekend. The only solution, of course, was to expand her budget, which she cheerfully did.

The tour bus reached their hotel, which was already packed with some of the thirty-five thousand other quilters who would double Paducah's population that weekend. Vinnie was sharing a room with another member of the tour, but she didn't mind, knowing she was lucky to have a place at all. Every hotel room within fifty miles was booked up; those in the Executive Inn itself had been given out by lottery a year before. Megan and Donna had taken advantage of the city's Bed and Breakfast program, in which local residents provided the visiting quilters with a room and a meal for about the same rate as a hotel. Vinnie wasn't sure what Julia's plans were, but she wouldn't be surprised if Julia had used her star power to finagle a room in one of Paducah's finest hotels.

On Thursday she rose early, eager to see as much of the show as possible before the crowds descended in full force. She rode the hotel's shuttle to the convention center in downtown Paducah, on the shore where the Tennessee River fed into the Ohio, and was among the first hundred viewers to enter the show. She was not disappointed. The quilts were breathtaking, inspiring; she saw examples of every style from watercolor to Baltimore Album to others so innovative she wasn't sure their styles had a particular name. There were quilts from every state and around the world, some made by professional quilters, others by amateurs, although Vinnie was puzzled by that distinction because she detected no difference in the quality of artistic expression or craftsmanship. She took snapshots of her favorites and wrinkled her nose at others, wondering what on earth that particular quilter had been thinking. But she figured one person's art was another person's drop cloth, and just because a quilt didn't suit her tastes didn't mean it wasn't a good quilt. She, for example, thought she might keel over dead if she had to look at another Sunbonnet Sue quilt, but she had friends who thought little Sue was the most adorable creature on the face of the earth. Vinnie figured there was room enough in the quilting community for all manner of tastes and styles. She wasn't as opinionated as some of the other viewers, who evaluated each quilt in loud, obnoxious voices, as if anyone listening gave a fig what they thought. Once, after an irritating old biddy had made a particularly thoughtless remark about a Mariner's Compass quilt, Vinnie said, "I'm sorry you didn't like it. I worked very hard on it, and tried to do my best." The old biddy's jaw dropped in horror, and Vinnie turned her back and walked away with a satisfied smile. That would teach her to be a little more sensitive. Honestly. They were fellow quilters, after all; if they were going to offer criticism, it should be constructive, and it should never be unkind.

By lunchtime Vinnie was fatigued from being on her feet all day, so she met up with a group of ladies from the tour and strolled downtown for lunch. Spring was much further along in Paducah than in Dayton, and the skies were clear and sunny above the blooming dogwood trees. The downtown streets were charming, as all the shops—from the hardware store to the women's clothing boutique—displayed quilts in their front windows. Vinnie considered it a thoughtful, friendly gesture, the way the entire city welcomed the visiting quilters.

After lunch Vinnie toured the Museum of the American Quilter's Society, then returned to the convention center to attend a lecture by one of her favorite quilters. She waited until later that afternoon, when most of the other visitors were at supper, before visiting the merchants' mall, so she could shop without too much jostling from the crowd. She quickly snapped up several yards of fabric and a pattern for a quilted pullover, then added a box of notecards and a few books to her purchases. She might have gone on until all her money was spent and her charge card melted from so much use, except her tote bag was getting too heavy to carry. She decided, reluctantly, to call it a day, because she wanted to be in top form when she met the Cross-Country Quilters the next afternoon.

Vinnie tried to sleep in Friday morning to make the afternoon come sooner, but she was up at dawn, bursting with energy and impatient to see her friends. She distracted herself pleasantly enough by seeing the rest of the quilts and continuing her shopping, but it was a miracle she made it to lunch. An afternoon class kept her busy for a few hours, and then, at last, it was time.

She arrived at their designated meeting place in the lobby of the Executive Inn a half hour early, but there were so many other visitors milling about, she worried that she might not see her friends. She managed to find one of the last empty chairs in the place and gingerly climbed on top of it, the better to scan the crowds, but before long, a security guard asked her to get down. She did, but only because he asked nicely and seemed genuinely concerned for her safety.

Four o'clock arrived, and at last Vinnie spotted two familiar faces. "Megan," she shouted, waving her arm in the air. "Donna! Over here!"

They worked their way toward her, and a moment later they were embracing. "It's so good to see you," Donna said, hugging her. "You look wonderful."

"Well, naturally. You look lovely yourself." She did, indeed; she had slimmed down some, and her skin had a healthy glow. "That California sunshine suits you."

"Oh, don't tell me that," Donna said, laughing. "I'm already tempted to move in with Julia permanently."

"And where is our Julia?" Vinnie asked, searching the crowd behind her friends. "Didn't she come with you?"

"No, she had to cancel. She was afraid of what might happen if she left the studio for too long."

"From what she writes about that Deneford character, that was probably a sensible decision." Vinnie smiled at Megan. "Megan, honey, how are you?"

"Fine." She hesitated. "I've been better."

Vinnie sensed her apprehension. She knew she shouldn't mention Adam, but she couldn't help herself. "I suppose you're upset about my grandson? I know you two had a falling out."

"You weren't even supposed to know about us."

"Grandmothers have their ways. Now, surely you know how disappointed I am. Can't you at least tell me what went wrong?"

"It's hard to explain." Megan studied her for a moment, then sighed. "It's true we never actually agreed not to see other people, but I thought we were seeing each other exclusively." Then her expression hardened. "I fail to understand how you can tell someone you love them, and at the same time, be involved with someone else. Keith did it, but I never expected Adam to."

Shocked, Vinnie said, "You think Adam cheated on you?"

"I didn't say he cheated on me. We never specifically said we wouldn't see other people. Is that still cheating?"

"Yes," Donna said.

"Megan, honey, I know my grandson. He's not perfect, but he isn't cruel. I know he wouldn't betray you like this."

Megan fixed her with a penetrating look. "Can you honestly tell me he isn't seeing Natalie?"

Oh. Vinnie glanced at Donna, but Donna's expression told her to expect no defense of Adam from her. "He is seeing her now," she admitted, "but I'm sure he only took up with her afterward."

Still Megan watched her, as if sifting her words to find the truth in them, or to find hope. Then she softened. "I wish I could be that certain, but I can't deny what I saw. I can't ignore evidence when it's right before my eyes. I did that with Keith for too many years, and I won't do it again."

Vinnie knew there had been a terrible misunderstanding, but she could not see how to resolve it. "I'm sorry it didn't work out." She took Megan's hand and gave her a sad smile. "But I hope that whatever happened between you and my grandson, you and I will always be friends."

"Of course we will," Megan said, without hesitation and so warmly that Vinnie felt her throat tightening with emotion.

"Okay, now," Donna said. "Let's not start weeping in the middle of the quilt show."

Vinnie and Megan laughed, and before they could become sentimental again, Donna launched into a narrative of her adventures on the set of *Prairie Vengeance*. Her story was so lively and full of fun Hollywood gossip that before they knew it, forty minutes had passed.

"I wonder what happened to Grace," Megan said. "Did she know where and when to meet?"

"I sent her the same E-mail I sent you," Donna said, scanning the crowd.

Vinnie shrugged and said, "There are always delays at that airport. She might be late, but she'll be here."

Their conversation broke off as they watched the quilters passing their way to and from the main entrance to the quilt show. Suddenly Donna pointed and cried, "Look who's here!"

Vinnie expected to see Grace, but instead discovered none other than Sylvia Compson. She was exiting the quilt show with a kind-looking man carrying a shopping bag in each hand. "Sylvia," Vinnie cried out. "Yoo hoo! Come say hello!"

She had to shout a second time before Sylvia turned their way, but when her eyes met Vinnie's, she smiled and waved. She and the man made their way across the busy lobby to the Cross-Country Quilters. "My goodness," Sylvia said, giving Vinnie a warm hug. "Vinnie Burkholder. Of all the people to run into."

"I should have known I'd see you here." Vinnie laughed, then indicated her companions. "I don't know if you remember these two from quilt camp. They were first-timers."

Vinnie re-introduced Megan and Donna, and in turn, Sylvia introduced them to the man, a friend from Waterford named Andrew. Then she gave them a quizzical frown and said, "Why are you three standing around in the lobby? Are you bored with the quilt show already, or are you waiting for a bus?"

"We're waiting for a friend of ours," Donna said. "Grace Daniels. She was at camp with us."

"Oh, yes, I know Grace," Sylvia said. "I haven't seen her yet today, but she should be around here someplace. She was at the banquet last night."

The Cross-Country Quilters exchanged a look. "She was here last night?" Megan asked. "We thought she wasn't coming in until today."

Sylvia shook her head, puzzled. "No, she's here. We sat together at supper." Suddenly her expression brightened. "There she is now. Grace!"

Vinnie saw her then, too, and she added her voice to Sylvia's. When Grace looked around to see who was shouting her name, Sylvia and the Cross-Country Quilters waved wildly. She spotted them through the crowd, and then, to Vinnie's astonishment, she froze. An indecipherable expression came over her face, and a heartbeat later, she had spun around and disappeared into the crowd.

Vinnie was too astounded to do anything but stare. "What on earth?" she finally managed to say.

Her friends seemed equally dumbstruck. "That was Grace, wasn't it?" Megan said. "I mean, there were a lot of people walking between us, and she was on the other side of the room—"

"No, that was Grace, all right," Sylvia said.

"Maybe she didn't recognize us," Donna said.

"I don't believe that for a minute," Vinnie declared. "She looked right at us."

"And even if she didn't remember you three, she would certainly remember me," Sylvia said. "We've been friends for fifteen years."

Vinnie didn't know what to think. One glance at Megan and Donna told her they were equally at a loss.

"Well," Vinnie eventually said, "I guess it's just us three, then."

Megan and Donna only nodded in reply.

They bid Sylvia and Andrew good-bye and went inside the conference center to enjoy the quilt show, as much as they could enjoy anything knowing that one of their friends hadn't shown up lest she jeopardize her career and the other had fled the building rather than speak to them.

Shaking, Grace walked as rapidly as she could away from the convention center, which was slow indeed, encumbered as she was by the two metal crutches she now needed to walk more than a few steps. She had no idea where she was headed, but the urgency to get away compelled her forward. She had waited an hour. That should have been long enough. They should have given up on her and left the lobby, allowing her to sneak upstairs to her room undetected. Now what was she going to do?

She tired too easily to go far, so she went to the Museum of the American Quilter's Society, which to her relief retained its air of contemplative serenity despite the excitement surrounding the quilt show. She found an unoccupied bench in front of one of the older exhibits and sat down, pretending to study the work in front of her, but in truth, resting and trying to sort out her thoughts. Had they seen her crutches? Then she had a more disturbing thought: Had they pursued her, but stopped when they saw her crutches? That was exactly what she had feared—and exactly what Justine insisted would never happen, not with true friends. "You shouldn't be ashamed of the tools that help you to live your life," Justine had admonished her, but Grace had been too exhausted by similar arguments to explain. She wasn't ashamed of the crutches, nor was she ashamed of strangers seeing her use them. As an African-American woman in a white world, she was used to sidelong glances from ignorant people; it mattered little whether they came because she was black or because she looked disabled. What she could not bear was the uncomfortable reactions of friends and acquaintances. At first even her own family had pretended to ignore the wheelchair, and the crutches in their turn until they got used to them, but at least her family soon resumed treating her as they always had. She could not say the same for her colleagues at the museum. Some ignored the crutches and spoke to her loudly, with false cheer in their voices; others looked askance at the crutches and avoided talking to her at all; most humiliating were those who assumed her mind was as weakened as her body, and either no longer entrusted important tasks to her or explained the obvious in slow voices as if she were a child.

And then there was Gabriel, who phoned at least twice a week, offering to pick up her groceries or run her errands or stop by to see if anything around the loft needed to be fixed. For her part, Justine seemed to have forgotten that Grace was the mother and she the child; she checked in every day to see what Grace was doing, where she was going that day, what she was eating, and how often she rested.

How would the Cross-Country Quilters have reacted? Grace couldn't say for certain, but judging by the reactions of her other friends, they would respond with nervousness, the sort of transparent phony encouragement one saw in cheerleaders for the losing team, or pity. Of the three, Grace despised pity the most.

She stayed in the museum for another hour, long enough for the Cross-Country Quilters to have given up waiting for her to return, enough for them to be well into their tour of the quilt show. Only then did she return to the Executive Inn, and she made sure her friends were nowhere in sight before she rode the elevator to her room.

She had planned to attend a dinner lecture that evening, but instead she ordered room service and read a book until it was time for bed. Saturday morning she had breakfast delivered, and then she hung the Do Not Disturb sign on the door and spent the entire day alone, watching a local cable station's continuous broadcast of quilt show highlights and wishing she had never left home.

Sunday morning she ventured out of her room, hoping the

Cross-Country Quilters had not changed their travel plans. According to their last E-mails, Vinnie's tour bus had departed the previous evening, Megan intended to drive home right after breakfast, and Donna's flight was due to take off at any moment. Since she didn't have to be at the airport until the afternoon, she could enjoy a few hours of the last day of the quilt show without worrying about running into them.

The crowds had dramatically diminished compared to Friday and Saturday, and Grace found that she was now able to get around the convention center rather easily. She viewed half of the quilts before having a quiet brunch of muffins and grapefruit in the convention center restaurant. She then browsed through the merchants' mall, which still displayed an impressive array of wares despite having most of their stock depleted over the previous three days. Grace saw several items she would have liked to purchase, but she did not want to attempt maneuvering with the crutches while toting a shopping bag. Next time she would plan for that—but then again, next year her condition might necessitate using the chair instead of the crutches, or she might not be able to come at all.

At the thought, she abruptly left the merchants' mall with its reminders of her limitations and returned to the quilt show, where she tried to lose herself in the beauty of the quilts. She found her own, a quilt she had completed three years before, the last full-size project she had made, and perhaps would ever make. With machine appliqué and silk ribbon embroidery she had created a portrait of Harriet Tubman encircled by folk-art motifs symbolizing events from her life. A second-place ribbon hung beside the quilt, and for a moment it brought her a small thrill of joy, which quickly faded when a voice in the back of her mind whispered that it could be the last award of her career.

"Well, my goodness," came a voice from behind her. "Second place. I would have given it first, myself, but no one asked me."

Grace recognized the voice, and didn't turn around. "Hello, Sylvia."

"Hello yourself." Sylvia walked around her, studying the

crutches, looking at Grace from beneath raised brows. "Is this some type of fashion statement, or do you actually need those contraptions?"

Grace's grip tightened on the handles. "I need them."

"I see." Sylvia nodded thoughtfully. "I suppose this is why you took off so suddenly the other day?"

Grace could only manage a nod.

"I must say you can move along quite quickly on them. I don't think I could have caught up with you at my sprinting pace. Granted, my sprinting pace isn't what it used to be."

Grace took a deep breath and slowly let it out. "Aren't you going to ask me why I need them?"

"I assumed you need them to walk."

"Well, yes, but . . ." Sylvia's dry matter-of-factness flustered her. "But don't you wonder why?"

"Of course I do. I imagine it must be something serious if you'd go to so much trouble to conceal it from your friends. I also assume it must have been afflicting you for some time, including when you visited Elm Creek Manor, which would account for your odd behavior there. On the other hand, I also realize it's none of my business, and if you wanted me to know, you'd tell me."

"I have MS," Grace heard herself say.

Sylvia's expression became grave. "Oh, dear. Grace, I'm so sorry."

Grace felt tears spring into her eyes. "Don't pity me. I hate pity."

"Grace, dear, it's not pity I feel." Sylvia's voice was warm with compassion, and she placed a hand on Grace's shoulder. "Let's find somewhere to sit down, shall we?"

Sylvia nodded toward a bench several yards away, and as they made their way to it, Grace composed herself. Grace marveled at how easily the truth had slipped from her when she had tried so hard for so long to conceal it. "Are you angry that I didn't tell you in August?" she asked as they sat down.

"Of course not. You're under no obligation to share your secrets with the world, or even with your friends." Sylvia looked at her appraisingly. "I do wonder how it's been for you, though, keeping this particular secret, having no one to talk to about it."

"It's been awful," Grace blurted out. "It's bad enough knowing I have this disease, knowing its prognosis, but seeing how other people react to me, how they change—sometimes I think that's worse."

"People deal with illness and disability in odd ways sometimes," Sylvia remarked. "After I had my stroke, Sarah—she's the young woman who runs Elm Creek Quilts—she's like a daughter to me, but she was so shaken up that she couldn't even visit me in the hospital. She avoided me after I returned home to recuperate, too."

"I don't want people to treat me any differently than they did before."

"Are you different?"

Grace's instinct was to say no, but Sylvia's bluntness forced her to think before responding. "Yes," she said, realizing that truth for the first time. "I have a sense of my own mortality. I have limitations I didn't have before. I see the world differently; I see other people differently. I'd be lying if I said my MS has left me unchanged."

"People probably see those changes in you, and they need time to get to know you as you are now."

"No, that's not it," Grace shot back. "They see the crutches; they see the wheelchair. They see the tremors and the clumsiness. Then don't see Grace adjusting to a disease; they see the disease."

"I'm sure some of them do exactly that," Sylvia admitted. "But others would not. It seems unfair not to let them show you. It seems wrong to deny yourself the comfort their friendship could bring you." Sylvia paused. "Especially since, as I'm guessing, your quilting brings you little comfort these days. Your MS is the root of your quilter's block, isn't it?"

"It *is* my quilter's block," Grace said bitterly. "It's stolen my creativity along with everything else."

"A disease can't take your art from you unless you let it."

"You don't understand. If you could see my studio, you'd find it littered with dozens of sketches, as shaky as if my grandson had drawn them. You'd see appliqués cut awkwardly and sewn with haphazard stitches." She held out her hands, the hands that had once created so much beauty and now betrayed her every time she held pen or needle. "My mind knows what to do—how to draw, how to cut, how to sew—but my hands can't do it."

Grace struggled to hold back the tears, but one slipped down her cheek, and she brushed it away angrily. The blood was rushing in her head, all the anger and helplessness that had plagued her for months, fighting to be let out. "I would give up walking forever," she choked out, "if I could just have my art back."

"It never left you," Sylvia said gently. "You tell me you can't do what you used to do. Very well; so be it. Accept that and move on."

"Move on to what?"

"Move on to what you can do now. Grace, you think your creativity is in your hands. It isn't. It's in your heart, your mind, your soul, and until you lose those three, you can never lose your art." Sylvia placed a hand on her shoulder. "You must find some other way to create."

"What other way?"

"I don't know. Only you can discover that for yourself."

"I don't know how. I don't know where to start."

"I know where. You admitted you're not the same person you were before this disease afflicted you, so stop trying to create the quilts that quilter would have created. Art is supposed to tell the truth. Don't use your quilts to hide your MS; use your quilts to expose it. Let us see your pain and frustration in every stitch. Let us see how you struggle to make beauty out of your grief. Tell the truth."

Tell the truth. The words rang in Grace's ears and resonated in her heart. She had been lying for too long, to herself, to her friends, and she knew suddenly that it was time to stop. It was time to tell the truth, and accept the consequences both certain and unpredictable, to let come whatever pain, rejection, or unhappiness must, and as an artist would, embrace it, and find the meaning in it.

❧

It was Sunday morning, and Adam had been listening to Natalie gripe about work for nearly fifteen minutes when his call-waiting clicked. "Hold on a minute. I have another call," he said, grateful for the momentary escape. He was trying to be a concerned friend, but Natalie taxed his patience. He hadn't seen her for weeks, not since his mother's birthday party and their argument in the car afterward, but every so often she would phone him to vent about the latest Lindsor's upheaval or indignity. He wondered if Natalie realized she knew nothing of what was going on in his life, both because she never asked and because she never gave him an opportunity to volunteer the information.

"Wait—" Natalie said, but he quickly switched to the other line before she could complain.

"Hello?" he asked.

"Before you say it's none of my business, just listen. I've had days to think about this, and I need to get something off my chest."

"Nana?"

"I know you care about Megan, and I know you aren't a scoundrel," Nana said. "But somehow you've done something to convince her otherwise. I don't know what you did, I don't know what happened, and frankly, I don't want to know. All I want is for you to talk to her and get this nonsense straightened out."

"Megan doesn't want to talk to me. She's made that perfectly clear."

"And you're going to leave it at that? She doesn't want to talk to you because she thinks you deceived her. Now, unless you did—"

"Of course I didn't."

"Then nothing's stopping you from patching things up."

Nothing except Megan's refusal to return his phone calls, her unwillingness to answer his E-mail, and her suspicions, which he understood but in another sense resented, because he had done nothing to earn her mistrust. He had never lied to her, but the first time she doubted his word, instead of giving him an opportunity to explain, she shut him out of her life—and Robby's life—forever. He loved her and he missed her, but he was angry, too, angry and hurt.

But he didn't think he could explain this to his grandmother. "It's not that simple," he said instead.

"I never claimed it would be simple. Nothing worthwhile usually is. But because it's worthwhile, you owe it to yourself to try."

"Nana—"

"I don't want to argue. I just wanted to speak my piece," Nana said. "And now I've done that, so the rest is up to you. I love you, Adam, but you can be a stubborn fool sometimes."

"I'm not stubborn," Adam protested, but he was talking to a dial tone. He sighed and switched back to Natalie.

"What was all that about?" Natalie asked, irritated.

"It was my grandmother."

"Still pestering you about coming to that Mother's Day thing?"

Suddenly he pictured Valentine's Day, and the way Natalie had acted the gracious hostess in his home when Megan came over. "No, she's not pestering me," he said, unable to keep the annoyance out of his voice. "She doesn't need to. I already said I'm going."

"She isn't your mother."

"I know she isn't, but my mother will be there, too. The Mother's Day brunch is a family tradition."

"I swear to God, you and your family have a tradition for everything," Natalie groused. "What about the luncheon?"

"What about it?"

"I asked you a week ago if you'd come with me."

"And I told you then I couldn't."

"But I need you there," she protested. "I can't show up without an escort."

"Why not?"

"It just isn't done. Forget the brunch. Your family won't disown you."

"That's not the point."

"Then what is the point? The CEO of the corporation that's buying Lindsor's is going to be there. This might be my only chance to impress him, and you want me to go alone?"

He struggled to maintain his patience. "Natalie, I'm sorry, but I can't take you to the luncheon."

"This is your last chance, Adam." Her voice was like ice. "If you don't come with me, I'll find someone else who will, someone unselfish, someone who is willing to support my career."

"I'm sure you won't have any trouble finding him," Adam said. "You've always been able to get what you want."

In response, she slammed down the phone. For the first time in the history of their relationship, she had let Adam have the last word.

It was late afternoon by the time Megan reached her parents' house to pick up Robby, so she gratefully accepted her mother's invitation to stay for supper. To her relief, Robby seemed glad to see her; lately his behavior toward her ranged in a wearying, unpredictable arc from loving to resentful. She had feared her trip to Paducah would set off a bad phase, or worse yet, frighten him as her trip to Elm Creek Quilt Camp had, but he was cheerful as he told her about his visit with his grandparents, and even remembered to ask her how her weekend had gone.

They drove home, stopping across the street to pick up the mail and newspapers their neighbor had collected for them in their absence. Most of the mail was advertisements and bills, but there was also something for Robby, a small card with his father's return address.

Robby sat down at the table as Megan sorted the rest of the mail on the counter. She watched him out of the corner of her eye as he opened the envelope, took out a card, and read it. His ex-

pression changed from the hopeful gladness any communication
from his father elicited to confusion, and he sat, brow furrowed,
studying the card in silence.

She didn't want to pry; she knew he was entitled to privacy in
his relationship with Keith, as much as she might long to monitor
every detail. Just as she thought she couldn't hold out another moment, Robby said, "I don't get it."

"What don't you get, honey?"

"Is this a birthday card?" he asked, still studying it. "My birthday isn't March twenty-second. Must be from Gina. She got my
middle name wrong, too."

"Mind if I take a look?" With a shrug Robby held out the card,
so she sat beside him and took it. "Oh. It's a birth announcement," she said, noting the baby bunnies and chicks pictured on
the front. "Gina must have had her baby."

Then she opened the card, and disbelief flooded her with the
numbing force of cold water.

"It's a boy!" the card declared, a boy seven pounds four ounces
in weight and twenty inches long, a boy born March twenty-
second to proud parents Gina and Keith Donohue. A boy named
Robert Keith Donohue.

Megan couldn't believe it. She prayed she had read the card
wrong; she desperately wanted to have read the card wrong. She
felt ill. She looked from the card to Robby, speechless, and tried
too late to disguise her expression.

"They named the baby Robert?" Robby asked, his voice disbe-
lieving, but his expression oddly blank.

Megan glanced at the card. "It seems so."

Robby looked away, silent. She had never seen him so stunned
before, and his stillness frightened her. "Maybe it's a mistake," she
said, groping foolishly for something, anything, to reassure him.
"Maybe Gina was thinking of you when she filled out the card,
and—"

"It's not a mistake." He slid off his chair and left the kitchen. A
moment later, she heard the door to his bedroom close.

Megan's heart pounded as she reached for the phone and dialed Keith's number. She couldn't believe he would do such a thing, not even after everything else he had done and had neglected to do. It had to be a mistake.

The phone rang twice before a woman answered, her voice weary and young. "Hello?"

"This is Megan Donohue," she said, stiff with formality. "May I speak with Keith, please?"

"Oh, Megan. Hi." Gina sounded startled. "Hi. Um, well, yes, Keith is here, but he's taking a nap. Can he call you back?"

Megan's anger became too much for her. "I suppose he can, but he probably won't. Would you put him on the line, please?"

A baby began crying in the background. "I really hate to wake him. He's been so tired lately—"

"Gina, I remember what it's like to have a new baby in the house, and if anyone should be taking a nap, it's you. I need to speak to Keith, and if he doesn't talk to me now, I'm going to keep calling back until he does."

Gina hesitated, and the baby's wails grew louder. "Okay, I'll get him." The phone clattered as if she had dropped it.

Megan waited, and heard the baby's cries subside. Long after she began to suspect Keith wouldn't answer, he did. "What is it?"

"Keith, this is Megan."

"I know. What do you want?"

"Robby just received the birth announcement." Megan took a deep breath. "I'm hoping there's been a mistake. Robby's card says you named the child Robert."

"Yeah, that's right. Robert Keith."

Anger made her words distinct and hard. "You already have a son named Robert."

"I know that."

"Isn't there enough danger that an older child will feel replaced by a younger sibling without giving that sibling the older child's name?"

"Not that it's any of your business, but I didn't give the baby

Robby's name. Robby's Robert Michael, not Robert Keith. So we won't call the baby Robby. We'll call him—I don't know, Bob or Rob or something."

"Why?" Megan managed to ask. "Why would you do this?"

"Ask Gina. Robert is her father's name, and her grandfather's, and so on and so on. Do you think this was my idea? I wanted to name him Keith, but I had to settle for the middle name."

"Robby is very hurt."

"It can't be that bad."

"It is."

"Well, he's a tough kid. He'll get over it."

"He isn't as tough as you think, and if he were, it would be because of the calluses he's had to develop because of how you treat him."

"Oh, don't start—"

"You're going to have to explain this to him, because I don't think I can when I don't understand it myself."

"Thanks, Megan," Keith snapped. "This is just what I need. I have a baby crying day and night, Gina moaning over every little thing, and now I have to listen to you. I don't have time for this." He hung up.

Slowly Megan replaced the receiver, wondering what she should do, how she would comfort her son. She went down the hallway to Robby's bedroom and knocked softly on the door. "Robby?" she called. "May I come in?"

"No."

Megan touched the door with her fingertips. "Honey, none of this is your fault."

Suddenly the door flew open. "I know it isn't," Robby shouted. His face was streaked with angry tears. "It's your fault. You made Dad go away and marry *her,* just like you made Adam go away. You won't even let him be my friend anymore. You ruin everything. Just leave me alone. I hate you!" He slammed the door shut with all his strength.

Tears sprang into Megan's eyes. *He doesn't mean it,* she told herself. Robby didn't really hate her; he was angry at his father and Gina—and, she admitted, at her, too, because of Adam—but she was the only one of the three he could confront. Her heart ached with the knowledge, but she decided to leave him alone. Tomorrow his rage would be mostly spent, and she could try again.

But in the morning, he averted his eyes and shoveled down his breakfast without even the smallest response to her attempts at normal conversation. He went out to the car without waiting to be reminded of the time, as if he couldn't get away from her quickly enough. When she dropped him off in front of his school, he pulled away when she tried to kiss him good-bye and jumped out of the car without a backward glance.

At work, she tried to lose herself in her research, but Robby's bitterness and accusations were always there, nagging at the back of her thoughts. She told herself not to take Robby's anger personally, because that would only interfere with helping him. Her resolution changed nothing, but somehow she felt a bit better. She was engrossed in the analysis of the burning rates of a new synthetic rocket fuel when her phone rang.

"Megan, honey?" her mother said.

"Mom?" Megan glanced at the clock. It was nearly four. "What's going on?"

"I don't want to alarm you, but did you make some other arrangements for Robby today?"

Fingers of cold dread crept around her heart. "What do you mean?"

"When your father went to pick Robby up from school, he wasn't there. We hoped . . . we thought maybe he stayed home sick, and you forgot to tell us."

"No, I dropped him off at school this morning." Megan's throat was dry; she tried to swallow. "Did Dad talk to his teacher?"

"She said he left with the other kids as always. Your dad didn't want to worry her, so he told her he'd check the playground."

"Oh my God."

"It's probably nothing," her mother hastened to say. "He probably went home with a friend. There's probably a message waiting on the answering machine."

Megan nodded numbly, as if her mother could see her. "I'm going home."

"We'll meet you there," her mother said, and hung up.

Megan snatched up her bag and left the building, pausing only to tell a co-worker that she had to rush home for an emergency. Twenty minutes later she pulled into her driveway beside her father's truck, not remembering a single mile of the drive. Her parents were waiting in the kitchen. She knew from their expressions that no message waited for her, and that Robby wasn't anywhere in the house.

Her mother embraced her, her face drawn with concern. "Are you certain he didn't tell you he was going anywhere after school?"

"I know he didn't," Megan said. Her legs felt too weak to support her, so she sank into a chair. "He hardly spoke to me at all this morning. We had a fight last night—well, not exactly a fight. He was angry, and he shouted."

"Angry about what?" her father asked.

Wordlessly, Megan gestured toward the birth announcement, which she had left beside the phone after calling Keith. Her father read it and scowled, then passed it to his wife. She sighed and shook her head. "No wonder he's upset," she said.

"He probably just ran off to be by himself for a while," her father said. "It's his way of punishing all the grown-ups who have let him down."

As hard as that would be to accept, Megan prayed it was true. Considering the alternatives, the horrible, nightmare alternatives . . .

In an instant her mother was at her side. "Megan, honey." She held her daughter tightly. "Everything's going to be okay."

Megan nodded and gulped air, squeezing her eyes shut and clutching desperately at her mother. She couldn't fall apart. It was too soon to fall apart. She had to stay in control to find Robby. He would be found; he would be home within the hour.

She reached for the phone. "Are you calling the police?" her father asked.

"Not yet," Megan said, hoping that wasn't a mistake. "I thought I'd call some of his classmates first."

Her father slipped on the jacket he had draped over the counter. "I'll walk around the neighborhood and look for him."

"I'll drive up to the school," her mother said, picking up her purse and glancing at Megan. "Unless you want me here?"

Megan preferred for them to be out searching, so her parents left. Megan tried to calm herself as she dialed Jason's number. His mother answered cheerfully enough, but her voice grew troubled when Megan asked if Robby was there.

"No, he isn't," she said.

"Would you mind asking your son if he saw Robby leave school?"

The other woman's voice telegraphed alarm. "Is Robby missing?"

"He isn't home," Megan managed to say, unable to get her mind around the darker possibilities. "Would you ask Jason, please?"

"Of course." There was a scramble on the other end of the line, and muffled voices. "Jason says he saw Robby on the soccer field after school playing football with some other kids."

"Does he know who these other kids were?"

There was another pause while she inquired, then she returned with a list of five names. Megan thanked her and hung up, already paging through the phone book for the first number. Her brief stirring of hope wavered and then flickered out when one by one, each of the children's parents told her that their children had come home long ago, and Robby had not accompanied them.

"I have the phone tree for the PTA," one mother said. "I'll call around and ask if anyone has seen him."

"You should call the police," the last father said. Megan decided to take his advice.

The officer who took her call tried to reassure her, saying that Robby hadn't been missing very long, and he would probably come home before the squad car arrived. Megan was not comforted. She paced around the kitchen looking out the windows and praying she would see her son walking down the sidewalk. Her mother returned just as the police arrived. Megan watched as the two officers spoke to her briefly in the driveway, then all three came into the house.

The two men introduced themselves as Officers Hasselbach and DiMarco. They began with a series of what Megan assumed were routine questions—Robby's age, height, weight, hair and eye color. Megan's mother hurried into the living room for a photograph, which Hasselbach studied and passed to DiMarco. "May we keep this?" Hasselbach asked.

Megan nodded.

"Is Mr. Donohue home?"

"Robby's father and I are divorced."

The two officers exchanged a look. "Have you tried to reach him?"

"No," Megan said, surprised by the question, surprised that calling Keith had not occurred to her. "But he's in Oregon. I don't think he'll be much help, and I'd hate to alarm him."

DiMarco picked up the receiver and handed it to her. "Let's just make sure he's still in Oregon."

Suddenly Megan understood. "It's not like that," she said, but she dialed the number. "Keith wouldn't take Robby. Not even for a visit."

The officers exchanged another significant look. "So the divorce was unfriendly?" Hasselbach asked.

"What divorce isn't?" Megan replied, then broke off as the phone was answered. It was Gina, and when she said Keith wasn't home yet, Megan remembered the time difference. "Could I have his number at work, please?"

"I really don't think you should be calling him at work."

"Please, Gina, it's an emergency."

"Like yesterday was an emergency?"

Megan closed her eyes and willed the churning in her stomach to subside. "Not like yesterday. Robby's missing."

There was a pause, and then Gina said, "I'll call him and have him call you back. You should keep your line open in case Robby tries to reach you."

Megan stammered her thanks and hung up the phone. "Keith's wife is going to call him at work."

DiMarco was watching her quizzically. "What did you mean when you said, 'Not like yesterday?'"

Megan sat down at the kitchen table and buried her head in her hands. "I phoned them yesterday to discuss another matter."

"Child support?"

"No. It's complicated." Suddenly Megan grew exasperated. "Why are you wasting time asking me about my ex-husband on the other side of the country when my son is missing?"

"We're just trying to cover everything, ma'am," Hasselbach said.

DiMarco said, "I'd like to look around the house, if you wouldn't mind showing me around."

"I'll take you," Megan's mother said crisply. She brought Megan a glass of water and hugged her before leading the officer out of the room.

Hasselbach eyed her thoughtfully before saying, "The call yesterday—was Robby angry at his father?"

"Yes." Megan forced herself to say the rest. "And at me."

"Why?" When Megan showed him the birth announcement and pointed out the baby's name, Hasselbach nodded and said, "Is it possible Robby might try to go see his father?"

"In Oregon?" Megan said, incredulous. "Robby's only nine, but he knows how far it is to Oregon."

"If he has an allowance, he might have raided his piggy bank for a bus ticket. I've seen it before."

"Not Robby."

"You said he was angry at you, too?"

Megan nodded, gulping the water and glancing out the window in time to see her father walking up the drive, alone. "He blamed me for sending away his father and for not letting him see Adam."

"Who's Adam, a classmate?"

"No." She glanced at the clock. It was approaching six; Robby had been missing for nearly three hours. "He's a friend of mine. Robby's fond of him."

"A boyfriend?"

Megan heard the front door open and shut. "Yes. He was. Not anymore." She rose as her father entered the room. Megan quickly made introductions, then asked, "Anything?"

Her father looked grim. "Not a sign of him. I talked to a few kids and some neighbors who were outside. No one saw him walk home."

Hasselbach asked Megan, "Any chance your former boyfriend might know where Robby is?"

"I don't think so."

Hasselbach nodded thoughtfully, then asked for Adam's name and phone number, as well as Keith's. After Megan provided them, he indicated the phone. "Mind if I call the precinct?"

Megan nodded just as her mother returned with DiMarco. "Nothing," he told Hasselbach. Hasselbach nodded and dialed the phone.

"Nothing what?" Megan's father asked.

"No signs of a struggle, no signs of forced entry." DiMarco nodded to Megan's mother. "Mrs. Levine found Robby's suitcase in his closet and said none of his clothes seem to be missing."

"I couldn't be certain, though," she said, giving Megan an apologetic look.

Megan nodded slowly, feeling panic rising in her chest. "You think he ran away?" The thought should have comforted her. If he had run away, he might come back on his own, but if he had been kidnapped . . .

"That seems the most plausible explanation," Hasselbach said.

"He was angry at you and his father. He might be trying to get back at you. We'll have officers checking the bus stations just in case."

The phone rang. Megan jumped, heart pounding, and glanced at Hasselbach. He nodded, so she picked up. "Hello?"

"Megan?" It was Gina. "I'm so sorry. I called Keith at work, but they said he left early for a dentist's appointment. I didn't know he had one, so I called the dentist, but they said he wasn't scheduled for any work. So I called the doctor, thinking maybe I had heard wrong, but he wasn't there either. I'm sorry, Megan, but I don't know where he is."

"I understand." More than anyone else in the world, Megan understood. "Will you have him call me when you hear from him?"

"Of course. The police have phoned here already asking to speak to him. Megan . . ." Gina sounded as if she were crying. "Robby sounds like such a sweet boy. I hope . . . I mean, I'm sure—"

"Thank you," Megan said quietly, and hung up the phone. The officers were watching her. "That was Gina. My ex-husband's wife."

"Still no sign of him?" DiMarco asked.

Megan shook her head, and nearly gasped aloud as the phone shrilled again. Without waiting for Hasselbach's signal, she answered. "Hello?"

"Megan?"

It was a man's voice, so altered by emotion that it took her a moment to recognize it. "Adam?"

"Megan, what's going on? The police just called, asking if I've seen Robby."

The warmth and concern in his voice dissolved her shaky courage into tears. "He's missing."

"Missing? What do you mean?"

"He wasn't waiting when his grandfather went to pick him up after school." She struggled in vain to regain her composure. "I don't know where he could be. He's angry at me. I think he ran away, but where would he go? Where would he go? He's only nine."

"Where was he last seen?"

"On the soccer field, at school. Another boy saw him playing football with some classmates."

"Are you alone? Is anyone with you?"

"My parents are here. And the police."

A pause. "I'm coming over."

"Adam—"

"I'll be there as soon as I can." Before she could protest, he hung up the phone. He was coming. The control she had fought so hard to maintain crumbled, and she began to sob, shaking, until her mother came and wrapped her arms around her.

Another hour crept past. Around her, the officers talked quietly, making arrangements, checking in with other officers. Hasselbach agreed that Megan's father could help by going door to door in the neighborhood, asking if anyone had seen Robby. Megan's mother remained with her, saying little, but comforting Megan with her presence.

A neighbor called; she had been contacted by the PTA phone tree and wanted to know if there was anything she could do to help. Another woman Megan didn't know, but whose name she recognized from the phone list, phoned to pepper Megan with questions until she began to feel dizzy and nauseated. After that, DiMarco began taking the calls. Still no one had heard from Keith.

As darkness fell, Megan felt herself becoming still and numb. Robby was out there somewhere, lost or hiding, hungry and cold. The police had searched everything within a child's walking distance of Robby's school, to no avail. She could not believe Keith had taken him, and yet if Robby had run away, surely he would have been found by now, unless something far more malevolent had befallen him.

Then, suddenly, headlights shone through the kitchen window

as a car pulled into the driveway. As Megan watched, a figure exited the driver's side and came around to open the front passenger door to let out a much smaller figure.

"Robby," she breathed, and bolted to the door. In a heartbeat she was outside embracing him, tears running down her face. "Robby. Thank God."

"I'm sorry, Mom," he said, his voice muffled against her shoulder.

She loosened her desperate grip to get a better look at him. "Are you all right? Are you hurt?"

Behind her Hasselbach asked, "Was he with you?"

"No," came the answer, and only then did Megan look up to see who had brought Robby home. Adam gave her a reassuring look before returning his attention to the officer. "I found him at the middle school, practicing his kicking."

"And you are?"

"Adam Wagner. A friend of the family."

Megan rose, clutching one of Robby's hands. She placed her other hand on his shoulder and steered him inside. Robby was home, home and safe, and nothing else mattered.

The rest of the evening passed in a blur. The officers remained while she fixed Robby some supper and phoned in their report to the station as she took him upstairs to get him ready for bed. She lingered in Robby's room for a while, stroking his hair as he drifted off to sleep. When she returned to the kitchen, she thanked the officers for everything they had done, and saw them, along with her parents, to the door.

In the sudden quiet, Megan realized that she had not said a word to Adam the entire evening. "Thank you for finding him," she said, and felt her emotions welling up until it was almost impossible to say any more. "I don't know what I would have done if he hadn't come home tonight."

"He's safe. That's all that matters," Adam said, his voice an echo of her own thoughts.

"How did you know where to look?"

"When I was driving here, I remembered that you said he was last seen playing football. We had a lot of fun that day we practiced kicking at the middle school. He talked a little about his dad while we were there, and about you. Somehow it seemed right to check."

"I'm very grateful," Megan said, and she meant it with all her heart.

Adam shrugged and gave her a smile that was encouraging and yet sad. They stood for a moment in awkward silence. Megan didn't know what to do or say, but Adam told her good-bye and left.

Julia was sorry when shooting ended and Donna and Lindsay went home. Except for her maid, Julia had lived alone since her second divorce, and she had forgotten how pleasant it was to have company around the house. She consoled herself by thinking of Elm Creek Quilt Camp, where she would be reunited with her friends. By then *Prairie Vengeance* would be out of postproduction, and Ares might even have a new project lined up for her.

To reward herself for surviving Deneford, she spent a week at Aurora Borealis. When she returned home, pampered and refreshed, she found two new scripts Ares had sent for her review— and a note from Deneford summoning her to a meeting.

She met Ares outside the studio, and together they entered Deneford's conference room just as they had so many months ago for the first script meeting. Deneford wasted no time in small talk. "I have bad news," he said when the principal actors, their agents, and the assorted assistants were seated. "We played some scenes for a test audience, and it didn't go well."

A collective mutter of frustration went up from the table. "You have a first cut already?" Julia asked, surprised.

"Not a complete cut. Like I said, just a few scenes."

Julia sensed the people around her relaxing. "What's a few scenes?" Rowen's agent asked. "That doesn't sound like any cause for concern."

Deneford fixed him with a piercing look. "You of all people should be concerned, for your client's sake. Our test audience was our target demographic."

"Men eighteen to thirty-five?"

"Exactly. They hated it."

Rowen paled. "Even the cattle-rustling scene?"

Deneford hesitated. "No. Actually, they liked that."

Rowen smiled and sank back into his chair, relieved.

"Hold on," Ellen said. "Since when is our intended audience eighteen- to thirty-five-year-old men?"

Deneford ignored her. "The numbers are low, but I have hopes that the project is still salvageable. Sorry, people, but that means we reshoot."

Above the groans, Samantha's agent said, "What's your timetable? Samantha is the guest VJ on MTV all next month."

"We'll work around her. We might need that much time for the rewrites anyway." Deneford looked at Ellen, slouching unhappily in her chair at the far end of the table. "Is your calendar clear?"

"Clear enough," she said. "I'm almost afraid to ask, but what sort of changes did you have in mind?"

"I've decided to ax all the quilting stuff."

Julia started. "I beg your pardon?"

"We're going to lose the quilting." Deneford regarded her, puzzled. "Surely you don't have a problem with that. Now you won't have to admit to the world you hired a stunt quilter for your scenes."

"I could live with that," Julia retorted. "Whatever would compel you to get rid of the quilting? It's the heart of the story."

"Rick Rowen is the heart of the story," his agent said.

"Give me a break," Samantha's agent muttered.

Julia was in no mood for their bickering. "Stephen, do you really think such a drastic change is necessary?" she asked in her most reasonable tone. "Quilting is the metaphor that binds the entire story together."

"Not to mention that it's how Sadie supports her family and saves her farm," Ellen added.

"I had some thoughts about that, too," Deneford said. "Our test audience thought earning money from quilting was, well, a little tame. I decided she'll run a bordello instead."

Deneford's assistant held up his hands as if framing a sign. "Think *Little House on the Prairie* meets *Die Hard* meets *Pretty Woman*."

Julia gaped at them. "Sadie is going to be a hooker?"

"At least at first," Deneford said. "Later, when the money starts rolling in, she'll become the madam."

"I don't believe this," Julia said, disgusted.

"It might not be so bad," Ares said in her ear. "You're still sexy. With the right lighting and costumes, you could still carry it off."

Julia wanted to slug him, but she kept her attention on Deneford. "I don't think this is a good idea. Maybe you're not choosing the right test audience for this picture. Why don't you show those scenes to women? I'm sure you'll get much better numbers in all age groups."

Deneford shrugged. "We might, but that's not the audience we're going for."

"That's not the Rick Rowen audience," Rick's agent chimed in, and Rick nodded.

Julia felt her anger rising. "Women do attend movies, you know."

"Come on, Julia," Deneford said. "Don't go all feminist on me. We both know women will go see a man's picture, but men won't go see a chick flick unless they're dragged there kicking and screaming."

"As long as they buy their tickets, does it matter how they go?" Ares countered.

Julia glared at him. "Thanks for that brilliant contribution."

Deneford raised his hands. "All right, all right. Everyone take a deep breath. We all want to do what's best for the movie, right?

We all want to salvage the hard work we've already put into it. This is the way to go. I'm staking my career on it."

Not only his career, Julia thought, but hers as well. She knew she could balk and complain all she wanted, but ultimately Deneford would have his way. Her only choices were to cooperate or to quit, and she couldn't afford to quit.

"I quit."

Julia spun to face the back of the room.

Ellen, her expression weary, had risen from her chair. "I can't do this anymore."

"Ellen," Deneford said quietly, "sit down."

But Ellen remained standing. "I can't do this. Sadie Henderson was my great-grandmother. I can't let you make my great-grandmother into a prostitute. That's not the way it happened. I won't do that to her memory. I won't do that to my family."

All eyes were upon her as she walked around the table toward the door.

"Think carefully before you do this," Deneford warned.

Ellen removed from her bag a battered, dog-eared script marked with dozens of bright sticky notes and threw it into the wastebasket beside the door. "Think *This Script* meets *The Trash Can*."

"Think *Another Dime-a-Dozen Nobody Writer* meets *Unemployment*," Deneford shot back icily. "Don't forget, Miss Henderson, I was giving you a break based upon a student film and the minuscule talent you displayed in that abominable first script despite the fact that you've never done anything and no one's ever heard of you. If you think you'll ever get another chance like this again, you're gravely mistaken."

Ellen blanched and swallowed, but reached for the doorknob.

"You're not that important," Deneford said, his voice rising. "I bought your script. I own it. This movie will be made with you or without you. There are four people essential to this project—me, Rick, Samantha, and Julia. I need them, but you need us much more than we need you."

Ellen's hand trembled—and she released the doorknob. Her gaze went from Deneford, around the table, and came to rest on Julia. She said nothing, but her gaze pleaded with Julia as loudly and as clearly as if she had shouted.

Julia remembered how she had loved that young woman's original story, how she had longed to know Sadie, to be her, and she thought of how drastically her history had been altered since then. She thought of Donna, and how thrilled she had been to work as a stunt quilter; she thought of the extras around the quilt frame in Kansas and the quilters at Elm Creek Manor, and how much they would have loved a movie about their passion and their art. Most of all, she thought about the Cross-Country Quilters, and how they stood by each other and supported each other in their times of greatest need.

"I'm out, too," she said softly.

Deneford stared at her. "What did you say?"

"I'm out." Julia pushed back her chair and rose.

Ares seized her arm. "Are you out of your mind?"

She freed herself and gathered her things. "Sorry, Ares." She looked around the table. "My apologies to all of you. But I'm ashamed of what we've done to Ellen's story, and I can't be a part of it anymore."

She thought she heard Ellen let out a glad sob, but Ares held her attention. "If you do this, it will mean the end of your career."

"I know that."

His eyes narrowed with fury. "It also means that you and I are through."

Julia smiled. "Why, Ares, you just made my decision that much easier."

She turned, went to the door, linked her arm through Ellen's, and led the dumbfounded young woman from the room.

Deneford pursued them as far as the doorway. "Your leaving will only improve the project," he snapped at Ellen. "But you, Julia, you'll be hearing from my lawyer."

Julia felt a tremor of queasiness, but she disguised it by waving her hand and saying airily, "Oh, very well, Stephen, if you must litigate, litigate. As if you don't have more important things to do with your time. As if you don't have Samantha ready and waiting to take over my role, as she has already done to some extent. You took a few liberties with our contract, too, did you not?"

She glimpsed the speechless consternation on Deneford's face as she spun around and strode away, half propelling Ellen along, half leaning upon her for support.

She kept smiling as they walked down the hallway to the exit, and nodded as Ellen thanked her over and over, but her thoughts were of the career she had thrown away, the resurgence in fame she would never see, the Academy Award she would never hold, gleaming in all its golden beauty.

Then she thought of the Cross-Country Quilters. She imagined them cheering her on, proud of her, assuring her she had done the right thing.

She and Ellen left the building together, and as Julia stepped into the bright California sunshine, a flicker of joy rose in her heart, growing until it burned away her remorse and misgivings, until her smile transformed the mask of an actress into the face of a true friend.

Twelve

ONNA'S FLIGHT arrived in time for her to catch the first shuttle from the airport to Elm Creek Manor. She settled into her seat with a happy sigh as the van full of excited quilters left for Waterford. When Donna's status as a veteran camper came up in the course of conversation, the first-timers peppered her with questions, which she tried her best to answer. But when they asked her what Elm Creek Quilt Camp was really like, she could only tell them, "You'll have to discover that for yourself."

She indulged in a contemplative mood and spent much of the trip gazing out the window at the rolling, forested hills of central Pennsylvania, daydreaming about the week to come. For more than an hour they drove, past farms and small towns, past historical markers and a sign for Waterford College, until at last the van turned onto a gravel road that wound its way through a forest. This Donna remembered; she looked for the bridge over the crystal waters of Elm Creek, and when they reached it, she knew they were almost there.

Not far across the bridge, the forest opened suddenly into a broad clearing from which a lawn sloped gently upward toward the gray stone manor. Donna felt a pang at the sight of it, a sense of homecoming and nostalgia she couldn't quite explain.

"There it is," the driver announced. "Elm Creek Manor."

The travelers who had not yet broken off their conversations did so then, peering through the windows expectantly. Donna heard murmurs of delight, and she smiled to herself, remembering how she had first reacted at the sight of the gray stone walls and tall white columns. Now the scene was colored by memories of picnics in the gardens, quilting with friends on the broad verandah, and passing through the tall double doors to and from her morning walks.

As the van approached the manor, Donna searched in vain for a familiar face among the women unloading cars parked in the circular driveway. She waited on the sidewalk as the driver unloaded their suitcases, hoping the other Cross-Country Quilters would arrive soon.

Suddenly from behind her a voice cried out, "Donna!"

Donna whirled around. "Vinnie," she exclaimed with delight. "It's so good to see you."

"You, too, honey. My goodness, you're looking sharp."

"Thanks," Donna said, pleased. In the past twelve months, she had lost twenty pounds, and she now felt years younger. She had hoped her friends would notice. "You look great, too."

"Tell me something I don't know," Vinnie said, primping her hair. The two friends laughed and embraced.

Megan arrived not long after Donna had checked in and settled into her room. Two hours later, Julia's limousine pulled up in front of the manor, creating a stir just as it had the year before. As the four friends welcomed each other with laughter, hugs, and tears of gladness, Donna was struck by how everything felt so comfortably familiar and yet so new and full of promise.

Only Grace's absence cast a shadow on their reunion. After months of silence following Grace's inexplicable behavior at AQS, each had written asking her to meet them again at Elm Creek Manor as they had planned. No one reproached her for her actions or even asked her to explain; all they wanted was her company, and each had tried in her own way to show her how eager they were to see her again. She had never responded.

When they had finished unpacking, they gathered in Vinnie's room for show-and-tell before supper. Donna was the first to unveil her block for the Challenge Quilt. She had abandoned the Hen and Chicks block and made a Bear's Paw instead, with the autumn leaf print as the four feet, and a rich purple for the claws and the small square in the center. Julia and Megan admired her piecing, but Vinnie said, "What does a Bear's Paw have to do with your challenge? You should have chosen a block with 'Daughter' or 'Mother' in the name."

Donna was quiet for a moment, thinking of the fierce mother-bear rage that had filled her as she brought Lindsay from the apartment where Brandon had beaten her, and the protectiveness that had compelled her to spirit her daughter away to California, where at last Lindsay remembered who she truly was. "To me, Bear's Paw symbolizes how I overcame my obstacle. Wasn't that how we were supposed to choose?"

"If that's what this block means to you, then it's perfect," Megan reassured her.

Julia agreed, too, so Vinnie accepted her explanation grudgingly, but added, "I would have settled for a block with 'University' or 'Student' in the title. You could have made a Schoolhouse block, only in the University of Minnesota's colors." Vinnie's eyebrows rose. "Lindsay *is* returning to school this semester, isn't she?"

"She is, but not at Minnesota. She's transferring to the University of Southern California's film school."

Her friends burst into exclamations of delight, and Julia's was the most joyful of all. "You'll have to come visit her," she said, "and whenever you do, you and Paul can stay with me. Becca, too."

Donna agreed, and immediately Megan and Vinnie pretended

to pout over their exclusion. Julia teased them at first, but soon expanded the invitation to include them all. "Come in winter," she suggested. "Get away from that awful cold."

To the others, Donna said, "She thinks anything below fifty degrees is arctic."

"I do not," Julia protested, but joined in the laughter.

Next Megan showed her block, a beautiful Snow Crystals pattern with diamonds cut from the autumn leaf print and a lovely blue floral. In the center, eight diamonds formed a LeMoyne Star; in each corner, six diamonds fanned into a partial star, so that the design seemed to radiate from the center. Julia gasped at the perfect precision of Megan's sewing. "How did you make all these points so sharp?" she asked, tracing the tip of a diamond with her finger.

"Sharp points or not, she should have chosen something else," Vinnie protested. "Snow Crystals. What on earth does that have to do with helping your son?"

Megan's smile faded, and a wistful look came into her eyes. "It's hard to explain," she said. "I suppose my situation is like Donna's. Maybe there isn't a literal connection between this block and my challenge, but this is what I was inspired to make." She paused, gazing at her block, and quietly added, "The pattern just came to me on a night when I finally realized that I could be happy again."

Donna reached over and squeezed her hand, wondering what secret Megan kept, and wishing she could do something to remove the sorrow from her friend's voice.

Vinnie sighed in exasperation. "I don't think you two followed the rules very well."

"At least I met my challenge," Megan said. "Robby's counselor says he's making great progress."

"Has Keith helped?" Donna asked.

Megan hesitated. "A little. He invited Robby for a visit in June, and Robby said they had a good time. He's crazy about his little brother, and he said Gina's not so bad, either."

"That's good news," Julia said.

"It's a start, anyway. A lot depends on Keith, but I'm hopeful. Robby's disappearance shook him up. I think . . ." Megan paused, thoughtful. "I think he'll be a better father from now on, despite the geographic distance between them. I think he'll be a better father to little Bob, too, and maybe even a better husband."

Donna was glad to hear it, but she wished that Megan had added something about her own happiness. Megan had never mentioned Adam since the day he had found Robby at the middle school, but Donna remembered how his affection had transformed her, and hoped she would know as great a happiness soon.

"My turn," Vinnie said, and reached into her red canvas tote bag. Before bringing out her block, she pursed her lips and glared around the circle of friends. "Now, no laughing," she scolded them. "I finished my block in January, when circumstances were quite different." Donna caught the quick glance she gave Megan as she unfolded her block, sighed, and held it up for them to see.

It was a Wedding Ring block.

Donna, Julia, and even Megan burst into laughter. "All right," Vinnie said, with just the barest hint of a smile. "You're all very amused, I'm sure. But you have to agree this burgundy complements the autumn leaf fabric well."

"It's a lovely block," Donna assured her.

"I know that, and that's why I wasn't about to throw it away just because I didn't meet my challenge." Then she frowned, thoughtful. "Although in a way I did meet at least part of it."

Donna and Julia exchanged a look of surprise, but Megan's gaze was fixed on Vinnie. "What do you mean?"

"I wanted my grandson to get over his broken engagement and find someone new. Well, perhaps he hasn't found someone new, but he must have gotten over his former fiancée, and if he hasn't, I'm sure he will soon."

Megan's voice was a study in nonchalance. "What makes you think so?"

"Because she's marrying someone else," Vinnie said. "He's a

big shot, too, and almost twice her age. He's the owner of the company that bought the store where she works."

"You're kidding," Donna exclaimed.

"That's one way to insure your job security," Julia remarked.

"Now, I'm not saying that's why she did it," Vinnie said. "She might truly love him. On the other hand . . ." She shrugged. "Well, she's stopped pestering Adam, and that's what counts."

"Pestering him?" Megan said.

"Oh, my, yes. She was always showing up unannounced making a nuisance of herself. Once she even came to his school because she was upset about one thing or another that had happened at work. Would you believe she didn't understand why he wouldn't interrupt his class to console her?" Vinnie shook her head, exasperated. "He can be too kind for his own good. If I were him, I would have told her to buzz off a long time ago."

"That doesn't seem like Adam's style," Donna said, giving Megan a sidelong glance. Megan didn't notice, as she was staring at Vinnie's block, her expression reflecting her conflicting emotions.

"Then I suppose I'm the only one who failed to meet her challenge," Julia said with a sigh. She held up her Friendship Star block for inspection, and smiled as the others admired it.

"I'm glad you didn't meet your challenge," Vinnie said. "It was a far better thing you did, sticking up for that poor girl."

"I am disappointed about the movie, though," Donna remarked. "I was looking forward to seeing it."

"I was looking forward to starring in it," Julia said. "But that's show biz."

"Show biz sounds like a lot of malarkey to me," Vinnie said. "When's *Prairie Vengeance* coming out? I want to know so I can be sure to boycott it."

They laughed, and Megan put a comforting arm around Julia's shoulders. They all knew how disappointed she was, how much she had counted on this movie to revitalize her career. After watching Julia on the set and seeing how devoted she was to her craft, Donna knew perhaps better than anyone how bravely she had persevered in the face of disappointment and humiliation. Deneford and his cronies had treated her shabbily, and Donna considered Julia well rid of them. She hoped Julia was wrong, and that Deneford didn't have the power to blacklist her, as Julia was certain he had done. Her sacrifice for Ellen merited a reward, and Donna believed wholeheartedly that good deeds eventually brought rewards, especially when the doer wasn't expecting them.

"May I still include my block in the quilt, even though I didn't accomplish my goal?" Julia asked.

"Of course," Vinnie declared. "You earned your place. Besides, we're going to need all the blocks we can get, now. . . ."

She left the thought unfinished, but Donna suspected they all understood her meaning: They would need every block to complete their quilt, now that Grace would not be contributing hers.

Just then, there was a knock on the door.

"Come in," Vinnie called out, but the door remained shut. She brightened. "Maybe someone was passing by to call us to dinner."

"She would have said so," Megan said, and called out in a louder voice, "Come on in. It's not locked."

After a pause, someone on the other side of the door said, "It would be much easier if you would open it, please."

Donna looked to Vinnie for permission, since it was her room. When Vinnie shrugged and waved her toward the door, she rose and opened it.

Grace stood in the hallway, supporting herself upon two metal crutches.

"Grace," Donna exclaimed. "What happened? Were you in an accident?"

"Not exactly." In the room beyond, Grace saw the others rising and coming to the door, then hesitating as they spotted the crutches. She fought the urge to run away—not that she could run. "May I come in?"

"Of course," Vinnie said, pushing the door open wider and assisting her into the room.

"My bag—"

"I have it," Megan said. She brought it into the room and shut the door.

Vinnie led Grace to the bed and helped her sit down as the others settled into chairs or on the floor. Nervously, Grace waited for them to ask her about Paducah, about the crutches she unfastened from her arms and leaned against the bed, but they sat watching her expectantly, waiting for her to speak. Grace intended to tell them everything, but now, facing them, she didn't know where to begin.

Vinnie broke the silence. "It's good to see you, dear."

"I guess you weren't expecting me."

"No," Donna said, "but it's a wonderful surprise."

The others nodded, and suddenly Grace couldn't bear their polite caution, their tentative attempts to draw her out when they had always been so open with her. "I'm sorry about Paducah," she said.

Vinnie waved it off. "Don't worry about it. We probably got the time mixed up or something."

The others nodded, but Grace wasn't about to let herself off so easily, not when she had come to make amends. "No, I saw you, and you know it. I saw you and I ran away." She glanced at her crutches and let out a small laugh. "Or tried to run."

Megan's voice was gentle. "What happened, Grace?"

"I didn't want you to see me. I didn't want you to see me with these." She indicated the crutches. "I didn't want you to know I needed them."

"But why?" Donna said. "We're your friends. You don't need to hide from us."

That was precisely what she had been doing for far too long: hiding from her friends, from everyone who cared about her, from herself. "I have MS." She watched their faces as this sank in. "It's gotten worse since last year, when I could hide it, and it will probably continue to worsen."

"Why didn't you tell us?" Vinnie said. "Honestly, dear, to go through something like this alone . . ." She shook her head.

"I didn't want anyone's pity."

"We wouldn't have given you pity," Megan said. "We would have given you friendship. A shoulder to cry on, if you wanted it."

"I know that now," Grace said. "But I'm not used to needing people. Whatever problems life has sent my way, I've always handled them alone. My ex-husband tells me I'm the most stubborn and fiercely independent woman he's ever met. If I am, he's partly responsible, but I can't ignore the fact that sometimes even fiercely independent people need to share their burdens."

Vinnie reached out and patted her knee. "That's not an easy lesson to learn."

"No, but it's easier than lying." She looked around the circle of friends and felt herself warmed by their compassion. "And I've lied to you from the beginning. I knew what caused my quilter's block, and it wasn't my daughter's supposed romance. It was my MS and my refusal to admit that it had become a part of my life." She quickly bent over her bag until she could blink back tears. "All this time I've been trying to live in spite of MS, to quilt in spite of MS. It wasn't working, because living a lie never works for long. It took a good friend to show me I need to live and quilt *with* my MS, not in spite of it."

She reached into her bag and brought out the quilt she had begun the day she returned home from AQS, Sylvia's words still resonant in her heart. Her friends reached forward to grasp the edges, unfolding the quilt so all could see.

It was a wild, chaotic work, a whirlwind of angry reds and oranges and yellows, blazing on a black background. Sharp, jagged lines conflicted with uncontrolled spirals over the barely recognizable outline of a woman crouched beneath a burden of grief. Into every uneven, undisciplined piece and crooked stitch Grace had poured all her rage, her anguish, her loss. She felt the emotions nearly overpowering in their intensity, but as she gazed upon her handiwork, she reminded herself that creating this quilt had freed her from pain, and that if she permitted it, she could sustain the peace that had come from completing the final stitch, filling up the empty spaces in her heart, until the grief subsided beneath a blanket of calm.

Her friends held the quilt tenderly, as if they were cradling a piece of Grace's soul in their arms.

"This is the quilt that helped me get through my quilter's block," Grace said. She meant that this monument to her pain was the only quilt powerful enough to smash through the barriers she had erected around herself. Looking into her friends' eyes, she knew they understood.

She set the quilt aside lovingly, as if it had been a joy to make, although she had often succumbed to tears of rage and anguish as she worked upon it. "Since I faced my challenge, even though I wasn't completely honest with you about the true nature of that challenge, I decided I was allowed to complete my Challenge Quilt block." She smiled, reached into the bag, and brought out a Carpenter's Wheel block made in burgundy and green and the autumn leaf fabric Vinnie had given her.

"Not you, too," Vinnie said. "Why Carpenter's Wheel?"

"Because she discovered she's the architect of her own fate," Megan said.

Grace laughed, delighted at the hidden meaning she herself had not considered. "I like that answer, but I admit I didn't think of that at the time. I chose this pattern because a carpenter taught me it's possible to transform your life even when all manner of obstacles are placed before you."

Vinnie nodded in approval, and as Grace's friends admired her block and showed her their own, she knew the quilt they would make together would be as strong as its creators and as enduring as their friendship, which had been tested by time, distance, and misunderstanding, yet on that day shone brightly, untarnished, as if newly minted.

All that week the Cross-Country Quilters worked on their quilt, attending only a few seminars and spending most of their time in a vacant classroom Sylvia had set aside for them. First they arranged the blocks in a three-by-three grid, separating their pieced blocks with solid setting squares of background fabric. Donna's Bear's Paw block was in the upper left corner, and a solid setting square separated it from Megan's Snow Crystals block in the upper right. Julia's Friendship Star occupied the center position, with setting squares on either side. The Carpenter's Wheel block Grace had made took the lower left corner; Vinnie's Wedding Ring, the lower right.

They united the sampler blocks and setting squares, then encircled the finished unit with a narrow border of background fabric. Together they scrutinized the quilt and decided that it needed something more. They considered prairie points, or solid fabric borders, and several other ideas before Donna had a brainstorm. One of her infamous unfinished projects was a quilt made of Autumn Leaf blocks in autumn colors. She had brought those blocks with her for a seminar entitled "Finishing Your UFOs," a class she suspected Sylvia Compson had added to the program with her in mind. Since Donna had completed eight blocks already, they would only need to make sixteen more to create a pieced Autumn Leaf border to surround their sampler blocks.

"*Only* sixteen?" Julia said, alarmed.

"With all of us working together, we'll finish in no time," Megan reassured her. "We can use some quick-piecing techniques, too."

Julia shuddered. "Please, no quick piecing." They all laughed, remembering Julia's disastrous first class the previous year.

Grace shook her head, smiling. "It's a wonder you stuck with quilting after that introduction."

"It is a wonder," Julia agreed, "but I'm glad I did."

Their laughter rang through the halls of Elm Creek Manor, as it had so often that week. Other campers, made curious by the noise and their feverish excitement, stopped by to see what they were doing. The Cross-Country Quilters took turns telling on-lookers the story of how their project had come to be, how each had faced a challenge in her life and had commemorated her success with a quilt block. Some campers asked what those challenges were, but by unspoken agreement, the Cross-Country Quilters refused to divulge the confidences of their friends. Grace had the final word that put an end to the persistent inquiries: "Think of the challenges you face as a woman, as a wife, as a mother. The problems we faced were no different than those any woman faces."

They completed the pieced top on Wednesday just before lunch, and interrupted the meal with a special unveiling. When the other campers burst into cheers and applause, the Cross-Country Quilters exchanged smiles and knowing looks. The other campers celebrated them for their hard work that week, little realizing that the real work had taken place over the course of an entire year.

After lunch, Sylvia invited the Cross-Country Quilters to a far corner of the ballroom, a place that had not been converted to classroom space. There she showed them a wooden quilt frame that had been polished both with a craftsman's care and with usage over time. The rectangular frame was the height of an ordinary table, with slender rods running along the longer sides, and knobs and gears at the corners. As the others placed chairs around it, Megan returned to her room for the batting and backing fabric she had brought from home. They placed the layers in the frame: backing fabric on the bottom, batting in the middle, and the colorful pieced quilt top last of all.

They took their places around the frame, but not long after they had begun to quilt, Sylvia returned to tell Julia she had a phone call. Julia followed her to the formal parlor and discovered that Ellen was on the line.

"Ellen," she exclaimed, astonished. They had spoken only once since walking out of Deneford's meeting in April. "It's good to hear from you."

"It's good to hear your voice again, too. I hope you don't mind my interrupting your vacation. Your assistant gave me the number."

"That's fine," Julia assured her, and she meant it, surprised by how pleased she was that Ellen had tracked her down. "How are you? Are you working on anything new?"

"As a matter of fact, I am. How about you? Is your schedule full?"

"Hardly," Julia said. "I guess you could say I'm semiretired. I've looked at a few scripts—all of them awful—but without an agent soliciting work for me, I don't expect to be working again anytime soon." She smiled, thinking how a year ago she would have trembled in fear at the very thought.

"If a good project came your way, would you consider it?"

"Oh, certainly. But I'm not as hungry as I used to be. I won't settle for another *Prairie Vengeance* to make a quick buck, that's for sure. There's been some talk about doing a *Home Sweet Home* anniversary reunion, and if it comes together, I'd do that for a lark. Otherwise I only want serious, high-quality work, something worth the time and effort I'll put into it."

"Would you consider playing Sadie Henderson in *A Patchwork Life*?"

Julia laughed. "In a heartbeat, but that's not an option, is it?"

"Actually, it is."

Julia almost dropped the phone. "What do you mean?"

"PBS wants to produce it. I'm going to direct, and I'd like you to star."

"But how is this possible?" Julia stammered. "Deneford bought the rights to Sadie's story."

"Ah. But he didn't. He bought the rights to my original script.

I own the rights to Sadie's diaries, and therefore, her story. I'll have to rewrite the script to make it all nice and legal, but it will be legal. My father's an attorney, and I had heard enough nightmare stories about Hollywood to be very careful when I signed over my script."

Julia was impressed. "Ellen, my dear, I underestimated you."

"So did Deneford."

His name reminded Julia of a new worry. "Deneford might object to your releasing a film so similar to his. He might even sue."

Ellen laughed. "First of all, *Prairie Vengeance* barely resembles *A Patchwork Life*. Second, I don't think Deneford will want to remind anyone of *Prairie Vengeance*. It's caused him enough damage without him airing his failures in the media again."

"I don't understand. Wouldn't the publicity help the release of *Prairie Vengeance*?"

"Didn't you hear?"

"Hear what? I've been somewhat out of the loop."

"*Prairie Vengeance* went so far over budget in the reshooting that Deneford had to promise the studio he'd take no salary and cover the extra expenses himself. He thought he'd end up making a profit, but the test audience response was so negative that the studio sent the movie straight to video."

"No," Julia said, with only the smallest wicked surge of glee.

"Yes. There are even rumors that he's going to be, shall we say, encouraged to void his contract with the studio." Ellen paused. "So what do you think? It won't be the feature film you wanted, and it certainly won't pay what you were getting from Deneford, but are you interested? Do you want to think it over and call me back in a few weeks?"

Julia didn't need a few weeks. "I'm interested. Send a contract to my home."

"You mean it?"

"Of course."

"You won't be sorry."

Julia laughed. "That's what you said last time."

"This time will be different," Ellen promised, and Julia knew in her heart it would be.

Julia returned to the quilt frame with a heart so light she wanted to skip across the marble floor of the grand foyer singing the Hallelujah Chorus. A new project, something she could be proud of. Whatever Ellen's terms were, she would accept them, although she might ask Maury to come out of retirement to read over the contract first, for old times' sake.

She couldn't wait to tell her friends.

Each morning, the Cross-Country Quilters met for an early breakfast before gathering around the quilt frame. As the hours passed, their stitches added dimension and texture to their sampler, and their progress urged them on despite sore fingers and tired eyes. They talked as they worked, baring their hearts and unburdening their souls as they felt they could with no other friends, even ones they had known all their lives. There was a sanctity about the quilt frame that promised that secrets could be shared there, and no confidence would be broken or judgment passed.

On Friday afternoon, they finished the last quilting stitch and removed their masterpiece from the frame. Megan made a long strip of bias binding; Donna machine-sewed one of the long sides a quarter inch away from the edge, all around the front of the quilt. They decided a change of scene would invigorate them, so they carried the quilt outside to the verandah, where they arranged chairs in a circle, the quilt in the center. Each woman took one section of the edge, and together they folded the binding around the raw edges of the quilt and blind-stitched it in place on the back.

By late afternoon, they were so close to finishing their project that they decided to skip dinner and work all through the night if necessary. A half hour into the dinner period, Sylvia came looking for them.

"Aren't you ladies going to take a break?" she asked.

They shook their heads, and Grace said, "Not when we're so close to the end."

"Some rest might give you more energy to finish."

"Or it might make it all the more difficult to continue afterward," Julia said.

Sylvia sighed. "Very well. You're forcing me to pull rank. As the founder of Elm Creek Quilts, I'm ordering you to put down those needles and join me in the banquet hall. Now."

The Cross-Country Quilters exchanged looks of surprise and dismay. "We'll grab a snack later," Megan said, but Sylvia would have none of that. Ignoring their protests, she ushered them inside. Resigned, they allowed themselves to be herded along, realizing that they were a bit hungry after all, and that maybe a minute or two of rest wouldn't hurt.

When they walked into the banquet hall, they were greeted by dozens of women of all ages shouting, "Surprise!"

Vinnie nearly reeled from astonishment.

One by one, the Cross-Country Quilters began to laugh as other campers surrounded their friend, hugging her and wishing her a happy birthday. Sylvia led them in singing "Happy Birthday" as she led Vinnie to a place of honor, a seat at a table with a birthday cake in the middle.

"I can't believe we forgot," Donna whispered to Megan in dismay as Vinnie made a short speech thanking everyone for their good wishes.

"Don't feel bad," Megan said with a shrug. "Vinnie forgot, too."

And it was true. This year, Vinnie's Elm Creek Quilt Camp surprise birthday party was indeed a surprise.

Sylvia's prediction came true; after the birthday party, the Cross-Country Quilters were in such good spirits that they finished the quilt in no time. Each signed the back with her name, her city and state, and the name of the block she had made. All that remained was to admire their handiwork and praise themselves for the hard work, quilting and otherwise, they had put into their masterpiece.

But then Vinnie frowned. "Who gets the quilt now?"

All they could do was look at each other. Somehow, the thought of what would become of the quilt after its completion had never occurred to them. They could hardly divide it into equal shares, as they had the autumn leaf fabric the year before.

"Maybe we should ask Sylvia to display it here," Donna suggested. "To inspire other campers."

"Not on your life," Vinnie retorted. "If that's our best option, I'm taking it home."

"Why you?" Julia protested, nudging her.

"I have seniority," Vinnie said in a lofty voice, and they all laughed.

"We could draw straws," Megan said, but she didn't look satisfied with that solution.

"We should take turns," Grace said, and soon it was decided that Vinnie would be allowed to take the quilt home first, since it was, after all, her birthday. Next year, and every year after that, they would meet at Elm Creek Quilt Camp to renew their friendship and pass on the quilt to the next in line.

Vinnie was pleased that she got to be first, but she still looked doubtful. "A year is an awfully long time to wait."

Donna smiled. "Not if we keep busy with a new project."

She reached for her bag and brought out two yards of fabric she had been saving for exactly this occasion.

Good-byes were even more difficult and tearful than they had been the year before, even though each knew she would be seeing her friends again the next summer. Megan reflected that if their friendship had survived that first, most difficult year, it would surely endure as long as they nurtured it.

Julia left first, waving her fat quarter of Donna's fabric out the window at her friends as her limousine pulled away. Donna and Grace rode the shuttle to the airport together, able to postpone their farewells for another two hours. Then only Megan and Vinnie remained in the parking lot behind Elm Creek Manor, waiting for Vinnie's ride and watching other campers load their cars.

Megan's heart began to pound with nervousness as a familiar car crossed the bridge over Elm Creek, slowing as it approached them.

"Well, there's my ride," Vinnie said, sighing. She hugged Megan and added, "Take care of yourself, dear."

"You, too," Megan said. "I'll see you next year."

Vinnie nodded, and they both fell silent as Adam got out of the car. "Hi, Nana," he said, bending over to kiss her cheek. His eyes went to Megan. "Hi."

"Hi."

"My goodness, my legs are so tired," Vinnie said, hurrying toward the car with a speed that belied her words. "I'd better sit down." She let herself in the passenger side and shut the door.

Megan and Adam watched her, then looked at each other. "She's still at it, I see," Megan said.

"She doesn't give up easily."

Megan nodded, unable to think of anything more to say.

"How's Robby?" Adam asked.

"Good. He's good."

"Good."

Megan nodded again, pained by the deep loss she felt seeing him again, and wishing that things had turned out differently. "Well," she said, when she could no longer bear the awkwardness between them. "I'd better get going."

"Me, too," he said, indicating his car with a tilt of his head. Suddenly he extended his hand. "Have a safe trip."

She shook it. "You, too."

"Say hello to Robby for me."

"I will."

He nodded, and gave her a smile that was both wistful and understanding, then placed Vinnie's suitcase in the trunk, got into his car, and drove away.

Megan watched him go, then sighed and carried her bag across the parking lot to her own car. It had been difficult seeing him again, as she had imagined it would be, but her heart ached only a little, and she would get over it. Next year, she promised herself, she would be able to face him without the slightest hint of regret.

Or maybe she would spare them both another awkward scene. Someone else could wait with Vinnie next time.

"Well?" Nana asked as they drove through the forest toward the main road.

"Well what?"

"Did you apologize?"

Adam glanced at her. "I apologized months ago. It didn't do any good."

"So you're just going to give up? Don't you sit there and tell me you don't care about her. I know you still love her."

At first Adam said nothing, reluctant to discuss the deepest feelings of his heart with his grandmother, who, it had to be said, didn't always recognize the importance of keeping a secret. Then, suddenly, he didn't care whom she told. She could tell all her quilting friends if she liked—she could even tell Megan if she was determined to do so. It was the truth, and he was tired of pretending otherwise.

"I never stopped loving her," he said quietly.

Out of the corner of his eye, he could see Nana glaring at him. "You should have told her."

"She doesn't want to hear it. She doesn't want me in her life, Nana. She's made that perfectly clear."

"You should have told her anyway."

Frustrated by the suspicion that maybe she was right, Adam shot back, "Maybe I'm tired of humiliating myself."

"I'm ashamed of you," Nana retorted. She folded her arms and turned her head firmly toward the window, as if she would have turned her back on him if the seat belt permitted. "My only comfort is that your grandfather isn't here to witness this appalling display of cowardice. You are a prideful, ignorant young man, and because of it, you're going to lose that lovely young woman."

Adam was about to protest when suddenly, with a flash of insight, he realized that if he let Megan drive away without attempting to talk to her, he would deserve every word of his grandmother's criticism.

He turned the car around.

Nana started. "What are you doing?"

Adam said nothing. Determined now, he sped along the highway back the way they had come and turned onto the road through the forest. He passed the fork that led to the front entrance of Elm Creek Manor and continued along the narrow road that wound through the trees toward the back of the building. Megan would have taken the same road he had traveled on, and since he hadn't seen her, she must still be back here—

"You're driving like a madman," Nana shrieked. "Do you want to crash us into a tree? If another car comes—"

But just then the forest gave way to a clearing. Ahead of them on the right was a two-story red barn built into the side of a hill, and coming around it at that moment was Megan's car.

Adam honked his horn and flashed his lights, slowing his car and pulling off the narrow road onto the bordering grassy meadow. He parked and kept honking, knowing she would recognize his car, but watched with a sinking heart as she drove toward him without slowing, and then passed.

She didn't even stop, he thought, bitter with disappointment. She had kept driving as if he were invisible. He reached for the keys and was about to start the engine when a glance in the rearview mirror told him he was mistaken.

Megan had pulled her car off the road.

Quickly he left his car and went to meet her. By the time he crossed the distance that separated them, Megan had exited her car and stood, arms folded, beside it.

He waited until he reached her before saying, "I'm glad you stopped."

"I thought it might be an emergency."

"It is." He searched for the words, but before he could think of something gentle and romantic to say, the truth spilled out. "Megan, you haven't been fair to me. I never gave you any reason to doubt me, or to doubt how I feel about you. I know you've been lied to in the past, but not by me. Never by me."

She watched him, her green eyes wide and calm. "I know that."

"Then how could you have assumed the worst instead of believing me when I told you what happened? You know what Natalie's like; I *told* you what she was like. Couldn't you see she was baiting you?"

"Not at the time, I couldn't."

"What about now?"

"Now . . ." She hesitated and looked away. "Now I think I gave Natalie exactly what she wanted."

"Not everything she wanted."

"You went back to her."

"No, I didn't," he said firmly. How he regretted every minute he had tried to soothe his loneliness for Megan by giving in to Natalie's requests to try again. "Not in the way you think."

She fixed him with an inscrutable look. "And how is that?"

"You think I love her, but I don't. I couldn't. How could I love her, when I'm still in love with you?"

She was silent. "Are you?" she asked softly.

"Yes, I am. And you'd better get used to it, because you can doubt me as much as you like, but I'm not Keith and never will be. And I'm not going to stop loving you no matter how much you want me to. And if you don't want to see me again, you'd better forget about ever coming to back quilt camp, because I'm going to be here every year to drop off Nana and pick her up again, and every time I see you here, I'm going to ask for another chance."

He had to pause to take a breath, but her expression would have cut him short anyway.

She was smiling.

❦

Two sisters pulled out of the parking lot behind the manor and drove across the bridge over Elm Creek, discussing whether they should stop at the charming quilt shop in downtown Waterford on their way home, or if the delay would cause their husbands to worry. They had just decided to drop by for a moment when they rounded the bend beside the barn and spotted two cars parked at the bottom of the hill where the road disappeared into the trees. A man and a woman stood beside the car closest to the forest.

"What's this?" said the elder sister, who was driving.

"I have no idea," said the younger, who looked more carefully and added, "Isn't that Vinnie in the first car?"

Sure enough, Vinnie's familiar cloud of white hair was visible above the front passenger seat headrest.

"Has there been an accident?" the elder sister wondered aloud. Vinnie smiled brightly through the window and waved as they passed.

They waved back, puzzled. "Should we stop and offer to help?" the younger sister asked.

The elder sister, her eyes on the young couple by the second car, suddenly broke into laughter. "They must be all right," she said. "She's kissing him."

The younger sister let out a wry chuckle. "Maybe we should ask *them* to help *us*."

Laughing, the two sisters drove past the couple in their warm embrace and into the shade of the forest, while behind them, within gray stone walls just down the road and across the creek, Sylvia Compson and the Elm Creek Quilters were congratulating themselves on another week of camp successfully concluded, and preparing to welcome the next group of quilters, friends, and friends-to-be.